P.I. DADDY'S PERSONAL MISSION

BY
BETH CORNELISON

AND

COLTON'S SURPRISE FAMILY

BY
KAREN WHIDDON

MILLS
BOON

First published in Great Britain 2011
by Mills & Boon, an imprint of Harlequin (UK) Limited,
Eton House, 18-24 Paradise Road, Richmond, Surrey TW9 1SR

© Harlequin Books S.A. 2010

ISBN: 978 0 263 88520 0

46-0411

Harlequin (UK) policy is to use papers that are natural, renewable and
recyclable products and made from wood grown in sustainable forests. The
logging and manufacturing processes conform to the legal environmental
regulations of the country of origin.

Printed and bound in Spain
by Blackprint CPI, Barcelona

P.I. DADDY'S
PERSONAL MISSION

BY
BETH CORNELISON

To my parents—thanks for all you do!
And in memory of Samson, our lovable goofball,
who exuded awesomeness into our lives and left three
big paw prints on our hearts. You are missed.

Beth Cornelison started writing stories as a child when she penned a tale about the adventures of her cat, Ajax. A Georgia native, she received her bachelor's degree in public relations from the University of Georgia. After working in public relations for a little more than a year, she moved with her husband to Louisiana, where she decided to pursue her love of writing fiction.

Since that first time, Beth has written many more stories of adventure and romance suspense and has won numerous honors for her work, including a coveted Golden Heart award in romantic suspense from Romance Writers of America. She is active on the board of directors for the North Louisiana Storytellers and Authors of Romance (NOLA STARS) and loves reading, traveling, Peanuts' Snoopy and spending downtime with her family.

She writes from her home in Louisiana, where she lives with her husband, one son and two cats who think they are people. Beth loves to hear from her readers. You can write to her at PO Box 5418, Bossier City, LA 71171, USA or visit her website at www.bethcornelison.com.

Chapter 1

His father had been murdered—*twice*.

Peter Walsh ground his back teeth together and shifted uncomfortably in the front seat of his truck. Stakeouts were tedious enough without nagging concerns over a crime that should never have happened. His father had been killed fifteen years ago—or so his family had thought. But then, just a few months ago, Mark Walsh's body had been found in Honey Creek. All evidence pointed to murder. A *recent* murder.

So where had Mark Walsh been for the last fifteen years if he was not dead? Who had known Peter's father was still alive and hated him enough to murder him—again?

Explaining to his son, Patrick, that Grandpa Walsh had been murdered—for real this time—had confused and upset the impressionable ten-year-old. Peter could see the strain all of the turmoil was causing Patrick. He'd become withdrawn, sullen. One more concern to keep Peter awake at night.

Peter rubbed warmth into his cold hands. The November morning was brisker than average thanks to the cold front that had dumped several inches of snow overnight. The first signs of winter had come to Honey Creek, Montana, with a snowfall in October. But that snow had been followed by unseasonably warm weather, a tornado and then more cold air. Peter shook his head, musing over the crazy seesawing weather.

Raising his camera with its telephoto lens to the open truck window—a necessity for a clear view despite the frigid temperatures—Peter focused on the front porch, then the barn door, of the Rigsby residence. Still no activity. Still no proof that Bill Rigsby was defrauding his insurance company with false injury claims.

With his surveillance of Rigsby's farm yielding little evidence to take back to his client, Peter's thoughts returned to the numerous troubling events his family had dealt with in recent months, the most glaring being the shocking reappearance and murder of his father. Peter's stomach rumbled, and he lifted his travel mug to sip coffee that had long ago gotten cold. Maybe he should pack it in, get some lunch and head to the hospital to visit Craig.

When a woman stepped out on the Rigsbys' porch to feed a pair of mutts, he lifted the camera again. He clicked a few shots, just because, as his thoughts mulled the latest hit the Walshes had taken.

Craig Warner, the man who had been more of a father to Peter than Mark Walsh had ever been, had suffered his own mysterious attack in the last few weeks. The stomach virus Craig thought he had turned out to be arsenic poisoning. Lester Atkins, Craig's assistant, had tried to kill the CFO of Walsh Enterprises within months of Mark Walsh's murder.

Then his sister Mary had been blatantly run off the road after visiting Damien Colton in prison. Coincidence?

Not likely.

Peter's gut tightened. He smelled a conspiracy. The Walsh family, the people he cared about, were under attack. Someone in Honey Creek had viciously—

Click-click.

Peter froze as the pumping sound of a shotgun filtered into the open truck window.

"Who the hell are you and what are you doin' on my land?" a low voice growled.

Peter turned slowly, his hands up, and stared down the barrel of a Remington 870. Silently he cursed the distracting thoughts that had allowed this armed farmer to approach his truck without Peter noticing. That kind of inattention could get him killed. An unsettling thought when the Walshes and their business associates seemed to be the target of a murderer.

Peter took a slow breath that belied the speed of his thoughts as he analyzed the best way to diffuse this situation. "Is that a Wingmaster?"

The armed farmer lowered the muzzle an inch or so to narrow a curious gaze on Peter. "Yeah."

Peter smiled. "Man, I've been wanting to buy a Wingmaster for years. Remington sure knows how to build a beauty of a shotgun, don't they?"

The farmer hesitated then snarled, "I asked you who the hell you were! What are you doin' out here?"

Peter's pulse kicked. The last thing he needed was an irate farmer with a twitchy trigger finger blasting a hole in his truck—or his head. Palms out in a conciliatory gesture, Peter tried again to calm the man. "If you'll put the gun down, we'll talk. I don't want any trouble."

The man shifted his weight nervously. "Get out of the truck."

Hell. If he got himself killed, who'd raise Patrick? His motherless son had already lost too many people in his short life. Peter gritted his teeth. Screwups like this weren't like him. Proof positive that he needed to get the disarray of his private life in order before he could be effective for his clients.

He nodded his compliance before he reached down to open the driver's door of his truck. As he stepped down from the cab, he resisted the urge to stretch his stiff muscles. Better not give the jittery farmer any reason to shoot. As he slid out of the truck, he pulled his identification wallet out of the map pocket and flipped it open.

If people didn't look too closely, his private-investigator license looked pretty intimidating.

"I'm Peter Walsh, and I'm here on official business." The vague statement usually made people think he meant *police* business, which won their cooperation.

The farmer looked skeptical. He wouldn't be bluffed. "What kind of official business?"

Peter wasn't about to show his hand until he could determine whether the farmer was likely to report to the Rigsbys on Peter's surveillance operation. If Rigsby had a heads-up that the insurance company was on to his fraud, he could cover his tracks. Peter needed to catch the man who claimed to have a disabling injury in the act—horseback-riding, snowmobiling, shoveling his front sidewalk. Anything that would prove he wasn't bedridden with a back injury as he claimed.

"Lower the gun, and we'll talk."

Farmer tensed. "I'm giving the orders here, buddy. You've been sittin' out here on my property for hours, and I want to know why. Now!"

Technically the road was county property, but Peter didn't feel quibbling over that point was wise, given the man's mood. And his weapon.

Peter's priority was getting the shotgun barrel out of his face. He was already plotting his next move as he asked, "We had reports of some suspicious activity at your neighbors' house. When was the last time you saw Bill Rigsby?"

"Bill Rigsby? What kind of suspicious—?"

Peter made his move.

While the farmer's attention was focused on answering the baited question, Peter swept his arm up, knocking the shotgun away from his face, then followed through by grabbing the gun by the barrel and yanking it from the startled farmer's grip.

"Hey!" the man shouted.

Peter tossed the weapon on the front seat of his truck and slammed the door. "I asked you to lower the gun. You didn't, so now we'll do things my way. You'll get the gun back once you answer *my* questions."

The farmer stepped closer, glowering, but his nose only reached Peter's chin. "You sonofa—"

"Answer the question!" Peter barked, seizing the upper hand. He loomed over the shorter man, squaring his broad shoulders and narrowing a hard stare. "When was the last time you saw Bill Rigsby?"

The farmer's Adam's apple bobbed. "Yesterday."

"What was he doing?"

The farmer shrugged. "Nothing. Just out riding, checking his fence."

"On horseback?"

The man gave him a no-shit-Sherlock look. "Yeah. Horseback. Why?"

Peter kept his expression blank, although he sensed the

farmer could prove a wealth of information. The sooner he finished the Rigsby case for his client, the sooner he could look into the questions surrounding his father's murder. "Does Rigsby ride often?"

The farmer cocked his head, sending Peter a dubious frown. "He has to. Got a farm to run."

Peter catalogued the information, then hooked his thumbs in his jeans pockets. "Ever see him shoveling snow?"

The farmer snorted. "There a law against that?"

"No. Does he shovel the front walk or does his wife?"

"He does. Why does that matter? What kind of suspicious activity is he into?"

To keep Rigsby's neighbor off balance, Peter asked, "You ever see a black van parked in front of Bill's house?"

The farmer took a step back and squinted at Peter with deep creases in his brow. Lowering his voice, the farmer asked, "Is he dealing drugs?"

Deflecting the question and turning it to his advantage, Peter responded, "Why? Have you seen evidence that Rigsby has acquired a large unexplained sum of money recently?"

The other man folded his arms over his chest and frowned. "Well, he did buy a new four-wheeler a couple of weeks ago. My wife and I were puzzling over how he afforded it, what with the economy being the way it is and all." He shook his head, his scowl darkening. "Are you telling me Bill Rigsby is a drug dealer?"

Peter raised a palm, keeping his expression neutral. He'd feed the farmer's paranoia without outright lying if it would get him the information he needed. "Let's not get ahead of ourselves. My investigation isn't finished." He glanced meaningfully toward the Rigsby property. "Do you have any idea where I might find Bill Rigsby now?"

The man lifted one shoulder. "Can't say for sure, but I think I heard him and his son leave by snowmobile at first light this morning. My guess is they headed down to the south pasture for the day."

Peter blew out a deep breath that clouded in front of him in the chilly November air. "So Bill's still able to drive a snowmobile since his injury?"

The farmer looked confused. "What injury? Did that good-for-nothing liar tell someone he was laid up again?"

Bingo.

"Again?" Peter eyed the man carefully. "He's pulled a scam before?"

"And brags about it." The farmer glared in the direction of the Rigsby farm. "I hate cheaters."

"If you knew your neighbor was involved in the kind of insurance fraud that means you have to pay higher premiums, would you be willing to testify at a deposition on behalf of the insurance company?"

The man arched an eyebrow. "Testify?"

"That you've seen him shoveling snow, horseback-riding and snowmobiling."

The farmer jerked a nod. "Damn straight."

Peter turned and took the shotgun out of his truck. He handed it back to the farmer. "Is there a road that will take me to the Rigsbys' south pasture? I'd like to get a few pictures of Bill Rigsby snowmobiling."

The farmer gave Peter a gloating grin. "There sure is."

An hour later, Peter drove toward the hospital in Honey Creek to see Craig Warner. He had a dozen or more incriminating photos of Bill Rigsby and his son riding snowmobiles, chopping wood and loading hay bales in the south pasture. More than enough evidence for his client to prove that Rigsby's disability claim was false. With that matter behind him, Peter focused his attention on the problems that had kept him awake at night in recent weeks—the attacks on his family.

While he hadn't been close to his father before Mark had disappeared, believed to be dead, Peter took personally the recent discovery of Mark Walsh's body and apparent murder. Any ill will he had for his father because of his numerous affairs and his desertion of the family didn't offset Peter's hunger for justice. Mark Walsh *was* his father, bad one though he'd been, and his murder cut too close to home for Peter to rest easily. Was the murderer's vendetta just against Mark or was there a broad conspiracy at play? Knowing that Craig, the man who'd run Walsh Enterprises for years and been like a second father to Peter, had been deliberately poisoned made the conspiracy theory more valid to Peter.

After parking in the hospital lot, Peter slammed his truck door as he headed inside.

Craig was alone in his hospital room when Peter arrived, which suited Peter just fine. He really didn't want to have the conversation he intended to have with Craig in front of his mother, who had been hovering by her lover's bedside since he'd been admitted.

"Afternoon, Craig. How's tricks?" Peter worked to keep his smile in place when he saw how pale and drawn Craig still looked even after several days of chelation therapy to rid his body of the arsenic in his system.

"Peter, good to see you. I was just about to call you." Craig rearranged the tubes that fed fluids and detoxifying agents into his blood and tried to sit up.

Seeing Craig, who'd been the picture of strength and

virility before his poisoning, laid low by the arsenic sent a chill deep into Peter's bones. *We could have lost him.*

"Looks like I saved you a call then, huh? What can I do for you?" Peter removed his coat and took a seat beside the narrow bed.

"Keep an eye on your mother for me. She's still so upset over this poisoning mess. I've told her I'm going to be fine, but you know how she worries. She's wearing herself out dividing her time between me and all her regular responsibilities with the company and her family—especially that son of yours. Her grandson is the world to her."

Guilt kicked Peter in the shins. He'd long known he depended too heavily on his mother for babysitting Patrick after school, but Jolene insisted on watching her grandson rather than hiring someone else. As a single father, Peter was grateful for the help and didn't argue the point.

"Come on, now, Craig. I thought you knew by now, no one tells Jolene Walsh to slow down. She's happiest when she's taking care of her chickadees." Peter forced a grin. He, too, had seen the strain his mother was under. Who could blame her? Having her husband's body discovered and her closest friend poisoned…

"Are you calling me a chickadee?" Craig said weakly, a smile playing at the corner of his mouth.

Peter laughed. "Never. But you know what I mean."

Craig nodded. "So what brings you around today?"

"I can't stop by to see how you're feeling?"

Sinking deeper into the stack of pillows behind him, Craig sighed. "I know you better than that, Peter. Something's on your mind, so spill."

Peter rubbed his temple and stared at his boots. "Have you heard anything else from the sheriff about who is behind your poisoning?"

"Lester Atkins is the only arrest the sheriff's made."

"Yeah, and we both know he didn't act alone. Someone paid him. Someone supplied the arsenic."

Craig nodded. "Sheriff Colton said he'd look into the possibility Atkins had help."

"Sheriff Colton is first and foremost a Colton," Peter scoffed. "I'd bet anything the Coltons had a hand in this. Maybe Damien was wrongfully convicted fifteen years ago, but I wouldn't put it past his family to have arranged my dad's *real* murder—and your poisoning—as revenge. Or to cover some other crime. Or…hell, the possibilities are endless when it comes to the Coltons."

Darius Colton and his offspring knew how to wield power and intimidate the right people. They'd been a thorn in the Walsh family's side since before Mark disappeared and Damien Colton was accused of his murder.

"I've considered the possibility that the Coltons could be involved myself. Finn's been treating me for the poisoning, so I don't think he's our man." Craig closed his eyes and sighed. "But if another Colton is responsible, how do we prove it?"

Peter gritted his teeth and shook his head. "Not through official channels, that's for sure." Because Wes Colton was the sheriff, Peter needed to find a way to circumvent the sheriff's department and get to the bottom of his father's murder and Craig's poisoning.

"I can hire someone to look into the matter. Money is no object for me." Craig paused for a breath, his weakness from the poisoning still evident. "You and your mother are family to me, and I have a feeling we haven't seen the last of these attacks. Until whoever is behind this mess is stopped, we're all still in danger. That includes you and Patrick."

A chill shimmied through Peter. Craig was right. He had to protect Patrick.

Despite his heavy case load—cheating spouses, insurance fraud, missing teenagers, adopted kids looking for their birth parents—Peter had to find the person behind the attacks.

He met Craig's dark eyes with a level stare. "I'll do the legwork myself. I have resources at my disposal, law enforcement and investigation training." *If not much time.*

He hated that taking on a private investigation into his father's death would mean more time away from Patrick. But how could he let Craig's poisoning, Mary's attack and Mark's murder go unsolved?

Craig's wan face creased with worry. "Are you sure you want to dig into your father's business and expose yourself to his skeletons?"

Peter's gut churned at the thought of the dirt he was likely to uncover on his father if he undertook this investigation of his murder. "I'm sure. But I'll need your help."

"My help?" Craig lifted the numerous IV tubes and tipped his head. "I'd love to assist you, but I'm kind of tied down at the moment."

"I need information from you. I need you to try to remember anything suspicious that may have happened at Walsh Enterprises in the weeks before my dad was murdered. Did my father contact you? Did you know he was alive?"

Craig's gaze softened. "If I'd known that, I would have told you and your brother and sisters and your mother, Peter. You know that."

"Okay." Peter waved that issue away. "Then what about the company? Any suspicious activity in the accounts or operations?"

"I'll check on that, but…my memory is a little muddled. The arsenic caused me a bit of confusion and lapses in my memory." He twitched a wry grin. "Thank God it was just poison. I thought I was getting senile."

Peter forced a grin, but reminders of how close he'd come to losing the man who'd been a surrogate father was no laughing matter. "What about threats? Had anyone contacted you—"

When Peter's cell rang, he scowled, checked the caller ID.

Honey Creek Elementary.

His pulse spiked. If the school was calling in the middle of the day, it couldn't be good news. Was Patrick sick? Hurt?

Had his father's killer come after his son?

He jabbed the talk button, his heart in his throat. "Peter Walsh."

"Hello, Mr. Walsh," a sweet female voice began. "This is Lisa Navarre. I'm Patrick's teacher."

"What's happened? Was there trouble at school?" Peter was already out of his chair and putting on his coat.

"Well, yes, there's been an incident. I need you to come to the school as soon as—"

"I'll be right there." He disconnected the call and squeezed his eyes closed. Patrick was his whole world. If anything happened to his son—

Panic rising in his throat, Peter met Craig's concerned gaze.

"Is Patrick all right?"

"I don't know. His teacher said there'd been an accident. I have to go." He backed quickly toward the door. "But we'll talk more later. I want the people responsible for doing this to you caught, Craig. I won't rest until I find everyone involved in this conspiracy."

Chapter 2

"Eyes on your own paper, Anthony." Lisa Navarre gave the student in question a firm but kind look to reiterate her directive.

Cheeks flushing, Anthony DePaulo lowered his head over his geography quiz and got back to work.

Lisa checked the clock. "Fifteen more minutes. Pace yourselves. Don't spend too much time on a question you don't—"

Her classroom door slammed open, and a tall, dark-haired man—an extremely handsome man—burst through. His eyes were wide with alarm, his manner agitated. Even before Mr. Handsome Interruption's gaze scanned the room and landed on Patrick Walsh, Lisa knew this had to be Peter Walsh. The father was the spitting image of his son. Or vice versa, she supposed. Dark brown hair roguishly in need of a trim, square-cut jaw and a generous mouth that was currently taut with concern.

"Mr. Walsh, I—"

"Patrick!" Peter Walsh rushed to his son's desk and framed his face, tipping his head as if checking for injury. "Are you all right?"

"Da-ad!" Patrick wrestled free from his father's zealous examination, while the class twittered with amusement.

"Settle down, kids. Finish your work." Lisa hustled down the row of desks to rescue Patrick from further embarrassment. "Mr. Walsh, if you would?" She tugged his arm and hitched her head toward the hall. "We can talk in the office. As you can see, the class is in the middle of a test."

Peter Walsh raised dark, bedroom eyes—okay, not bedroom eyes. He was a student's parent, so maybe that descriptor was inappropriate…but, gosh, his rich brown eyes made her belly quiver. Confusion filled his expression, then morphed to frustration or anger. Now her gut swirled for a new reason. She hated dealing with angry parents.

"Fine." Mr. Walsh gave one last glance to his son before stalking out to the hallway.

"Keep working, kids. I'll be right back." Lisa swept her practiced be-on-your-best-behavior look around the room, meeting the eyes of several of her more…er, *loquacious* students before she joined Mr. Walsh in the corridor.

He launched into her before she could open her mouth. "What's going on? You called me here because there'd been—"

"Mr. Walsh." Lisa held up a hand to cut him off, then caught the attention of the school librarian who was walking past them. "Ms. Fillmore, would you mind sitting with my class for a few minutes while I talk with Mr. Walsh in the office?"

"Certainly," the older woman said with a smile.

"They're taking a geography quiz. You'll need to pick up the papers at exactly two-thirty if I'm not back."

"Got it. Two-thirty." Ms. Fillmore gave a little wave as she disappeared into the classroom.

When Lisa turned back to Patrick's father, she met a glare that would freeze a volcano. "You lied to me. You said Patrick had been in an accident. Do you have any idea how worried I was on the way over here?"

Patience. Keep your cool. Let him vent if he needs to.

Drawing a deep breath to collect herself, she flashed him a warm smile. "Let's go to the office where we can speak privately." She motioned down the hall and started toward the front of the school. When Mr. Walsh only stared at her stubbornly for a moment, she paused to wait for him to follow. Handsome or not, the man clearly had a temper when it came to his son.

Lisa could understand that. Most parents had an emotional hot button when it came to their children. Sweet, soft-spoken members of the quilting club became growling mama bears when they thought their cubs needed protecting or defending.

Finally, Peter Walsh fell in step behind her, his long-legged strides quickly catching up with hers. "Why did you tell me there'd been an accident?"

"I didn't," she returned calmly.

"You di—"

"I said *incident*. With an *i*. You hung up before I could explain the nature of the problem."

Mr. Walsh drew a breath as if to mount an argument, then snapped his mouth closed. His brow creased, and his jaw tightened as if replaying their brief phone conversation and realizing his mistake.

"I'm sorry if I alarmed you. Patrick is fine, physically."

They reached the front office, and Lisa escorted him into a vacant conference room. "Please, have a seat."

Patrick's father crossed his arms over his chest and narrowed a suspicious gaze on her. "Thanks, I'll stand."

Okay. She faced him, squaring her shoulders and staring at his forehead…because looking into those dark eyes was just too distracting. Too unnerving.

Darn it all, she was a professional. She couldn't let this man rattle her.

"Mr. Walsh, I called you because Patrick was disrupting class today and—"

"Disrupting how?" he interrupted, his back stiffening.

"He burped."

Mr. Walsh's eyebrows snapped together in confusion. "Excuse me? He burped?"

"Yes."

He shifted his weight and angled an irritated look toward her. "You called me down here to tell me he *burped?*" His angry tone and volume rose. "Kids will burp sometimes, lady. It's a fact of life. Maybe you should be talking to the lunch ladies about the food they're serving instead of calling parents away from important business to report their kids' bodily functions, for crying out loud!"

Patience. Lisa balled then flexed her fingers, struggling to keep her cool. She made the mistake of meeting his eyes then, and her stomach flip-flopped. Good grief, the man had sexy eyes!

"It wasn't just a small, my-lunch-didn't-sit-right burp, Mr. Walsh. It was loud. Forced. Designed to get a rise out of his classmates."

Peter Walsh rocked back on his boot heels, listening. At least, she hoped he was listening. Some parents wore blinders when it came to their kids' behavior. Their little darling couldn't possibly have done the things she said.

Lisa took a slow calming breath, working to keep her voice even and non-confrontational.

"He'd been disruptive all morning—talking, getting out of his seat without permission, making rude noises, even poking the girl in front of him for no apparent reason. The loud belching was just the final straw."

Peter Walsh had the nerve to roll his eyes and shake his head. Lisa gritted her teeth.

"With all due respect, Ms. Navaro—" he started in a tone that was far from respectful.

"It's *Navarre,* Mr. Walsh."

"Navarre," he repeated, lifting his hand in concession, but his disposition remained hard and challenging. "It seems to me keeping order in your classroom is *your* job. Send him to the principal's office if you need to, but don't drag me down here every time my son acts up in class… or *burps.* You shouldn't have to call a kid's parent away from their job to handle a minor behavior problem. If you can't keep a ten-year-old boy in line for a few hours a day, perhaps you're in the wrong profession."

Lisa's hackles went up. She'd already wondered if teaching children was the best place for her, but for reasons that had nothing to do with her ability to discipline her class. She suppressed the ache that nudged her heart and focused on the matter at hand.

"I'm perfectly capable of maintaining order in my classroom, Mr. Walsh." She drilled him with a look that her students knew well, the one that said she'd reached the limits of her patience. "Especially if I have the cooperation of the children's parents in addressing at home any issues that may be at the root of behavior problems."

He scoffed. "My son does not have a behavior problem. He may be having a bad day today, but you know as well as I do that he's not a troublemaker."

"Which, if you'd let me finish explaining, is why I called you to come down for a conference. Usually Patrick is quite well-behaved. In fact, since the beginning of school, it seems he's become more quiet, even withdrawn. His grades have slipped in recent weeks. Did you know that? I've sent home his test papers to be signed, but you never sign them. His grandmother does."

"My mother babysits him most afternoons until I can get home from work. My job keeps me on the road a lot, and I've had to work longer hours lately, so Patrick's grandmother handles his schoolwork."

"But you're his parent, Mr. Walsh. You need to be involved."

His face darkened, and he narrowed a glare on her. "Are you telling me how to parent my kid?"

Why not? You were just trying to tell me how to do my job! Lisa bit back the caustic retort that would serve no purpose other than make her feel better for five minutes. Then she'd feel bad that she'd lost her temper and kick herself for being reactionary.

"No, sir. I'm not." She purposefully infused her tone with calm and concern, enough to capture the agitated father's attention. She had to be sure he heard and understood the importance of her next statement. "But earlier today, when I warned Patrick that I would have to call you if he didn't behave, his response was, 'Go ahead. Call my dad. He won't care. He's too busy to care about what I do.'"

Peter Walsh jerked back as if slapped, his expression stunned. "That's…crazy! He knows I care about him. He knows I *love* him! More than anything in this world."

"Maybe up here he knows that." She tapped her head. "But kids need to see that love and affection in action to reaffirm what you say. He needs to see you express interest in his schoolwork, in his friends, in his life to really believe it here." She moved her hand to her heart.

A muscle in his jaw twitched, and he shifted his glowering gaze to a bulletin board on the far wall. "The last few months have been...especially difficult for my family, Ms. Navarre. I've tried to protect Patrick from most of the fallout, shield him from the worst of it, but..." He heaved a sigh and left his sentence unfinished.

"I read the newspaper. I know about your father's murder, and I'm terribly sorry for your loss."

His eyes snapped to hers. Pain shadowed his gaze, and her heart went out to him. She'd seen a similar sadness in Patrick's eyes too many times since the school year had started. "The reason I called you here is not because Patrick was acting out. I can handle disciplining students when it is called for."

Chagrin flickered across his face, and he shifted his weight.

"I called because I'm worried about Patrick. I think the recent events in your family have upset him, and he doesn't feel he can talk to you about it. He feels alone because he thinks you're too busy for him. He's confused and scared."

Worry lined Peter Walsh's face. "He said that?"

"His withdrawal said that. His grades said that. His misbehavior today said that. I've been a teacher for six years. I've seen this before. He just needs reassurance from you that his world is safe, that you care, that he is your priority. Mr. Walsh, more than discipline, what Patrick needs is his father."

Peter squared his shoulders, a bit of his temper returning. Obviously, he took her last comment as an indictment. "I'll talk to him tonight. You won't have problems with his behavior again."

Lisa's heart sank. Had he heard her at all?

Peter Walsh, his square jaw tight and his back stiff, turned to stalk out of the conference room.

"Mr. Walsh, I—"

But he was gone. All six feet plus of seething testosterone and brooding eyes. Lisa inhaled deeply, hoping to calm her frazzled nerves, but instead drew in the enticing scents of leather and pine that Peter Walsh left in his wake.

She had no business thinking of her student's father in the terms that filtered through her head—sexy, virile—but with a man like Peter Walsh, how could she not?

Lisa dropped into a chair and raked fingers through her raven hair. She needed to collect herself before she returned to her class.

But five minutes later, as she headed back to her room, her mind was still full of Peter Walsh and his smoldering dark eyes.

Patrick tossed his backpack on the floor of Peter's truck and gave his father a forlorn glance as he climbed onto the seat. "So I guess I'm in big trouble, huh?"

Peter shrugged. "Depends on what you call big trouble. I understand you gave your teacher a good bit of grief today. You were loud and disruptive in class. You know better than that, sport."

"Am I grounded?"

"Do you think you should be grounded?"

Patrick hesitated, got a scheming glint in his eyes. "No? I think I've learned my lesson, and we can skip the punishment?" He lifted hopeful dark eyes to his father.

"Seriously? I think I hear a question mark in your answer. You know I can't just let this slide. What if I'd been working a big case out of town when I got called to the school? Huh?"

Patrick scowled. "You're always working big cases out of town. Why can't you have a regular job like everyone else?"

Peter's chest tightened. He'd heard Patrick complain about his work hours before, but in light of his teacher's concerns, Peter took his son's comments more seriously this time. "Patrick, you know I'd spend more time with you if I could. There's nothing in the world more important to me than you are, but I have to earn a living and pay our bills. My job demands that I be gone a lot. I can't change that."

But even as he said as much, a niggling voice in his head argued the point. He *could* rearrange his schedule or be more selective in the cases he took on so that he could have more time at home with Patrick. Even if the more lucrative cases took him out of town, couldn't they tighten their monetary belts a bit in order for him to be more attentive to his son's needs?

He glanced over at Patrick's long face, slumped shoulders. Guilt pricked Peter.

"Tell you what—I'll make a special effort to cut back on my hours and do more stuff with you—"

Immediately, Patrick's eyes brightened, and he snapped an eager gaze up to his father's.

"If—"

Patrick rolled his eyes and groaned. "I knew there was a catch."

Peter shot his son a stern glance. "Don't interrupt. You have to promise me you'll work hard at bringing your grades up. Mrs. Navarre said your work has been slipping."

"*Ms.* Navarre, Dad. She's not married."

Peter quirked an eyebrow, mentally flashing to when he'd been corrected by the woman herself on the pronunciation of her name. He worked to school his expression and hide his intrigue with this new tidbit of information. He'd been too worked up, too worried about Patrick during his altercation with the attractive brunette to look for a ring. But even as upset as he'd been, he hadn't missed Ms. Navarre's shapely curves or model-worthy face.

Hell, he couldn't blame Patrick for being distracted and having faltering grades with a teacher as hot as Lisa Navarre. Any male over the age of nine would be distracted by Patrick's teacher.

Peter squeezed the steering wheel and cleared his throat. "Ms. Navarre also said that you were talking back to her, being rude." Peter cast a disapproving look to his son. "Burping."

Patrick chuckled. "Yeah, it was a good one, too, Dad. Really low and loud and—"

"Patrick," Peter said, a warning clear in his tone. "It was rude and inappropriate."

"But Da-ad—"

Peter raised a hand, anticipating the coming argument. "I know that we sometimes goof around at home and do stuff like that, but…there's a time and a place for that kind of behavior and school is *not* the time or place."

God, when had he started sounding like his father? No. Not his father. More like his *mother*. Egad. *That* was scary. Peter cringed internally.

But Mark Walsh had never been interested in teaching his son wrong and right. He'd been too busy cheating on his wife. Acid burned in Peter's belly at the memory, and he swore to himself, again, that he'd be a better father to Patrick than Mark Walsh had been to him.

Mr. Walsh, more than discipline, what Patrick needs is his father.

"Patrick, I think the thing I find most disturbing about what happened at school today is that you sassed your teacher. I didn't raise you to disrespect adults and especially not a lady."

"That's no lady, that's my teacher," Patrick said in a deep voice, mimicking the comedian they'd watched on television together the past weekend.

Peter had to bite the inside of his cheek so that he wouldn't laugh. He couldn't encourage Patrick's misbehavior, even if he did find his son's sense of humor amusing.

Instead, he gave Patrick the look all parents have instinctively. The I-mean-business-and-you're-treading-on-thin-ice look.

"Tomorrow, first thing when you get to school, you will apologize to Ms. Navarre for being rude and disruptive."

Patrick gave a dramatic sigh and stared out the window.

"Look at me." When he had his son's attention he added, "And you're grounded for…" Peter did a quick calculation. What length of punishment suited the crime? And why *wasn't* there an instruction manual for parents? Raising his son alone was, hands-down, the hardest thing he'd ever done.

And the most rewarding, he thought as he held his boy's dark gaze. "For the weekend. No video games, no TV, no going to your friends'."

"What!" Patrick grunted. "What's left?"

"Try reading a book, or catching up on your schoolwork. Or…going fishing with me."

"Hello? Dad…it's November. It's freezing."

"What, you don't think fish get hungry in November?" He tugged up the corner of his mouth. "Okay, so…we'll save fishing for spring, and we'll…" Peter turned up his palm as he thought. "Catch a football game together."

"You said no TV."

"I know. I'm talking about going *to* a game. Live. I bet

I can still get us tickets to see the Bobcats play. What do ya think?"

Patrick's face lit with enthusiasm. "Montana State? Seriously, Dad? Can we?" Patrick whooped.

"I'll take that as a yes," Peter chuckled as his son bounced in his seat. "But remember our deal."

Patrick screwed up his face. "What deal?"

Peter shook his head in frustration. "You're going to bring up your grades, apologize to your teacher and promise me that your days of clowning around in class are over. Got it, buddy?"

Patrick slumped back against the seat, a contrite expression pulling his mouth taut. "Yes, sir."

On the way home from school, Lisa stopped at Salon Allegra for a pedicure. Sure, it was November and no one except her would likely see her bare feet until next spring, but after standing all day and dealing with Patrick Walsh's aggravated father, she figured she deserved a little pampering. Heck, she might get a manicure, too.

Lisa pulled the collar of her parka up around her chin as she bustled into the beauty shop. The bell over the front door tinkled as she entered, announcing her arrival to the staff. The shop's owner, Eve Kelley, looked up from the appointment book at the front desk and sent her a bright smile.

"Afternoon, Lisa. What brings you in on this blustery day?" Eve's blue eyes shone warmly, her girl-next-door-meets-cheerleader friendliness in place as always.

"Hi, Eve. I need a pick-me-up in the worst way. I thought I'd get a pedicure if you could work me in."

"Well…" Eve glanced to her beauticians, each with a customer already, and gnawed her bottom lip.

"If you're too busy, I'll—"

"Nonsense. I'll get you fixed up myself." She picked up a tube of salted crackers and motioned for Lisa to follow. "So...bad day at school?"

"Not for the most part. Plans for the rescheduled fall festival are going well. But one of my better students decided to act out today, and when I called his father in for a conference, I got an earful. Dad settled down a little once I got the chance to explain myself, but...whew! Confrontations with parents always leave me wrung out."

"I bet." Eve patted an elevated chair, showing Lisa where to sit, and set her crackers on a nearby table. As Eve took her seat, Lisa noticed the former prom queen and cheerleader had unbuttoned her jeans at the waist, as if they didn't quite fit anymore.

Had Eve put on a couple of pounds? Lisa couldn't really tell.

The beauty shop owner look as gorgeous as ever to her. Eve turned and caught Lisa staring, speculating. "So who was this irate father?"

"Oh, uh...Peter Walsh."

Eve paused in her preparations for Lisa's pedicure. "Peter Walsh? But Peter's always struck me as the laid-back, easygoing sort." Eve flashed her a devilish grin and wiggled her eyebrows. "The *extremely hot,* laid-back, easygoing sort."

An image of Peter Walsh's broad shoulders and rough-hewn jawline taunted her as Lisa returned a smile. "Oh, he is good-looking, no lie. But when it comes to his son, he apparently has a bit of pit bull in him."

"Hmm." Eve hummed as she nibbled a cracker and tipped her head in thought. "I've known the Walsh family for years. Peter has never been overly social, but also never anything but kind and polite. He's had a tough road, raising Patrick on his own."

When Eve paused to munch another cracker, Lisa asked, "What happened to Patrick's mother?"

A shadow crossed Eve's face, her sculpted eyebrows puckering with some dark emotion. "She died...in childbirth." Eve's gaze drifted away, across the room, as she recalled the details. She rubbed a hand over her belly almost without thought.

An odd tingle of recognition nipped Lisa's nape. She glanced at Eve's crackers then studied the pretty blonde's glowing face. Could she be...?

"Katie and Peter were so young," Eve said and shook her head sorrowfully. "Probably only nineteen or so, but they'd been high-school sweethearts and married right after graduation. Katie's death crushed Peter. And after losing his father a few years earlier...well, we *thought* his dad was dead..."

Eve gave her head a shake and puffed out a breath. "But that's a whole other can of worms. One more freak tragedy for him and his family to have to deal with." Jamming one more cracker in her mouth, Eve turned on the jets of the steaming foot bath for Lisa to soak in.

Lisa slipped off her shoes and socks, giving her sore feet a little rub before sinking them in the warm water. Her fatigue now pressed on her with a more somber note, but she couldn't blame Peter Walsh for her gray mood.

Mention of childbirth gone wrong and the subtle clues that Eve was pregnant stirred up painful memories. Memories that were better locked away where they couldn't haunt her.

Shoving down thoughts of the baby she'd never have, Lisa wiggled her toes in the steaming foot bath and redirected her thoughts to the subject at hand. "So Peter has raised Patrick alone since his birth?"

"Yep. Although I'm sure his family gives him plenty of help and babysitting services. Jolene can't say enough glowing things about Patrick when she's in here." Eve smiled wistfully. "Like any good grandma would." She started working on Lisa's right foot, buffing, trimming and shaping. "Anyway… don't let this first impression of Peter Walsh color your opinion of him. He really is a great guy. Any gal would be lucky to have him."

"Whoa!" Lisa held up her hands. "I never said anything about dating him. I'm not looking for a husband."

Eve flipped her blond hair over her shoulder and flashed Lisa a saucy look. "Who said anything about *you?* He might be ten years younger than me but…hoo-baby! When a guy looks that good, who cares about age?"

They both laughed, and Lisa felt a little of her tension melt away.

"So what color on the toes?" Eve asked, pulling out a large tray of nail polish.

"Oh, just a basic pink or mauve is fine."

Eve scrunched up her nose. "Pink is so boring, girlfriend. How about this new sexy red I got in last week? Or…oh, I know! Electric purple!"

Lisa snorted. "Me? Purple?"

Eve wiggled the bottle and raised her eyebrows with enthusiasm. "Come on. Be daring! It looks really sexy."

Lisa shrugged. "What the heck. Paint me purple. Not like anyone but my cat is gonna see my toes anyway."

And thanks to her inability to have children, Lisa thought with a pang of sorrow, that was how things were likely to be for a long time. Even her attempt to adopt once had ended in heartache.

No children. No husband. No family.

A lonely ache settled over her. Her infertility hadn't just robbed her of a child, but also the future she craved.

Peter flipped his wrist to check the time. "Better get a move on, sport. School bus will be here any minute."

"Do you gotta work out of town again today?" Patrick asked around a mouthful of cereal.

"Nope. I wrapped up the legwork on a case yesterday, so I'll mostly be working from home today to get the paperwork finished. Why?"

His son shrugged. "Just wonderin' if you'd be here when I got home or if Grandma would."

He feels alone, because he thinks you're too busy for him.

Lisa Navarre's assessment rang in Peter's head, and he studied the droop in Patrick's shoulders as he slurped sugary milk from his breakfast bowl.

"I'll make a point of being here when you get off the bus today. Okay, sport? After you do your homework, we'll do something together. Your choice."

Patrick gave him a withering look that said parents were the stupidest creatures on earth. "Dad, it's Friday. I don't have homework on Fridays."

"Good," Peter returned with good humor. "Then we'll have more time to do something together."

"Can we play on the Wii?"

Peter was about to agree when he remembered yesterday's punishment. "Aren't you grounded for the weekend?"

Patrick's face fell. "Oh, yeah."

Outside, the bus tooted its horn.

"Time's up. Grab your backpack!" Peter hurried to the front door to wave to the bus driver, while Patrick struggled out. "Don't worry. We'll find something fun to do that doesn't include the TV. And… I haven't forgotten about taking you to see the football game tomorrow."

Patrick's face brightened as he rushed past. "Cool. Bye, Dad!"

"Don't forget to apologize to Ms. Navarre!"

His son gave a wave as he climbed on the bus, and Peter sighed. Patrick wasn't the only one who owed the attractive brunette an apology. He'd been pretty hostile, when Patrick's teacher had only had his son's best interests at heart.

Peter scrubbed a hand over his unshaven cheeks as he went back in his house. His only lame excuse for his shameful behavior was that he'd already been pumped full of adrenaline after the brush with Bill Rigsby's shotgun-toting neighbor, and he'd been spoiling for a fight after his meeting with Craig, where the Coltons, his least-favorite family, had been high on the list of suspects. But he should never have let his bad mood taint his treatment of Patrick's teacher.

Peter took Patrick's half-eaten cereal to the sink and ate a few bites himself before dumping the rest.

Jamming his thumbs in his jeans pockets, he headed into the den where he had his PC set up in one corner. Perhaps on Monday, he'd drive Patrick to school and make a point of speaking to Ms. Navarre. His pulse spiked a notch, a bump that had more to do with his anticipation of seeing Patrick's teacher again than his morning caffeine kicking in. He thumbed the power button on the computer and leaned back in his chair as the monitor hummed to life.

In the face of his shouting and sarcasm, Lisa Navarre had not only held her own, but she'd kept her tone calm and her arguments constructive and focused on Patrick's needs. He respected her for her professionalism and grace under fire.

And the fact Lisa Navarre had sexy curves and a spark of stubborn courage in her dark eyes only made her more intriguing to Peter. Knowing her observations of Patrick in the classroom mirrored his own suspicions about Patrick's difficulty processing the most recent family troubles gave him reason to call on her expertise. Perhaps the attractive teacher would give him a bit of her time and help him figure out the best way to handle the recent family crises with Patrick.

When his computer finished loading the start-up programs, Peter opened his case file on Bill Rigsby and got to work, but his mind drifted again to the same family issues that had had him distracted yesterday on his stakeout. His visit with Craig at the hospital only confirmed that someone outside the Colton family needed to be looking into his father's murder and who'd paid Atkins to poison Craig.

Peter lifted his coffee mug and squeezed the handle until his knuckles blanched. How could Sheriff Wes Colton possibly conduct an unbiased investigation when his own family was most likely at fault? What secrets and evidence was Wes suppressing to protect his brood of vipers? Craig may have ruled out Finn, since Finn was his doctor, but Peter wasn't willing to make that leap of faith yet.

Peter gritted his teeth and shoved away from the computer. Enough waiting for answers. He'd go down to the sheriff's office and demand answers from Wes Colton.

Even if Mark Walsh had been a half-hearted father and a two-timing husband, he deserved justice. And Craig Warner, the man who'd managed the reins at Walsh Enterprises for almost two decades and who'd been a father figure to Peter, deserved answers about who'd poisoned him.

Peter refused to rest until he had the truth.

* * *

As Peter strode up the front walk to the county courthouse, he huddled deeper into the warmth of his suede coat. A chill November wind announced the approach of another bitterly cold Montana winter, a bleak time of year that reflected Peter's current mood. He glanced up to the steepled clock tower in the red brick and natural stone edifice where the sheriff's office had told him he could find Wes Colton that morning, waiting to testify in a court hearing. The woman at the sheriff's office had said she thought Wes was due at the courthouse by 9:00 a.m.

But if he wasn't, Peter would wait.

He nodded a good-morning to an elderly man who shuffled out the front door of the courthouse, then shucked his gloves as he entered the lobby and got his bearings. The scents of freshly brewed coffee, floor cleaner and age filled the halls of the old building. Peter could remember thinking how old the courthouse seemed when he'd come down here with his mother to get his driver's license when he was sixteen. Little about the building had changed in the intervening years, even if Peter felt he'd lived a lifetime since then.

Jamming his gloves in his coat pocket, Peter spotted Wes Colton down a long corridor and headed purposefully towards him. "Sheriff?"

Wes turned, lifting his eyes from the foam cup of coffee he sipped. The sheriff stilled, his expression growing wary, before he lowered his cup and squared his shoulders, taking a defensive stance.

"Peter." Wes gave a terse nod of greeting. "Something I can do for you?"

"Yeah. You can tell me why no one's been arrested yet for my father's murder." Peter stood with his arms akimbo, his chin jutted forward.

A muscle in Wes's jaw tightened as the sheriff ground his back teeth. "Because we don't have enough evidence to make an arrest stick yet."

"You've had more than four months. What the hell's taking so long?"

"We're doing all we can." The sheriff lifted one eyebrow, his blue eyes as cold as his tone. "I'm sure you wouldn't want us hauling anyone in prematurely, just to lose an indictment due to lack of good evidence." Wes paused and canted his head to the side, his eyes narrowing. "Unlike the last time your father was *murdered,* I intend to build a case based on solid evidence. Forensics. Facts. Not the circumstantial tripe and suspicion they used to railroad my brother when your father pulled his disappearing act years ago."

Peter stiffened. He should have known this discussion would deteriorate to a rehashing of the Walsh and Colton families' ancient feud. Even before Mark Walsh had forbidden his eldest daughter, Lucy, to date Damien Colton, the families had been rivals. Two powerful families in the same small town couldn't help but butt heads every now and then, in business, or in politics, or, in the case of Lucy and Damien, in the personal lives of their children.

"Your brother may have been innocent of murder, but even your family can't deny he looked guilty as sin."

Wes curled his lip in a sneer. "Thanks to your family greasing the skids of the judicial system to see that the prosecutor's flimsy circumstantial case slid by the judges and jury."

Peter stepped closer, aiming a finger at Wes's chest. "We did no such thing!"

The sheriff sent a pointed gaze to Peter's finger before meeting his eyes again. "Want to back off before I charge you with assaulting an officer?"

Drawing a deep breath, Peter dropped his hand to his side, balling his fingers into a fist. "Just tell me where the current case stands. Who are you investigating? What clues do you have?"

Wes shrugged casually. "Everyone's a suspect until the investigation is closed."

"Don't give me that crap. I want answers, Colton!" Damn, but the Coltons could push Peter's buttons.

He paused only long enough to force his tone and volume down a notch. A public brawl with the sheriff would serve no purpose other than to land him in jail for disorderly conduct. "What are you doing to catch my father's murderer?"

"I'm not at liberty to discuss an ongoing investigation."

When Peter shifted his weight, ready to launch into another attack, another round of questions, Wes lifted a hand to forestall any arguments. "And I'm not just saying that to get you off my back or because there's no love lost between our families. I truly can't answer any question for you right now."

"That's not good enough."

"It has to be."

Peter clenched his teeth. "I have a right to know who killed my father."

"And you will. As soon as I know." The sheriff pinned a hard look on Peter. "But I won't blow this case by tipping my hand prematurely or letting you or anyone else pressure me into making an arrest for the sake of making an arrest. My brother knows all too well what happens when vigilante justice is served rather than reason and law. My deputies and I are conducting a thorough investigation. We'll find the person responsible. Don't doubt that."

Scoffing, Peter shook his head. "Well, forgive me if I

don't take you on your word, Sheriff *Colton*. I haven't seen any progress on the case in weeks, and now Craig Warner's been poisoned, too."

"And you think the two incidents are connected." A statement, not a question.

"Damn straight. And I'd hardly call my father's murder and the attempted murder of a family friend 'incidents.' They're felonies. Need I remind you that someone ran Mary off the road a couple months ago? How do we know that whoever is responsible won't come after someone else in my family?"

"We don't."

The sheriff's flat, frank response punched Peter in the gut. When he recovered the wherewithal to speak, he scowled darkly at Wes. "And that doesn't bother you, Sheriff? You may not like me or my family, but I have a ten-year-old son at home. How are you going to feel if he gets hurt because you didn't do your job and find the scumbag who killed my father?"

Wes hooked his thumbs in his pockets and rolled his shoulders. "Believe it or not, I'd feel terrible—and not because I didn't do my job, because I am doing everything humanly possible to catch the bastard. No, because I'm not the inept, hard-hearted fool you seem to think I am. I don't want to see anyone else hurt. But I have to work within the law. A proper investigation takes time. There are forces at work behind the scenes that you may not see, but which are busy 24/7 looking at this case from every angle."

Peter gritted his teeth, completely unsatisfied with the runaround and placating assurances he was getting from the sheriff. "Here's an angle you may have missed. Not only do I think Craig Warner's poisoning is related to my father's murder, I think your family is involved. I'd bet my life a Colton is behind everything."

Wes's glare was glacial. "Do you have any proof to back up that accusation?"

"Not yet. But I can get it."

The sheriff's eyes narrowed even further. "I'm warning you, Walsh. Don't interfere with my investigation. If you so much as stick a toe over the line, I'll throw the book at you."

Peter pulled his gloves from his pocket, signaling an end to the conversation. "I would expect as much."

Chapter 3

Thanks to a new missing-person case on Friday and his promise to take Patrick to the game on Saturday, Sunday afternoon was the first chance Peter had to follow up on his suspicions regarding the Colton family's connection to Craig's poisoning and his father's murder. The best place to start, Peter always figured, was the beginning—in this case, the circumstances and events surrounding the Coltons at the time of Mark Walsh's first "death" in 1995.

He left Patrick in the capable hands of his mother, Jolene, and headed to the library to begin his research. In 1995, when his father went missing and was presumed dead, Peter had been a typically self-absorbed teenager. He hadn't cared what political causes or social events his family or the rival Coltons were involved in. But in hindsight, he thought maybe he could glean some helpful information to focus his investigation.

As he headed into the library from the parking lot, he

noticed a number of large limbs and debris still cluttered the lawn. He frowned at the reminders of the tornado that had struck Honey Creek recently. Most of the brick and stone buildings in town had survived with minimal or no damage, but many homes, including his own, had sustained varying degrees of damage. He scanned the library's brick exterior searching for signs of damage before mounting the steps to enter the front door.

He spotted his younger sister, Mary, near the front desk and made a beeline toward her. "Well, if it isn't the future Mrs. Jake Pierson."

Mary's head snapped up, and a broad smile filled her face. "Peter! How are you?"

Love—and Mary's recent, significant weight loss—looked good on his sister. She positively glowed with her newfound happiness.

"Clearly not as well as you. Look at that radiant flush in your face." He tweaked his sister's cheek playfully, and she swatted his hand away. "So what are you doing here? I thought your days as librarian were over now that you and Jake are opening the security biz."

She leaned a hip against the front desk and grinned. "I may not work here, but I have friends who do. And I volunteer to lead the story time in the children's area on Sunday afternoons. What brings *you* in today, and why didn't you bring my favorite nephew with you?"

"Mom's watching Patrick so I can get some research done." Peter unbuttoned his coat and glanced around at the tables where people were scattered, reading and studying. An attractive dark-haired woman at one of the corner tables snagged his attention.

Lisa Navarre.

Patrick's teacher was hunched over thick books, scribbling in a notebook and looking for all the world like a college co-ed the night before exams. Her rich chocolate hair was pinned up haphazardly, wisps falling around her face. A pencil rested above her ear, and a pair of frameless reading glasses slid down her nose. Chewing the cap of her pen, she looked adorably geeky and maddeningly sexy at the same time.

Peter stared openly, his pulse revving, and his conscience tickling. No time like the present to apologize for his oafish behavior on Thursday afternoon.

"Hello? Peter?" Mary waved a hand in front of him and laughed as he snapped back to attention. "I asked what kind of research you were doing. Geez, bro, where did you go just then?"

Peter shifted awkwardly, embarrassed at being caught staring. "Sorry. I saw someone I need to talk to."

Mary glanced the direction he'd been looking. "Would that someone be an attractive single female who teaches at the elementary school?"

Peter ignored the question and his sister's knowing grin. "Say, where do they keep the microfiche around here? I need to look through old issues of the *Honey Creek Gazette*."

Mary shifted through a stack of children's books, setting some aside and discarding others. She thumbed through the pages of a colorful picture book, then added it to her growing stack.

He tipped his head and smirked. "Just how many books are you planning on reading to the story-time kids?"

Pausing, she looked at the tall pile. "Looks like about fifteen to me. But I could always add more later." She gave him a smug grin. "How far back do you want to go with the *Gazette?* Anything older than two years is filed in a room at the back. Lily will have to get it for you."

When she nodded toward the other end of the check-out

desk, Peter shifted his attention to the raven-haired woman who'd earned a bad reputation before leaving town years ago. Now Lily Masterson was back in town, repairing her reputation after being hired as the head librarian. She was also Wes Colton's fiancée.

Tensing, Peter took Mary by the elbow and led her several steps away from the front desk. "I want everything from 1995."

Mary stilled and cast him a suspicious look. Clearly she recognized the time frame as when their father disappeared. "What are you doing, Peter?"

He rubbed the back of his neck and sighed. "Looking for the answers that the sheriff either refuses to find himself or is covering up to protect his family."

Mary's shoulders drooped, and she lowered her voice. "You make it sound like Dad's disappearance was part of a big conspiracy with the Coltons."

He twitched a shoulder. "Maybe it was."

She looked skeptical. "Look, Peter, I don't know what you're up to, but be careful. When Jake and I dug into Dad's death this summer, we clearly rattled some skeletons. This research you're here for could lead to trouble for you if word gets out. I don't want to see you or Patrick in any danger."

Craig had said as much, too, when he'd visited him in the hospital. Peter's gut rolled at the suggestion his investigation could threaten Patrick's safety.

"And considering that Damien was proven innocent of killing dad, since dad wasn't really dead all these years," Mary added, "I'm not sure what sort of conspiracy you think the Coltons are involved in. But Jake trusts Wes, and that's good enough for me. What makes you think Wes isn't doing his job?"

Peter glanced around the bustling library, his gaze

stopping on Lily. "That's a conversation for another day and another, more private place." He shoved his hands deep in his jeans pockets. "So do you still have access to the *Gazette* microfiche? I really don't want the sheriff's new girlfriend knowing I'm digging into his family's history."

She frowned and flipped her red hair over her shoulder. "I can't access the back room anymore, but I'll ask Lily to get the microfiche you need. Meet me over by the film reader." She jerked her head in the general direction of the microfiche machine on a far wall, then headed across the room to speak to Lily.

Peter noted the machine she indicated but headed the opposite direction. He had to eat a bit of humble pie.

Wiping his suddenly perspiring palms on the seat of his jeans, Peter headed toward the table where Lisa Navarre sat. As he approached, she paused from her work long enough to stretch the kinks from her back and roll her shoulders. When her gaze landed on him, he saw recognition tinged with surprise register on her face, along with another emotion he couldn't identify. She seemed uneasy or flustered somehow as he stepped up to her table and flashed her an awkward grin. He couldn't really blame her for being disconcerted by his presence. He'd been rather gruff and unpleasant last time they met.

Ms. Navarre snatched off her reading glasses and smoothed a hand over her untidy hair. "Mr. Walsh… hello."

He rocked back on his heels and hooked his thumbs in his front pockets. "Hi, Ms. Navarre. I'm sorry to interrupt. Do you have a minute?"

She closed the massive book in front of her and waved a dismissive hand over her notepad. "Sure. I was just doing a little studying for my class."

Peter read the title of the book. "*Critical Evaluation in*

Higher Education. Huh, I didn't know fourth grade was considered higher education nowadays."

She tucked one of the stray wisps of hair behind her ear and sent him a quick grin. "It's not for Patrick's class. I'm working on my PhD in Higher Education. I'm thinking of moving to teaching college-level classes instead of elementary."

"Because at the college level you won't have to deal with jerk fathers who read you the riot act for doing your job?" He added a crooked smile and earned a half grin in return.

"Well, there is that." Her expression brightened. "Although, for the record, the term *jerk* is yours, not mine. *Concerned, somewhat overwrought fathers* might be a better term."

"Call it what you want, but I still acted like a jerk." He met her golden-brown eyes and his chest tightened. "Please forgive me for taking you to task. I do appreciate your concern for Patrick and your willingness to bring his errant behavior that day to my attention. I'd already had a rather stressful day and was on edge about some family matters, but that's no excuse for the way I bit your head off."

She blinked and set her glasses aside. "Wow. That's, um… Apology accepted. Thank you."

Peter noticed a pink tint staining her cheeks and added her ability to blush to the growing list of things he liked about Patrick's teacher. "So if jerk fathers aren't why you're thinking of moving up to higher education, what *is* behind the career change?"

"Well…" Her dark eyebrows knitted, and she fumbled with her pen. "My reasons will sound really bad without knowing the whole long, boring personal story behind my decision. Let's just say teaching older students would be less…painful." She winced. "Ooo, that sounded more melodramatic than I intended." She laughed awkwardly and waved her hand as if to erase her last comment. "Forget I said that."

"Forgotten." But Peter had already filed both the comment and the shadow that flitted across her face in his memory bank. He had no business delving deeper into her personal life, but he couldn't deny he was intrigued. And sympathetic to her discomfort. He had painful things in his past that he avoided discussing when possible.

"Is Patrick with you?" she asked looking past him toward the children's section.

"No. Not today. I'm here on business matters, looking for information for a case I'm working on."

He could tell by the wrinkle in her brow that his working on the weekend away from Patrick bothered her. A jab of guilt prodded him to add, "But yesterday, Patrick and I took in the MSU game and spent most of the evening playing Monopoly together."

"Oh, good." Her lips curved, although the smile didn't reach her eyes. "I'm sure he enjoyed that."

"I hope so. You made some valid points the other day at school."

She blinked as if surprised, and Peter chuckled. "Despite how it may have seemed, I was listening. I heard what you said about Patrick's withdrawal and falling grades."

She held up a finger. "Um, *slipping*. I believe I said his grades were slipping."

He scratched his chin. "The difference being…?"

"His grades are still good. They've come down a bit, just a few points. But *falling* to me is more dramatic. Big drop, by several letter grades."

Peter chuckled. "You are a master of nuance, aren't you? *Incident* not *accident*. *Slipping* not *falling*."

She flushed a deeper shade of pink, and Peter's libido gave him another hard kick.

"I'm not trying to be difficult. I just believe in saying what I mean. Exactly what I mean."

Mary caught his attention from across the room. With an impatient look, she held up the microfiche Lily had retrieved for her.

"Well, I don't want to keep you from your studying." Peter motioned to her books then took a step back. "I just wanted you to know I'm sorry for shouting at you."

"Thank you, Mr. Walsh." She held out her hand, and he grasped her fingers. Her handshake was firm and confident, and the feel of her warm hand in his sent a jolt of awareness through him.

Ms. Navarre, Dad. She's not married.

As he turned to walk away, Peter hesitated. The woman was beautiful, intelligent and *single*. "Uh, Ms. Navarre…"

Good grief. Suddenly he was thirteen again and asking Cindy Worthington to the Valentine dance. He was a geeky ball of jittery nerves and sweating palms. He hadn't asked a woman on a first date in more than thirteen years. Not since he'd asked Katie out for the first time in high school. Since Katie's death, he'd preferred to be alone, to focus on Patrick and losing himself in his work.

But somehow Lisa Navarre was different from the other women in Honey Creek. She'd managed to stir something deep inside him that had been dormant since Katie died—an interest in getting back into life.

She raised an expectant gaze, waiting for him to continue.

His heart drummed so loudly in his ears, he was sure she could hear it. "I was wondering if you might be free next Saturday to—"

Wham!

A loud thump reverberated through the library, drawing his attention to the front desk. When he saw the source of the noise and the ensuing commotion, he tensed. Maisie Colton was not only a Colton, reason enough for Peter to steer clear of her, but the *Vogue*-beautiful woman was well-known in town as being eccentric and unpredictable.

Maisie angrily slammed another stack of books on the counter, and Lily Masterson rushed over to quiet Maisie.

"No respect!" Maisie steamed, full voice. "Do you know how many times I've called that damn show? And they *still* won't talk to me!"

Lily murmured something quietly to Maisie, who retorted, "The *Dr. Sophie* show, of course. My God, this town has enough dirty secrets and public scandals to fill the show's programming for weeks! But the ninny they have working in PR not only wouldn't listen to me, but told me to stop calling or she'd contact the police!" Maisie tossed her long dark hair over her shoulder and scowled darkly.

Peter gritted his teeth, mentally applauding the *Dr. Sophie* show's PR rep for recognizing a kook when they heard one and having the guts to stand up to Maisie. Not too many people in Honey Creek did. She was, after all, a Colton, and Coltons held a great deal of power in the town.

He knew he should ignore Maisie's outburst as most of the other library patrons were, but watching Maisie Colton was a little like watching a train wreck. Despite knowing better, you just can't look away.

In hushed tones, Lily tried to calm Maisie, but she bristled and railed at Lily, "Don't tell me what to do! This is a public building, and I have every right to be here and speak my mind."

Mary edged up to the front counter to give Lily backup, and Peter groaned. This could get ugly.

Mary spoke quietly to Maisie, and, as he'd predicted, Maisie rounded on his sister in a heartbeat. He heard a hateful, derogatory term thrown at his sister, and he'd had enough. Turning briefly to Lisa Navarre, Peter said, "Excuse me. I have to go." He hustled up to the front desk, where Maisie was bristling like an angry cat, flinging insults at Mary.

"…Walsh slut like your sister! Lucy ruined my brother's life the instant she hooked her talons into Damien and seduced him. I pity poor Jake Pierson. You damn Walshes are all the same!" Maisie huffed indignantly.

Peter stepped up behind his sister, not saying anything but drilling Maisie with a warning look.

"And you!" She aimed a shaking finger at him. "You killed Katie, same as if you'd pulled a trigger."

Peter stiffened, bile churning in his gut. "That's enough, Maisie. Go home."

"She died having your baby! Or don't you care? Your father sure didn't care how many women he hurt, how many hearts he broke, how many lives he ruined!"

Mary gasped softly, and Peter sensed more than saw the shudder that raced through his sister. He stepped forward, prepared to bodily throw Maisie from the library if needed, just as another woman brushed past him to confront Maisie.

Lisa Navarre. Startled, Peter caught his breath, as if watching a fawn step in front of a semi-trailer.

"It's Ms. Colton, right?" Lisa smiled warmly and held her hand out for Maisie to shake. "I don't know if you remember me, but I taught your son Jeremy a couple years ago."

Maisie gaped at Lisa suspiciously, then shook her hand. "Yeah. I remember you. Jeremy loved your class."

"Well, I loved having him in my class. He's such a sweet

boy. Very bright and well-mannered. I know you must be proud of him."

Maisie sent an awkward glance to Lily, Mary and Peter, then tugged her sleeve to straighten her coat. "I am. Jeremy is the world to me."

Lisa smiled brightly. "I can imagine." Then, gesturing with a glance to Mary and Peter, Lisa continued. "Somehow I doubt he'd be happy if he knew you'd been yelling at these nice people, though."

Maisie lifted her chin, her eyes flashing with contempt. "There is nothing nice about these or any of the Walshes." Nailing an arctic glare on Mary, Maisie added, "I'm glad your father is dead. One less Walsh for the world to suffer."

Peter had never struck a woman in his life, but Maisie tempted him to break his code of honor. He squared his shoulders and would have moved in on the hateful woman if Lisa hadn't spread her hand at her side in a subtle signal asking him to wait.

"Ms. Colton, the town is justifiably upset over the murder of Mark Walsh. Emotions are running high for everyone. I know there is a lot of bad blood between your families, but this kind of name-calling and finger-pointing serves no good. Think about Jeremy. I'm sure the last thing he needs is to hear from his friends that you were causing a scene here today."

Maisie crossed her arms over her chest and moisture gathered in her eyes. "Their family has caused me and my brother years of heartache. Damien spent fifteen years in jail for something he didn't do!"

"I'm sorry for that, truly. But do you really think Damien wants you adding salt to the wounds now, or would he rather put the past behind him?" Lisa's calm tone reminded

Peter of the tactful way she'd handled his tirade earlier in the week.

While he hated to consider himself in the same category as Maisie Colton, he had to admire Lisa's people skills. Already Maisie's ire seemed to have cooled. Incredible.

Maisie glanced away and quickly swiped at her eyes before returning a less militant gaze to Lisa. "You're right. I just get so mad when—"

She shook her head, not bothering to finish. Dividing one last cool glare of contempt between Mary and Peter, Maisie tugged the lapels of her overcoat closed and breezed out the front door.

To Peter, it seemed the entire population of the library sighed with relief.

Lisa turned to Peter and twitched a lopsided smile. "I'm sorry. I probably shouldn't have butted in, but—"

"No apology necessary. You handled that…beautifully. You have a real talent for talking people down from the ledge, so to speak."

"If I have a talent, it's simply for keeping a cool head. And, spending most of my day with a room full of rowdy fourth-graders, it is a skill I've practiced and have down to a science."

Peter laughed. "I bet."

"So before…you were saying something about next Saturday?" She tipped her head in inquiry, inviting him to finish what he'd started.

Peter blew out a deep breath. "Right. To say I'm sorry, I'd like to take you to dinner."

Lisa's eyes widened in genuine surprise. "You're asking me out? Like…on a date?"

Somehow the notion of a date seemed to bother her so he backpedaled. "Well, not really a date. I thought you could give me some advice about how to handle all the stuff that's been happening in my family. You know, with Patrick. You aren't the only one who's seen changes in him lately. I'm worried about him, too. I want to help him but… I don't know where to start."

Patrick's teacher eyed him suspiciously. "Hmm. Good cover."

Peter feigned confusion. "Excuse me?"

When she laughed, the sound tripped down his spine and filled him with a fuzzy warmth like the first sip of a good whiskey. "I'd love to go to dinner with you. But—" she held up a finger, emphasizing her point "—it's not a date."

Peter jerked a nod. "Agreed. Not a date."

Yet even as he consented to her terms, a stab of disappointment poked him in the ribs. *Not a date* wasn't what he'd had in mind and seemed wholly insufficient with a woman like Lisa Navarre.

But for now, it would do.

Chapter 4

After setting a time to pick Lisa up on Saturday, Peter ignored Mary's querying looks and got started skimming through the microfiche of old newspapers to see what he could learn about the Coltons. Lisa returned to her table to study, but just knowing she was nearby was enough to distract Peter from his tedious research. He found himself repeatedly glancing in her direction and wondering where they should go for dinner next weekend.

Perhaps a restaurant in Bozeman would be better than the local fare if they wanted to avoid starting rumors. He knew several high-end restaurants in Bozeman that were sure to impress Lisa, but perhaps, for their first date, he should keep things low-key.

Their *first* date? *First* implied there would be more than one, and since Lisa insisted it wouldn't be a *date* at all, he was definitely getting ahead of himself.

Peter drummed his fingers as he scrolled through the want ads and comic strips looking for the local society page.

Who was he kidding? He might be attracted to Patrick's teacher, but he wasn't in the market for a girlfriend. He and Patrick were getting along just fine on their own. Weren't they? Sure, he didn't have as much time to spend with his son as he'd like, but his mom had been more than accommodating, helping him with babysitting most afternoons and evenings when he had to work late.

He hadn't been on a date since Patrick was born, because he didn't want to get involved with anyone. Involvement meant investment. Investment meant attachment, bonds, intimacy. And the deeper the attachment, the deeper the pain when the bonds broke.

Katie had died ten years ago, and he still felt the loss of his first love, his young bride, his son's mother, to his marrow. How could he risk that kind of pain again?

He flicked another glance to Lisa's table in time to see her look up at him. She sent a quick smile before returning to her studies. A funny catch hiccupped in his chest.

He was getting ahead of himself.

Not a date. *Check.*

Shifting his attention back to the microfiche reader, his eye snagged on a headline about a business deal Darius Colton had signed fifteen years ago, buying out another local rancher who was on the verge of bankruptcy. The *Gazette* reporter heralded the move as the kind of bold, risk-taking business move that had grown the Coltons' ranching empire from relative obscurity twenty years earlier.

Peter's jaw tightened. What the newspaper called bold and risk-taking, Peter called greedy and cut-throat. In the 1990s the Coltons had run most of the local ranches out of business, then swooped in to gobble up the smaller ranches and turn their business into a multi-million-dollar enterprise. Forget the fact that Darius Colton turned around and employed the ranchers he bought out, Peter hated the idea of the Coltons having a monopoly in ranching in and around Honey Creek. The size of the Colton ranch gave them too much power in the town, too much influence over the city council. Yet the money they poured into local projects, charities and businesses elevated the Coltons' stature in the eyes of the community. Honey Creek residents loved the Coltons.

At least, all of Honey Creek except the Walshes.

He moved on to the society page featuring Darius and his third wife, Sharon, who had celebrated their anniversary with a huge gala party at their ranch. He scanned pictures of the Colton brood, including Wes, Maisie and Finn mugging for the camera. Next was a candid shot of Brand Colton, Darius's only child with Sharon, eating cake. Nothing helpful there.

Peter scrolled down farther…and froze. The last shot was a picture of Damien and Lucy, arms around each other, gazing into each other's eyes on the dance floor and smiling with pure love and joy.

Peter forgot to breathe. His pulse pounded in his ears as he stared at the photo of his sister with the young man who'd later shredded their family. Damien's relationship with Lucy had been at the root of Mark Walsh's dispute with the Coltons. The teenagers' love affair had been dissected and publicly examined when Damien went to trial for Mark's murder later that year.

Peter swallowed hard, forcing the bile back down his throat. Old news. Rehashing Damien and Lucy's star-crossed relationship didn't help him figure out what happened to his father in 1995. The simple fact that his father's body had been found in Honey Creek this summer meant that Damien had been innocent of the crime for which he'd been convicted.

Or did it? Damien could still be part of the conspiracy that included poisoning Craig. But even if he didn't pull the trigger, Damien could be complicit in the murder of Mark Walsh via a conspiracy with his family for revenge.

Peter paged through several more weeks of newspapers before he found a tidbit about Finn Colton receiving a science award at Honey Creek High School, another society article about Maisie winning a beauty pageant at the state fair rodeo, and a business article about Darius investing in a real-estate deal near Bozeman. Peter blew out a tired breath and kept scanning.

More society-page drivel about Duke Colton dating the prom queen, Darius and Sharon attending the Cancer Society fund-raiser, Finn Colton winning a scholarship... yada yada.

Peter rubbed a kink in his neck, checked his watch. How long had he been at the library? He'd promised his mother he'd only be gone a couple of hours. She'd been eager to get back to the hospital and spend the evening with Craig.

Peter skipped through several more weeks of farm reports, wedding announcements and sales fliers to search the *Gazette*'s reports from the weeks just prior to his father's disappearance and presumed death.

While there was no shortage of information about the Colton sons' achievements and dating exploits, Maisie Colton's leaving town for an extended vacation and Darius Colton's continued ventures in expanding his ranch and real-estate holdings, Peter saw nothing that pointed to a motive for murder.

"Okay, my curiosity finally got the best of me."

Peter jerked his head around at the sound of Lisa's voice.

She wore her coat, held a stack of books and notepads in her arms, and had her purse slung over her shoulder.

He pushed his chair back and shoved to his feet. "You're calling it a day?"

"Yeah. Think so. I have spelling tests to grade before tomorrow." She rolled her eyes. "That and a bowl of tomato soup are my exciting plans for tonight." She nodded toward the film reader. "So what are you up to over here?" She squinted and read the headline he'd stopped on. "Darius Colton Inks Land Deal." Her eyes ticked up to his. "So what else is new? Darius Colton is the king of ranching around here from what I understand. Is that what you're researching?"

Peter frowned. "Lord, no. Trust me, I'm well-versed in how large the Coltons' ranching business has grown. Naw, I was looking for something else."

She hesitated a beat, as if waiting for him to elaborate, before her brow rose with understanding. He wasn't going to say more. "Oh."

"I, uh…can explain more Saturday, but I'd rather not go into it here." He nodded with his head toward the other library patrons.

"I don't mean to pry. You just looked so…*absorbed* by what you were reading. And intensely frustrated at the same time. It's been most intriguing to watch you over the last hour."

She'd been watching him? Interesting.

He grinned. "Sorting through pages of dross looking for the one bit of gold that will turn my case can be very frustrating."

"Ah, Patrick told me you're a private investigator. Is that what you mean when you say *case?* Something you're researching for a client?"

He shoved his hands in the back pockets of his jeans. He

didn't want to lie to her, but the truth was bound to raise more questions than he was prepared to answer. "I am a P.I., yes. Unfortunately, it's not as glamorous as the movies make it seem." He hitched his head toward the microfiche reader. "This…is not business, though. It's personal."

"Oh." Her tone was more embarrassed now, and she shifted the books in her arms from one side to the other. "I'm sorry I interrupted."

He held up a hand. "Don't be. I was just about finished. I need to get home." He paused, then added, "But I'd love to have your thoughts on this project on Saturday. Maybe a fresh perspective is what I'm needing to put the pieces together."

She lifted a shoulder. "I'll do what I can." Backing toward the door, she gave him a warm grin. "Tell Patrick I said hello."

Her smile burrowed into Peter's chest, chasing away the bitterness and chill left by his walk down Colton-memory lane. "I will. See you Saturday."

"That and a bowl of tomato soup are my exciting plans for tonight," Lisa mimicked herself in a goofy voice as she drove home. Rolling her eyes, she groaned and knocked her fist against her forehead. "Could you sound any more pathetic?"

If that line didn't sound like a pitifully obvious hint that she wanted him to ask her out for tonight, then she was Queen Elizabeth. She'd wanted to eat her words the minute she heard the sentence tumble from her lips.

Peter Walsh was probably already regretting their dinner plans on Saturday, wondering what kind of desperate female she was. She'd babbled like a schoolgirl around the football jock.

And maybe she *was* that pathetic. She hadn't dated

anyone since Ray had left her four years ago. The scars from her marriage, her infertility, the angry accusations Ray had flung at her before storming out, still stung. All it took was an innocent question such as "What's behind the career change?" to pick the scabs of the old wounds.

How was she supposed to tell Peter Walsh that being around children all day only rubbed salt in her wounds? As much as she loved teaching, loved her class, loved making a difference in the lives of her young students, being around children all day only reminded her of what she could never have. The one thing she couldn't give Ray. The one thing she could never give any man.

A baby.

Some days she felt as though she wore a scarlet *I* on her forehead, branding her as infertile. A giant warning sign to keep men away.

Then, quite unexpectedly, Peter Walsh had waltzed into her life and planted a seed of hope. He'd seemed genuinely interested in her. And despite their inauspicious first meeting, she liked Peter Walsh, just as Eve had said she would. His gracious apology, his wry humor, his charming grin made her knees weak and her spirits light. He made her forget, for a few foolish moments, why she hadn't dated in four years. She couldn't impose her infertility on another man.

Lisa parked in her driveway and sighed. Her small house, with its gray siding and shutterless windows, seemed especially lonely tonight and the cloudy November sky didn't help her mood.

She'd met a handsome, interesting man this week, the kind of man who should have her hopeful and energized by the possibilities for the future. Yet she refused to give her heart to another relationship only to suffer the same frustrations and the agony of a childless marriage that she'd been through with Ray. Even the friendship she'd had with Ray had been eroded by the tedious tests, the fruitless attempts at in vitro fertilization, one heartbreaking attempt at adoption and the small fortune they'd spent with nothing to show for their efforts. Lisa had decided years ago that a second marriage would surely end as disastrously as the first. Romance and happy endings were for women lucky enough to be fertile.

Thus the no-dating rule. If she didn't date, she couldn't fall in love, couldn't lose her heart to a relationship that could have no future.

Which left her where she was tonight. Eating tomato soup with no other plans but to grade spelling tests. Alone, except for her cranky cat, Samson.

As she entered her house, juggling her stack of textbooks and notes, said cranky feline was asleep on her couch, a big brown ball of Maine coon fluff and attitude.

Lisa set her books on the kitchen counter and walked over to Samson. "Working hard again, I see."

When she ruffled his fur, Samson raised his head and chomped her hand, letting her know he didn't appreciate her sarcasm or having his nap disturbed.

"Ow." Lisa shook her offended hand and chuckled. "Ingrate." Despite his less-than-sunny disposition, she loved her irascible cat, her only company on cold nights like tonight.

Lisa clicked on the televison to fill the house with other voices, then headed back to the kitchen to heat her soup and fix sourpuss his dinner.

Patrick Walsh's spelling test was on the top of the stack of papers she had to grade after dinner. She paused and stared at the boy's neat script.

What were Peter and Patrick doing tonight? Was Peter helping Patrick with his homework or hiding out in a home office or behind a newspaper, cut off from his son? Peter seemed genuinely interested in seeking her advice on how to help Patrick through the family's recent rough patch. Maybe—

She shook her head and pushed the school papers across the counter. She needed to stop dwelling on Peter and Patrick Walsh.

But as the quiet November evening passed, Samson snoozing beside her as she graded tests, Lisa found keeping her mind off Peter and their upcoming dinner was easier said than done.

Peter had difficulty concentrating on his P.I. cases that week. Not only was he anticipating his dinner with Lisa Navarre on Saturday, but he also was plagued by thoughts of his father's unsolved murder and the dead ends he kept running into. On Wednesday afternoon, a comment that Mary had made Sunday at the library filtered through his brain and struck him with an idea. Abandoning the unfaithful-spouse case he'd been working on, he drove over to the new security firm that Mary and Jake Pierson were running to grill his sister.

When he strode into the office, Mary glanced up from the desk where she was working and sent him a bright smile. "Peter, what a nice surprise! Imagine seeing my reclusive brother twice in one week."

"Reclusive?"

She raised a palm. "I just call them as I see 'em. You just don't get out much."

Peter rocked on his heels. "I have a son to take care of and a business to run. Who has time to socialize?"

"Although I did overhear something Sunday about you and Lisa Navarre. What's the story there, big brother?"

"The story is there is no story. And if there was it would be none of your business."

Mary pulled a face and raised her hands in surrender. "Touchy, touchy. Forgive me for being interested in the fact that you've got your first date in ten years."

"It's not a date."

Mary flashed a smug grin. "Sure, it's not."

He scowled and pulled up a chair opposite her. "Can we move on to why I'm here?"

"Why are you here?"

Peter leaned forward, holding his sister's gaze. "On Sunday you mentioned the trouble you encountered when you and Jake looked into Dad's disappearance back in '95. I know about the FBI agent that was killed and that you think Jake was the real target, but did you ever get a sense of who was behind the murder?"

"We know who pulled the trigger. Jake killed him to save me. But he died before he could tell us who hired him, and we've left that case and the arson investigation up to Sheriff Colton."

Peter stiffened. "Arson? Are you telling me the fire at Jake's house wasn't an accident?"

She raised a hand to quiet him. "We're trying to keep that info on the down-low until the person behind all of these attacks on us is caught."

"You should have told me! I'm your brother, for crying out loud!"

She waved a hand of dismissal. "Wes and Perry are looking into the arson angle. There was no point in dragging you into it. And you need to stay out of the investigation now. Give Wes room to work."

"Wes and Perry are *Coltons*, Mary! If a Colton is behind the attacks—"

"Look, I know you don't trust Wes, but Jake does and that's good enough for me."

Another attack involving his family that was unsolved. He was sure this was no coincidence. All the more reason to step up his investigation.

Restless, he scratched his chin and struggled to rein in his thoughts. "Tell me again what Jake found out about Dad and where he went fifteen years ago. Don't leave anything out."

Mary sighed and rubbed her freckled forehead. "There's nothing else to tell you, Peter. Like I said months ago, we found out Dad had a lover in Costa Rica. We know he was there for a while, then…we hit a brick wall."

A shadow crossed Mary's face, and she cut her glance away. Peter knew his sister well enough to know she was hiding something. No surprise. Mary had always had secrets she wouldn't share with him. He'd always figured secrets were part and parcel of having a younger sister. But he hated the idea of her holding back information on something as critical as what had happened with their father fifteen years ago.

He propped an arm on the edge of her desk and canted further forward. "Mary, if our family is in danger, I deserve the whole truth. How can I protect Patrick if I don't know what I'm up against?"

"The best way to protect your son is to leave this investigation alone. There is more at work here than you know, more than I can tell you. You have to believe me when I tell you trustworthy people are working to find our father's killer and straighten out this whole squirrely mess."

"This involves me, too." Peter jabbed the desk with his finger. "I have a right to know what is going on."

Mary gave him a pleading look. "And you will, Peter, as

soon as everyone else knows. But if you investigate on your own, you could ruffle feathers and step on toes that could bring some dangerous people to your front door. Please, Peter, back off. Give up this vendetta you seem bent on. Let the authorities do their job."

"I can't, Mary. Not when the authorities belong to the very family I suspect is behind all of this." Peter shoved to his feet, frustrated by his sister's refusal to help him.

"Wes Colton isn't the enemy. He's doing all he can to solve Dad's murder. Don't you think with all the suspicion hanging over his family ever since Damien was accused of killing Dad years ago that Wes wants to find the *real* culprit and clear his family's name once and for all?"

Peter stormed to the office door and paused with his hand on the knob. "Circumstances may have cleared Damien of murder once, but the Coltons are a large family. They haven't forgiven or forgotten their grudges against our dad any more than you or I have."

Mary's spine straightened, and her face paled. "I may not have forgotten everything Dad did to us and to Mom. But I've moved on. Jake is my future, and I've put the past where it belongs. In the past. For Patrick's sake, I wish you could do the same."

A sharp stabbing sensation arrowed to his chest. Were his complicated feelings toward his father messing up his relationship with Patrick? If anything, Peter had tried hard to be the kind of father Mark Walsh had never been for his children—warm, involved, supportive. He had a good relationship with Patrick, even if his caseload had kept him preoccupied of late. Didn't he?

He stewed over Mary's comment as he drove home. On the heels of Lisa's comment that Patrick needed his father to be more involved in his life, he tried to see his life from Patrick's perspective. They ate breakfast together, but conversation, if any, revolved around Peter hurrying his son and double-checking the usual laundry list of morning requirements—brushed teeth, homework in backpack, lunch money.

In the evening, Patrick spent most of his time in his room playing video games and when he did come out to try to talk to Peter, he got only half of Peter's attention while he read the newspaper or worked on the computer or watched a football game on television. Maybe their time together *didn't* equate to the kind of relationship he thought he had with Patrick.

Peter squeezed the steering wheel. He had to do better. He couldn't repeat the mistakes his father had made. He didn't want Patrick growing up with the kind of distance and disconnect he'd had in his relationship with his father. A distance that grew to resentment.

Although, as Peter got older and realized *why* his father wasn't around, heard rumors of his father's many affairs and shady business deals, resentment became disgust, anger. Hatred.

Yet beneath the bitter layers was the little boy who still craved his father's love and attention. The sharp pang in his chest returned. Patrick would never know that double-edged sword of love and hate if he could help it. Gritting his teeth, Peter resolved to change his habits, rearrange his work schedule, make a conscious effort to give Patrick the attention he needed. Nothing mattered more than his son.

His mother and Patrick were in the yard when he pulled in the front drive. As Peter climbed out of his truck, Patrick loped over and showed him the carcass of a giant beetle he'd found. "Look how big this thing was, Dad!"

His mother, Jolene, gave a shudder. "I'm glad you're home. Big dead bugs are not my cup of tea!"

Peter examined the black beetle and raised an eyebrow. "Impressive, sport. What are you gonna do with it?"

"I should take it to school tomorrow and put it in Missy Haynes's locker!" Patrick laughed. "She'd be so grossed out."

Peter gave his son a firm look. "The bug does *not* go to school. Torturing girls is not gentlemanly behavior."

"Can I take it to show Ms. Navarre for science?"

Just the mention of Lisa's name caused his pulse to kick. "As long as that's all that the bug is used for. No tricks or pranks."

Patrick gave him the universal parents-are-such-a-drag look but nodded. "Okay."

"Better get inside and finish your homework now, Patty-boy," Jolene said, giving her grandson a side-hug. His mother's fiery red hair shimmered with the same orange and gold colors of autumn as the trees in the late-afternoon sun, and her amber eyes shone with her love for her only grandchild.

With a grunt of displeasure, Patrick turned to go inside, dragging his feet through the clutter of dead leaves and slushy snow.

"So," Jolene said, stepping forward to greet Peter with a hug and brief kiss on his cheek, "how was your day?"

"All right, I suppose. Frustrating though. I just can't seem to get anywhere with my investigation of Dad's murder."

Jolene blinked her surprise. "You're doing what? Did the sheriff ask for your help?"

Peter scoffed. "Hell, no. In fact, he warned me away. But Wes Colton sure isn't making any progress finding Dad's killer."

"And you know this how?" Jolene asked, crossing her arms over her chest.

Peter started inside, hitching his head to ask his mother to follow. "Has he given you any reason to think he's learned anything? That he's any closer to an arrest now than he was months ago?"

"Well, no. But then I've been much more concerned with Craig's condition and finding out who poisoned him, who tried to kill Mary."

As they entered the foyer, Peter pitched his voice low to keep Patrick from overhearing. "Craig and I think Dad's killer and the person responsible for the other attacks on the family may be one and the same."

Jolene didn't act surprised. "Craig mentioned his conspiracy theory to me. I didn't realize he'd gotten you involved in investigating it, though."

"He didn't have to ask me. If I'd known the sheriff was going to be so remiss in doing his job, I'd have gotten involved months ago. But maybe Wes's lack of progress is all the evidence we need that a Colton is involved, and Wes is covering for his family."

Jolene pulled off her coat and hung it on the coatrack by the door. "You know I have no love lost for the Coltons myself, but you should be careful throwing around accusations like that. Do you have any proof the Coltons are behind anything that's happened?"

"Nothing I can take to court. But my gut tells me—"

"Peter, your gut is biased. Don't get so focused on taking down the Coltons that you miss evidence right under your nose."

Peter tensed. "What are you saying? Do you know something you haven't told the police?"

She waved him off and moved to the stove to start the kettle heating. "No, nothing like that. Just don't limit your investigation to the Coltons. Plenty of folks had reason to hate your father. He hurt a lot of people." Grief and heartache filled her tone, and Peter heard her unspoken, *including me.*

"Well, if I had other leads I'd follow them, but even Mary is being a brick wall. She won't talk to me about what she found when she and Jake looked into Dad's disappearance back in '95."

His mother faced him with a stern look in her eye. "Don't pester Mary about your father. She's happy, truly happy for the first time in too long."

"I wasn't pestering her. I just wanted to know more about what she and Jake learned. But all she'll say is that Dad went to Costa Rica with a woman before his trail went cold." Peter realized what he'd said and kicked himself mentally. "Sorry. I shouldn't have brought that up."

"What, that your father had other women? Good grief, Peter, I knew about his women well before you kids ever did." Though she tried to dismiss Mark's affairs with a casual brush-off, Peter could see the shadows that crept into her eyes. Knowing about her husband's infidelity didn't mean Jolene Walsh hadn't cared, hadn't been hurt. She turned her back to Peter to pour hot water over the tea bag in her mug.

Peter crossed the kitchen and squeezed his mother's shoulder. "You all right?"

She glanced up, then firmed her mouth and gave a confident nod. "I am. Better than all right, in fact. I've moved on, and I have Craig in my life now."

Peter tugged up a corner of his mouth, wondering what his mother would say if he told her he'd known about her once-secret relationship with Craig for years. In recent months, they'd been more public about their love for each other, and Peter couldn't be happier for her.

Jolene set the kettle back in place and lifted her chin. "Craig's ten times the man your father was, and he makes me feel cherished." She beamed at him. "I'm a blessed woman."

"I agree." Peter kissed his mother's temple then walked to the kitchen table to sort through the day's mail.

"Peter."

He glanced up at his mother and waited for her to blow on her tea before she continued. "This woman down in Costa Rica…"

"Mom, you don't need to—"

She waved a hand to hush him. "Wait a minute. Hear me out." She stared into her mug and knitted her brow. "She was just one in a long line of women your father had. If you ask me, you should look into his liaisons and see who might have motive to kill your father. Maybe one of his women wasn't as willing to overlook his numerous affairs as I was."

Peter rocked on his heels, pondering his mother's suggestion. "But…why would one of Dad's women have any reason to hire Atkins to poison Craig?"

"No one said they did. The two crimes could be unrelated."

"And the attack on Mary and Jake? Did you know the fire at Jake's was arson?"

Jolene shrugged. "I don't know how it all fits. I'm just saying don't get tunnel vision when it comes to the Coltons. Consider everything and everyone."

Peter rubbed a hand over his chin. "Okay, so how do I find the women with whom dad had his 'liaisons,' as you call them. I don't want to cause a ruckus in town by asking women, 'Did you sleep with my father or know anyone who did?'"

Jolene chuckled. "Yeah, that'll go over like a lead balloon."

"And would likely tip off the killer that I'm on his, or

rather her, tracks." He paused. "Unless it was a jealous husband." Pulling a face, Peter shook his head. "Well, you're right about the fact that Dad made plenty of enemies."

From the next room, the sounds of Patrick settling his books on the dining-room table and dragging out a chair to start his homework drifted in.

Jolene set her tea on the counter and stepped closer to Peter. Lowering her voice to barely more than a whisper, she said, "Tess Cantrell."

Peter furrowed his brow, not sure he'd heard correctly. The name didn't mean anything to him. "Who is that?"

"She lives in Bozeman. Your father had a long-term relationship with her just before he disappeared. The only reason I know her name is because she confronted me once many years ago. I think she was hoping that by revealing herself to me, I would be shocked by Mark's affair and divorce him." Jolene paused and arched an auburn eyebrow. "She was the one surprised when I told her not only did I know about Mark's affairs, she was kidding herself if she thought she was his only fling." She gave him a wry grin and an insouciant shrug.

Peter stared at his mother, marveling at her strength and resilience, her ability to make light of a situation that had caused her so much pain in the past. For years she'd endured the humiliation of her husband's perfidy in order to keep her family together and minimize the scandal. She deserved every bit of happiness she'd found with Craig, and then some.

Sticking his hands in his pockets, Peter shot his mother a quizzical look. "And you think this Tess Cantrell could have something to do with Dad's disappearance years ago or his murder a few months ago?"

"I wouldn't know. But she's as good a place to start as

any. Last I knew, she was still living in Bozeman, not far from the apartment Mark kept there for his trysts."

"Dad! Gram!" Patrick hollered from the next room. "Can one of you help me with this stupid math?"

Jolene turned to head into the dining room, but Peter caught her arm. "I've got it. You can go on to the hospital and see Craig. I've taken enough of your day."

"I don't mind. In case you haven't noticed, I'm a little crazy about my grandson."

Peter lifted the corner of his mouth. "I've noticed. And I appreciate the help more than you know. But I've been told recently that I'm not spending enough time with Patrick. Helping him with his homework is a good place to start changing that."

Jolene cocked her head. "Who told you that?"

"Long story." He nudged her toward the door. "Tell Craig I said hello, and I'll keep him posted on any leads."

A knowing gleam sparked in his mother's eyes. "Interesting. You don't want to talk about it. Could it involve a woman? Say, an attractive schoolteacher?"

Peter frowned. "How—" *The library.* "Mary?"

Jolene nodded. "I think it's wonderful that you're finally dating someone."

"We're not dating."

"Not what I heard…" his mother replied in a sing-song tone as she left through the front door, then called, "Bye, Patty-boy!"

Peter dragged a hand down his face. Having a large family in a small town could be a mixed blessing. While he could never have raised Patrick as a single father without his family's ready support, the Walsh grapevine rivaled Eve Kelley's beauty salon for the lightning speed gossip traveled through it.

As he headed into the dining room to help Patrick with

his math, a tangent thought stopped Peter. *Large family in a small town.*

The Coltons.

Were all of the Coltons privy to the rest of the family's secrets? Was there another tack he could use to learn what the Coltons were hiding?

Don't get tunnel vision when it comes to the Coltons. Peter pinched the bridge of his nose. Maybe his mother was right. She had known the Coltons longer than he had and knew more about his father's potential enemies.

Stepping over to a notepad on the kitchen counter he jotted the name *Tess Cantrell* and underlined it.

He stared at the name, and his gut clenched. Did he really want to find and interview his father's former mistress? Now, *that* would be awkward. He was no stranger to questioning witnesses, but Tess Cantrell's relationship with his father made interrogating her deeply personal and potentially painful. And he wasn't the most tactful man alive. He was sure to do something to get the Cantrell woman's back up.

His thoughts flashed to Lisa Navarre's smooth handling of Maisie Colton at the library. Bozeman. Dinner Saturday.

A beat of anticipation and possibility jumped in his veins. Could Lisa Navarre's people skills help him get the information he needed from Tess Cantrell?

Chapter 5

Late Saturday afternoon, Peter arrived at Lisa's house a few minutes earlier than they'd arranged, and she checked her hair in the entry-hall mirror as she hurried to the door. The sight of him, his square-cut jaw and cheeks slightly red from the cold and his broad shoulders filling the door frame, stole her breath. Peter Walsh was a handsome man, no denying. And at that moment, his bedroom eyes, peering at her from under the brim of a black Stetson, and his lopsided grin were directed at her.

"Hope I'm not too early." His breath clouded when he spoke.

"Not a problem." She stood back to usher him inside. "Come in from the cold while I get my purse and coat."

Peter seemed even taller, his shoulders wider, when he stepped into her cramped foyer. A hint of pine-tinged cologne and the leather scent of his suede coat filled the air and hijacked her pulse. The masculine scents that surrounded him reminded her how long it had been since she'd spent time alone with a man.

"I hope it's not inappropriate for me to tell you how nice you look."

Her heart gave a nervous thump. "A lady always appreciates a sincere compliment, Mr. Walsh."

"Peter, please. And I'm completely sincere."

"Thank you." Heat pricked her face as he swept another appreciative gaze over her. "I'll be right back. Make yourself at home." She hoped her voice didn't betray her jitters. Backing down her hall, she turned and scurried to her bedroom to collect her purse. *Deep breath. Settle down. It's not a date.*

"You have a nice house," he called from the front room.

"Thank you. It's small, but it's all I need." Lisa pulled her dress coat from the closet and took her cell phone from her nightstand.

"On the way in, I noticed you had a broken window on the west side and a patch of broken shingles on the roof right above it."

Lisa poked her arms in the sleeves of her coat as she headed back down the hall. "Yeah. Had a branch from my neighbor's tree hit the house during the tornado last month." She reached the living room and caught her breath again at the sight of him. He might be a private investigator but with his Stetson, his suede range coat and his rugged good looks, he could easily be mistaken for one of the ranchers who populated Honey Creek.

She cleared the sudden thickness from her throat. "I've been too busy to call a repairman, and I figured there were folks with bigger repairs than mine first in line following the storm. For now the cardboard fix will have to suffice on the window."

He pointed to the couch where Samson sat staring at Peter. "I don't think your cat likes me. He's been giving me the evil eye since I arrived."

Lisa grinned. "Don't mind him. He acts tough, but under all that fluff, he's just a big marshmallow."

She walked over to scratch the Maine coon under the chin, and Samson gave a loud *mrow* before hopping off the couch and stalking away.

"You know, with this cold weather settling in, you should see about getting the window fixed soon or your heating bill is going to eat your lunch." He crossed to her, lifting a hand for her to proceed him to the door. "If you want, I can take care of those repairs for you. Shouldn't take more than a couple hours one afternoon. Did you have any other damage?"

Lisa led him out to her front stoop and paused long enough to lock her door. "No, the branch was about the extent of it, thank goodness. Other folks weren't as lucky." She flashed him a smile as they walked to his truck. "And though I appreciate the offer, I couldn't ask you to do my repairs."

"You didn't ask. I offered." He opened the passenger door for her and sent her a sheepish look. "Besides, I have a favor to ask you, and doing a few repairs for you is the least I can do to repay you."

Lisa lingered in the open door, enjoying standing so close to Peter's body heat and his tempting masculine scent, and she tilted her head. "What kind of favor?"

"I, uh…have a side trip I need to make tonight before dinner. Business-related." He paused and firmed his mouth. "Actually, it's more personal business." He knocked his Stetson back and scratched his forehead, stalling.

She gave him a patient smile of encouragement. "What's the favor, Peter?"

"I have to interview a woman in Bozeman. She had a, uh…a relationship with my father when I was a kid, and…I think she might have information that would help me find the person responsible for my dad's murder."

Lisa frowned. "Why aren't the police talking to her then?"

"She's not a suspect or anything. I'm just following a hunch, tracking down any possible leads. I'm conducting my own investigation into recent events. This has nothing to do with the case the sheriff's building." He hitched a shoulder. "Unless I find something significant."

Lisa drew a deep breath of the crisp autumn air. "And you want me to help you somehow?"

"I saw how you handled Maisie Colton at the library the other day. You're good with people and—"

Lisa chuckled her surprise, then covered her mouth with her hand. "I'm sorry. I don't mean to laugh. I've just never considered myself a "people" person. If you knew how nervous I get about talking to parents, how nervous I am even right now—" She stopped and swallowed hard.

Oops. Maybe she shouldn't have said *that*.

Sure enough, when she ticked her gaze up to Peter's, his eyes were warm, and a grin tugged his cheeks. "Don't be nervous. Remember, this isn't a real date."

The low, husky quality of his voice made her quiver low in her belly. Goose bumps that had nothing to do with the nip in the air rose on her arms.

She twitched a grin. "Right. Not a date."

"So will you help guide the conversation and smooth the rough edges for me when I talk to Tess Cantrell? Knowing that she was my father's former lover makes me more than a little uncomfortable."

"I can imagine." Lisa raised her chin and squared her shoulders. "I'd be happy to help however I can."

The smile of gratitude and relief that spread across Peter's face was all the reward she needed, but Peter still insisted he would tend to her home repairs later that week.

As they drove to Bozeman, Peter filled her in on the recent turbulence in the Walsh family. Besides the death of Mark Walsh, a tragedy she was familiar with only through the reports in the *Honey Creek Gazette,* Peter's sister had been forced off the road, her fiancé's house torched. Then a close family friend, a man Peter considered a second father, had been hospitalized after being poisoned.

"And you think all the incidents are related?" Lisa gave him a skeptical frown. Honey Creek had its share of petty crime, but the kind of conspiracy to commit multiple murders seemed a bit much for their small town.

"I can't prove it yet, but I intend to. Thanks to my line of work, I've learned not to believe in coincidence. Generally, if someone in your life is acting suspiciously, there's usually a reason." Peter glanced across the front seat to her. "Three attacks on my family in four months is no coincidence."

An uneasy flutter stirred in her belly. "Do you think you and Patrick are in danger?"

A muscle in his jaw bunched as he gritted his teeth. "I can't say for sure, but I wouldn't rule it out. I can take care of myself, but I'd appreciate it if you kept a close eye on Patrick when he was at school."

"Of course." She nibbled her bottom lip as she studied Peter's profile. "So how have you explained all the recent trouble for the family to Patrick?"

Drawing his eyebrows together low over his eyes, Peter shot her a dubious look. "I haven't told him anything. He's a kid. I didn't want him worried or upset."

Lisa gaped at Peter. "Nothing? You've told him nothing?"

"Well, when his grandfather was found murdered, I had

to tell him about that. It was in the newspaper and all the talk around town. I didn't want him to hear about it from someone else. But he didn't go to the funeral. I figured it would be the media circus it proved to be."

"So he doesn't know about Mr. Warner being in the hospital or the attack on your sister?" Lisa gripped the armrest, goggling over what Peter had shared. No wonder Patrick was acting so withdrawn, so insecure.

Peter rolled up his palm on the steering wheel. "Well… he knows Craig is in the hospital, because my mom babysits Patrick, and she leaves our house to go sit with Craig in his hospital room. But nothing about the arsenic. I told Patrick Craig was just feeling a little ill and was in for tests. Which is the truth…in a sense."

Lisa sighed and laced her fingers in her lap. "Peter, may I be candid?"

He sent her a startled look. "Please."

"I think keeping Patrick in the dark is causing more harm than good. He's a bright boy, and he's old enough to sense when there's unusual stress and upheaval in the family. I think the reason he's been withdrawn lately at school, the reason he made the comment he did about you not caring about him and the reason he decided to act out the other day is that he's feeling excluded, shut out."

Dark clouds filled Peter's expression. "I didn't tell him, because I was trying to protect him."

"I understand that. I'm not telling you this to point an accusing finger. But the other day at the library you asked for my help with your son. I feel like it's my duty as his teacher to look out for his best interests."

He whipped his head toward her. "No, it's my job as his *father* to look out for his best interests. That's what I thought I was doing!"

"We *both* want what's best for Patrick. But that doesn't mean we have to be at cross purposes."

Peter heaved a sigh, sent her a concerned glance and nodded. "You're right. So…go on. I'm listening."

Lisa stretched the fingers of one hand with the other, fidgeting as she gathered her thoughts. "Well, my guess would be he's worried because he knows you're worried, but he doesn't understand why. The underlying tension in the house, the extra time you have to spend away from home, and the hints he picks up about trouble facing the family are all affecting his performance at school. And his mental well-being. He senses something is wrong, and without any explanation from you, he fills in the blanks for himself. He's scared, uncertain. Knowing fourth-graders the way I do, I suspect he's probably thinking the problems are his fault."

"His fault? No…" Peter shot another deeply worried glance at her before returning his attention to the road.

"I know they're not, but he doesn't. Just think how his young imagination must be running wild, conjuring up all form of frightening possibilities to explain the grim mood in your house."

He shook his head and frowned. "If something is bothering Patrick, he knows he can come to me with it. We've always had that kind of open communication between us."

"You mean until recently?" Lisa met Peter's startled look. "You just said you weren't telling him about the family's recent crises. Communication is a two-way street. How can you expect him to be honest and forthcoming with you if you aren't with him?"

"That's different. There are things kids don't need to know. Things he's too young to hear, too young to grasp."

"True. So give them to him on a level he can understand. Weed out the stuff he's too young to hear. But don't pretend nothing is happening and that everything is fine when it's not. You don't have to be gloom and doom. That *will* scare him. But be honest with him and let him know that he's not to blame and that you are still there for him, protecting him. Give him back his sense of security. Let him know you love him and that you'll handle the trouble facing the family together."

Peter said nothing for a while, clearly mulling over all she'd laid out for him. As they neared the Bozeman city limits, he turned to her with a gentle smile. "That makes a lot of sense. Thank you, Ms. Navarre."

"Lisa."

His eyes warmed, and a flutter stirred deep inside her.

"Lisa." He quirked a wry grin. "So if you don't have kids of your own, how'd you get so smart about parenting?"

He meant the question to be teasing and light-hearted. She could see that much in the playful spark in his eyes, the devilish grin tugging his lips.

But his words sent a sharp ache straight to her heart.

So if you don't have kids of your own…

She swallowed the knot that rose in her throat and forced a smile to her face. She would not, would *not* let him see how his innocent words had slashed through her. Curling her fingers into fists, she sucked in a calming breath to steady her voice. "Six years of teaching and a minor in college in child psychology. I thought it would be a good complement to my teaching certificate."

"That'd do it," he replied with a wink.

Fighting down the grief that threatened to spoil her mood, she focused her attention on the Rocky Mountains silhouetted against the setting sun, beyond the lights of Bozeman. Montana had a rugged beauty and majesty that never failed to take her breath away. When Ray had left her, she'd never once thought of leaving Montana and going back to Texas, where her family lived. Even when the ice and snows of winter buried Honey Creek, Lisa saw the landscape as a wonderland.

"When we get to Tess Cantrell's apartment, just follow my lead, okay? I need her to feel comfortable enough to speak freely with me, to tell me everything she remembers about my dad and any enemies he had when she knew him."

Lisa angled her body back to face Peter. In the fading daylight, his profile had the same rugged appeal as the Rockies.

Peter rubbed a hand over his jaw. Although she could tell he'd shaved before he picked her up tonight, the calluses on his palms still scraped against the rugged cut of his chin with a soft scratching sound. Lisa's nerve endings crackled, imagining those wide, rough palms gliding over her skin.

Her mouth dried, and she gave herself a mental shake. Peter Walsh might be handsome as the devil, but entertaining any notions of a physical relationship was…dangerous. She didn't believe in casual sex, and a deeper, more personal relationship could only end badly. Ray was proof enough of what men thought of sterile women. Though most men would deny it until they were blue in the face, the ancient biological imperative to procreate still ruled men on some subconscious level. That primitive drive would eventually rear its head with any man she got involved with and cause the kind of resentment that had ruined her marriage to Ray.

Leaning her head back on the seat, she gave Peter another surreptitious scrutiny. He might be off limits in reality, but my-oh-my, Peter Walsh was fodder for some pretty steamy daydreams.

"This is it," he said, pulling his truck into the parking lot of a sprawling apartment complex and yanking her out of her musings.

While she gathered her purse from the floorboards, Peter circled the truck to open her door for her. He offered her a hand to help her down from the high front seat, and Lisa's heart tap-danced as his large hand closed around hers. Secure. Warm. Strong.

"Is Ms. Cantrell expecting us?"

"No. I didn't want her to have a chance to get cold feet and bolt on us before we arrived."

"You really think this meeting will go that poorly?" Lisa fell in step beside him, and Peter placed a hand on her back, guiding her around a pothole in the sidewalk.

"My father was a brilliant businessman. He built the family brewery into a thriving business. But I'm afraid that's the kindest thing I can say about him. He left a trail of broken hearts and ill will. I'm not expecting much different with Ms. Cantrell."

Lisa read the tension that crept into Peter's face, creasing his forehead and tightening lines around his mouth. She wondered briefly if Peter, like his father, had left a trail of broken hearts. Eve Kelley told her he'd married his high-school sweetheart. But how much had he dated since his wife's death?

They mounted the steps to the second floor and found apartment 208. Peter hesitated, staring at the door with a troubled expression for long seconds.

Lisa's heart went out to him, and she wrapped her hand around his and squeezed. When he glanced at her, startled by her gesture, she smiled her encouragement.

Peter returned a dubious grin. "Guess this won't get any easier by stalling, huh?"

Squaring his shoulders, he knocked firmly and raised his chin to wait. The door was answered promptly by an attractive dark-haired woman whose age Lisa estimated at around fifty-five.

She gave them a friendly, if curious, look. "Yes?" Then Tess Cantrell's gaze froze on Peter, and her smile faded, replaced by wide-eyed dismay. She raised a hand to her mouth and took a step backward. "Oh, my God."

"Tess Cantrell?" Peter asked. "My name is Peter W—"

"Walsh," Tess finished for him. "I see your father in you. The resemblance is…uncanny."

Hearing that he looked like his father didn't seem to sit well with Peter. He stared at Tess Cantrell with a furrowed brow and a stunned expression.

Lisa stepped forward and extended her hand. "I'm Peter's friend, Lisa Navarre. Would you mind if we spoke to you inside for just a moment? We promise not to take much of your time."

Both Tess and Peter rallied when Lisa spoke. Tess shook her hand and gave her a tight smile, then stepped back to invite them in.

"I heard about your father's murder. I wish I could say I was sorry to hear of his death, but… I can't. I was more shocked, really. I thought he'd died fifteen years ago."

Peter grimaced. "We all did."

"I didn't do it, if that's what you're here to ask." Tess closed the door and faced them with her hands on her hips. "Though I'd like to congratulate the person who *did* kill him."

Peter sucked in a breath, his nostrils flaring.

Feeling the tension rising in the room, Lisa jumped in,

hoping Peter would forgive her if she was overstepping her boundaries.

"Ms. Cantrell, we know Mark Walsh hurt a lot of people, and we're not here to make excuses for him or point fingers of blame. But we need information that we think you might have. Because you were involved with Mark Walsh just before his disappearance in 1995, you have a unique perspective on his state of mind, his activities and the people he had business with."

Tess moved past them and took a seat in her living room without inviting them to join her. She stared at the floor with a dark, distant expression, as if recalling past hurts. "What do you want to know?"

"I need a glimpse of my father's life before he disappeared." Peter stepped into the living room and sat on the edge of the couch. "Do you remember him mentioning anyone he was having trouble with? Anyone who was angry with him for some reason?"

She gave them a bitter laugh. "Where do I start? He didn't talk much about his business dealings with me, but more than once we had our dinner interrupted in restaurants by someone who had a bone to pick with your father."

"What do you think happened in '95? Could someone have tried to kill him and botched it? Is that what sent him into hiding? Did he ever mention leaving, ditching his life and making a fresh start?" Peter fired his questions in rapid succession, not giving Tess a chance to answer.

Lisa sidled onto the sofa beside Peter and laid a hand on his knee. He cast a puzzled look to her hand then raised his gaze to meet hers, and with her eyes, she silently warned him to slow down and not push Tess.

"Like I said, I didn't know much about his business life. He always spent a lot of time on the phone talking to his office or working on some new deal, but he was real private about what he was doing. I gave him space to conduct his business and never asked questions. That's not what our relationship was about."

The unspoken what-their-relationship-was-about hung in the air like a specter for the span of a tense heartbeat. Peter grunted churlishly under his breath, and Lisa squeezed his knee to hush him.

Tess apparently heard him, too. She sat straighter in her recliner and lifted her chin. "I make no apologies for the way I lived my life back then. Maybe I was naive to believe all the things Mark Walsh told me, but I did. I gave him the benefit of the doubt more times than I can count. But I honestly thought he cared about me. I loved him, and to me, that was all that mattered."

"Why?"

Peter's question surprised Lisa, and based on her confused and offended expression, it caught Tess off guard as well.

"Excuse me?"

Peter's dark eyes were shadowed, sad. Not hostile. "Why did you love him? What did you see in him?"

Lisa's chest contracted. Peter's expression reminded her of a young boy looking for some reason to cling to hope, some shred of evidence that his father hadn't been the disappointment he remembered.

Tess blinked rapidly and toyed with the charm on her necklace. "He treated me well, made me feel special. He told me things I wanted to hear, bought me presents. We laughed together and traveled together and had great sex."

Lisa felt the sudden tensing of Peter's muscles under her hand.

"He told me he loved me, and I ate it up. Looking back, I can see how shallow I was being. How easily I bought into his lies. We were together for three years before I learned the truth."

"What truth?" Lisa asked.

"He was never gonna leave his wife. He was using me. Didn't really love me the way he said. Maybe he cared in his own way, but I wasn't the love of his life, the way he was mine." She huffed indignantly. "I wasn't even his only woman." She waved a hand toward Peter. "And I don't mean your mother. I knew Mark was married. I mean the young tootsie he was seeing behind my back. Lord only knows how many others there were. But when I found out about the other woman being pregnant with his baby—"

Peter jerked.

"—I gave Mark an ultimatum. Me or her. He said he couldn't dump—"

"Whoa, whoa, *whoa!*" Peter shot to his feet, his body tense. "Back up."

Lisa's pulse kicked up. Not only did mention of pregnancies and babies always set her on edge, but she could tell by Peter's expression, Tess had just dropped a bomb on him.

"What other woman?" he asked hoarsely. "What *baby?*"

Chapter 6

Tess gave him a wary look. "You didn't know?"

Peter's jaw tightened, his eyes widening with shock.

Before he could respond, Lisa rose and wrapped her hand around his wrist. Shoving down her own raw emotions regarding pregnancies, she flashed Tess a smile. "I'm sorry. You've caught us by surprise. Obviously Peter didn't know, and this is a rather big bombshell for him to absorb. I… what can you tell us about this other woman and her baby?"

Tess shifted on the recliner, clearly uncomfortable with the direction of the conversation and eyeing Peter cautiously. "Just that whoever she was, their relationship was a big secret. And I'm not talking secretive like we were. I mean, big-time scandal and hush-hush. And he warned me not to try to find her or confront her because she was…what was the word he used? Oh, yeah…*volatile*. He said she tended to get really possessive and emotional and could be overly dramatic. He was having to dance really fast to deal with her once she found out she was pregnant. He didn't want anything to do with her baby and was already regretting having messed with this woman. He called her 'one of his worst mistakes.'"

"So you don't know her name?" Peter asked, his tone remarkably calm.

Tess shook her head, then sighed heavily. "So when I gave him the ultimatum, he said, 'No one is going to tie me down. Not you and not her.' And he left. Just like that. Never heard from him again." She firmed her mouth and squared her shoulders, but her eyes reflected her warring bitterness and pain.

Lisa moved closer to Tess and crouched next to her chair. She put a sympathetic hand on the other woman's. "I'm sorry. I know this is difficult for you, and we appreciate your candor."

Tess sniffed loudly and nodded.

"Do you think this woman, whoever she is, could have been upset enough to seek retaliation against Mark?" Lisa asked.

Tess lifted a shoulder. "If she was as much of a loose cannon as Mark said, who knows? But I know she was as determined to keep her child's paternity a secret as Mark was. He told me that much. Did she try to kill him to keep her secret?" Tess turned her palm up. "Did she run him out of town to keep him quiet?" Another shrug.

Peter paced across the room, his face grave, then he turned toward Tess, inclining his head in inquiry. "Do you think he could have gone to Costa Rica with her? Set her up there with a house?"

"Costa Rica?" She frowned. "No. As far as I know she stayed in Honey Creek and had the baby."

Peter jolted again, his mouth agape. "Honey Creek? She's from *Honey Creek?*"

Lisa could practically see the wheels in Peter's mind spinning, trying to figure out which woman from his hometown had given birth to his half-sibling.

Tess pushed to her feet now and moved restlessly across the floor. "After Mark left me, I didn't care what happened to the highfalutin' floozy he got pregnant. The crazy woman and her baby were not my problem."

Peter was staring out the front window, his expression shell-shocked, so Lisa continued to carry the questioning. She fumbled to decide what else might be relevant to Peter's investigation, what information Tess might have about Mark's enemies that she didn't realize she had.

"Ms. Cantrell, I know you said Mark didn't discuss his business deals with you, but can you remember a time during the years you were together when he seemed especially worried or upset over a deal? Did he ever indicate a deal had gone wrong and he had to handle the repercussions?"

Tess's shoulders sagged, and she rubbed her neck tiredly. "No. He was always upbeat about his brewery. It was thriving and growing and making him a ton of money. He even started branching out into new industries. He'd started dabbling in oil and ranching, anything he thought he could make a profit on."

Ranching. If Mark Walsh was moving in on Darius Colton's domain, there could have been trouble there. Lisa glanced toward Peter to gauge whether he'd drawn the same conclusion, but his expression was inscrutable.

Finally Tess stopped her restless shuffling and faced them with a determined set in her jaw. "Look, I don't know what else I can tell you. I had nothing to do with Mark's disappearance or his murder. I haven't seen or talked to him in fifteen years." She turned fully toward Peter. "But I can tell you this. You kids were important to him. He wouldn't divorce your mother because he wanted to keep your family together. He didn't want to lose the right to see his children. He loved you…in his own way."

Peter's face reflected a mix of skepticism and longing. The poignant battle of his emotions tugged Lisa's heart.

A gasp from Tess brought Lisa's attention back to the older woman. Tess snapped her fingers and waved a finger. "I just thought of something. In the months before he left, he was real upset about Lucy."

"Lucy?" Lisa asked.

"My sister," Peter supplied. His face said Tess's revelation was old news.

"Lucy was dating some boy he thought was trouble. He said he laid down the law to her that she couldn't see him, but he knew she was sneaking around behind his back."

Peter sighed and shoved his hands in his coat pockets. "Damien Colton."

Recognition lit Tess's face. "I know that name."

"He's who they charged with Dad's murder fifteen years ago." Peter shuffled toward the door, signaling an end to the conversation. "But since my dad wasn't actually dead, but in hiding, Damien just got a get-out-of-jail card from the state. So, thanks, but…that doesn't help."

Tess spread her hands. "I've got nothing else."

Lisa nodded and moved close enough to grasp the woman's hands. "Thank you. For your time and for indulging us when we stirred up bad memories. You have been a big help, and we appreciate what you've told us."

Perhaps because he felt taken to task by her example, Peter also mustered a smile for Tess Cantrell. "Yes, thank you." He dug in his pocket and extracted a business card.

"If you do think of anything else you feel could be helpful, will you call me? Please."

Tess stared at the card for a moment then nodded. "Sure. And I hope for your sake that they catch whoever did it."

With that, Peter opened the front door and stood back while Lisa pulled her coat tighter around her and stepped outside.

The cold slap of the evening air matched Peter's mood as they drove to the restaurant from Tess's apartment.

"If you'd like to skip dinner tonight, I'd understand. You've just been handed a shock, and I can imagine—"

"I'm fine." He added a tense smile that contradicted his assurances. "And I'd still like your input about Patrick."

"My analysis of the problem on the drive to Ms. Cantrell's didn't scare you off, then?" Lisa kept her tone light, hoping to establish a less serious tone for the rest of the evening.

"Not a bit. You were dead on target, and I need all the candor and honesty I can get. Patrick means everything to me, and I'll do whatever it takes to protect him and give him a good childhood."

"I'm guessing your relationship with your dad wasn't so hot when you were a kid?"

"You'd be right. Although at the time, I really didn't know any better. I just knew something was missing in our relationship that other guys had with their fathers. I want to be sure Patrick doesn't grow up feeling the same way."

Peter pulled in and parked at a locally owned restaurant whose sign out front claimed they served the best steaks in the state.

"Best in the state?" Lisa lifted her eyebrows. "Pretty bold claim considering the size of Montana. And this *is* ranching country."

Peter sent her a devilish lopsided grin. "Prepare to be impressed."

He escorted her inside and gave his name to the hostess. Once they'd been seated at a private corner booth, Peter ordered them a bottle of merlot and settled back in his seat. His gaze drifted around the classic Western-themed decor of the restaurant, but Lisa could tell by his deliberative expression that his thoughts were elsewhere.

"So, what do you recommend?" She unfolded her menu and began studying the entree choices.

Peter's dark eyes shifted to her. "I always get the ribeye." He quirked a grin. "Best in the state."

Lisa chuckled. "So I hear."

His face sobering, he leaned toward her and lowered his voice. "Do you think the woman my dad got pregnant actually had the baby?"

Lisa set the menu aside and considered his question. "Why wouldn't she?"

Peter flipped up his palm. "Well, you heard Tess. His affair with this lady was super-secret, and my dad called the woman *volatile*. If she *was* trying to keep his paternity and their relationship a secret, what better way than to get rid of the baby?"

The thought of someone ending a pregnancy when she and Ray had so desperately wanted a baby and couldn't have one made Lisa's chest contract. She fumbled with her napkin, then, seeing her hands shaking, she laced her fingers tightly in her lap. "I suppose it's possible. It's just difficult for me to imagine anyone *not* wanting a baby, even if the circumstances are less than ideal."

Peter nodded, his expression thoughtful. "Assuming she did have the baby, the kid would be…what, fourteen now?" He dragged a hand down his cheek and blew out a deep breath. "I could have a half-sibling out there somewhere."

"Tess said the woman was from Honey Creek. Can you think of anyone who fits the description she gave? Emotional. Desperate to keep their relationship secret."

"With a kid who is now fourteen…yeah. A couple of possibilities come to mind. Lily Masterson for one."

Lisa blinked her surprise. "The new librarian? I thought she just moved to town."

"Moved back to town. She lived here years ago. Had a reputation that even high school boys like me knew about. She was a wild one back then." He hesitated, drawing his eyebrows together in a frown. "She's involved with Wes Colton now. If she had my dad's baby, if she was involved with my dad's disappearance or his death in some way…" Peter gritted his teeth, his dark eyes flashing. "I bet Wes knows about it. He could be covering for her. Seems mighty convenient that Lily shows up back in town at the same time my dad winds up dead."

"Whoa! Slow down." Lisa held her hands up. "Let's not convict her without a little more evidence. You said there was more than one possibility. Who else could it be?"

Peter picked up his spoon and tapped it idly on the table. Suddenly he tensed, and his complexion paled. "Ah, hell."

"What?"

"Maisie Colton. Her son is the right age, isn't he?"

Lisa did a quick calculation. "Yes, but just because her child is the right age—"

"She's also as good as Honey Creek royalty, being a Colton. Our families have been at odds for years. A relationship with my father would be beyond scandalous. And she's—" Peter laughed without humor. "Well, you saw how she acted at the library the other day. She's definitely volatile. Some people say she's borderline nuts."

"And she's gorgeous. I could understand your father falling for her."

Peter gave her a startled look. "Yeah, I suppose she's attractive. I never really thought about it before."

She cocked her head skeptically. "You never noticed that Maisie Colton is drop-dead beautiful? I don't buy it."

Peter leaned closer as if about to confide a dark secret. "She's a Colton." His tone said his statement was self-explanatory.

She waved him off. "Whatever. So there are at least two possibilities. And nothing says the woman, whoever she is, is even still in Honey Creek."

Peter flopped back against the booth again. "You have a point. But it's worth looking into. But could the complication of an unwanted pregnancy be motive for murder?"

Lisa's stomach flip-flopped. "I don't know. Children are a highly charged subject. A lot of very important decisions get made based on having a child with someone." She dropped her eyes to her plate and added under her breath, "Or not."

The waiter arrived with their wine and a basket of rolls, distracting Peter from the comment that had slipped out almost on its own. She hoped he hadn't heard her aside, but Peter's curious gaze stayed fixed on her, as if he were trying to decipher a puzzle, as he ordered their dinners. When the waiter left the table, the question she'd read in Peter's expression came.

"What does *or not* mean?"

Lisa sighed. "I shouldn't have said anything. I was… letting personal history sideline me. Forget it."

But his dark eyes narrowed on her, sharp and intuitive.

"Do you…have a child who's affected decisions you've made?"

Lisa's mouth dried, and she had to clear her throat in order to make her voice work. "In my case, it was the children we *didn't* have that had an impact. The children…I couldn't have. My husband and I divorced after five years of trying to have a baby."

His penetrating gazed softened, and he sat back, looking a bit poleaxed. "Oh." His mouth opened and closed, his struggle to find the right words obvious. "I'm sorry."

Lisa awkwardly forced a laugh. "Wow, talk about a conversation killer." Avoiding his sympathetic but uneasy expression, she fidgeted with the stem of her wine glass, her hand shaking. "Note to self—infertility and subsequent divorce are not fodder for first-date table talk."

Peter's hand closed around her fumbling fingers, and the warmth of his grasp tripped her pulse. With her breath stuck in her lungs, she darted her gaze back to his.

"I thought you said this wasn't a date." The hint of a grin twitched at the corner of his mouth, and his voice was a low, smooth rumble like approaching thunder.

A tingle raced over her skin. The piercing intensity returned to his eyes, shooting heat straight to her core. "I—It's not. I meant…"

His thumb stroked her wrist where her pulse fluttered. "Would a date with me really be such a bad thing?"

A nervous laugh hiccupped from her throat. "No. I just—" Unable to think clearly with the crackle of energy from his touch short-circuiting her brain, Lisa reluctantly pulled her hand from his. Drawing a breath, she gathered her composure. "I don't date. It has nothing to do with you. I just don't think I should get involved with *any* man."

He scrunched his face in disbelief. "Why on earth not? You're young and beautiful and—"

"Peter." She held up a hand to cut him off. "Thank you. I'm flattered, but…none of that changes the fact that…I can't have children." Her shoulders drooped. She really didn't want to get into this discussion. Why had she cracked the door on the topic with her stupid muttering?

He leaned toward her again. "I don't mean to be insensitive, but…I don't see why that should make any difference."

His tone was so gentle it brought tears to her eyes. Or maybe it was the reminder that nights like tonight, alone with a handsome, attentive man, could never be anything more that made her well up. She swallowed the knot of emotion that rose in her throat and blinked away the moisture blurring her vision.

"The only thing more difficult than having Ray walk out on our marriage was seeing the disappointment in his eyes every time an in vitro attempt failed. Not having the children I wanted hurt badly enough, without knowing how I'd let the man I loved down, too. I refuse to put another man through that pain. And… I can't put myself through the heartache of another childless relationship. So…" She paused and squared her shoulders again, reinforcing her words. "I've made it my policy not to start anything I know can't go anywhere."

Lisa held Peter's gaze, her heart thundering as if waiting for an official judgment to be passed down.

A muscle ticked in his jaw as, for several nerve-racking moments, he silently studied her with a shadowed expression. Finally, in a husky voice that slid over her like a lover's caress, he said, "I'm sorry to hear that. Because I think you're special, and…I'm very attracted to you. I'd have liked the chance to…get to know you better."

His deep timbre and the hungry look in his eyes said

he wanted to do much more than "get to know" her. The answering shimmy low in her belly concurred.

If she'd thought she could have meaningless sex simply to satisfy the feverish ache Peter stirred deep inside her, maybe she'd take him up on the promise implicit in his dark, seductive eyes.

Lisa squeezed the armrests of her chair, holding herself in place as the maelstrom of tangled emotions blasted through her. On the heels of her frank confession about her infertility and the shared shock of learning Peter had a half-sibling, the temptation to lose herself in mind-numbing sex pounded through her like a gale-force wind.

But sex could never be meaningless for her, and hiding from the harsh realities of her circumstances was not her style, even if spending a night in Peter's arms did hold great appeal. Her raw honesty had already created a sense of intimacy between them that was dangerous to her heart. Under other circumstances, Peter Walsh was just the kind of man she'd like to 'get to know,' too.

The waiter arrived with their food, allowing Lisa to shake herself from the hypnotic lure of Peter's gaze. But not even the 'best steak in the state' could satisfy the cravings Peter had revived in her tonight—the desire to be held in strong arms, the yen to share her life with someone, and the bittersweet longing for a child of her own.

Peter sipped his wine and studied Lisa over the rim of his glass. He shouldn't have pushed her to divulge the painful reasons behind her divorce, but after only a few hours in her company, he felt himself powerfully drawn to her and wanted to get past her no-dating rule. Considering his own reluctance to involve himself with a woman since Katie's death, his attraction to Patrick's teacher had blindsided him.

Was he ready to take the risks that came with dating? He had more than his own interests to think about now. What was best for Patrick? He and Patrick had been alone for so long, what would it do to their relationship to add a woman to the mix? And was the lack of a mother figure in Patrick's life at the root of his son's recent problems?

Peter cleared his throat before diving into the subject of his son. "So you promised to help me figure out what to do about Patrick. Your suggestion that I explain more of what's happening with the family is a start, but…the truth is, I've felt a distance growing between us for more than a year now. We used to be really close. We did everything together but now…he's pulling away."

Lisa held his gaze, listening attentively as she cut a bite of steak.

"Nowadays, he'd rather sit in his room and play video games than talk to me."

She smiled. "I think most kids his age are more interested in playing video games or sports than talking to their parents. He's ten, Peter. He's a preteen, and it's natural for him to start establishing some independence at his age."

"Preteen?" Peter let his wrist fall heavily to the table and groaned. "God, I hadn't thought about that. What am I going to do with a teenager?"

Lisa chuckled. "Scary as it sounds, you will survive."

"I just wonder sometimes if I've done enough, if I've been a good enough parent. I can't always be there and when Patrick starts doing things that are out of character for him—" he nodded toward Lisa "—like acting out at school, I feel like I've failed."

Lisa shook her head. "You haven't failed. Patrick is a great kid. He's bright and well-behaved…usually. He's a pleasure to have in my class. But his recent mood changes tell me he's just going through a difficult adjustment. Maybe because of the trouble your family has encountered, maybe because you've been working longer hours lately…"

Peter's gaze snapped up to hers. "He told you that?"

"No, you did. The day you came up to the school."

He scratched his chin slowly. "To be honest, I don't remember much of what I said. Only that I was pretty short with you." He sent her an apologetic look. "I'd just been at the hospital to visit Craig Warner, and we'd been discussing the recent chain of trouble my family's been going through. Discussing the fact that we believe the events are connected." Peter elaborated briefly on the attack on Mary, Craig's relationship with the family and his poisoning and the discovery of Mark Walsh's body. Lisa's expression reflected her growing concern and dismay for all the Walshes had endured.

"When I came to the school, I took my frustrations with the case out on you. I'm sorry."

"You've already apologized. The issue we need to solve is how do you reach out to Patrick during all of this, so he's not hurt by the ripple effects of these family problems."

Peter spread his hands. "I'm all ears. What do you suggest?"

"Well, the football game you took him to last weekend was a good start. He beamed like a Christmas light when he told me about the game on Monday."

Peter smiled. "I'm glad he had fun."

She leaned forward, her expression direct and serious. "I'd dare to say it wasn't the game nearly as much as the time with you that he enjoyed. You need to make an effort to do things with him outside of your normal routine. I know that's hard when you are a single parent with a busy job. But for Patrick's sake, try to *make* time."

Peter filled his lungs and nodded. "I can do that. Any ideas?"

"Well…" Lisa stabbed a bite of potato and flashed him a cagey glance. "I have an idea that is self-serving."

Intrigued, Peter arched an eyebrow. "Do tell."

"I'm in charge of the Fall Festival at school. We were supposed to have it last month, but the tornado hit that afternoon, and we had to postpone it until this coming Saturday."

"You want me to go to the festival with Patrick?"

"Better than that." She tugged her mouth into a sheepish, lopsided grin. "I'd like you two to help me set up and run a booth. I have to decorate, oversee all the activities and clean up afterward. I could use all the extra help I can get."

Peter did a quick mental check of his schedule. He'd have to rearrange a few things, but he could clear his calendar for next Saturday. "Done. We'll be there whenever you need us and stay until the last corn-dog stick is thrown away."

Her smile brightened. "Thank you. And did Patrick mention the Parents' Day Thanksgiving luncheon?"

"I think he gave me a note about that. The day before they get out for Thanksgiving break, right?"

She nodded. "I know it's a work day for most parents, but if you can get there—"

"Say no more. I'll do everything I can to be there. Can my mom come? I know she'd love it."

"By all means. Grandparents are welcome." Her expression darkened slightly, and her brow furrowed. "Peter, how much does Patrick know about his mother?"

Peter's gut pitched and for a moment he couldn't draw a breath. "I…told him the truth. That she died when he was born. Why?"

"That's all you've told him? You don't talk about what

kind of person she was or memories you have of her that he'd find funny or comforting?"

A fist squeezed Peter's heart and filled his chest with an ache that made it difficult to talk. "I don't...I mean...if he asks, I try to...be honest, but..." Peter closed his eyes and gritted his teeth, forcing down the surge of emotion Lisa's question brought.

Katie was the last person he wanted to talk about, but knowing Lisa had bared her soul to him concerning her infertility, he owed her a similar honesty. With a deep breath for courage, he faced his demon.

Chapter 7

"We don't talk about Patrick's mother much. Partly because he doesn't ask, and partly because…well, it's difficult for me. Still."

Lisa reached across the table to touch his hand, her eyes soft with sympathy. "I don't mean to cause you pain, but I think it is important that Patrick know about his mom. Even if he doesn't ask, he's bound to have questions. Not having a mom makes him different from the other kids in his class, and while you've done a commendable job raising him alone—"

"My mother helped a lot. Especially when Patrick was a baby."

She conceded the point with a turn of her hand. "Just the same, a grandmother isn't the same thing as a mom. My last piece of advice—" she quirked a self-conscious grin "—and then I promise not to offer anymore unsolicited opinions—Have a heart to heart with Patrick about your wife. He needs to know who he is, where he came from, what she was like. That she'd have loved him had she lived."

That she'd have loved him. Just when he thought he'd gotten his volatile feelings regarding Katie under control, Lisa's words sucker-punched him. His breath stuck in his lungs. A wave of grief and loss swept through him, shaking him to his marrow. Maybe he wasn't as over Katie's death as he'd thought, if one statement from Lisa could undo him so completely.

Peter fisted his hands and struggled to recover his composure. He nodded when his voice failed him, but finally managed to croak, "I'll keep that in mind."

When she withdrew her hand and resumed eating, Peter regretted the loss of her comforting touch. She clearly sensed she'd broached a sensitive subject and deftly turned the conversation toward more benign topics. Local sports, favorite restaurants, their shared interest in old movies. They chatted amiably through the rest of dinner, then split a decadent chocolate dessert. Peter found a rapport with Patrick's teacher that both put him at ease and filled him with the excitement of a promising new relationship.

He couldn't explain why Lisa Navarre had gotten under his skin when no other woman since Katie had, but the truth was unavoidable. Lisa challenged him, made him rethink aspects of his life he'd too long taken for granted. She reached deep into his soul with her honesty, her warmth, her understanding. Her beautiful smile and womanly curves woke a desire in him he'd denied for a long time.

Yet… *I don't date.*

If losing Katie still hurt after ten years, he couldn't imagine how much pain he'd suffer if he fell in love with Lisa, just to have her walk away. But Lisa had her own demons to battle, and Peter respected her honesty about her past, her reasons not to date.

After the waiter took their plates and left to get their bill, Peter leaned back in the booth and cocked his head. "You know what I wonder?"

Lisa wiped her mouth and sat back with a satisfied sigh. "What?" she asked, grinning.

"If we'd met years ago, before either of us married, before any of the mess we're both dealing with now ever happened..."

Her expression sobered, grew pensive, wistful. "Would we have had the same connection then that we have now?" she finished for him.

So she felt the bond, the magnetic attraction, too? Peter's spirits lifted...until he remembered the obstacles they faced.

Her infertility issues. His gnawing grief over Katie's death. The unsolved attacks on his family.

He flashed a small smile. "Yeah, that."

She held his gaze with eyes full of regret and longing, and a ripple of warmth tripped down his spine. "I guess we'll never know."

On Sunday, Peter took Lisa's advice and made a point of spending time with Patrick—making pancakes together in the morning, tossing the football in the back yard, helping him finish an essay and poster on the Boston Tea Party for school. Working with Patrick on his homework brought thoughts of his dinner with Lisa to mind. While they hadn't gotten the payoff tip from Tess Cantrell that he'd hoped would help find his father's murderer, his non-date with Lisa had been better than expected. He'd gotten an intimate glimpse of the woman who'd captured his attention as well as valuable insights to his relationship with Patrick. All of which served to make Lisa even more enticing, more intriguing and more desirable to him. He found himself restlessly anticipating the school's Fall Festival on Saturday, his next best chance to see Lisa and get to know her.

On Sunday evening as he said goodnight to Patrick, Peter sat on the edge of his son's bed and broached the topic he'd avoided for years. "Patrick, do you have questions about your mom that you want to ask me?"

Patrick's eyes widened, clearly surprised that his father had raised what was usually a taboo topic. "Well…yeah."

He nodded and squeezed Patrick's foot through the covers. "So let's talk. What do you want to know?"

His son swallowed hard and wrinkled his nose reluctantly. "Um…how did she die?"

Peter inhaled deeply, determined to keep his voice steady and reassuring. "There were…complications when you were born. Internal bleeding that the doctor's couldn't stop."

"Oh. Do you miss her?"

Peter squeezed the sports-print bedspread in his hands. "Every day. I wish you could have known her. She was terrific. Really fun, creative, loved to laugh."

Patrick's cheek twitched in a quick grin before sobering. His gaze dropped, and he stared at his hands.

"What is it, Patrick? You can talk to me about it. About anything."

"Do you…" Patrick gulped a deep breath. "Do you blame me for her dying?"

Peter's heart jolted. "What? No!"

Patrick's chin quivered, and Peter felt himself starting to unravel. He scooped his son into a bear hug and crushed him to his chest. "No way, sport. Not one bit. I love you, and I thank God for you every day. Don't ever forget that."

"But she died because of me." Patrick muttered, his voice tight with tears.

"No, she died because her iron was too low and they couldn't stop the bleeding. That's not your fault. No one blames you. No one. Especially not me."

Patrick shuddered and sniffled, and Peter kissed his son on the top of his head. "What's more…" He paused to gather his composure before finishing. "Your mom would have loved you as much as I do. More even. I have no doubt she is looking down from heaven and smiling because she is so proud of you."

"Really?"

"Really."

Patrick wiggled free of Peter's embrace and wiped his face on his pajama sleeve. "Dad, are you dating Ms. Navarre?"

Peter leaned back to get a better view of his son's face. "Would it bother you if I was?"

Patrick groaned. "You're not supposed to answer a question with a question!"

He grinned. "You're right. And no, I'm not dating her. We had dinner the other night, but it was strictly business."

"Business? With my teacher?" Patrick narrowed a skeptical glare on him. "Does that mean you were talking about me?"

"Part of the time. But she also helped interview someone for a case and dinner was my thank-you to her." That much was mostly true.

But Peter heard Lisa's voice in his head, urging him to be completely honest with Patrick.

"But, uh… I do like Ms. Navarre."

Patrick tipped his head. "Just like, or *like* like?"

Peter chuckled. "I think she's pretty and very nice, and

I'd like to see her some more, be her friend. Would that bother you?"

Patrick's grin spread. "That'd be okay. You can even date her if you want. I like her, too."

Peter laughed. "Well, thanks. It's good to have your permission."

Patrick slid back down in his covers with a shrug, missing Peter's sarcasm. "No problem."

Ruffling his son's hair, Peter rose from the bed and snapped off the bedside lamp. "Night, sport. Sleep well." He turned at the door and added, "And anytime you want to talk about Mom or school or anything, you can come to me. Okay?"

"Okay. 'Night, Dad."

Peter headed back to the living room, where he logged onto his computer to catch up on email correspondence and research for a couple cases he had pending. He was at the Montana state records website searching for documents regarding a client's recent divorce when it occurred to him that he could look up May Masterson's and Jeremy Colton's birth certificates to see exactly when the young teens were born and if either certificate listed Mark Walsh as the father. His internet search led him to the usual red tape, but Peter hadn't been a private investigator for seven years without learning a few tricks to get what he needed. A copy of the kids' birth certificates should be on file with their official school records. If he could find a way to steal a peek…

Thoughts of the local schools brought him back to his dinner with Lisa. The pain in her eyes when she'd described her heartache over her broken marriage and her inability to have children gnawed at him. He couldn't imagine his life without Patrick, and if he was honest, he'd always imagined that someday he'd have more kids. He'd come from a large family and wanted Patrick to know the joys of brothers and sisters.

But having more kids meant remarrying. Remarrying meant putting his heart on the line again. Getting involved with a woman meant he must overcome the icy ache deep in his bones when he remembered losing Katie. If he hadn't been able to move past his loss in ten years, what chance did he have of ever putting his wife's death behind him?

And yet…for a few hours Saturday night, Lisa had made him feel as if a future relationship might be possible. The chemistry was definitely there. He'd seen the same attraction burning in her gaze that had sizzled through him when they touched.

I can't put myself through the heartache of another childless relationship.

Peter sighed and rubbed his eyes. He couldn't push Lisa into a relationship she didn't want, and belaboring the point tonight wouldn't help him. He was better off concentrating on his caseload. And on his promise to Craig to find the link between the poisoning and his father's murder.

Setting aside his circular thoughts concerning Lisa Navarre, Peter typed *arsenic sources* into the search engine and looked for something that he could use to prove the Coltons supplied Lester Atkins with the poison used to make Craig sick. Most of what he found he already knew—arsenic is used to make insecticides, fungicides and rodent killer, all of which could have been purchased in bulk from one of the many farm- and ranch-supply stores in the area. While the Coltons had access to these poisons, so did everyone else. Peter raised an eyebrow when he read that a large number of commercially raised chickens were fed a compound containing arsenic. He dismissed this as the source of Craig's illness. Plenty of people ate chicken and didn't wind up in the hospital from it. Craig's poisoning had been deliberate and heavy-handed, intended to kill him.

By midnight, Peter's vision was blurring from reading the small print of the web pages he'd searched and he hadn't learned anything significant to help track down his father's killer.

Shutting down his computer, he decided to pursue the trail of his father's romantic liaisons in the morning. Perhaps someone in town could confirm whether Mark Walsh had gotten involved with Maisie Colton or Lily Masterson fifteen years ago.

As he turned off the lights and headed to bed, Peter recalled his trip to the library last weekend and Maisie's tirade.

Your father sure didn't care how many women he hurt, how many hearts he broke, how many lives he ruined! Did that number include Maisie?

Peter frowned as he climbed into bed. "Guess it is true—Hell hath no fury like a woman scorned."

But had his father's scorn driven one of his women to murder?

The following week dragged for Peter. His cases felt more tedious than usual, and his attention drifted frequently to the unresolved murder of his father. By itself, his father's murder would only be a general concern of wanting justice for his family. But the mounting evidence that Mark Walsh's death had only been the first attack of many directed at his family made finding the person responsible an urgent matter for Peter, a sentiment Sheriff Colton didn't seem to share.

He made a few casual inquiries around town with trusted

friends regarding the possibility that his dad could have had a brief, contentious affair in 1995 with either Lily Masterson or Maisie Colton. His straw poll overwhelmingly favored Lily Masterson as the most likely candidate.

"Face it, Peter. Lily earned the reputation she had back then. She was a wildcat," his barber said as he trimmed Peter's hair. "And Maisie? Well, the way she's storming around town, complaining to anyone who'll listen about the *Dr. Sophie* show not taking her calls, tells me she's not involved with what happened to your dad. Why would she want to go on national TV and draw attention to herself if she were guilty? Don't make sense."

Peter scoffed. "Not much about Maisie Colton makes sense. Besides, have you seen Dr. Sophie's show? Everyone who gets on there is airing their dirty laundry for fifteen minutes of fame."

He was still musing over his barber's comments, though, when he met his mother for lunch the next day at the Honey-B Café on Main Street. Jolene kissed his cheek before she settled in the booth across from him.

"Craig says hello. He's feeling better every day. Stronger."

Peter nodded. "Good. I plan on stopping by to see him later today. I haven't made much progress connecting his poisoning to Dad's murder or the attack on Mary, though."

"Whoever did this had plenty of help. Or they had lots of time to plan and hide themselves under layers of false leads. Like Lester Atkins. Atkins may have had his own reasons to poison Craig, but I'm not convinced he acted alone. But why our family? What do they have to gain by attacking us?" Jolene rubbed the joints of her hand where the earliest stages of arthritis often gave her trouble. "Did you talk to Tess Cantrell?"

"I did."

"And?"

Peter filled his mother in on the conversation with Tess about the volatile woman from Honey Creek Tess had mentioned. Jolene blanched and pressed a hand to her throat when Peter mentioned the mystery woman's pregnancy.

"I'm sorry. I shouldn't have brought that up."

Jolene waved him off. "Please. I'm past the days where your father's sins can hurt me anymore. I'm just startled. That's all. Something that big would be hard to keep a secret." She paused and tapped her fingernails on her coffee mug. "Unless…"

Peter leaned forward. "Yeah?"

"Well, in my day, when a girl got pregnant out of wedlock, the family sent her away to stay with family or stay at a special home for young mothers until the baby came. Maybe this girl left town."

Peter picked up his sandwich, took a big bite and chewed slowly as he thought. "Lily Masterson left Honey Creek back then."

"Hmm…yes. But so did Maisie."

Peter froze. "She did?"

Jolene's gaze drifted away as she tried to recall the specifics. "I think it was just before your dad disappeared. Or was it after? I know it was around then…."

Peter flashed to the newspaper columns he'd scanned through at the library concerning the Coltons. One of the headlines had been about Maisie taking an extended vacation. Ice seeped through his veins.

"Could it have been Maisie Colton, Mom? Could Dad have had a secret affair with the Colton princess and gotten her pregnant? I thought Dad hated the Coltons. All of them."

"It is certainly possible. And if he did, and if Darius

found out Mark had gotten his daughter pregnant? Well…"
Jolene tipped her head, her eyebrows lifted, as if to say,
"You fill in the blanks."

"Wouldn't have to have been Darius. Her brothers might
not have taken too kindly to someone Dad's age messing
with their sister. Don't think I haven't noticed Craig's
poisoning and the attack on Mary both happened right
after Damien was released from prison. Don't you think
he's got a grudge to settle with us?" Peter fisted his hand
and banged it on the table. "So once again we're back to
the Coltons. They seem to be the center of everything in
this investigation."

Jolene furrowed her brow and fiddled with her coffee
mug. "I know it seems that way to you, but I still think
you're focusing on them for personal reasons. Your dad was
involved with plenty of other people through his business,
his civic groups…his affairs." Jolene splayed her hand on
the tabletop and leaned toward Peter. "Honey, I'm worried
about you digging into this too deeply. I know you're trying
to help Craig find the person who poisoned him, and tie it
all to a bigger conspiracy but…I talked to Mary on Sunday
and—"

Peter grunted and looked away. "I know where this is
going."

"Peter, your sister's life was threatened when she and
Jake dug into your dad's business. She's worried about you,
worried you'll provoke the wrong people and get hurt. And
frankly, I'm worried too. Maybe the time has come to let
the matter go and—"

"I can't do that, Mom. Someone is coming after my
family. Dad, then Mary, then Craig…I can't sit back and do
nothing." Peter tossed enough money on the table to cover
their tab and a generous tip. "I have to go. I'm testifying in
a personal-injury lawsuit for a client this afternoon. And

if I finish at court early enough, I'm going to try to track down proof that Dad is the father of Maisie Colton's son, Jeremy. I know a Colton killed Dad. I just have to figure out which Colton."

Chapter 8

By Thursday afternoon, Peter had grown restless. He was tired of waiting for Saturday to arrive so he could see Lisa at the school's Fall Festival.

As he drove home from Billings, where he'd met with a new client regarding a private search for the woman's missing adult daughter, he had time to think. Two topics stuck center-most in his mind. The questions that still swirled around the attacks on his family...and Lisa Navarre. He couldn't do much more today to resolve the former, but seeing the damage to the trees and buildings on the outskirts of Honey Creek as he pulled back into town reminded him of his promise to fix Lisa's house.

Peter flipped his wrist to check his watch. School would be dismissing in ten minutes. He could pick Patrick up, stop by the hardware store and be at Lisa's house by four o'clock. He'd have about an hour of daylight to replace the roof shingles. A spotlight would be sufficient light to replace her broken window.

His anticipation ramped up as he headed for the elementary school. Once in the carpool line, Peter phoned his mother to let her know her babysitting services were not needed that afternoon. When the last bell rang and kids disgorged from the school, Peter stood beside his truck and scanned the mob of children for Patrick's blue coat and red knit hat. When his son scurried past him, making a beeline for the bus, Peter placed his finger and thumb in his mouth and whistled loudly. "Patrick!"

Stumbling to a stop, Patrick turned toward his father, then trotted over. Instead of the excitement of surprise Peter expected to see, Patrick's face was pale and wary as he approached.

"Dad, wh-what are you doing here?"

"Do I need a reason to pick you up?" Peter put a hand on Patrick's back and ushered him to the passenger's side.

"Is something wrong? Did something else bad happen?" Patrick's voice cracked.

Peter's breath caught. He mentally replayed the past several months, realizing the only times he'd picked Patrick up from school had been when Craig had been poisoned and when Mary had been attacked. "I…no. Nothing bad has happened, sport. I promise. I was just on my way into town from a business trip, and I thought we'd stop by the hardware store together then head over to Ms. Navarre's house to help her with some repairs." He took Patrick's backpack from him as his son climbed onto the front seat. "Does that sound okay to you? I can call Grandma back if you'd rather go home."

Patrick gave him a leery look. "You're sure nothing's wrong? I'm not in trouble?"

Peter smiled and hoisted his son's backpack into the back of the truck. "I'm sure."

But Patrick's wary concern niggled Peter all the way to the hardware store. He recalled Lisa's advice about being honest with his son about all the trouble the family had endured. After they bought the supplies they'd need, he headed to Lisa's house and searched for an opening to discuss the recent family crises with Patrick.

"Sorry I worried you this afternoon, buddy. I didn't realize I'd only picked you up from school on days when there was bad news for the family."

Patrick shrugged. "Whatever."

"Can we talk about what's bothering you?"

"I'm okay."

Peter patted Patrick on the leg. "I know I haven't told you much about what happened to Uncle Craig and Aunt Mary, but that was only because I didn't want to worry you. But I guess not knowing what happened can be just as bad, huh? Not knowing is scary, too."

Patrick glanced at his father with hooded eyes. "I'm not a baby, Dad. You can tell me the truth without me going ballistic."

He smiled at his son. "You're right. You're not a baby. So here's the deal…" Peter explained to Patrick in broad, general terms all that had been transpiring in recent months, careful to reassure him that he had nothing to fear. "The guy responsible for making Uncle Craig sick has been caught and Aunt Mary has given up her investigation of Grandpa's death, so there's nothing to worry about. Right?"

Patrick scrunched his face in thought. "Sorta. Are you investigating Grandpa's death?"

Whoops.

Be honest, he imagined Lisa telling him.

"Well, I'm looking into a few things that might help the sheriff find the person who killed Grandpa. But I'm a professional investigator. I know what I'm doing and how to be careful."

His son scowled. "Why does the sheriff need help? Doesn't he have deputies to help him solve murders?"

Peter squeezed the steering wheel. He hadn't anticipated these landmine questions. "Well, the sheriff didn't ask for my help. I'm doing this on my own. Because I want Grandpa's killer caught as soon as possible."

Patrick turned on the seat, his eyes wide and incisive. "But if Aunt Mary was attacked because she was trying to find out about Grandpa's killer, couldn't they come after you now that you're investigating?"

"I suppose there's a chance. But I'm being very careful." They stopped at a traffic light, and Peter reached over to catch Patrick's chin in his hand. He held his son's face and met his eyes squarely. "Listen to me, Patrick. If I get a sense that I'm in danger, I will quit my investigation without a second thought. Because being here for you and taking care of our family is what is most important to me. I will *not* let anyone hurt me, and more importantly, I will not let anyone hurt you. Ever. Okay?"

Patrick's throat worked as he swallowed. "Promise?"

Peter smiled. "Promise."

"Okay." Patrick returned, grinning. "So can I help fix Ms. Navarre's house?"

Peter released the breath he hadn't realized he'd been holding. "You bet, sport."

"I'm home, Samson!" Lisa called as she hustled in from the cold and left her bag of books by the front door. As she'd left school, she'd have sworn she saw Peter Walsh picking up Patrick, and the handsome father had preoccupied her thoughts ever since. Of course, Peter hadn't been far from her mind all week. When she thought about the Fall Festival and his promise to help set up and work the event, anxious butterflies swooped in her gut. Despite telling herself to take it slow with Peter, to remember her rule about not dating, she couldn't deny the smile that came to her face when she thought of him or the giddy rush of excitement when she looked forward to spending more time with him at the festival.

"Samson?" She shucked off her gloves and scarf and glanced down the hall. Her furry companion emerged from a back room, gave a lazy stretch, then loped with a kind of trot/hop down the hall to greet her. When she reached down to pat him, Samson gave her a cursory rub then headed over to his food bowl. He glared at her as if to say, "It's about time you got home. I'm starving!"

"Yeah, yeah. Let me hang up my coat."

Lisa had just finished feeding Samson, fixing herself a cup of hot tea and settling in her living room with a stack of papers to grade when someone knocked on her front door.

"Who in the world…?" she asked her cat, as he hopped in from the kitchen ready for a post-dinner nap.

She hurried to the door and yanked it open. When she found Peter on her doorstep, his cheeks ruddy from the cold and his jaw shaded with late-afternoon stubble, Lisa's heartbeat scampered.

"Peter." She hoped the breathless quality of her voice sounded more like surprise to him than the girlish giddiness that was, in fact, at fault. She gripped the edge of her door and collected her composure. *Steady, girl.*

"Hi, Ms. Navarre!" Patrick said brightly.

Caught staring at his father, she jerked her gaze to

Patrick and smiled warmly. "Hi, Patrick. What brings you by?"

Patrick held up the toolbox he carried. "We're gonna fix your house."

She glanced back at Peter for confirmation, and he gave her a lopsided grin that did little to help the breathless feeling squeezing her chest. He plucked the toolbox from Patrick's hand and ruffled his son's hair. "Correction. I'm going to fix her roof while you do your homework, and once you finish your schoolwork, you can help me with the window. But homework comes first."

Lisa gave him a sassy grin. "You're just saying that to impress the teacher."

Arching an eyebrow, he replied, "Maybe. Is it working?"

Her smile spread, and she had a playful retort poised on her lips when she caught the fascinated look her student was dividing between her and his father. "Patrick, you can use my kitchen table to do your homework if you want. And help yourself to one of the cookies on the counter if you're hungry."

"Thanks, Ms. Navarre." Patrick plowed through the door with his overstuffed backpack, jostling her into his father's chest as he bustled into her house.

Lisa turned to Peter. "You really don't have to—"

He touched a finger to her mouth to silence her. "But I want to."

The brush of his cold skin on her lips sent sweet sensations curling through her.

"How was I supposed to get any sleep tonight with that arctic front moving in and knowing your window is still broken?"

She hiccuped a laugh. "I don't know. I guess I'll have to let you fix it. We can't have you losing sleep."

An image of Peter, shirtless, restless and tangled in his sheets flashed in her mind, wiping the teasing grin from her face and overloading her circuits.

"I hope you don't mind me bringing him along?" Peter hitched his head toward her kitchen as he stepped inside. "My mom usually keeps him for me in the afternoon, but I thought I'd give her a day off."

Lisa had to swallow before she could speak, the image of Peter in his bed imprinted like a film negative in her brain. "It's fine. He won't bother me. I was just about to grade the history essays they turned in today." She rubbed her palms on the seat of her jeans. "Can I offer you anything before you get started?" *Like permission to have your way with me.*

Oh, mercy. Lisa shoved the provocative images aside. *What is wrong with you?*

"No, I'm good. I've got everything I need in my truck. In fact, I got the last package of black shingles Cooper's Hardware had in stock. Needless to say, they've had a run on building products lately."

"Well, thank you. I'll repay you for the supplies, of course."

He pulled a face and waved her off. "Forget it. My pleasure." He stepped toward her, and she held her breath. But instead of her, his target was the kitchen doorway. He leaned into the room just far enough to send Patrick a parental look. "You behave yourself for Ms. Navarre, and let her get her work done. Understand, sport?"

"Yep." Patrick returned without looking up.

"Yep, sir."

"Sir," Patrick groaned, apparently missing his father's sarcasm.

Peter lingered for another moment, the whisper of a smile on his lips and an affectionate glow in his eyes as he regarded his son. Peter's obvious love for his son nudged the empty ache in her soul for the children she didn't have, and reminded her why she couldn't burden Peter, or any man, with her infertility.

As he turned toward the door, Peter caught her eye. "I'll be on the roof if you need me."

For the next half hour, Lisa tried hard to concentrate on the history essays, but the thudding on her roof was an ever-present reminder of the man doing the repair, the man who made her pulse hammer.

"I can't think about spelling with all that racket," Patrick complained as he sauntered in from the kitchen and flopped on her couch.

"I know what you mean." Lisa set aside the essays and stretched her back.

Patrick cast a curious gaze around her living room, and his gazed stopped when he spotted Samson napping on the rocking chair by her fireplace. His eyes widened. "Is that your cat?" he asked, even as he crossed the room toward the snoozing feline.

Lisa chuckled. "No, it's my pet shark."

Patrick sent her a withering look and a grin as he knelt in front of the rocking chair. "Can I pet her?"

"That's Samson. You may pet *him,* but be warned, he bites."

Patrick stroked Samson's long fur, and the cat raised his head to greet him with a loud, short, *"Rrow."*

Lisa folded her legs under her, watching Patrick pat Samson and awaiting the inevitable.

Sure enough, Samson batted at Patrick's hand, pinned the boy's hand down with his paw, and—

"He's licking me!" Patrick laughed.

"Licking?" Lisa craned her neck for a better look. "Well, I'll be darned."

Peter's son continued playing with her cat, ruffling his fuzzy tummy and chuckling as Samson batted at his hand. After a moment, Lisa shrugged, baffled by Samson's uncharacteristic behavior, and returned her attention to the history essays.

"Hey, he's only got three legs!" Patrick sounded truly dismayed.

She glanced up again and met the boy's curious gaze. "Yep, I don't know what happened to his other foot. He lost a foot somehow before I rescued him as a kitten."

"Can he walk?" Patrick asked, his expression apprehensive as he continued to pat Samson.

"Oh, yeah, he—"

"Ow! He bit me." The startled but humored expression Patrick wore told her he wasn't hurt. Samson, for all his crankiness, never bit hard.

"I told you." Lisa flashed her student a smile. "He's a shark."

Patrick chuckled and reached for Samson again, but the feline decided he was done amusing their guest and hopped down from the rocking chair. The cat ran off toward the kitchen, answering Patrick's question regarding his mobility.

"Did you finish your homework?" she asked. "Remember, we're having a spelling test tomorrow."

Patrick rolled his eyes and sighed dramatically. "No. I still have to do my math. And my grandma usually helps me study spelling."

Lisa set aside the history papers and rose to scoot Patrick back to the kitchen table. "Your dad wants you to finish your schoolwork before you help with the window. If you want me to quiz you in spelling, I can."

Patrick looked up at her, his face brightening. "Really? Can you help me with my math, too?"

"What's your trouble with math? You've been doing well on all your assignments so far this year."

"I just hate fractions is all."

"If you're asking me to do your math for you the answer is no. But if you get stuck, give a holler. Okay?"

"Give a holler?" Patrick laughed. "You sound like a hick."

Lisa pretended to be affronted. "*Holler* is a perfectly good word down in Texas, where I grew up." She propped her hands on her hips and scowled playfully. "And I'm fixin' to open a can of whoop-butt on you if you don't get your hide into the kitchen and get busy."

Though he grinned at her southernisms spoken with a heavy drawl, Patrick's eyes widened, and he jumped up and scurried to the kitchen table. She followed him and paused to tousle his hair.

How many times had she imagined sitting around the table with her own family, sharing meals or tutoring on homework? She suppressed a pang of regret and focused on his cherubic face. In a few years, with the sculpting of maturity, Patrick would be the spitting image of his father.

While Patrick tackled fractions, she started a package of hamburger browning, glancing toward the table every now and then to check on her student. "How's it going?"

"Okay. Just two more to go. Then spelling."

She pulled a jar of spaghetti sauce from the cabinet and turned down the heat on the beef.

As she headed to the table, Patrick closed his math book and sighed. "Why do you give so much homework?"

"Patrick, ten math problems and twenty vocabulary words is not that much homework."

She slid his spelling book toward her and flipped to the right page. "Ready?"

He nodded. "If I get them all right, do I get a dollar?"

She laughed. "If you get them all right tomorrow, you'll get an A on your test."

"Grandma gives me a dollar if I spell all my words right."

"Hmm, well, you can take that up with your dad. For now, spell *abject*."

They made their way through most of the list before Peter sauntered in from outside, bringing the crisp scent of autumn leaves with him.

"Hey Dad, Ms. Navarre has a cool cat named Samson. He's only got three legs, and his fur is really soft. First he was licking me, and then he bit me!"

Peter frowned. "Bit you?"

Lisa opened her mouth to defend her cat, but Patrick rushed on enthusiastically. "Not hard. It didn't hurt. He's really awesome, Dad."

"Awesome? Wow. High praise for a cat." He pulled off his coat and hung it in the front hall. "So how's the homework coming?"

Patrick's shoulders slumped. "I'm still studying spelling for my test."

His dad twisted his mouth in thought. "Tell you what. Do as much as you can while I set things up for the window, then I'll finish quizzing you while we work. Deal?"

"Deal!"

"Peter?" Lisa said impulsively. "I'd love for you to stay and eat with me. I'm making spaghetti. It's the least I can do to say thank you."

"Spaghetti! Can we, Dad? Please?" Patrick's expression was enthusiastic and pleading. Lisa just hoped her own face didn't reflect the same expectant eagerness, despite the thump of adrenaline and hopefulness in her chest.

"You sure you have enough to share? Growing boys eat a lot."

She winked at Patrick. "I'm sure."

Peter's face warmed, and his smile sent a zing through her blood. "Thank you. We accept. Let me go get the new window out of the truck and I'll let you know when I'm ready to start, okay, Patrick?"

As Peter headed out to his truck, Lisa tried to tame the giddy smile that tugged her cheeks.

Patrick would be with them, chaperoning, so her dinner invitation couldn't be considered a date. Right? Repaying his kindness was the least she could do.

So why did having Peter and his son staying for dinner feel like something special, something significant?

Setting aside the nagging questions, she glanced down at Patrick's spelling list. "Okay, spell *dangerous.*"

Her pulse stumbled. An omen? Was pursuing this "non-relationship" with Peter a dangerous venture for her heart?

Not a date, she told herself. *It's not a date.*

Peter removed the cardboard Lisa had taped over her broken window and set it aside while the image of his son sitting at the kitchen table with the pretty brunette replayed in his head. Patrick seemed to be gobbling up the female attention. And why not? Lisa was attractive, kind, invested in seeing Patrick do well in school. Had he underestimated the importance of having a mother figure in his son's life?

Sure, his mom was there for Patrick every afternoon, but somehow that was different. Jolene was Patrick's grandmother, only available part-time. A whole generation older than Patrick's friends' mothers.

Lisa would make a great mother. As soon as the thought

filtered through his head, he remembered her painful confession at the restaurant on Saturday. A fist of regret squeezed his chest. Not only did her infertility troubles make her gun-shy about dating, reluctant to risk the kind of pain she'd known with her ex-husband, but she was missing out on one of life's truly great joys. Parenting Patrick filled his heart in unexpected and powerful ways.

When he and Katie had been anticipating Patrick's birth, they'd talked about how many more children they'd have.

Twelve, Katie had said, *just like in* Cheaper by the Dozen.

Peter had laughed and kissed his wife. *Let's see how this first one goes before we commit to a dozen.*

He sighed as the tightness in his chest gripped harder. Katie hadn't lived long enough even to see Patrick grow up. And deep inside he still harbored a desire for more kids. Maybe not twelve, but…

Peter removed the wrappings from the new window and was lining up the needed tools when Patrick bustled into the room. "Ms. Navarre says to let her know when to start the noodles. They take about ten minutes to boil."

Shaking off the melancholy that thoughts of Lisa's infertility and Katie's death had stirred, he managed a smile for his son. "Copy that. So did you bring your spelling words?"

Patrick handed him a thin book. "Page 44. We stopped at *extensive.*"

Flipping to the proper page, Peter scanned the list and read aloud, *"Exude."*

"Exude. E-x-u—" Patrick paused and took the screwdriver Peter handed him. "—d-e. *Exude.*"

Peter pointed to a screw on the existing window frame. "See if you can remove that screw, then tell me what *exude* means."

Patrick set to work on the screw. "We don't have to know the definitions for the test. Just spell the words."

"Yeah, maybe so. But *I* want you to tell me what the words mean while we work."

His son groaned. "*Exude* means...like...stuff coming out or oozing from something?"

"Basically, yeah." He watched Patrick struggle to loosen the screw. "Can you use it in a sentence?"

Another grunt. "Dad!"

"Patrick!" he returned mimicking his son's exasperated tone.

His son bit his bottom lip and leaned into his efforts to budge the stuck screw. When it turned, Patrick's face lit with victory. "Did it."

"Excellent." He gave his son's upper arm a light squeeze. "Yep, definitely getting some muscles there. Now... *exude.*"

Patrick tipped his head and wrinkled his nose. Then a sassy grin lit his face. "Ms. Navarre's cat exudes awesomeness."

A chuckle behind them drew his attention to the door. Lisa leaned against the frame watching them, looking beautiful with a mysterious little smile tugging her lips.

Peter's pulse kicked as the impulse to taste those lips slammed into him.

"Works for me, Dad. Although I'm not sure if *awesomeness* is in the dictionary," she said.

Patrick nudged Peter out of the way, pulling his dad from his lustful sidetrack, and set to work loosening the next screw holding the broken window in place. "Dad, can we get a cat?"

Peter pulled a dubious frown. "A cat? Wouldn't a dog be more...a guy's pet?"

Patrick shrugged. "I don't know. I like Samson. I want a cat like him."

Peter sent Lisa a look and caught her smirking, muffling a laugh. "Yeah, well…we'll see. I'm not much of a cat person."

Over the next twenty minutes, Patrick loosened all of the remaining screws and helped him lift down and replace the broken window. Lisa checked on them several times, complimenting Patrick on his handyman skills and smiling her approval to Peter. When they had secured the new window and sealed the edges with caulk, he cast a glance over his shoulder to Lisa. "All done here. Just need to clean up, if you want to start the pasta."

"Got it." She pushed away from the wall where she'd been leaning and stepped closer to examine their work. "Double-paned for extra insulation, even. Wow."

Peter handed his son a small bag of trash. "Please take this to her garbage can outside."

When Patrick reached for the old window, Peter and Lisa spoke at the same time.

"Wait!"

"Patrick, don't—"

He looked up at them, confused.

"Let me get the broken glass, sport. I don't want you to cut yourself." Peter ruffled Patrick's hair. "Take that trash out, then wash up for dinner."

After Patrick left, Lisa sidled closer to Patrick and pitched her voice low. The scent of her perfume teased his nose and made his body go haywire.

"You're good with him. Patient. Firm but loving. Instructing without being bossy or demeaning. I know I have no room to judge since I'm not a parent myself—"

"Lisa—" He furrowed his brow, sensing where this might be going.

She raised a finger to stop him.

"And it really isn't my business anyway, but…in case there is any question left about my opinion of the job you're doing with Patrick—" she flashed a gentle smile "—you're a great father. I can see how much you love him in the way you look at him."

He nodded. "He's everything to me."

A wistful look drifted over her face, and she turned back to the new window, ran her fingers over the glass. "It looks like a professional did this. Thank you, Peter." She lifted a corner of her mouth, an impish light sparking in her eyes as she nudged him with her shoulder. "And for the record, the teacher *is* impressed."

"I'm glad." The temptation to kiss her sucker-punched him again, making his body taut, as if his skin were too tight. He canted slightly forward, his gaze locked on hers.

And Patrick barreled back into the room, the bag of trash still in his hand. "It's too dark outside."

Peter jerked away from his son's teacher and cleared his throat. "What?"

"I can't see anything. Can you turn on a light for me?"

Lisa's expression reflected the same crushed anticipation as she ushered Patrick into the hall. She met his gaze as she left the room, her eyes full of the same regret that hammered him.

Trying not to resent the missed opportunity to sample her lips, Peter carefully picked up the broken window and followed them down the hall. Somehow, some way, he'd find another chance to show Lisa Navarre how he felt about her.

Chapter 9

Saturday morning, Peter and Patrick rose early and headed over to the school gymnasium to help Lisa decorate and set up for the Fall Festival. They arrived just as Lisa was unloading a large box from the back of her car, and Peter swooped in to take the box from her.

"I'll get that."

"Morning, Ms. Navarre!" Patrick said, a bounce of preteen energy in his step.

"Hi, guys!" Her face brightened as she passed the bulky load to Peter. "You came."

"Didn't I say we would?"

"Well, yeah, but…I guess I didn't expect you until later." She nodded to the box as she started for the gym door. "Looks like you arrived right on time, though. Thank you."

He flashed a broad grin. "I aim to please."

Patrick held the door as Peter carried the large box

inside and set it on a folding table near the door. A few other parents and teachers already milled about in the gym, hanging posters, unfolding chairs and shuffling volleyball nets off the main floor. Peter scanned the faces, recognizing a few. No Coltons.

He hoped to have a chance to question some of the other parents, and get a feel for what the local grapevine was saying about his dad's death. The Honey Creek gossip mill had an uncanny way of learning who did what long before official channels did.

"What is all this stuff?" Patrick asked, peering into the box.

Lisa started unpacking papers, baskets, balls, staplers, scissors and rolls of tape. "Decorating supplies. Odds and ends for the games." She handed Patrick three small rubber balls. "Will you take these to Mrs. Jones for the milk-can-toss booth?"

"Sure."

While his son scurried away with the rubber balls, Peter stepped closer to Lisa, mindful of the eyes watching him and the pretty teacher. "How is it you look so pretty at this hour on a Saturday morning?"

She gave him choked-sounding chuckle. "What? Are you kidding? No makeup, faded jeans and a ratty ponytail? Who are you kidding?"

He turned up a palm. "I just call 'em as I see 'em."

Patrick returned, gushing with the eagerness of a puppy. "Now what?"

"Well, will you help me make copies of these coloring sheets for the little kids?" Lisa pulled a couple of pages with black line drawings from a folder and held them out to Patrick.

"Okay. What do I do?"

"Follow me to the front office, and I'll show you how

to work the copy machine." After popping a few pieces of candy corn in her mouth, she pulled out a wad of keys and jangled them as she hitched her head, signaling Patrick to follow her.

The front office. Peter stilled. This could be his opportunity to get the information he needed on Maisie Colton's son.

"Hey, Patrick?" he called, trotting to catch up. "Why don't you help Mrs. Robbins set up chairs? I'll make the copies with Ms. Navarre."

Patrick divided a curious look between Lisa and his father. "You just want privacy so you can kiss, don't you?"

Lisa sputtered a laugh, her cheeks flushing. "Patrick!"

"None of your beeswax, sport. Now go help with the chairs." Peter took the coloring sheets from Patrick, curled them into a cone and swatted at his son's fanny as Patrick loped away, smirking.

Facing Lisa, Peter rolled his eyes. "Sorry about that. The boy never did miss a chance to embarrass his old man."

Lisa bumped him with her shoulder as they started down the corridor. "Not so old."

Peter gave her an appreciative grin. "Most men my age are only just now starting to have babies. When most guys were graduating from college and thinking about marriage, I was parenting a toddler. Alone."

Lisa grew quiet, pensive. He could guess where her mind was. *Stupid, stupid, bring up babies!*

"Sorry—" he said at the same time she started, "Peter, do you ever—"

He waved a hand. "Go on."

"Do you think about having more kids?"

He sighed. "The thought has crossed my mind. I came from a relatively large family. I enjoyed having a brother and two sisters to play with growing up. I'd love for Patrick to have that, but at this point he's already got a ten-year head start on any siblings he'd have, so they wouldn't exactly be contemporaries."

"But you do want more kids?"

They stopped in front of the front office, and when she reached for the knob to unlock the door, he caught her hand. "I know where this is coming from. I shouldn't have mentioned kids around you. I'm sorry."

Her eyes lit with a fiery intensity. "Wrong. The last thing I want you to do is dance around subjects with me. Especially when it comes to children. If we're going to see more of each other, then it's something we have to deal with up front."

He drew her closer, and her eyes widened with surprise. "*Are* we going to see more of each other?"

"I…I only meant—"

"Because I'd like that. A lot."

"I—" She licked her lips and cast her gaze toward his chest. "Peter, I like you. Really I do, but what's the point in dating if—"

He caught her chin and nudged her face up. "Here's the point."

Without a second thought, he dipped his head and caught her lips with his, shaping and molding them with a gentle persuasion.

Lisa stiffened in shock, then slowly melted into his embrace, answering the tug of his mouth with a reciprocal fervor. Her kiss tasted like the candy corn she'd been nibbling, and like a sugar rush in his blood, the sweet pressure of her lips made his pulse pound and wired his body with a surge of energy.

The clang of a locker closing down the hall startled them, and Lisa jerked back from his arms. Touching her lips, she glanced up from hooded eyes and sent him a devilish grin. "Are you trying to get me in trouble with the principal, sir?"

"Certainly not. But Patrick put the idea in my head, and...well, it was a good idea, so..."

She blushed a darker pink and turned to unlock the door. "The copier is in the far corner over there." She pointed out the device to Peter, then turned the thumb lock on the door. "Pull the door closed when you leave. It should lock."

"You're leaving?"

"I think you can handle the copier alone. I've got a mess of things still to do. See you back in the gym in a few..."

"Mm-hm," he called to her as she started back down the hall. "You're just scared to be alone with me. Aren't you? You know I'll kiss you again, and you won't want to stop."

She turned, grinning as she put a finger to her lips to shush him.

Peter lingered in the office door, enjoying the sway of her hips as she sashayed down the corridor. Once she disappeared around the corner, Peter crossed the office and powered on the copier. While it warmed up, he glanced around and located a long, low file cabinet with drawers labeled A-F, G-N, O-Z. He tested the top drawer and found it locked. Naturally. Did he really think the school left personal records for the students that vulnerable?

With a quick glance toward the door, Peter pulled out his pocket knife and jimmied the top drawer lock. When it snicked open, he slid the drawer out, flipped through the files until he found Jeremy Colton's, and spread the folder on the desk. He paged through transcripts, noting that Jeremy was a good student and had been given both academic awards and citizenship recognition. He paused to study the most recent school photo, clipped on the inside cover of the file.

Did Jeremy bear any resemblance to the Walshes? Peter's heart clamored in his chest. He imagined that he saw his father in Jeremy's eyes, in his crooked smile, in his chin. With a huff of disgust, Peter turned the page. He was only seeing what he thought he should see. The kid looked like his mother, like a Colton.

At the back of the file, Peter found what he was looking for. A photocopy of Jeremy's birth certificate.

A thump in the hall, followed by the sound of young voices chattering and giggling, called Peter's attention to the corridor.

Hurry.

He scanned the document, noting the date of birth— seven months after his father had disappeared in 1995—and the space for the father's name.

Blank.

Peter suppressed a groan. No help there.

Unless…Maisie had been unwilling to publicly acknowledge the boy's father due to the scandal it could cause.

I mean, big-time scandal and hush-hush. Tess Cantrell's assessment rang in his head, and a chill slithered down Peter's back.

The copier beeped that it was ready, and Peter carried Jeremy's file over, laid out the copy of the birth certificate and Jeremy's photo and pressed Copy. When the machine spat out the pages he wanted, Peter folded them three times and shoved the papers deep in his back pocket for closer inspection later. Returning the evidence to the file, Peter stuck Jeremy's file back behind Collins, Sara, jimmied the lock closed and set to work copying the coloring sheets for the festival.

* * *

Lisa was filling the apple-bobbing tub with water when Peter strolled into the gymnasium. Just the sight of him, his loose-hipped amble, his broad shoulders and form-fitting jeans stirred a restless hunger in her belly. Her lips twitched, remembering the mind-blowing kiss he'd startled her with in the hall.

He flopped the stack of coloring sheets on the table beside her. "Your papers, milady."

She grinned. "Thank you, sir."

He spread his hands. "What should I do next?"

Kiss me again. She bit down on her bottom lip to keep from blurting the reply that sprang to mind. Unlike the deserted hallway, the gymnasium buzzed with activity as more students and parents arrived to set up booths from a cupcake walk to a beanbag toss. Kissing Peter Walsh now would start rumors flying faster than the kamikaze bumblebees that even now were swooping in her stomach. Too bad they'd nixed the idea of a kissing booth when Mrs. Holloway raised her concerns about passing germs.

"You can help me hang the decorations. I have balloons, streamers to go up, and a banner needs to be hung over the main stage."

Peter clapped his hands together. "Great. Let's do it."

She directed him to the stepladder the custodian had left out for their use and collected the decorations that needed to be put up, a stapler, a roll of heavy-duty tape and a hammer.

As Peter brought the ladder over to the corner of the stage where she waited, Patrick ran up to him, followed at a more leisurely pace by Jeremy Colton.

"Dad, Jeremy's mom brought a ton of cupcakes for the cupcake walk, but she said I can have one now if it's okay with you."

Knowing Peter's feelings toward the Coltons, especially his suspicions about Maisie having an affair with his father, Lisa watched Peter's reaction closely. Setting the ladder down, Peter turned to Patrick, then, as if he'd just noticed his son's companion, lifted a sharp gaze to the second boy. He tensed slightly, his expression reflecting surprise, but he quickly schooled his face and sent the boy an awkward grin. "Hello, Jeremy." Then to Patrick, "I didn't know you and Jeremy were friends."

Patrick shrugged. "We ride the same bus, so we talk sometimes. So can I have one of the cupcakes?"

Peter sent his gaze across the room to the table where Maisie Colton was unpacking several bakery boxes and lining up cupcakes on a plate. "I, uh… Isn't it kinda early for sweets?" He checked his watch and sent Patrick a skeptical look.

"Da-ad!" Patrick groaned. "Please? I'm starving."

He sighed. "One. Only one."

"Yeah!" Patrick brightened, exchanged a high five with Jeremy, and loped off to collect his treat.

His hands balled at his sides, Peter watched his son approach Maisie. "What is she doing here? Her kid is in junior high."

"Because our festival was delayed, we combined with the junior high this year." She nudged Peter's shoulder. "You know, I taught Jeremy. He really is a good kid. You don't have to worry about Patrick hanging out with him."

The boys reached the table, spoke to Maisie, and she lifted a startled glance to Peter that morphed into a hostile glare.

"It's not Jeremy that bothers me," he muttered, turning away from Maisie's stare and shifting the ladder closer to where she stood.

"Wow, y'all are regular Hatfields and McCoys. What

started this hatefest anyway? Has your family always had a feud with the Coltons?" She scooted the ladder to where she needed it and handed him the decorations to hold while she climbed up.

He steadied the ladder and tipped his head back to meet her gaze from her perch on the top rung. "Not always. Seems like way back when I was younger, our families might have even been friends. But something happened a long time ago that made my dad really hate the name Colton. I'm not even sure what it was. Probably something business-related. Then when Lucy started dating Damien, the you-know-what really hit the fan. It just escalated from there."

She frowned and held out her hand for the streamers. "What a shame. The two most prominent families in town fighting. Think of all the good you all could do if you spent the same energy doing things to heal the town and help the needy."

Peter's spine stiffened. "The Walshes do tons of good for this town. Besides, do you really expect us to ignore the fact that a Colton was convicted of killing my dad in 1995?"

"He's since been cleared."

"Yeah, yeah. That doesn't erase the ill-will. A Colton could easily be responsible for real this time." Peter's jaw tightened, and he sent a dark look across the room to Maisie.

"Look, I don't mean to preach. I just hate to see you poison the next generation if there is no proof the Coltons are responsible for your family's trouble." She hitched her head to where Jeremy and Patrick stood licking the icing off their cupcakes and laughing together. "They don't have any ill will."

Peter glanced at his son, and his expression softened. "I

have no intention of interfering with my son's friendships. If Jeremy is a good kid, then—"

"He is." She pointed to the stapler. "Will you hand me that?"

Peter picked up the stapler and climbed several rungs to hand it to her.

When the ladder rocked slightly, Lisa gasped and groped for something to hold on to. "Hey, you're supposed to be steadying the ladder!"

He passed the stapler to her and gave her a wolfish grin. "I'd rather steady you." He demonstrated by splaying a wide, warm hand at the base of her spine. "The ladder's stable. Just be sure *you* don't keel over."

I'm more likely to fall off if you keep touching me like that.

Heat from his hand sent a sweet sensation tingling up her back. When he moved up a couple of more rungs, his arms surrounded her as he held on to the ladder, and his body heat wrapped around her like a hug. His freshly-showered scent tickled her nose and made her heart thump a wild cadence.

Her hand trembled from the adrenaline of having him so close, the memory of his seductive kiss still zinging through her. When she tried to staple a banner into place, her reach proved too short, and without her asking, Peter took the banner from her hand and held it in place. On her toes and stretching her arm, she slapped a couple of staples in the sign, then clutched at Peter's arm when the ladder wobbled again.

"I got you," he murmured close to her ear.

With a nervous chuckle, she released his arm. "Yeah, but who's got you? If this ladder tips, we'll both go down."

She started to move down the ladder, but Peter stayed put, putting him at eye level with her once she'd climbed down a couple rungs. She turned in the tight space between his broad chest and the ladder and met the smoky look in his eyes.

"I, uh, need to get some balloons." Her voice cracked, giving away the nervous flutter pinging in her chest.

"I want to see you again." His voice was low and husky, his dark eyes penetrating, smoldering.

Her head spun, and she groped behind her for a rung to cling to. Tugging her lips in a lopsided grin, she said, "You're going to see lots of me today. I'm going to need plenty of help with the booths once the festival opens."

"I want to see you again *alone*." He tucked a wisp of hair that had escaped her ponytail behind her ear, and a thrill raced through her. "Next weekend. Let me take you out to the Walsh family ranch. We can ride the horses out on the property or take the sleigh out and have a picnic."

"A picnic? In November?" She tried to sound light-hearted. A difficult trick considering her breath had lodged in her lungs the instant his bedroom gaze latched onto hers, and his proximity had her heart thundering for all it was worth.

He nodded. "Beside a bonfire. I'll bring blankets and hot coffee." He shrugged and canted closer to her. "Or we can stay in and eat by the fireplace. Your choice."

Lisa cast a glance over his shoulder to the other parents and kids milling about the gymnasium. She could already hear the tongues wagging over the cozy scene between the fourth-grade teacher and one of the fathers. "I…I'd like to but—"

"No buts. It's a date." When she opened her mouth to counter, he pressed his fingers to her lips, and a crackle, like heat lightning, fired from every synapse. "A real date. I know you're worried about getting involved with someone, but I think if we talk about it, we can figure something out."

A bittersweet pain swelled in her chest. She wanted to believe there was hope for her to build a relationship with someone someday. And Peter was certainly the kind of man she could see herself falling for. But the power of her attraction to him also rang warning bells. The harder she fell for him, the more it would hurt if they couldn't find an agreeable compromise about how the relationship would work.

"We can go slow," he said, seeming to read her mind. "But I want—"

"Dad, Jeremy and I are gonna shoot some hoops out on the basketball court, okay?" Patrick called from the foot of the ladder.

Peter jerked away from her and started down the ladder. "What about helping Ms. Navarre set up the booths? That's what we came to do."

Lisa struggled for a breath as she followed Peter down the ladder.

"Aw, Dad…" Patrick frowned and gave his friend a shrug.

"You'll have lots of time for playing later." He handed Patrick a package of balloons. "Why don't you guys blow these up for us? I know you boys are full of hot air, so…"

Jeremy chuckled, and Patrick groaned at Peter's joke.

Feeling much steadier and in control once her feet were again on the ground and Peter's heavenly scent wasn't scrambling her thoughts, Lisa handed Patrick some ribbon. "Once you blow them up, tie them in bunches of three and put them up all around. Tie them to chairs, doors, anywhere you think the place needs sprucing up."

"Okay," the boys answered together before wandering off with their new assignment.

Using the distraction to gather her thoughts, Lisa fumbled with a poster she'd made for the bean-bag-toss booth and kept her gaze on her hands. "Peter, I'm flattered by the invitation. Can I think about it and give you an answer later today?"

When she peeked up at him, he was still watching her with those dark bedroom eyes. She wanted to drown in those eyes, wanted to sink into their depths and forget that Mother Nature had cursed her with fibroids that had prevented her from getting pregnant and had eventually led to her hysterectomy.

"Sure." With a quick smile that said he knew he was being put off, he picked up the ladder and moved it down the stage to tack up the next section of the banner.

Lisa swallowed the lump that rose in her throat. When she'd divorced Ray, she thought she'd endured the most painful effect of her infertility. She hadn't counted on meeting a man like Peter, who made her want to be part of a family all over again.

"Come on, sport, give it your best shot!" Peter called from the dunking booth as Patrick wound up to throw at the target.

Since opening to the community three hours ago, the Fall Festival had been packed with children and their parents. The cheerful fall decor of pumpkins, dried corn stalks and colorful leaf collections gave the school a festive mood, and the scents of fresh popcorn and cotton candy that filled the air brought back memories of summer carnivals Lisa had attended as a child. Without a doubt, the festival had been a smashing success for the PTA.

For Lisa, personally, the day had exceeded her expectations, thanks in large part to the man sitting in the dunking booth and his son, winding up for his pitch.

"You're going down, Dad!" Patrick hurled the tennis ball at the target, hit the bullseye, and Peter splashed down into the water to the cheers of the crowd gathered around the booth.

Lisa saw Peter shiver as he came up from the cold water, although he hadn't complained once. He'd been a good sport about sitting in the dunking booth for almost an hour. "Okay, I think poor Mr. Walsh has had enough. Who is our next volunteer? Principal Green?"

A cheer went up from the gathered kids, who scrambled to be first in line to dunk the principal.

Laughing at the kids' enthusiasm, Lisa walked around to the back of the dunking booth just as Peter was stepping down from the perch and peeling off his sopping T-shirt. Her steps faltered, and she nearly swallowed her tongue.

Peter Walsh's muscled chest and arms, flat stomach and arrow of dark hair that disappeared into his wet jeans were fodder for any woman's most sensual fantasy.

"Can you hand me that towel?" he asked, pointing to the stack of clean towels waiting for the dunkees to dry off.

She had to mentally shake herself from her gaping stupor in order to process his request and respond. "Uh, sure."

Patrick wheeled around the corner of the booth. "Ha! I got you good, huh, Dad?"

"That you did, buddy. Along with several dozen other folks." Peter shook his head like a dog, spraying Patrick and Lisa with droplets of water. Lisa raised the towel she was about to hand Peter as a shield.

"Hey!" Patrick laughed.

Peter tossed his son his keys. "Run out to the truck and bring me the dry clothes in my gym bag, will ya, sport?"

"Sure, Dad."

As Patrick trotted off, Lisa offered Peter the towel. "Thanks for doing that." She hitched her head to the booth where Mr. Green was now taunting the kids trying to dunk him. "I know it was a cold job."

Peter shrugged. "Not too bad. Glad to help. Patrick really seemed to get a kick out of it."

"He wasn't the only one. I think you're lucky Maisie Colton was stopped when she was." She rolled her eyes, thinking of the way Maisie Colton had elbowed people out of the way when Peter climbed in the booth, then spent twenty minutes and fifty dollars throwing balls, trying to soak Peter. Had other parents not intervened and insisted Maisie give someone else a chance, Lisa had no doubt Maisie would have soon started throwing the tennis balls right at Peter's head. Yet Peter had been a good sport, keeping a smile on his face, despite the daggers in Maisie's eyes as she'd dunked him over and again.

"More money for the school. Glad my family's feud with the Coltons proved lucrative for the Festival." He flashed her a wry smile.

When he shivered again, Lisa winced. "Let me buy you a hot chocolate at least. You need something to warm you up."

He stepped closer and arched a dark eyebrow. "I bet a kiss would do the trick."

Her breath caught, and she felt her cheeks heat.

"But I guess there are too many spectators here for that, huh?" His smile was devilish. "I'll take the hot chocolate for now."

With a jerky nod, she hurried off to join the concessions line, winding up behind two women deep in conversation.

"If Maisie Colton doesn't shut up about the *Dr. Sophie* show, I think I'm going to have to shut her up!" The first woman complained loudly to her friend. "I know they say the rich are eccentric, but sometimes I think Maisie takes eccentric to a new level!"

"I know it. Did you see the way she knocked Emily Waters out of the way to be first in line to dunk Peter Walsh? She's an embarrassment to the school."

Lisa looked at her feet, pretending not to listen. But the women didn't seem to care who heard them as they fussed at full volume.

"Did you hear what she said when Mr. Green finally pulled her out of line so the kids could play?"

"No. What?"

"She said, and I quote, 'You Walshes deserve that and more! I thought I was rid of Mark Walsh the first time, but at least he's gone for good this time. He got what he deserved!'"

A chill skittered down Lisa's back.

The other woman gasped. "She did?"

"No lie. The Walsh family is mourning Mark's murder, and she has the nerve to say he got what he deserved." Now the woman did pitch her voice lower. "Although, from what I hear, Mark Walsh was a reprobate who slept with anything in a skirt."

Lisa tensed. Was this the kind of catty gossip Peter had grown up hearing? She glanced across the gymnasium floor in time to see Peter take his gym bag from Patrick and speak to an older woman with red hair as he headed into the locker room to change. The woman gave Patrick a big hug then, when Patrick pointed at Lisa, the woman smiled and waved.

Lisa waved back, then turned to move up in the line and place her order. She carried a tray with four hot chocolates back to where Patrick and the older woman waited for Peter. "Cocoa for everyone!"

"Oh, thank you, honey," the woman said with a smile. "I'm Jolene Walsh. Patrick's grandmother."

And Peter's mother.

Still shaken by the exchange between the gossipy women, Lisa forced a grin and balanced the hot chocolate tray as she offered her hand to Jolene Walsh and introduced herself.

"Thanks, Ms. Navarre. Dad said to tell you he'd be right back." Patrick helped himself to a cup and handed one to his grandmother. "Can we do the cupcake walk again? I'm getting hungry."

"Do it *again?*" Mrs. Walsh asked Patrick. "How many times have you done the cupcake walk?"

He shrugged. "A couple."

Lisa laughed. "You mean a couple of dozen?"

By her count, she, Peter and Patrick had made the rounds of all the games and booths at least eight times, and for Patrick's favorites, like the cupcake walk, the number was much higher.

Jolene gave her grandson a crooked smile. "Tell you what. We'll do the cupcake walk, but if you win the cupcake, you save it for after dinner."

Patrick cocked his head as if considering the deal. "Okay!"

"Want to come?" the redhead asked Lisa.

"No, I'll wait here for Peter," she replied, indicating the hot drink in her hand was for him.

Patrick dragged his grandmother off to the cupcake booth, and Lisa sighed contentedly. The afternoon had passed quickly and been filled with laughter, good-spirited competition between the father and son, and a growing sense of family. Which was ridiculous, because Peter and Patrick weren't her family. Technically, she wasn't even dating Peter. But…

I want to see you again alone.

Heaven help her, she wanted to see Peter again—alone—too. She wanted to explore the familial warmth their time together today had nurtured, wanted to share more steamy kisses like the one Peter had stolen in front of the office, wanted to give Patrick the motherly love and attention a boy his age deserved.

But mostly her day with Peter and Patrick had woken her soul-deep desire for her own child, a yearning that could never be fulfilled. Spending more time with the Walsh family could only exacerbate the painful longing. So why was she actually considering Peter's invitation for another date? A real date. A date that would acknowledge that they shared an electric attraction and had fun together.

And today had been fun. More fun than she'd had in years.

"That for me?"

She startled when Peter's voice broke into her reverie. The hot cocoa sloshed onto her hand, and she gasped.

"Whoa, sorry. Didn't mean to spook you." He took the hot chocolate and flashed a smile that did more to warm her inside than the sweet drink. Peter had changed into dry jeans and a flannel button-down shirt that reminded her of Paul Bunyon, and had combed his wet hair back from his face. With his five o'clock shadow and dark hair peeking from the collar of his shirt, he looked woodsman-rugged and thoroughly sexy.

She was in trouble. She was falling fast and hard for this man and his son. Even as she told herself she should turn and run, she heard herself saying, "Yes, I'd love to see you again next weekend."

Peter blinked as he took a gulp of his cocoa and played mental catch-up to her out-of-context comment. But soon a satisfied grin tugged his cheek and his eyes warmed.

"Great. I'll get my mom to watch Patrick, and we'll have the whole day."

Lisa's stomach flip-flopped with anticipation and giddy delight. A whole day alone with Peter Walsh.

A whole day.

Alone.

With Peter.

What had she done?

Chapter 10

Before the Fall Festival officially wound down, Peter could tell Patrick had reached his limit of fun and frosting and would soon reach critical mass if he didn't go home and decompress. Peter's mother volunteered to take Patrick home so that Peter could stay and help tear down the booths and haul some of the larger materials back to Lisa's house in his truck.

"How did you get this *to* the school?" he asked as they carried a tall plywood backboard for the bean-bag toss out of the gymnasium. "I know this didn't fit in your car."

Lisa puffed a wisp of her dark hair out of her face. "Nope. Harvey brought it over for me in his truck."

"Harvey?" Peter couldn't help the prick of jealousy that poked him at the idea of another man going to Lisa's house, winning one of her bright smiles for his helpfulness.

"Principal Green," Lisa clarified.

Peter pictured the short, aging principal and felt somewhat better. Not that he had any right to feel possessive of Lisa's attention.

"Bye, Ms. Navarre!" a young voice shouted, and Peter glanced over his shoulder to find Jeremy and Maisie Colton headed out to their car. He tensed and turned away.

Lisa waved back with a bright smile. "Bye, Jeremy."

He'd managed to avoid Maisie for most of the day, until she'd fought her way to the front of the line at the dunking booth. He'd been tempted to leave his post as dunkee before he'd really started his shift, but he'd promised Lisa he'd help. When he'd seen what a bad shot Maisie was, and that his good-natured grin riled her more than jeers, he'd had fun watching the Colton princess make a fool of herself.

Lisa met Peter's gaze and lowered her voice. "I overheard some ladies talking about Maisie earlier."

Peter raised an eyebrow. "Something related to my dad's murder?"

"Perhaps."

Peter closed his tailgate and stepped closer to Lisa. "What did you hear?"

Lisa told him about a conversation between two ladies in the concession line. He'd already known Maisie's reputation for being a loose cannon, but statements the women claimed Maisie had made regarding his father rankled. Maisie's tirade, as repeated by the women, was hearsay and not admissible in court. But it confirmed Peter's suspicion that Maisie held more than a passing grudge against his father. Question was, was Maisie's hostility rooted in family loyalty and her brother's murder conviction, which now appeared to have been a mistake? Or did Maisie have more personal reasons to hate his father? Reasons enough to kill Mark Walsh?

He mulled those questions over as he followed Lisa

back to her house and unloaded the festival miscellany into Lisa's garage.

"Can I offer you something hot to drink as a thank-you?" she asked as they finished moving the last box from his truck.

Peter consulted his watch. Despite the early darkness of the fall evening, it was still early. "Sure."

More than something to drink, he wanted a few minutes with Lisa, without the eyes of the town watching or his son around as a chaperone. He helped Lisa with her coat and hung both his and her coats in the front hall while she started a kettle of water heating.

Peter paused by the rocking chair in the living room long enough to give Samson a ruffle on the head. The cat greeted him with a loud meow, stretched sleepily and half-heartedly bit at his wrist. "Goofy cat," he chuckled as he settled on the sofa, then decided Patrick wasn't off the mark. The fluffy Maine coon had personality to spare. He was no dog, but...

"Here you go." Lisa carried in two mugs of spiced tea and handed one to him as she sat beside him. "Thank you for your help with the festival. I think Patrick had a good time."

"Well, spending time with Patrick wasn't the only reason I went." Setting his mug aside, he scooted closer to Lisa and stroked her cheek with the back of his fingers. "I enjoyed spending the day with you, too."

She smiled sadly then lowered her gaze to her drink. "Peter, I..."

His chest tightened, knowing where her thoughts had drifted. He hated the idea of their relationship hitting a roadblock before it had even started. Turning his hand, he cupped her chin in his palm. "I know you're worried about getting involved with me because of the way your marriage ended. But can't we talk about it?"

She lifted a wistful gaze, her fingers tightening around her mug until her knuckles were bloodless. "Talking doesn't change the facts. I'll never be able to have children, Peter. I can't saddle you or any man with that."

He stroked her bottom lip with his thumb, and her breath hitched. "What if I told you your infertility isn't an issue for me?"

Lisa covered his hand with hers, squeezing his fingers. "I'd say you were either lying to ease my mind, or you hadn't really thought the issue through thoroughly. I've seen how you are with Patrick, heard you talk about your family and how much they mean to you. You can't tell me you don't want more children. I can see the truth in your eyes when you watch your son."

Peter started to deny her assertion but stopped. If he wanted a relationship with Lisa, it had to be based in total honesty. Starting now. He took her drink from her and put it aside, then wrapped his fingers around hers.

"Okay, the truth is I'd like to have more kids one day. Yes. I've always pictured myself with a large family."

With a defeated-sounding sigh, she started to withdraw, and he slid his hand to the base of her skull to keep her from backing out of his reach.

"But more than that, the idea of having more children scares the hell out of me."

Her gaze snapped up to his, dark with concern and confusion. "Scares you?"

"The woman I loved died giving me my son. I know, in here—" he pointed to his head "—that it was a fluke thing. I know the chances that something like that would happen again if I had a baby with another woman are low. But in here—" he splayed a hand over his heart "—I'm terrified of losing someone else I care about. It's been ten years since Katie died, and I still miss her every day. I see her in Patrick, the sacrifice she made to give me my son. That's what you see in my eyes when I look at my boy. Love for him, but also longing for what could have been…if Katie had lived."

Tears glistened in Lisa's eyes. "The children that could have been."

He drew a deep breath. "Partly. But also sadness for all the events Katie is missing. His first steps, first Little League game…school carnivals. Katie would have been a great mom."

With a hiccupping sob, Lisa's face crumpled. "Oh, God." She covered her face with her hands, her shoulders shaking.

Peter's gut pitched. He'd known this conversation would be emotional and difficult, but her breakdown wrenched his gut. "Lisa, honey, what is it?"

She peered up at him with a heartbreaking melancholy etched on her face. "I want all that. I want the first steps, the ball games, the PTA. I want a baby so much it hurts. But I can't. Ever. I had fibroid tumors that necessitated a hysterectomy, so I'll never have my own children—"

"Aw, honey." Peter closed the distance between them and reeled her into his arms, pressing her head to his shoulder. "I'm so sorry. I won't pretend I know how much that must hurt."

"I thought I'd come to terms with it, thought I was doing all right, b-but…" She sniffled and swiped at her damp cheek. "Every day when I go to school and see those young faces in my class, I'm reminded of what I can't have. And I hurt all over again."

She tipped her head back and looked up at him, her expression beseeching him to understand. "That's why

I'm getting my PhD in higher education. I love teaching elementary school, but at the same time it's too painful to continue."

The grief in her voice stabbed him. Peter's chest ached as if sharp talons had raked his flesh and sliced open his heart. He could do nothing to ease her pain, and his sense of helplessness chafed his male ego. Tucking her under his chin again, he squeezed her tighter. "I don't begin to understand why these things happen. It's not fair."

Lisa backed from his embrace and narrowed her wet gaze on his. "I'm not looking for answers why. I know life is unpredictable. You have to take the bad with the good. I've learned to appreciate my blessings—my family in Texas, my health, my home." She stroked his cheek. "Friends who care about me. I just want you to understand why getting involved with you would be a mistake for me."

He dried the moisture on her eyelashes. "Why would it be a mistake?"

She sniffed again and lowered her gaze to her hands. "Being in a relationship would be a lot like teaching elementary school for me. As wonderful as parts of the relationship might be, I'd have a daily reminder of what wasn't possible. Loving a man would make me ache for the children we wouldn't have. There'd always be a gulf between us, something missing. You can't build a future when you start with such a giant hole in the relationship."

Peter held her gaze, his heart pounding wildly. "Then… we have a problem. Because my feelings for you have already grown past simple friendship."

A bittersweet surprise, then regret flittered over her face. "Peter…"

He framed her face with his hands. "I know you feel the same connection between us that I do. The same heat. The same pull." He clenched his teeth and drilled his gaze into hers. "Damn it, Lisa, don't tell me we can't try to make this work. Because I don't think I can stay away."

She sucked in a sharp breath that hissed between her teeth. "But how—"

"I don't know how we'll make it work. I just know we have to try." He nudged her chin up. "I don't want to hurt you, honey. I swear I will do everything in my power to make this work somehow."

Tears sparkled in her eyes. "I'm scared."

He nodded. "I am, too. Putting my heart out there after so many years terrifies me. But I'm in too deep now to do anything else."

She blinked, and fresh tears escaped onto her cheek. Lifting her hand, she raked fingers through his hair before settling her hand on his neck. "Me, too."

Lisa leaned forward and brushed her mouth across his. The brief contact shocked his system like a jolt from a taser. His nerve endings crackled and danced, and his muscles tensed.

Hovering scant inches from him, she angled her gaze to his. "I feel like I'm diving into a murky lake on a hot day," she whispered. Her breaths came quick and light, mingling with his. "I know the water will be cool and refreshing, but I don't know what hidden dangers wait below the surface."

He skimmed her lips with his and murmured, "Go ahead and jump, Lisa. I'll catch you. I'll keep you safe."

"Peter." His name was a sigh as she found his mouth again and kissed him deeply. Desperately. Tenderly.

With one hand cradling her head and his other arm wrapped around her waist, Peter held Lisa close and indulged in the lips he'd been thinking about all day. Heat flashed through him, chasing the chill of past losses from his bones. Lisa's flesh-and-blood kiss was ten times more potent than his daydreams about the stolen kiss by the school office.

Her lips tasted sweet, like spiced tea and warm seduction. She met the pressure of his mouth with her own fervor. When he traced the seam of her lips with his tongue, she opened to him, her contented sigh stoking the fire inside him with promises of future passion.

His body screamed for him to lay her back on the couch and stake his claim to her. But he'd promised not to let her get hurt, and he knew that meant they had to move slowly. His muscles trembled with restraint as he pulled away and finger-combed her hair behind her ear. "I don't want to wait a whole week to see you again."

Smiling, she tipped her head back to meet his gaze. "What do you propose to do about that?"

He grinned, hearing the breathless quality to her voice. Their kiss had left him feeling winded as well. Stunned. Reeling. "Well…my mom and sisters are meeting Patrick and me for dinner tomorrow at Kelley's Cookhouse. Why don't you join us?"

Her eyes widened. "Wow. Meeting the family. Isn't that usually at least a third- or fourth-date kind of thing?"

Her tone was teasing, but he heard an anxious tension behind it as well.

Nudging up her chin with his thumb, he met her dark-eyed gaze. "I don't want to pressure you. I promised we'll take this as slow as you need to."

Lisa caught her bottom lip with her teeth. "I do love barbecue."

He cocked an eyebrow. "Is that a yes?"

She tipped her head and flashed him a lopsided smile. "It is."

"Good." Splaying his fingers, he slid his hand to the

nape of her neck and nudged her forward. "May I kiss you again?"

"Yes, please." She leaned into him, angling her head to seal her mouth with his.

When a tremble shook her, he tightened his hold on her and nuzzled her ear. "We'll figure this out, Lisa. Somehow."

Her fingers dug into his back, and she sighed sadly. "That's the same thing my ex-husband promised…a year before he walked out on our marriage."

Kelley's Cookhouse, owned and operated by the Kelley family for years, was a Honey Creek institution. Everyone who was anyone gathered at the barbecue restaurant at some point during the week to drink a Walsh-brand beer and savor the best smoky ribs and coleslaw west of the Mississippi River. Tonight was no exception. The restaurant, with its dark wood-panel walls and hardwood floors, was packed with Honey Creek residents, family and friends.

Lisa squeezed Peter's hand tighter, so as not to lose him in the crowd, as he led her to a table near the bar where his sisters, Mary and Lucy, were already seated. Mary bore a striking resemblance to Peter's mother, whom Lisa had met yesterday at the festival, but Lucy, with her girl-next-door sweetness and brown eyes, looked more like Peter. Next to Mary, with a possessive arm around her, sat a ruggedly handsome blond-haired man Lisa assumed, based on the coaching Peter had given her on the drive over, was Jake Pierson. The chair beside Lucy was conspicuously empty, a situation Patrick quickly remedied, sliding into the ladder-backed chair and giving his aunt a bear hug.

"Evening, folks," Peter said, as he held out a chair for Lisa. "Everyone, this is Lisa Navarre, Patrick's teacher.

Lisa, this is the motley crew I warned you about in the truck." He gave Lucy a curious glance. "Where's Steve?"

Lisa mentally recalled the list of names Peter had supplied on the drive. Lucy was happily involved with a man named Steve Brown.

"He's caught a nasty cold and didn't feel like coming out tonight." She turned to Patrick and wrapped an arm around the boy's shoulders. "But I didn't want to miss seeing my favorite nephew!"

"I'm your *only* nephew," Patrick groaned.

"But you're still my favorite!"

Lisa turned to Mary, who sat across the table from her. "Peter tells me you and Jake have opened a private security business. How is that going?"

Mary's smile brightened. "So far so good."

As the conversation continued with polite small talk and inquiries about each other's jobs and Lisa's family in Texas, she noticed Peter's gaze roaming the faces in the crowd, his expression speculative, guarded.

"Something wrong?" she whispered to him during a brief lull in the conversation when the waitress arrived to deliver drink orders.

"No, I'm just—" He stopped abruptly, and his expression changed. Shadows of suspicion clouded his face, and his stare grew icy. "I stand corrected. Look who just arrived."

Frowning her concern and curiosity, Lisa pivoted in her chair to glance toward the front door. Darius Colton strode into the main dining room, leading his wife Sharon by the arm. Behind them, Damien, Maisie, Jeremy, Brand and Joan Colton followed, each sweeping the restaurant with gazes ranging from excited, in Jeremy's case, to hostile, in Damien's.

Lisa tensed. "Is this a problem? Can't your family eat

in the same restaurant without it leading to World War Three?"

Peter cut a side glance to his family, presumably checking to see if they'd noticed the new arrivals. "Depends. I don't intend to start anything, but I won't let a slight pass unchecked either."

Lisa sighed. "Peter..."

Darius, the patriarch of the clan, gave the room an imperious glance and, spying the Walshes, glared darkly and spoke to the hostess. He aimed a thumb to the opposite side of the dining room, and the hostess glanced toward the Walsh table and nodded.

The message was clear enough. Darius wanted a table far from the Walshes. Darius took his mousy wife by the arm and led her from the door.

Across the table from Lisa, Lucy's head came up, her gaze darting to the door. She gasped softly, staring at the Colton family. Lisa held her breath, remembering that the youthful infatuation between Damien and Lucy had been a key factor in the families' feud.

"Lucy?" Peter said, leaning toward his sister. "Do you want to leave?"

His sister sent him a sharp look. "Don't be silly. I can't spend the rest of my life ducking and running for cover every time my path crosses his. This is a small town, and we need to figure out how to share it."

"I know, but—" Peter started, but Lucy caught them all off-guard by rising slightly from her chair, smiling and signaling Damien to come to their table.

Peter frowned. "What are you doing?"

Lucy squared her shoulders. "Making peace with my past so I can move forward."

At the front door, Damien nodded, grim-faced, but headed their way. When Maisie grabbed his shirt to stop him, he disengaged his sister's fingers and gave her a push in the opposite direction.

"Damien!" Maisie called after her brother in a panicked voice loud enough to carry through the restaurant.

The din of voices quieted to a murmur as heads swivelled to follow the unfolding drama.

Lisa reached for Peter, who looked ready to jump Damien with the slightest provocation, and wrapped her hand around his wrist. When he met her eyes, she sent him a quelling look.

Damien's boots scuffed the hardwood floor as he stepped up to their table and cast a dark look to the Walshes.

Chapter 11

Despite Lucy's warning look, Peter rose to his feet and raised his chin, as if putting Damien on notice. Lisa held her breath, much as she sensed everyone else gathered in the restaurant did.

But when Damien's gaze landed on Lucy, a flicker of warmth lit his eyes, though his mouth stayed pressed in a firm line. "Lucy."

Lucy flashed a nervous smile. "Hello, Damien. It's nice to see you."

Damien's brow furrowed, and he grunted. "Right."

Lucy squared her shoulders, her smile dimming. "It is. I...I never wanted you to suffer because of—"

"Whatever." His tone was cool, flat. "You wanted something?"

Mary, Jake and Peter exchanged worried looks. Lisa could have cut the tension with a knife. Even Patrick seemed to notice the hostile undercurrent. Sidling closer to Lucy, Patrick eyed the tall, dark-haired stranger looming over their table.

"Just…to say hello." She cleared her throat, and her fingers trembled as she fidgeted with her silverware. "And I'm sorry about…everything that happened. I—"

"Sorry? You never wrote, never came to see me. Not once," Damien interrupted. Lisa swore she heard pain laced heavily throughout his hard tone, and her heart broke for the star-crossed high-school sweethearts Damien and Lucy had been.

Lucy dropped her gaze for the first time and drew a deep breath. "I'm sorry for that, too. I was as hurt and confused about everything as you were, and—"

Damien scoffed. "You think so? I was in prison, Lu. Accused of a murder I didn't commit. Abandoned by you, by members of my family. You really think you were hurting as much as I was?"

Lisa wondered if anyone else noticed Damien's use of a nickname for Lucy. That he still thought of her in terms of the intimate pet name spoke volumes to Lisa.

Peter took a step toward Damien. "Look, Colton, if you think—"

"Peter." Lucy's firm tone stopped her brother. Shoving her chair back, she circled the end of the table to where Damien stood. When she lightly touched Damien's arm, he jerked, as if jolted by lightning.

Lisa's fingers clutched the arm of her chair. She recognized the raw emotion that filled Damien's face. Bitterness clashed with longing, betrayed love, remorse and regret battled anger and disappointment. When Ray had walked out on their marriage, she'd felt many of the same conflicting feelings that marched across Damien's face. His jaw tightened, evidence that he was working hard to maintain a stony facade and shove down the rioting feelings.

"I know we can't change the past," Lucy said softly. "But I don't want to be enemies going forward. I won't ask you to pretend we're friends again, but can we at least be civil when we meet in town?"

Damien shifted his feet slightly, and the hard line of his jaw relaxed a degree. "That shouldn't be a problem, seeing as how I'm leaving town."

Lucy frowned. "Leaving?"

"This town holds too many ghosts. I'm planning on heading down to Nevada. Maybe starting my own ranch." He paused and sighed wearily. "I need a fresh start. That's not possible here in Honey Creek."

"Oh…" Lucy fumbled. "Well, good luck. I…" She hesitated as if torn what to do next, what to say. Then, taking a deep breath, she grabbed Damien's hand, rose on her toes and kissed his cheek.

A murmur rolled through the restaurant, and Lisa sensed more than saw Peter stiffen.

"Take care of yourself, Damien," Lucy said quietly before sinking back on her heels again. When she would have withdrawn her hand, Damien squeezed Lucy's fingers, drawing her gaze back to his. For several seconds he said nothing, his green eyes boring down on Lucy with an intensity that sent a shiver through Lisa.

"Goodbye, Lu," he said at last, while still clinging to her hand. His throat worked as he swallowed, before he added a rasped, "and thanks" as he turned quickly and strode away.

Lucy watched him leave, her expression poignant and filled with wistful regret.

Lisa's heart thudded, touched by the bittersweet goodbye between the former lovers.

The gazes of the other diners followed Damien's retreat, dividing speculative stares between Lucy and the brooding ex-con Colton. Lisa wanted to shout at the room to mind their own business. She couldn't imagine being a member of one of the town's prominent families and having so much attention drawn to her every move. Yet if she started dating Peter, wouldn't that put her in the gossip limelight? She wasn't sure how she felt about that.

Peter stepped closer to his sister and touched her arm. "You okay?"

Lucy rallied, flashing Peter a bright smile. "I'm fine. Hey, I've got Steve now. And my store, my family. I'm great!" She clapped her hands together as she spun back to the table. "So what are we ordering? I'm starved!"

Peter continued to watch his sister with his brow knitted, so Lisa leaned over to him and put a supportive hand on his arm. "She's not the vulnerable teenager she was back then, Peter. She's okay. And I think they both needed that closure."

He shifted his worried look to Lisa. "Maybe, but he—"

"No maybes. Look at her." Lisa nodded her head toward Lucy, who was laughing with Mary over something Patrick said. "She's doing all right. She's putting the past behind her. So is Mary. Please, Peter, they have a right to move on and be happy with where their lives are taking them now."

Peter drew a slow sigh and nodded. "You're right. But seeing him here after all these years just…shook something loose deep inside. I didn't do enough to protect her fifteen years ago, and I don't intend to make the same mistake again."

Peter's obvious love and protectiveness for his sister touched a tender spot in Lisa's heart. If she gave in to the call of her heart, if she let herself fall for Peter, would he be that supportive of her? She'd been on her own, away from her family in Texas so long, the idea of someone looking out for her, having her back through the tough times in life held tremendous appeal. Carrying the load alone grew wearisome at times. She missed having someone close to lean on in difficult times. And the months since her divorce had been *very* difficult.

Knowing how much Peter cared about his family and looked out for their best interests spoke volumes regarding his character and priorities. Had she really accused him of having his priorities mixed up the day she called him to the school about Patrick's misbehavior?

She saw now that Peter was, in fact, a single father, juggling his son's needs with his career and a cascade of recent family tragedies. That was a lot for anyone, and if Peter was overwhelmed by it all, that only made him human, not irresponsible.

Lucy caught Lisa's eye, pulling her out of her thoughts briefly. "Save room for dessert. The chocolate cake here is the best! Right, Patrick?"

"Oh, yeah!" Patrick gushed.

She smiled at them. "Oh, I'm well acquainted with the chocolate cake here. In fact, maybe I'll skip dinner and go straight to dessert."

Peter arched an eyebrow. "Can't recommend that. You don't want to miss the barbecued ribs."

Jolene Walsh arrived at last, took a seat next to Peter, and pulled off a pair of leather driving gloves. "Sorry I'm late. The doctor came in right as I was leaving Craig at the hospital. He said Craig's making good progress and can likely go home on Monday." Her smile lit her face, pure relief radiating from her every pore. "Craig sends his love to everyone, by the way." She sent a glowing look around the table to her children and grandson. "So what did I miss?"

"Oh, nothing much," Lucy chirped. "We were just discussing what to order." Without any further mention of Damien or the Coltons, Lucy waved to their waitress.

Once their order had been taken, conversation turned to yesterday's Fall Festival at the school, and the upcoming Thanksgiving holiday.

"I want everyone to plan on coming to the ranch for our family dinner next Thursday," Jolene announced, then turned to Lisa. "You're welcome to come with Peter, dear. We'd love to have you join us."

Lisa blinked, startled—and flattered—by the invitation. "Oh, well, thank you. I—"

Peter and Patrick both sent her expectant, eager looks.

"Can you, Ms. Navarre? Please?" Patrick asked.

Her gaze shifted to Peter, who lifted a dark eyebrow in query. "No pressure. If it's too much too fast…"

"I'd love to join you," Lisa said, facing Jolene. "What can I bring?"

"I have a new recipe for a low-sugar, low-fat pie I want to bring," Mary interjected.

As the conversation continued, planning the menu for Thanksgiving dinner, Lucy pushed her chair back and rose. "If you'll excuse me for a minute, I'm going to make a quick trip to the ladies' room."

Mary pushed her chair back, too. "Want some company?"

"Sure. Lisa?" Lucy hitched her head, inviting Lisa to follow her.

Mary gave Jake a teasing stern look. "No comments from the peanut gallery about women traveling in packs to the restroom."

Jake turned up a palm. "What? Did I say anything?"

Mary gave her fiancé a quick kiss and a smile as she stepped away from the table, then hooked her arm in Lisa's as they fell in step behind Lucy. "I have to tell you, I haven't seen my brother smiling as much in years as he has been these last couple weeks. I'd bet money you are the reason."

Lisa felt heat sting her cheeks. "I, uh—"

Lucy came to an abrupt stop in front of them, and Mary and Lisa ran into her.

"You!" Maisie Colton blocked their entry to the women's restroom, hands on her hips, glaring at Lucy with a venomous snarl. "You have a lot of nerve hitting on my brother like that after what you and your family did to him!"

Lucy fell back a step, clearly startled by the attack. Mary moved up next to Lucy, and Lisa flanked Peter's sister from the other side, her heart thumping anxiously. Maisie's infamous volatility worried Lisa. She didn't want the families to engage in a public brawl.

Lucy raised her chin, and calmly replied, "I didn't hit on Damien, Maisie. Not that it is any of your business."

Maisie puffed out her chest and narrowed her eyes. "My brother will always be my business. And I'm warning you to stay away from him! Haven't you hurt him enough?"

"Come on, Luce." Mary nudged her sister's arm. "Ignore her."

But Lucy squared her shoulders and faced Maisie's challenging glare. "I have no intention of hurting your brother. For your information, I'm happily engaged and moving on with my life."

Maisie gave a disgruntled sniff. "Yeah, I heard you were engaged. Poor guy doesn't know what he's getting himself into." Her gaze suddenly shifted to Lisa's. "Be warned, Ms. Navarre. The Walshes are cold-hearted and self-serving. If you were smart, you'd run the other way. Peter may seem like a catch, but he will break your heart. It's just what the Walshes do."

Lisa was so stunned by Maisie's unwanted advice, she didn't notice Damien's approach until he loomed over the women with a dark expression. He wrapped a firm hand around his sister's arm and tugged her away from her confrontational stance in front of Lucy. "Go back to the table, Maisie. You're out of line."

Maisie sent her brother a hurt look. "I'm just defending you. You can't let the Walshes push you around!"

"No one is pushing me around. Don't hassle Lucy ever again. Understand?" Damien's tone brooked no resistance.

Maisie stared at her brother as if he'd lost his mind. "Do you not remember what they did to us? The Walshes—"

"Maisie." The deep resonant voice of Darius Colton interrupted Maisie's tirade.

Lisa lifted her gaze to the senior Colton who now stood behind Damien. A muscle in Darius's jaw jumped, and he narrowed a warning stare on his daughter. "Don't make a scene and embarrass the family."

Maisie frowned. "But, Daddy—"

"You heard me." His tone was final.

With an indignant huff, Maisie lifted her nose and stormed back to the Colton's table. Darius said nothing else before turning and walking away, but Damien divided an uneasy look between Mary, Lucy and Lisa. "I'm sorry about that, ladies."

"Forget it. Come on, Lucy." Mary gave Damien a tight, stiffly cordial nod, then wrapped her arm in her sister's and steered Lucy toward the restroom.

Lisa knew she should follow the Walsh sisters, but the look on Damien's face gave her pause. The man, for all his gruff posturing, was clearly hurting. He'd had a less-than-warm welcome home from his family, if the rumor mill was correct, and after witnessing the scene between him and Lucy earlier, Lisa felt compelled to say something to him. But what?

Damien Colton's problems and heartaches weren't any of her business. But being no stranger to pain and rejection herself, Lisa felt an empathetic tug for him.

"I—" she started then stalled when his jade gaze met hers.

"You're Lisa Navarre, aren't you?"

She gaped at Damien, stunned that he knew her name. "Uh, yes."

"You teach at the elementary school, right?"

Lisa laughed nervously. "How did you—?"

Damien's cheek twitched in a quick grin. "My nephew said something earlier when he saw you at the Walshes' table. You were, apparently, his favorite teacher."

Lisa's cheeks heated, and she smiled. "I think pretty highly of Jeremy, too. He's a bright boy and well-mannered."

Damien's expression warmed with obvious affection for his nephew. "Thank you."

Lisa shifted her feet awkwardly, fully aware of Peter's hawk-eyed gaze watching her exchange with the ex-con.

Sticking his hands in his back pockets, Damien angled his head and gave Lisa a speculative look. "I know what Peter's probably telling you about my family."

Lisa's heart thudded. She didn't want to be drawn into this conversation…

"I know there is no love lost between your families."

"Yeah. You could say that. But…" He paused, glancing away, as if looking for the right words. As he brought his gaze back to her, Damien did a double take. His attention snagged on someone at the front door, and though he tried to cover his distraction, Lisa didn't miss the obvious signs of male interest in the lift of his brow and widening of his pupils. She turned to see who had caught Damien's eye.

Eve Kelley, looking especially radiant with her hair upswept and wearing a high-waisted blue dress that complemented her coloring, stood by the hostess desk waiting to be seated.

Lisa hid the grin that tugged her lips. "That's Eve Kelley. She owns Salon Allegra. Would you like me to introduce you?"

"Huh. Oh, no, I—" Damien rolled his muscled shoulders and furrowed his brow, as if embarrassed to have been caught ogling the blond beauty. "I remember her. She was in Perry's class. Cheerleader. Beauty queen. Miss Popular." He shook his head. "Not my type." He clenched his back teeth, his jaw tensing. "Anyway, just remember there are two sides to every story. Anything Peter tells you about my family is only half the picture."

That Damien would defend his family to her, be concerned about her perception of the Coltons—especially in light of what she'd heard through the grapevine about the family's strained relationship with Damien when he went to prison—only bolstered her instincts about the brooding man. Despite the gruff persona he projected, she sensed the wounded soul behind the dark scowl and shadowed eyes. And her heart went out to him.

She held his gaze and nodded. "I'll keep that in mind. Good night, Damien. It was nice to meet you."

He jerked a nod, then headed back to his table just as Lucy and Mary emerged from the restroom.

Mary gave her a concerned look. "More trouble?"

"No, we were…talking about his nephew. I taught Jeremy and…" Lisa shrugged and let her sentence trail off.

"We'll wait for you if you still need the facilities."

Lucy hitched her thumb over her shoulder toward the bathroom door.

"Naw. I'm good, and—" she glanced back at their table "—it looks like our dinner has arrived."

Peter stood as she approached and pulled out her chair. "Should I be jealous of your heart-to-heart with Damien?"

She smiled brightly and kissed his cheek. "Not at all."

Though she could tell he wanted more explanation of what she'd discussed with the ex-con, she said nothing else.

The rest of their dinner passed uneventfully. Despite the drama that had started the evening, the Walshes shared a sumptuous meal, laughed over stories they told on each other, and made plans for a family Thanksgiving. Being included in the family's camaraderie filled an empty place in Lisa's heart that had been languishing in the years since her divorce. But her inclusion in the Walsh family plans was bittersweet. As much as she craved the connections of a large family, the evening only demonstrated to her how much Peter loved his family, needed his family, deserved to have the family she couldn't give him.

Last night, she'd promised Peter she'd give their relationship a chance. Yet the closer she got to Peter and his family, the clearer it became to her that she was headed to another heartache. She simply couldn't give Peter the kind of relationship he deserved.

Chapter 12

Monday morning, Peter finished up a case report earlier than he'd expected and found himself downtown with time on his hands before he was due to meet with a new client. He sat in his truck, drumming his fingers on his steering wheel and considering the best use of his time.

He wished he could surprise Patrick by stopping by the school for lunch but the class didn't break for lunch for another hour.

Peter smiled, remembering the family dinner at Kelley's Cookhouse the night before. Lisa had fitted right in with his sisters and mother. And they seemed to like her, going so far as to make plans for shopping on Black Friday together. He'd gotten a chance to get to know Jake Pierson better and knew the former FBI agent was a good match for his sister. Jake would keep Mary safe.

The evening had been nearly perfect. Nearly. Peter gritted his teeth, remembering Damien Colton's glowering indignation and Maisie's repeat performance, confronting Mary, Lucy and Lisa. The Coltons were like a bad rash, a constant source of irritation. Some days, Peter just wanted to meet the Colton clan in the center of town and have an old-fashioned duel. The town just didn't seem big enough for both families. Something had to give.

Peter cranked his engine, which sputtered to life, protesting the Montana cold. Without conscious decision, he headed for the sheriff's office. Two weeks had passed since he'd last confronted Wes Colton, and he hadn't seen any hint of progress in the investigation in that time. Nothing in the *Honey Creek Gazette*. No calls from the sheriff's office. Zilch.

Acid churned in Peter's gut as he parked in front of the redbrick building that housed the sheriff's office. He recognized Wes Colton's vehicle in the lot, telling him the sheriff should be in his office.

He strode inside and approached the receptionist's desk. "I want to see the sheriff."

The female officer looked up, clearly recognized him and hesitated before paging her boss's office. "Sheriff Colton, Peter Walsh is here to see you."

Wes didn't reply for several seconds. Finally a mumbled curse word filtered through the intercom, followed by a grudging, "Send him back."

The sheriff was on his feet behind his desk when Peter entered his office.

"Morning, Peter. What can I do for you?" he said with strained civility.

Peter braced his feet and squared his shoulders. "I still haven't heard anything from you about the investigations into my father's murder or Craig Warner's poisoning. I can only assume that means nothing's being done, no progress is being made."

Wes gave him a patronizing grin. "You'd be wrong. I'm not required to report my findings to you or anyone until my case is wrapped up. So don't assume my silence indicates anything other than the facts of the case are a police matter and not for public consumption."

"I'm family of the victim." Peter jabbed Wes's desk with a finger.

"Which makes you a possible suspect."

Peter gaped at the sheriff. "You've got to be kidding. My alibi was confirmed months ago."

Wes shrugged. "I'm still not discussing the case with you."

"I have a right to know what's happening!"

"I disagree."

Peter clenched his back teeth and swallowed the retort on his lips. Clearly getting into the same argument with Wes wouldn't get him anywhere. He thought a moment and decided on a surprise attack.

"Who fathered Maisie's son?"

Wes blinked. Frowned. "Excuse me?"

"Who is Jeremy's father? There is no name listed on his birth certificate."

Wes tensed and drew himself taller. "How did you get a copy of Jeremy's birth certificate?"

"I'm a private investigator. I have resources, tricks to get around red tape."

"If you've done something illegal—"

"You'll never prove it." Peter braced his hands on the sheriff's desk and leaned toward him. "Answer my question. Who is Jeremy's father?"

Wes hesitated. "Maisie would never say."

"Why did she leave town so abruptly back in 1995, right after my dad disappeared?"

Wes scowled and folded his arms over his chest. "I think you know the answer to that."

"The obvious answer is because she was hiding her pregnancy to avoid scandal. But when she returned with a son in tow, she kinda blew that cover, didn't she?"

The sheriff sighed wearily. "What's your point Walsh?"

"I think your sister had an affair with my father that went sour." Peter smiled his satisfaction when the color drained from Wes's face. "I think Jeremy is Mark Walsh's son, and that your sister killed him to keep her secret a secret. Or out of revenge for his dumping her."

Wes twisted his mouth in a dismissive frown. "That's insane. My sister is brash and confrontational, but she's not a killer."

"You sure about that? She's been rather vocal around town, saying how glad she is that my dad is gone and that he got what he deserved."

The sheriff lifted a hand in concession. "Not particularly discreet of her, I admit. But I know my sister. She's not a killer."

"Does she have an alibi for the time of my father's death?"

Wes dragged a hand down his cheek. "I'm doing my job, Walsh. I don't need you to back-seat drive."

Peter aimed a finger at Wes. "You do if you are driving with blinders on concerning your family. They should be at the top of your suspect list."

Wes drew in a deep breath and blew it out, his jaw tense. "So you've said. Your five minutes with me are up. Goodbye, Peter."

The sheriff sat down behind his desk, flipped open a file and bent over it, signaling an end to the discussion.

Peter didn't budge. "At least tell me what direction you're

going with the case. Who are you investigating? What are your leads? God, give me something!"

Wes leaned back in his chair, tapping his pen on his desk in visible irritation. "Walsh, this case is bigger than just a murder investigation or a case of intentional poisoning. There are people working this case from more angles than you could imagine. But because of the sensitive nature of the ongoing investigation, and because I don't want to jeopardize the case, I can't tell you anything more. I told you once and I'll tell you again. Butt out." Wes leaned forward, stabbing the air with his pen to punctuate his demand. "If you interfere with the investigation or compromise the case in any way, I'll write you up for obstructing justice."

"If so many people are on this case, why is it taking so long to close it? Three members of my family have been attacked in five months. I refuse to sit by while your officers chase their tails and let my family get hurt again. I want answers, Wes. I deserve answers. And my family deserves justice. If you can't get it for us, then by God, I will."

Wes narrowed his eyes and lowered his voice. "Don't do anything rash, Peter. You'll have your justice soon enough. We just need a little more time."

Jamming his hands in his coat pockets, Peter met Wes's stare. "You've had five months. Time is up." With that, he turned and stalked from the sheriff's office.

In the parking lot, he slammed his truck door and sat for a moment brooding.

…this case is bigger than just a murder investigation or a case of intentional poisoning. There are people working this case from more angles than you could imagine.

What did Wes mean by that? How big was the investigation? He gritted his teeth as he backed out of his parking space. He hated being kept in the dark. Wes knew something, and it irritated the hell out of Peter that Wes wouldn't tell him. For that matter, Mary and Jake had been awfully cagey when he questioned them a couple weeks ago. They knew something they weren't sharing as well. And his mom—what did she know about his dad that she was keeping secret?

He slammed his hand on the steering wheel in frustration. He loved his family, but they had more secrets than the CIA. They might think they were protecting him by keeping him in the dark, but information was power. How was he supposed to protect his family if he didn't know what he was up against?

That Tuesday, Peter and Jolene met Patrick at his school for the class Thanksgiving feast. As he sat at the long lunchroom table eating his cafeteria-prepared turkey and stuffing, Peter watched Lisa greet the other parents and mill about the crowd, wishing students a happy holiday.

When she finally made it to their table, she slid into a seat and blew out a tired breath. "Whew! I'm ready for our holiday break. How about you, Patrick?"

He nodded. "I ain't gonna do nothing all day tomorrow but watch TV and play video games."

She arched an eyebrow and laugh-sighed. "Good to know my grammar lessons have made a difference for you, Patrick."

Peter ruffled his son's hair. "Sounds to me like you need to crack a school book instead of cranking up the games, sport."

His son's eyes rounded. "What? Not on vacation, Dad."

Jolene nudged her son with her shoulder. "So what are your plans tomorrow? Will you need Grandma to ride herd on the little anti-grammarian?"

Peter caught Lisa's gaze. "Are we still on for the sleigh ride and picnic at the ranch?"

"You really want to picnic in this weather?" She aimed her thumb toward the cafeteria window. Outside, a light snow fell and blanketed the ground.

He reached for her hand. "I promise to make a bonfire and have plenty of blankets and hot coffee."

She turned her palm over and gave his fingers a squeeze before withdrawing her hand. "Then I accept."

He smiled and cast a side glance to his mother. "Then I'll need your services with the anti-grammarian."

Patrick took in the adults with an encompassing glance and shook his head. "Parents are so lame."

Peter chuckled and had a bite of turkey halfway to his mouth when Patrick said, "Ms. Navarre, when we're not at school, is it okay if I call you Mom?"

The question kicked Peter in the gut, and he lowered his fork to his plate with a clatter.

Lisa choked on the fruit juice she sipped. Her panicked eyes darted to Peter's, and she had to cough a few times before she could speak. "Uh, well, Patrick, isn't that a little premature? Your dad and I aren't married."

"Yet. But you're dating now, right? Isn't it just a matter of time?"

"Patrick." Peter sent Lisa an apologetic look. "It's rather rude to put Ms. Navarre on the spot like this. If and when she's ready to have you call her anything besides Ms. Navarre, she'll tell you. Until then, it's Ms. Navarre. Capisce?"

Patrick's shoulders drooped. "Yes, sir."

Peter's heart performed a slow roll in his chest. Was Patrick's eagerness to call Lisa Mom an indication of his son's longing for a mother or of his growing attachment to his teacher as a mother figure? Or both? When he'd asked

Lisa to give their relationship a chance, Peter hadn't fully thought out the ramifications where Patrick was concerned. And what kind of father did that make him? Why hadn't he realized that his involvement with Lisa meant his son would be forming delicate bonds to her as well? Patrick stood to get hurt if things didn't work out with Lisa.

An uneasy apprehension crawled through Peter. Tomorrow, he and Lisa needed to reach an understanding. He couldn't let her fears regarding their budding relationship come back to haunt Patrick. The tragedies of the past months with his grandfather's murder, the attack on his aunt, and Craig Warner's poisoning had already shaken Patrick's world. Losing a mother figure would be too much. Peter had to make sure that didn't happen.

The day before Thanksgiving dawned sunny and cold. The fresh layer of snow made perfect conditions for the horse-drawn sleigh.

"The family bought the sleigh from an antiques dealer about ten years ago for days just like today," Peter told her as he hitched the ranch's strongest horse to the sleigh and helped Lisa climb onto the seat.

She pulled one of the lap blankets around her legs as she settled in. "Peter, this is pure Currier and Ives! I can't think of a better way to start my Thanksgiving holiday."

"Glad you think so," he replied, his breath forming a white cloud between them when he spoke. "Patrick was chomping at the bit to come with us. I had to promise him he could ride our stallion, Lightning, on the property when we come for dinner tomorrow as consolation."

"You should have let him come. He'd have had fun today."

He sent her a side glance as he gathered the reigns. "Maybe so. But today is about us."

His emphasis on the word *us* stirred a flutter in her chest. Peter had arranged a romantic setting, a sumptuous picnic and complete privacy. He'd carefully planned a perfect day. So why was she so apprehensive about where their picnic would lead?

Despite her promise to give her relationship with Peter a chance, she was scared of serious involvement, terrified of repeating the cycle of pain that had broken up her marriage. Even the thought of it left a pit in her stomach and a cold sweat on her lip. She couldn't go to that dark place in her life again.

Regret settled in her chest, colder than the ice and snow crusted over the sprawling fields. She hated being of two minds regarding Peter—wanting him and his son in her life, yet fearing what seemed inevitable: more heartache and devastation.

With a flick of the reigns, Peter sent the horse clopping over the snow-covered fields of the Walsh family ranch. Tiny bells on the horse's harness jingled, reminding Lisa of numerous Christmas carols. She snuggled closer to Peter as the sleigh whisked over the open land toward the woods on the far side of the property. She could already see a large stack of firewood he'd set up for their bonfire.

When they pulled to a stop, Peter jumped to the ground, then turned to lift Lisa down from the sleigh. Even through thick layers of clothing, the contact made her skin tingle. Or maybe it was the look of pure seduction in Peter's gaze as he let her body slide along his as he lowered her feet to the ground. Before he released her, he caught her mouth for a body-warming kiss that promised much more to come. Lisa's heart pattered with anticipation.

Peter lifted down a large basket and a tarpaulin from the back of the sled. "I had the Honey-B Café fix our lunch. I hope you're hungry."

Yes, but for you. Not food. Lisa squelched the thought and took one end of the tarp to help him spread the ground cover next to the pile of firewood.

"Cold weather always gives me a good appetite."

Peter grinned. "Good. If you'll get that blanket and lay it out on top of the tarp, I'll light the fire."

"You've already lit my fire." Lisa shook out the quilt Peter indicated, and as she smoothed the wrinkles, she glanced up to find Peter looking at her with a devilish smile tugging his mouth. She hesitated a beat, then gasped. "Did I say that out loud?"

Peter threw back his head and laughed. "Funny how I was thinking the same thing."

He tossed a match on the firewood, which instantly roared to life. Clearly he'd soaked the wood with lighter fluid earlier. Peter dropped onto the blanket beside her, pulling her into his arms. "Do you know what I'm most thankful for this Thanksgiving?"

The answer shone from his eyes, and Lisa's chest filled with a happiness she hadn't known in years. She wanted to bottle the feeling and save it for days to come when she knew the loneliness and disappointment would creep back into her life.

With a teasing grin, she smoothed her cold hands over his warm, bristly cheeks. "I'll take a guess and say delivery pizza."

He cocked his head as if considering her answer. "Hmm, good point. But no." His dark eyes honed in on hers, his gaze hot and enticing. "You, Lisa. I'm so thankful that I met you."

A bittersweet ache throbbed in her chest. She wanted to believe meeting Peter was meant to be, that maybe her luck had turned for the best. But doubt demons bit hard, spoiling the tender moment. *It can't last. You can only give him heartbreak and grief.*

Ducking her chin, she battled the surge of melancholy. "Peter, I can't—"

"Don't." His finger touched her lips, and her pulse scampered. His gaze drilled hers with a steely conviction. "You promised to give me a chance. No second-guessing, no regrets. Let me in, Lisa. Let me be the man who gives you back your hopes and dreams."

In that moment, she knew she'd lost another little piece of her heart to Peter. His determination to be with her, despite the costs she'd laid out, burrowed into the cracks Ray had left in her soul.

She leaned in to him and brushed her lips on his. "I'm thankful for you, too, Peter."

Peter deepened the kiss, locking her in a firm embrace and sandwiching her body between his hard chest and the unyielding ground. In his arms, Lisa savored a sense of security and protection she'd missed in recent years. Yet at the same time, she felt as if she were spinning along a race track, out of control, headed for a crash. The dichotomy wrestled uneasily inside her.

When Peter broke the kiss and sat up, she sucked in unsteady breaths, trying to regain her balance, yet cherishing the dizzying rush of sweet sensation he stirred in her.

He pulled a bottle of champagne and two flutes from the basket. The cork exited with the appropriate *pop,* and after pouring two glasses, Peter shoved the bottle down in the snow and handed her a flute. "To new beginnings and seeing where this path leads."

He touched his glass to hers and drank deeply, his bedroom eyes holding hers. Even before she sipped the bubbly wine, warmth and longing flowed through her. The champagne tickled her tongue and, on her empty stomach, soon had her head feeling muzzy.

"I think we should crack open that basket of goodies, or I'm going to be tipsy in a minute."

Peter wiggled his eyebrows. "Ah, my evil plan is working…"

Chuckling, she curled her fingers into his suede coat and snuggled closer. "Evil but genius. Kiss me again, you dastardly man."

He did, and soon lunch was forgotten.

Beside the crackling fire, with a crisp blue winter sky above, Lisa lost herself in Peter's kisses, the tenderness of his touch and the seductive rumble of pleasure that vibrated in his chest. When they finally did open the lunch basket, they lingered for hours, feeding each other cheese and crackers, grapes and sinfully rich cream puffs. They nibbled sandwiches and savored an artichoke dip and tortilla chips.

And through it all, they shared intimate chit-chat about their hopes and dreams, their hurts and heartaches, while restless hands roamed and tantalized. The exchanged slow, sultry kisses that intoxicated her more than the champagne ever could.

As their passion grew, Peter slid his hands under Lisa's coat and sweater, his touch shockingly cold against her warm skin. She gasped at the contact, as a shiver chased through her, then moaned her delight when his hand cupped her breast and grazed her nipple. In turn, she unbuttoned the flannel shirt he wore and raked her fingers down his bared chest, memorizing the feel of his taut skin and muscle under her hands. When he shivered, she couldn't be sure whether it was from the cold or her touch.

Nuzzling his ear, she whispered, "As lovely as this picnic

is, I'm not sure this is the weather or the best location for what I think is on both our minds."

Beneath her hands, a shudder rippled through Peter. "Let me douse the fire, and we'll head back to the ranch. Since my mom is with Patrick, we'll have the place to ourselves."

Anticipation ramped through Lisa, leaving her body jangling and flushed. "Perfect."

When Peter returned from settling the horse in its stable, Lisa was waiting beside the fire she'd lit in the living-room grate.

"Can I get you anything from the kitchen?" he offered, still playing the perfect host.

She twisted her mouth in a come-hither smile and tugged her sweater off over her head. "What I want isn't in the kitchen."

Peter cocked an eyebrow and returned a simmering grin. "Do tell."

Instead she showed him.

His gaze heated as she lowered the zipper on her jeans and stepped out of them. Crossing to him, she slid her hands over his broad chest, then looped her arms around his neck. "Where were we?"

His palms skimmed down her back and cupped her bottom. Sinking his fingers into her, he pulled her flush with his body. "This seems like a good place to start."

Angling his head, he sealed his mouth over hers and swept his tongue in to duel with hers. With greedy hands, she untucked his shirt and pulled it, still buttoned, over his head. Tossing the shirt aside, she canted back to fumble with the zipper at his fly. In seconds, he'd helped her strip off his jeans, and they stood flesh to flesh, warming the chill from their bones with deep lingering kisses and the eager exploration of their hands.

Dragging a quilt from the couch, Peter made them a hasty makeshift bed on the floor in front of the fireplace. She knelt beside him on the quilt and sank into his open arms, shutting out the nagging doubts about their future. Right now, all she wanted was Peter. She wanted to be a sensual, sexual woman and not the barren vessel she'd felt like at the end of her relationship with Ray. She wanted carnal, satisfying sex, not the mechanical, result-oriented process that had dominated most of her marriage. She wanted to feel desirable. Alive.

And in return, she held nothing back. Lisa tuned out her inhibitions and let herself indulge in the passion Peter awoke in her.

Their legs tangled, their mouths fused, their hands explored.

While Peter nibbled the curve of her throat, she curled her fingers into his back and writhed sensuously against him. A pounding heat built in her core, crackling in her blood like the fire in the grate. She savored the sensation of his skin against hers, the way his chest hair teased her nipples. Peter moved his kisses down her collarbone and into the valley between her breasts, while his hands traced the curve of her hip and trailed lightly along her thigh, his fingers stirring tendrils of desire in their wake. When he levered himself up to gaze tenderly into her eyes, her heart performed a forward roll. Without her protective shields in place, she could fall hard and fast for this loving man.

"You're beautiful," he murmured, his expression echoing his words.

And you're the answer to a prayer. She closed her eyes, when the sting of unwanted tears gathered in her sinuses. *Don't think. Just feel. Savor.*

Dipping his head, he drew her peaked breast into his mouth and she arched her back, offering herself to him. Ribbons of tingling heat shot through her as his tongue lashed and aroused. She sighed her pleasure and worked her hands between them to stroke the hard shaft that he pressed against her thigh.

He drew a sharp breath as her fingers skimmed the heat and length of him. "Lisa…"

"Now," she whispered, opening herself to him.

With a throaty groan, he sank into her, filling her—fulfilling her.

Their bodies swayed and rocked in the rhythm as old as time, and as the coil of need tightened in her core, Lisa felt a connection to Peter that went beyond the joining of bodies. Something elemental, spiritual, intimate.

And frightening.

She was falling in love with Peter Walsh.

Peter shuddered as he climaxed, the release so powerful it shook him to his marrow. His whole body throbbed and every nerve ending sparked. It had been a long time since he'd been with a woman, but he couldn't blame his recent celibacy for the surge of emotions that battered him in the wake of the hottest, sweetest lovemaking he'd known in years.

Peter wrapped his arms around Lisa, holding her close to the heavy thud of his heart. Pure joy and a sense of completeness swelled in his chest until he thought he might burst with it. He remembered feeling like this when he'd married Katie. He'd known then, as he did now, that he'd found someone he would love the rest of his life.

Love. He smiled as the word tickled his mind, and he kissed the top of her head.

Lisa drew lazy circles on his chest with her finger, and

his body answered with a fresh surge of heat and desire. He wanted her again.

He wanted her forever.

He'd sidestepped and ignored the truth for days, trying to give Lisa the time and space she needed to be comfortable with their growing closeness. But after making love to her, sharing the ultimate union of body and soul with her, he couldn't deny his feelings any longer.

"Lisa," he murmured, his lips pressed softly to her temple.

She tipped her head back and met his gaze through a drowsy screen of eyelashes.

"I know what we talked about the other night…about how we should take things slow, give you a chance to get comfortable with our relationship, but this—"

He stroked a hand down her back and felt her tremble as she hummed her pleasure. "No regrets, Peter. We both wanted this. Despite our haste, I knew what I was doing."

He thought about their eager battle to shed their clothes, and a chuckle rumbled from his chest. "Yes, you did. And you did it well."

She flashed an impish grin, and he couldn't resist kissing the sassy smile. Fire licked his veins, his hunger for her returning in force. The magic of her lips was almost enough to make him lose his line of thought. But four words pounded in his brain, demanding to be shared.

After raking her hair back from her face, he held her head between his hands and stared deeply into her warm eyes. "I love you, Lisa."

Lisa gasped softly, and her brow twitched in a frown. Though she grew still outside, frozen by shock, her insides were a farrago of emotions. For a moment, she wondered if she'd misunderstood Peter. But with a glow in his gaze, he repeated the words that sent a frisson of fear to her marrow.

"I haven't felt like this for anyone since Katie died, and I can't pretend this is just a casual thing for me. I want you in my life, Lisa. Always."

She struggled for a breath, pushing against his chest to free herself from his grasp. He'd promised not to rush her, to give her time. She'd made love to him because she was powerfully attracted to him, and the moment had felt right. Yet suddenly their relationship was careening down a path she hadn't intended. Faster than she could keep up.

"P-Peter, I—"

"We don't have to get married right away. I don't mind waiting for you, but I can't deny my feelings anymore."

Tears burned her sinuses and spilled onto her cheeks. "Peter, slow down!"

He swiped at her cheeks with his thumbs. "Aw, sweetheart, don't cry." A soft laugh laced his voice, and he pulled her close to kiss her wet cheeks.

"Please stop, Peter. I can't—" Her thoughts scrambling, her stomach bunching, she backed out of his embrace. Suddenly cold to the bone, she tugged the corners of the quilt around her shoulders.

He furrowed his brow, his expression guarded. "What's going on, Lisa? Why are you crying?"

"You promised not to push." She waved a trembling hand and blinked hard as more tears pooled in her eyes. "Is this your idea of not rushing me?"

"You just said you had no regrets about us making love. We both wanted it."

She raked her hair back with both hands then pressed the heels of her palms into her temples. "I know. But saying you love me…talking about marriage. I'm not ready for that kind of commitment!"

He sat up slowly, his gaze wounded. "I had to be honest with you about what I feel. You're an amazing woman, Lisa, and I want to be with you, build something lasting together."

"But we can't!" Anguish sharpened the cry that wrenched from her breaking heart. "I was wrong to think we could dabble with a romance and not regret it. But I've told you from the beginning that I can't have children. My infertility ruined what had been a beautiful marriage. I can't go through the motions of a relationship that I know will end in resentment and loss again. You want more kids. You've said as much. You deserve the big family I can't give you."

He stared at her silently for long seconds, her nerves stretching tauter.

"What about adoption? Surrogacy? There are other options," he murmured.

She pinched the bridge of her nose. How many million times had she gone around this rollercoaster with Ray. Hashing and rehashing. Debating and arguing.

"Red tape keeps good parents from adopting. Surrogates grow attached to the fetus. Every option has so many potential problems and roadblocks."

"You're just borrowing trouble. That's a cop-out."

"No, it's reality, Peter. We tried to adopt once, and the biological mother changed her mind. The disappointment was devastating. It was the straw that broke Ray. He left soon after that."

"I'm so sorry, sweetheart." He stroked her cheek, his own eyes damp.

Lisa drew a deep breath for courage. "Peter, I care too

much about you to let you throw away your life with a barren woman."

Grasping her chin, he narrowed a stern but loving look on her. "Maybe you should let me decide what is right for me and my life. I love you. Just the way you are. No, it doesn't make me happy to think of never having more children, but I can deal with it."

She tugged her chin free from his grasp. "Well, I *can't* deal with it, Peter! I'm still haunted by the ghosts of my first failed marriage. I ache every day for the babies I'll never carry. I don't think I'm strong enough to survive another broken heart when the reality of my situation catches up with you." When he opened his mouth, clearly ready to deny her claim, she held up a hand to silence him. "It will catch up. Just like it caught up to Ray."

Peter tightened his jaw, his eyes dark. "I'm not Ray."

With a weary sigh, Lisa slumped her shoulders. A sense of defeat crashed down on her. With her back to the wall, she was faced with truths she couldn't outrun. "But I'm still me, and I still can't have children. Nothing has changed for *me*. I care about you, Peter, but I'm scared! I'm so afraid of winding up in the same place I found myself five years ago when Ray had enough and left me. He thought he loved me enough to wade through the pain and disappointment, too. But he was wrong." Her voice broke, and she paused long enough to wipe her tears on the corner of the quilt. "I'm scared of loving you, Peter."

Peter scowled, but his eyes reflected the pain of heart-break. "Well, that doesn't say much for your trust in me, does it?"

"It's not you I don't trust. It's me. I don't know if I can ever be happy without my own children, and I won't drag you down in my pain."

He scrubbed his hands over his face and shoved to his

feet. Snatching up his boxers and pants, he started dressing, his motions jerky. "You know, if it were just me, I'd tell you that I had the patience to wait for you to see what we have together. I've waited ten years to find someone I loved enough to put myself out there for, so what's a few more months or years?"

A sharp ache slashed through her chest as she watched him jam his arms into the sleeves of his shirt. The scene unfolded as if under water—blurry, slow motion, surreal. In her head a voice screamed, begging her to make him stop. To go back and unsay what had been said.

"But I have to think about my son." Peter met her gaze with a pained gaze. "He's already forming bonds with you. He lost one mother already. I can't let him grow attached to you, only to have you walk away down the road because you're *afraid* of committing to me."

Afraid. The disappointment and disgust that filled his tone with that word reverberated inside her. Was she throwing away the best thing to happen to her in years because of fear? She was already planning to change her career path to avoid facing her personal pain and loneliness.

Bile churned in her gut. She was a coward, letting the best of life pass her by while she licked her wounds and mourned her misfortune. But she didn't know what else to do. She couldn't change her infertility. And she was sinking in the tar pit of her own dejection.

Peter finished dressing and pinned a penetrating stare on her. "You have to choose, Lisa. For Patrick's sake. But we can't do this halfway. I have *all* from you—or we have nothing. What will it be?"

Her heart sank. She couldn't blame him for issuing his ultimatum. He had to protect Patrick from further heartbreak.

The quilt still wrapped around her like a shield—though a worthless protection that had allowed arrows to pierce her heart—Lisa rose from the floor on shaky legs and gathered her clothes.

Her heart breaking, she gave Peter the only answer she could. "Nothing. I can't do this halfway either, Peter. And I can't promise you what I don't have in me to give."

Before he could respond, Peter's cell phone rang. The harsh tones jangled her already frayed nerves. At first she thought he'd ignore it, but after several rings, he stepped over to the end table where he'd left the cell phone and checked the caller ID.

Frowning, he flipped open the receiver and pressed it to his ear. "Hello?"

Numb with loss and trembling with regret, Lisa tugged on her jeans and bra while Peter took his call. Her head buzzed with tangled emotions.

As she pulled her sweater over her head, Peter's tone, more than his words, alerted her to trouble. She faced him and found his face pale with shock and worry.

"Do your best to calm him down. I'm on my way home." He snapped his phone closed and spun to face her. His eyes were bright with anxiety. "Get your shoes. We have to go."

Lisa's heart climbed into her throat. "What's happened?"

"A note was left on our porch, and Patrick found it." Peter's hands shook as he rammed his feet into his boots. "It was a death threat."

Chapter 13

Nothing.

Lisa's blunt response to his ultimatum echoed hollowly in Peter's head, tumbling with his mother's frightened voice. *Someone's threatened your life, Peter. Patrick found the note. He's hysterical.*

His world seemed to be crumbling, and he was at a loss what to do about any of it.

Across the cab of his truck, Lisa sat with her hands knotted together and the strain of the past half hour creasing her face. He'd offered to drop her at her house but she declined, stating that she would go crazy not knowing what was happening with Patrick.

Her interest in Patrick's well-being and concern over the death threat proved to Peter that she cared about him and his family.

She just didn't care enough to fight her fears and look for a way through the morass of her infertility. Peter's chest contracted until he couldn't breathe. Why had he let himself fall for Lisa when he knew the risk to his heart? Her skittishness about getting involved with him should have been enough warning that with her he'd end up nursing the pain of rejection and loss again.

Yet he couldn't be angry. Couldn't resent her decision. Because his heart broke for her pain. He understood the depth of her trepidation and the roots of her reluctance.

He simply had nothing that could assuage that fear and convince her to take a chance on love again.

As he pulled into his driveway, Patrick bolted through the front door and was clambering at the driver's door before Peter even had the engine shut off.

Peter stepped out of the truck, and his son threw himself against Peter.

"Dad, someone wants to k-kill you! They sent a letter with a bullet in it. You said your job wasn't dangerous. Why would someone want to hurt you? Who would want to kill you?" The flurry of questions that Patrick lobbed at him in a tear-choked voice battered Peter like fists.

He wrapped Patrick in a fierce bear hug intended to calm his son, but which he found he needed just as much to soothe his tattered nerves. He clung to Patrick, battling the sting of his own tears, the fear of something happening to Patrick, the heartache of losing Lisa, and he cherished the feel of his baby—his son—in his arms.

A feeling Lisa had never, would never experience. The grief that shot through him on Lisa's behalf nearly brought Peter to his knees. Living daily with an unrequited yearning for a baby, dealing with the neverending emptiness on top of her husband's abandonment… Peter staggered under the weight of her losses. No wonder she was so terrified of another failed relationship, of reviving the ache of being a childless couple.

"Hey, calm down," he crooned. "I'm okay, sport. No one is going to kill me. And I won't let anyone hurt you either."

Jolene crossed the yard, her face lined with stress and worry, and she handed him a folded sheet of paper. "It was taped to the front door."

With a final squeeze, he stepped back from Patrick. "Did you preserve the tape? We might get a good fingerprint off it."

She grimaced. "No. I didn't think about that. I was so worried about you and about Patrick's reaction—"

Peter stepped back from Patrick and unfolded the note. From the corner of his eye, he saw Lisa round the front of the truck and sweep his son into a firm embrace, mothering Patrick despite her breakup with Peter.

The letter had been addressed to Patrick and read, *Tell your father to butt out or he'll be the next to die.*

"Butt out," Peter muttered under his breath, the message ringing bells in his memory. Wes Colton had warned him away from his investigation with the same words.

Fury burned through Peter, vibrating in every muscle.

Had the sheriff stooped to making criminal threats to children to drive home his point?

For all his distrust of Wes Colton's handling of the murder investigation, Peter felt the sheriff didn't seem the sort to resort to such juvenile and gutless tactics of intimidation. But Peter knew with a certainty *some* Colton was behind the threat.

And his money was on Maisie.

Judging by the number of vehicles parked in the main drive of the Colton ranch, Peter guessed most of the clan had gathered for some family event. Logical, seeing as it was the day before Thanksgiving, and convenient, seeing as how he couldn't be sure which Colton was responsible for the threatening note.

Most of the lights inside the sprawling, rustic-wood ranch house were ablaze, illuminating the home like a Christmas tree at the foot of the majestic Rockies. The scene was homey, inviting…deceptive.

As he climbed out of his truck and braced himself against the stiff, cold wind, Peter reminded himself that the magnificent stained-wood-and-mountain-stone mansion housed a brood of vipers.

Remembering the terror in Patrick's eyes because of the death threat, Peter squared his shoulders and strode to the front door. His knock was answered by a young voice calling, "I'll get it!"

When the door opened, Jeremy Colton greeted Peter with a puzzled look. "Oh, uh, hi, Mr. Walsh." He looked behind Peter. "Is Patrick with you?"

Peter faltered. He hadn't counted on Jeremy witnessing his showdown with the adult Coltons. Jeremy, who was Patrick's friend. And who could easily be his own half-brother.

Acid roiled in Peter's gut. "No, Patrick's at home. Is your mother or Wes here?"

"Well, sorta. They're kinda busy. We're just about to eat a big family dinner."

So the gang was all here. Perfect.

Peter took off his gloves and jammed them in his coat pocket. "It's important that I talk to them."

"Who is it, honey?" A slim, older blond woman Peter recognized from newspaper pictures appeared in the foyer behind Jeremy. Sharon Colton, Darius's current wife in a string of many. When she spotted Peter on the porch, Sharon came up short, her expression wary. "Mr. Walsh, is…is there a problem?"

Peter glanced to Jeremy. He refused to air his wrath in front of the boy unless the Coltons gave him no choice. "Why don't you run along, Jeremy, and tell Wes and your mother I need to see them."

Jeremy sprinted away, calling, "Mom! Uncle Wes!"

Sharon gripped the edge of the door as if it were all that supported her. "What's going on, Mr. Walsh?"

The heavy thud of footsteps signaled the arrival of not one, but several, Colton men. Leading the way, Darius spotted Peter and scowled darkly. When he reached the door, he shoved his wife back into the shadows, growling, "I'll handle this, Sharon."

Sharon turned meekly and faded into the background.

Peter scanned the other faces that gathered in the foyer. Duke, Damien and Finn stood behind their father like the goon squad, ready to remove Peter bodily on cue from Darius.

"What do you want, Walsh?" Darius's voice rumbled, low and menacing, like thunder announcing an approaching storm.

Peter thrust the letter toward Darius. The patriarch was as good a place to start as any.

"I want to know which one of you bastards sent this to my son."

Darius ignored the paper Peter shoved at him and glowered. "Care to rephrase that?"

Peter returned a stony glare. "No, I don't. Because terrorizing a ten-year-old boy is the kind of vile move only a sorry coward would make. I won't stand by and let you Coltons harass my family any longer."

More family members appeared from the back rooms. Susan Kelley joined Duke, lacing her hand in his with a curious frown. Perry, Wes and Lily Masterson arrived right behind Susan. Spying Peter, Wes pushed his way to the front of the group. "What's going on?"

"Mr. Walsh was just leaving, Wes." Darius tried to shut the door on Peter, and Peter's hackles went up.

Ramming his shoulder into the door, he plowed his way into the Colton's front hall, fully aware of the angry glares and hostile stance of the many Colton alpha males. Peter didn't care if he was outnumbered. One of the Coltons had come after his son, terrorizing Patrick, making dire threats. He wouldn't let such an offense pass. "I'm not going anywhere until I know who sent this!" Again he waved the letter. He could feel his blood pressure rising, and he fought to keep it in check. He had to keep his wits about him against the Coltons. "Although I have my suspicions."

Wes took the note and read it. Furrowed his brow. "Where did you get this?"

"It was left at my house with a bullet. Patrick found it."

Darius took the note from his son, and Damien and Duke crowded closer to read over his shoulder.

Wes braced his hands on his hips. "I'll need that bullet, too. I'll start an investigation, if you want."

"You won't have to look far. Ask Maisie what she knows about it."

"Maisie?" Darius asked.

Peter faced the patriarch. "Do you know that she had an affair with my father back in 1995? I have reason to believe Jeremy is my father's son."

The women gasped softly, and a murmur of discontent rose amongst the men.

"I'm aware of Maisie's mistake," Darius said coolly, confirming Peter's suspicions. The man's face remained hard, emotionless.

"What does that have to do with this note?" Wes asked.

"Why don't you ask her?" Peter divided a dark look between Darius and Wes. "A spurned lover could have reason to murder, to seek revenge. Especially if she's trying to cover her tracks, hide an illicit affair, the paternity of an illegitimate son."

An uneasy silence filled the foyer until Darius bellowed, "Maisie!"

The clop of hard-soled shoes sounded in the hall, and Maisie pulled up short when she saw her family clustered around Peter. "What's all this about?"

Darius thrust the letter in her direction. "What do you know about a death threat sent to Patrick Walsh?"

Maisie stiffened. Her hands balled at her sides. "Why are you accusing me?" her tone grew shrill.

As she shuffled cautiously forward, her brothers and their girlfriends parted to let Maisie through.

Peter regarded Maisie with a narrowed gaze. Disgust and fury churned in his gut. "I think you know. Your secret is out, Maisie. Jeremy is Mark Walsh's son, isn't he? Did you kill my father to keep him from telling the world your dirty little secret?"

Maisie drew a sharp breath, her eyes widening in horror. "How did you find out? You can't—"

In an instant, her shock morphed to rage. With a keening, animalistic wail, she charged at Peter. She attacked him, arms swinging, fingernails raking, feet flailing. A blur of fury and wrath, vicious strikes and battering kicks. "I hate you! I hate you! You've ruined everything! You'll pay for this!"

Wes bit out a scorching obscenity and, with Damien's help, peeled Maisie off Peter. Finn stepped forward to help subdue Maisie, who fought their hold like a rabid wildcat.

Stunned, but not really surprised by Maisie's outburst and attack, Peter dabbed at his bloody lip, where Maisie had clawed him with her fingernails. His cheek throbbed, and his shins ached from her assault, and he'd likely have a shiner in the morning thanks to a well-placed jab.

With his brothers restraining Maisie, Wes stepped toward her and pointed to the note with the death threat Darius still held. "Did you send Patrick Walsh that threat, Maisie?"

Her eyes narrowed on Peter with a venomous glare. "Yes!" she hissed. "I hope all of the Walshes die! They're nothing but heartless animals."

Wes closed his eyes, and his shoulders drooped wearily. Finn and Duke exchanged guarded looks.

"First Lucy betrays Damien and stomps on his heart," Maisie continued ranting, red-faced with anger, "then Mark knocks me up and tells me to get an abortion when he finds out. He never really cared about me. He just used me and abandoned me! The cold-hearted rat deserved to die!"

Peter shuddered. He might be bleeding and bruised, but he had what he wanted. The truth.

He turned to Wes with a level gaze. "Your sister assaulted me. She's admitted to sending a death threat to my son and murdering my father." He aimed a finger at Maisie. "I want her arrested."

"What!" she shrieked. "No! Wes, you can't—"

Wes held up a hand to hush his sister. "I can charge her with battery and sending the threat, but I didn't hear a murder confession."

"Neither did I," Damien added. His brothers shook their heads in agreement.

Peter raised his chin and moved toward Wes. "Sounds

like you should add her to your suspect list at least." He gritted his teeth and cast a side glance to the grim faces around him. "I told you if you'd look at your own family you could solve my father's murder and the other attacks on my family without your lengthy investigation."

Wes shot a glance to his sister. "Did you kill Mark Walsh, Maisie?"

"No!" She struggled against the hands that still held her.

Wes arched an eyebrow. "Maisie didn't kill anyone. This changes nothing about my investigation."

Peter tensed. "Bring her in for attacking me then. I'm pressing charges for assault."

Maisie grunted indignantly and cut her gaze to Darius, who stood back, arms folded over his chest, watching the proceedings with a disapproving glower. "Dad, you can't let him do that!"

"Lily, call my office, please," Wes said, "Ask them to send a cruiser out here." He sighed and faced his sister. "Maisie, you have the right to remain silent—"

"Wes, no!" Maisie sent another pleading look to her father. "Daddy, please! Do something! This town owes you. You can't let them arrest me!"

"You made this bed for yourself. Now lie in it." Darius shoved the threatening letter toward Wes then strode into the bowels of his ranch house.

Damien squared his shoulders and moved to block Peter's view of Wes reading Maisie her rights, of Maisie crying and begging her brothers to let her go. "You've done enough damage here tonight. I think you should go." His tone, black glare and rigid stance left no doubt his suggestion was actually an order.

Swiping a trickle of blood from his mouth and rolling the ache of tension from his shoulders, Peter gave Damien a curt nod. "I'll go. But your family hasn't heard the last of me. I won't rest until I know which one of you killed my father and declared war on my family."

"Planning to railroad through false charges like your family did against me?" Damien asked, his tone bitter.

"No, this time I'll make sure we get the right person, and I'll see that the charges stick." Turning on his heel, Peter stormed through the front door and across the lawn to his truck, parked at the far end of the driveway.

As he passed one of the bunkhouses where several ranch hands had gathered outside for a smoke, the sound of Maisie protesting her arrest to Wes in shrill tones wafted through the November chill. The ranch hands shook their heads, and Peter heard one man say, "Just goes to show—money can't buy happiness."

"You can't pick your family, but I bet ol' Sheriff Wes sure wishes he could right about now," another hand added with a scoff.

Peter paused with his hand on the door handle of his truck and looked back up at the main house. The Coltons spilled out the front door as Wes took Maisie out to meet the arriving patrol car.

You can't pick your family...

Or could you?

As Peter pulled onto the highway that led back to Honey Creek, the old ranch hand's statement tumbled in his head, tangling with a collage of snapshot memories of his own family. His heartache over Lisa's choice to end their relationship without giving it a fair chance. Patrick's haunted expression over the death threat when he'd arrived home this afternoon. Mark Walsh's womanizing and disinterest in his wife and children. Mary's and Lucy's newfound happiness with upstanding men who would love and protect them. Craig Warner filling the role of father for Peter in recent years. Katie's death as she gave Peter the greatest gift in his life, his son.

Peter hadn't chosen some members of his family, wouldn't wish his absentee lothario father on anyone. Yet he'd chosen his young bride, just as Mary had chosen Jake. Lucy had chosen Steve.

He'd chosen to count Craig as a father figure, and Craig treated him like an adopted son.

Adopted.

Peter tightened his hands on the steering wheel, and his heart pounded harder.

We tried to adopt once, and the biological mother changed her mind. The disappointment was devastating. It was the straw that broke Ray.

Earlier today, he'd been so caught up in Lisa's pain, his own emotions and desperation to change Lisa's mind that he hadn't fully analyzed all the ramifications of their situation. He'd been so confident in his own feelings for Lisa, so cocksure about their future that he hadn't given real thought to how to make it work. Lisa needed that reassurance, not ultimatums.

Peter squeezed his eyes shut and cursed his blindness and stupidity.

He prayed she'd still be at his house when he arrived. They couldn't leave things unsettled between them.

Jolene met him at the door. Her troubled expression asked what she didn't verbalize.

"Maisie admitted sending the note," he told her in soft tones before going inside. "I was right about her having an affair with Dad. Jeremy is his son."

"Why are you bleeding?" Jolene reached for the cut on his lip, and Peter pulled away.

"She attacked me when I told her the secret was out.

She swears she didn't kill Dad, but her assault on me and the threatening note were enough to have her arrested."

"Wes allowed his sister to be arrested?" Jolene sounded stunned.

"He's the one who took her into custody…until his backup arrived."

Jolene touch a hand to her temple. "I'm so ready for all this drama to be behind us. You know, years ago, the Walshes and the Coltons were friends. I miss those days." She sighed and shook her head, then raised a firmly loving gaze to Peter. "Enough dwelling on our troubles. Thanksgiving is about counting our blessings. And the Walshes have plenty. Craig is stronger every day. Mary and Lucy have never been happier. And you have a healthy, growing son. And Lisa—"

His heart twisted. Hadn't Lisa filled his mom in on their break-up?

"Mom, about Lisa…"

Jolene gave him a quelling look and put a finger to her lips. "Shh. Come here. There's something you need to see."

Wes rocked back in his desk chair waiting to hear from his deputy that Maisie had been processed, printed and photographed. What a night!

Maisie had always been a handful for their parents. The oldest child and only girl in the family until Joan had come along when Maisie was fifteen, Maisie had been spoiled yet also strangely isolated among all those Colton sons, especially after her mother had died when she was five. With her unrivaled beauty, men twice her age had showered her with the wrong kind of attention at too early an age. Yet Maisie had sought more and more outrageous ways to attract attention from her family. She'd pushed every envelope, courted danger and invited scandal but, to Wes's knowledge, had never crossed the line of legality. Until tonight.

He rubbed his chest where a raw ache had settled. He hated bringing Maisie in, but what choice had he had? She'd admitted to threatening Peter Walsh's life, had viciously attacked him. His sister was out of control, headed for a bigger fall if he didn't intervene.

Like he needed something else to worry about. This mess with Mark Walsh's murder, Craig Warner's poisoning, money-laundering schemes that had brought the FBI to his tiny town…the stress wore on him. Something had to break soon.

"Sheriff, your sister is in the interrogation room," one of his deputies said from the door. "She's asked to see you."

Wes nodded. "Thanks."

Bracing his hands on his desk, he shoved to his feet, feeling far older than his thirty-three years tonight.

Maisie had her head buried in arms folded on the table when he walked in and sat across from her. She raised a teary gaze to him, her luminous aqua eyes rimmed in red, lined with distress and fatigue. Despite her taller-than-average height, his sister seemed smaller tonight, child-like, drawn into herself, vulnerable.

Wes's chest clenched. "What's going on with you, Maisie? What possessed you to send Patrick Walsh that death threat against his father?"

She swiped at her cheek and shook her head slowly. "I don't know, Wes. I was in town earlier today, picking up a few last-minute things for our dinner, getting an early start on my Christmas shopping…" She lowered her gaze to the table where she restlessly twisted a used facial tissue. "Everywhere I went, people told me Peter Walsh had been asking about me last week. Did anyone know who Jeremy's father was? Did anyone remember who I'd been involved with in 1995? Could Mark Walsh be Jeremy's father?"

Her hands trembled, and she shredded the tissue into bits. "If I'd wanted people to know the mistake I'd made with Mark Walsh years ago, I'd have told people myself. But I never wanted anyone to know that that cretin, Mark Walsh, was my son's dad. I never wanted Jeremy to have to live with that burden."

Wes leaned forward and placed a calming hand over Maisie's fidgeting fingers. "Go on. What did you do then?"

"I got mad. I'd heard you complain earlier about how he was nosing around in the death of his father and could jeopardize your investigation. I knew he had to be stopped. I knew a warning would be ignored. He hadn't listened to you after all. So I thought…if I involved Patrick—"

Wes frowned and squeezed Maisie's hand. "Patrick Walsh is just a kid, Maisie. How would you feel if someone sent a letter like that to Jeremy?"

Her eyes filled with fresh tears. "I'd hate it. I never wanted to hurt Patrick. He seems like a sweet kid—despite being a Walsh. But I didn't think—"

"Yeah. You didn't think." Wes gritted his teeth. "And now look where your temper has gotten you. You'll have plenty of time to think tonight. I've got to put you in the holding cell until your bond comes through."

As he scooted his chair back and stood, Maisie's shoulders slumped.

"Wes?" Her voice cracked, high and thin, full of pain.

Wes stopped at the door and faced his sister. "Yeah, Mais."

"Damien is talking about leaving town. Going to Nevada to start over."

Wes sighed. He hated to see Damien leave when the family had only just gotten him back. "Yeah, I know."

"I think that may be what I should do, too." Maisie lifted her aqua eyes, puddled with tears. "I have a horrible reputation in this town that I won't soon lose. Being a Colton in Honey Creek is hard. People expect so much, watch your every move, talk about you as if you don't have feelings. I should move far from here and make a fresh start."

"Are you sure? You'd be uprooting Jeremy from every-thing and everyone he's ever known."

"Maybe that's not such a bad thing. I don't want him living under the pressures I've known living here." She tucked her hair behind her ear. "Don't we have some cousins in Texas?"

"I think so. But…you know you can't leave town until these new charges against you are settled."

Maisie closed her eyes slowly and sighed. "I know." She rubbed her temple and said softly, "Go home, Wes. Lily's waiting for you."

Peter followed his mother into the living room. She put her finger on her lips, signaling for him to be quiet, then pointed to his sofa.

Under a shared quilt, Patrick lay huddled against Lisa, his head on her shoulder, her arms around him. They were both asleep.

The touching scene wrenched Peter's heart. Patrick needed a mother. Lisa needed a child. The solution seemed so obvious, but how did he convince Lisa to step out on faith, to give their love a chance? Her pain was deep and stubborn.

He took a step toward them, but Jolene caught his arm,

crooked a finger to motion him to the kitchen. Again he followed, curious.

Jake Pierson and Mary sat at his kitchen table nursing mugs of hot tea, their expressions grim.

Peter wasn't sure he could take any more bad news tonight. His world was already falling apart, his heart broken, his child terrorized. "What's going on?"

He heard the shuffle of feet as his mother backed out of the room, giving them privacy to talk.

Jake spoke first. "I hear you paid a visit to the Colton ranch tonight."

"My life had been threatened. My child scared witless. I couldn't sit back and do nothing."

"You could have called the authorities, Peter."

"Not when the authorities are the problem. Wes is a Colton. They're the ones behind all this. Maisie admitted to sending the note."

Mary frowned. "Just the same, there are proper channels for this kind of thing, so that citizens don't go off half-cocked seeking vigilante justice."

Peter sighed heavily. "So you came to lecture me? 'Cause I'm not in the mood."

"No," Jake said. "We came to level with you, before you do real damage to this case."

Peter tensed, raised his chin. "Level with me?"

Mary nodded. "But you have to keep this in the strictest confidence. Please, Peter. It's critical to the case that nothing leak about what's going on behind the scenes. Do you hear me? Do you understand?"

Apprehension stirred a drumbeat in his chest. "Talk to me."

Jake and Mary exchanged a troubled look.

"Your father's murder may be related to other crimes

that the FBI is investigating," Jake said. "Same with Craig's poisoning. You're right that they are probably linked."

Peter pulled out a chair and sat without breaking eye contact with Jake. "What kind of other crimes?"

"Money-laundering, real-estate fraud, a whole list of smaller related charges." Jake turned his mug idly and shook his head. "We don't know yet how it all fits together, but Wes has been cooperating with the FBI and their undercover investigators now for months."

"When we started digging, asking questions, we became a target," Mary said. "Remember when Jake's partner was killed? We think the murderer was really after Jake. The attempt on our lives a few days later cinched it for us. The case wasn't worth our lives, not when we'd just found each other and had a chance for real happiness."

"The FBI has someone in place, an undercover operative who can bust this case wide open in time." Jake tapped the table with his finger to emphasize his point. "But you have to back off. You can't interfere. You could ruin everything, right when Wes and the FBI are nearly ready to make arrests."

Wes had said much the same thing the last time Peter confronted him. *Walsh, this case is bigger than just a murder investigation…*

"Who is the undercover agent?" Peter looked to Jake. "You?"

Jake shook his head as Mary said, "We don't know who, don't care who, as long as it all gets settled. Soon. We trust Wes, Peter. He's a good lawman."

Peter propped his elbows on the table and raked both hands through his hair. "Why didn't you tell me this sooner?"

"It's classified. We shouldn't be telling you now, but when you go off and confront the Coltons at their ranch…" Mary heaved a sigh. "We asked you to drop your investigation weeks ago. For your safety as well as Patrick's. If what we've told you tonight isn't enough to convince you to leave this case to the authorities, then think about Patrick. Don't you want him to be able to sleep at night without fearing his father will be shot or run off the road or poisoned?"

Peter thought of his son, already facing the heartache of losing Lisa thanks to their break-up. He raised his gaze to Mary and Jake. The decision was easy.

"All right. I'll drop my investigation."

Jake gave a satisfied nod. "I'll try to keep you informed, but honestly we don't know that much ourselves now that we've backed off. I trust Wes and the FBI, Peter. And you can too."

Peter drew a cleansing breath. "Let's hope so."

Careful not to disturb the sleeping pair, Peter sat on the edge of the couch. He studied the tear tracks on his son's cheeks, and his stomach bunched. Patrick had needed comfort tonight, and his father had not been there for him. Peter had let his grudge against the Coltons get the better of him. Making a scene, disturbing a family holiday meal, all to satisfy his own sense of retribution.

Thank God Lisa had stayed. Not that Jolene couldn't have handled Patrick's tears, but his mother had been through so much recently herself. And Patrick had really bonded with Lisa.

...is it okay if I call you Mom?

Peter curled his hand into a fist of frustration. He had to change Lisa's mind about ending their relationship. Somehow.

You can't pick your family...

The old ranch hand was wrong. You *could* pick the people you loved, the people you surrounded yourself with, the people who became your family, even if not by blood.

Patrick had chosen Lisa to be his mother. And Peter wanted her as his wife. Needed her. Loved her more than anything—except his son.

Taking a deep breath and saying a prayer that he'd find the right words, he stroked Lisa's cheek and whispered, "Hey, Sleeping Beauty. I'm home."

Her eyelids fluttered open, and a smile graced her lips briefly before shadows crept into her gaze. "Are you all right? Your face—"

"Turns out Maisie Colton has a vicious right hook."

"Peter…"

"I'm okay. Help me get this guy to his bed. We need to talk."

A wary concern narrowed her eyes as Peter jostled Patrick lightly. "Wake up, sport. I'd carry you to your bed, but you've gotten kinda big for that."

Patrick grunted and rolled away from Peter.

"Patrick." Peter jostled his son again, and this time Patrick's eyes sprang open and he bolted up, alarm on his face.

"Dad? Did you find the guy who sent the letter? Are you okay?"

He tousled Patrick's hair and helped him up from the couch. "Everything's fine. No one is going to hurt you or me. I promise."

"Or Mom…I mean, Ms. Navarre?"

Peter's gaze darted to Lisa's. She bit down on her bottom lip, her eyes sad.

"I intend to keep all of us safe." Peter's gaze included Lisa. "No matter what. Okay, sport?"

Patrick nodded sleepily, his eyelids drooping again. Peter ushered his son to bed, kissed his forehead and bade him goodnight before returning to the living room. His mother puttered about his kitchen, still discreetly giving him time and space to sort things out with Lisa.

Lisa sat on the edge of the sofa, putting her shoes back on as if preparing to leave. "If you would drive me home, Peter, I'll get out of your hair and—"

"Don't go." He wrapped his fingers around her wrist, halting her progress. "Please talk to me."

"I don't know what we have left to say. You asked me to decide on *all* or *nothing*, for Patrick's sake. And I saw tonight why you had to make that call. Patrick doesn't deserve to have his heart broken. He's an impressionable boy who needs a mother and I—"

"He needs *you*, Lisa. He's bonded with you. Just like I have." He squeezed her hand, his expression pleading. "We love you."

Tears bloomed in her eyes. "Peter, don't make this harder than it already is."

He swiped moisture from her cheek and locked his gaze with hers. "Listen to me. I was wrong to give you an ultimatum. I see that now. I have no excuse except…I wanted assurance that we were both dedicated to making our relationship work…because I want us to work so desperately. But instead of supporting you and giving you the understanding you needed in facing the pain from your past, I pressured you and forced you to make a hard choice. I'm so sorry, sweetheart."

She flashed a weak, sad smile. "Apology accepted. But—"

"No. Not *but*. I learned something else tonight. Figured it out really…" He captured her face between his hands. "I overheard a comment that made me really think about what family is, who my family is, why we love our family. And blood is only a small part of deciding who we love."

Her brow wrinkled. "Peter, what does this have to do with us?"

"Everything. My dad was related to me by blood, but Craig Warner is more a father to me than Mark Walsh ever was. Patrick wants so badly to call you Mom, because he sees you in that role, wants you to be his mother. He loves you, even though there is no blood relationship."

Lisa's chin trembled as new tears spilled from her eyelashes. "I love him too. He's a great kid, Peter. But I—"

"Please, Lisa. Stop saying *but*. I know you're scared, but I'm not ready to give up on us. Think about what we could have together. We *are* a family—you, me and Patrick."

Her expression grew more wistful, more pained.

"And we can adopt more children. If you're worried about a birth mother changing her mind, then we'll adopt children already in the system, kids who are desperate for the kind of love we can offer."

She was softening. He saw the yearning that flashed brightly in her eyes.

"We *can* choose our family. I chose Craig to be my father figure. Patrick chose you to be his mother. And we can choose to adopt children who need us as much as we need them. Maybe they'll be babies, maybe not. But we will adopt as many children as you want. I swear it."

She began to shake, and he pressed her trembling hands between his. "The…approval process can be long and full of red tape."

He heard the years of dejection and frustration in her voice, still holding her back.

"Good thing I'm a stubborn and persistent man then."

She grinned finally, laughing through her tears. "You are that!"

Peter framed her face in his hands and touched his

forehead to hers. "And I choose you, Lisa Navarre, to be my wife. I want you to grow old with me, no matter what else happens in our lives."

She drew a quick, shallow breath and curled her fingers into his hair. "Oh, Peter..."

"If we never have any children besides Patrick, I will still be happy as long as you are beside me. And I will do everything in my power to make you happy until your dying day. I love you as you are. And if you give me a chance, I'll show you how much every day for the rest of our lives."

She grew still, her gaze searching his as if assessing his sincerity. "You still want me, even knowing what my infertility will mean in our marriage?"

He gave her a quick kiss. "Unlike Ray, I'm prepared to stand by you, support you, be a team, even through whatever bad times may come our way. Marry me, Lisa. We belong together. I want to build a family with you."

Lisa felt her world tilt as the possibilities Peter was offering her sank in and shifted her whole perspective on her future. Adopt children with Peter? Be Patrick's mother? Grow old with Peter at her side?

In a matter of hours, minutes really, she'd gone from facing dismally lonely days of heartache without the man she loved to a bright future with everything she'd dreamed of and wanted. Because of Peter. The man she loved. The man with whom she wanted to build a home.

The answer was clear, but she hesitated. She'd had her hopes dashed so many times, and as wonderful as Peter's proposal was, she had to be sure she wasn't dreaming.

Peter's brow puckered in a frown. "That's an awfully serious face, Lisa. What's wrong?"

"I just have to be sure... I—" She lifted her chin and laid a hand along his cheek. "Kiss me, Peter."

"Gladly." He caught her lips with his, and she wrapped her arms around his neck, holding him close, as if she'd never let him go. Because she had no intention of letting this loving man out of her life. His lips stirred a sweet hunger inside her, but more important, his kiss touched the vulnerable part of her soul, a place she'd spent years protecting.

She wasn't dreaming, and she wasn't alone anymore.

She sagged against him, feeling the weight of the world lift from her. Her arms tightened around him, and she whispered, "I choose you, too, Peter. I love you, and I want very much to be part of your family."

Peter held her as she cried happy tears. "Consider it done."

Epilogue

Later that night, Wes returned to his office, eager to wrap up the paperwork associated with Maisie's arrest and get back home to Lily and their interrupted family dinner. Several minutes later, a knock roused him from his work, and Damien opened Wes's office door a few inches and slipped inside. "Got a minute?"

Wes shrugged. "I guess. You here to post Maisie's bond?"

"That, and…we need to talk." As Damien took a seat in a visitor's chair, his brother's dark gaze sent a chill through Wes.

"Can this wait until we get home?"

A muscle in Damien's jaw flexed as he ground his back teeth. "No. It's official business."

Wes set his pen aside and leaned forward. "Okay. You have my attention. What's this about?"

"It's about the person responsible for all that's been

happening around Honey Creek lately. Mark Walsh's murder, Craig Warner's poisoning, the money-laundering—" Damien's expression darkened. "I think I know who is behind all of it."

COLTON'S
SURPRISE FAMILY

BY
KAREN WHIDDON

First published in Great Britain 2011
by Mills & Boon, an imprint of Harlequin (UK) Limited,
Eton House, 18-24 Paradise Road, Richmond, Surrey TW9 1SR

© Harlequin Books S.A. 2010

ISBN: 978 0 263 88520 0

46-0411

Harlequin (UK) policy is to use papers that are natural, renewable and
recyclable products and made from wood grown in sustainable forests. The
logging and manufacturing processes conform to the legal environmental
regulations of the country of origin.

Printed and bound in Spain
by Blackprint CPI, Barcelona

Dear Reader,

I've always wanted to travel to Montana, so I loved spending my time on the Colton family ranch in my imagination. Add the Christmas holiday into the mix, and you have this writer's idea of heaven. Snow and mountains and Christmas trees—oh, my! And let's not forget the most important part—family and friends and love. So much love.

Writing a hero as damaged as Damien Colton was a challenge. Imagining how much this man must have suffered while imprisoned for a crime he didn't commit, and realizing that the scope of his loss was so much more than just time, broke my heart. Like many of you, I can't resist a gorgeous, damaged man. Luckily for him, Eve Kelley has always secretly had a thing for him, and her love just might be enough to save him.

It was a double blessing that I was able to write this story during the holiday season and many times I wrote sitting by my own decorated Christmas tree. Love makes such a wonderful Christmas gift, don't you agree?

Karen Whiddon

To my three faithful writing companions, Daisy Mae, Mitchell Thomas and Mac Macadoo. These three dogs (two miniature schnauzers and one boxer) have kept me company through so many books, barely opening their eyes when I talk to myself or pace as I try to figure out a scene. I couldn't do it without them.

Karen Whiddon started weaving fanciful tales for her younger brothers at the age of eleven. Amidst the Catskill Mountains of New York, then the Rocky Mountains of Colorado, she fueled her imagination with the natural beauty of the rugged peaks and spun stories of love that captivated her family's attention.

Karen now lives in North Texas, where she shares her life with her very own hero of a husband and three doting dogs. Also an entrepreneur, she divides her time between the business she started and writing the contemporary romantic suspense and paranormal romances that readers enjoy. You can e-mail Karen at K.Whiddon1@ aol.com or write to her at PO Box 820807, Fort Worth, TX76182, USA. Fans of her writing can also check out her website, www.KarenWhiddon.com.

Chapter 1

Reeking of whiskey, cigar smoke and some fast woman's cheap perfume, Darius Colton barely resembled the dignified patriarch Damien Colton remembered from his youth. Glaring at his prodigal son with red-rimmed eyes, Darius's upper lip curled in derision as he pondered Damien's question.

It was a question that deserved to be answered. Cursing his bad timing, Damien elaborated. "I'd like to see the bank statements for my account."

"Are you questioning my word?" Darius snarled, his consonants slightly slurred.

"No." Damien crossed his arms. "But that money should have been earning interest the entire time I was in prison. Now you're telling me there's nothing left?"

"That's exactly what I'm telling you, boy." With a dismissive smile, Darius turned away, only to glance back over his shoulder. "You've got nothing."

Damien checked his rising temper, one of the many neat tricks he'd learned while incarcerated. Who knew it would serve him so well here in the outside world?

He kept his voice level. "I never signed anything authorizing you—or anyone else—to touch that money. I need an explanation. Hell, I deserve an explanation."

In response, his sixty-year-old, white-haired father let loose with a string of curses vile enough to make a sailor blush. Darius's face went red, then purple as he glared at his son with rage-filled eyes.

So much anger. So much hate.

Fists clenched, Damien waited it out. When Darius finally ran out of steam, Damien stepped back. "We'll talk about this again when you're sober," he said. "As soon as possible."

In the act of pouring another glass of Scotch, Darius turned on him so fast the expensive liquor sloshed all over his sleeve. He didn't appear to notice or care, so intent was he on giving his son what the Colton kids used to call the death stare. If looks could kill…

"You will not mention this to me again. The subject is closed."

"Later," Damien insisted. "I promise you we will discuss this later." He'd been saying this for months now. Enough was enough.

Though Damien halfway believed if he persisted, Darius would haul off and slug him, he'd been through hell and back already. Since the day he'd been set free and the prison gates had disgorged him, he'd known that no event life might have in store for him could ever be as heinous as the day he'd been convicted of a crime he hadn't committed.

None. Ever.

So Darius blustering and trying to tell him that he'd somehow lost a three-million-dollar inheritance didn't even compare. Especially since Damien didn't believe a word his dear old father said. He needed to talk to his brothers. And Maisie, he amended silently. All of them.

And quickly. Though he'd been home for three whole months, he hadn't seen this coming. When had the old man become so…unstable and deceitful? Something had to be wrong. Darius didn't need his son's money—he had enough of his own. But why lie? Round and round Damien's mind went, trying to adjust to what had just happened. Darius couldn't have stolen his inheritance. The money had to be here somewhere. All Damien had to do was find it.

Watching as his father, whiskey glass in hand, staggered from his office to the master bedroom suites, Damien was left frustrated and empty-handed, wishing he could punch something.

Gradually, sounds from the great room penetrated his consciousness. Christmas carols, rustling and clinking and talking and laughter. He remembered now—the family was gathering for the annual Colton family Christmas-tree-decorating ceremony.

When he'd been in prison he'd dreamt of this event. Now, he wasn't even sure he'd bother to attend. He really just wanted to head out to the barn and saddle up Duncan, his favorite quarter horse gelding, and ride out to the back pastures. As a matter of fact—

"Damien!" His sister Maisie, grinning like a gleeful small child, bounced into the room. "Come on! Hurry! Wes and Duke are bringing in the tree. Finn's getting the stand ready and checking the lights. Even Perry, Brand and Joan are here along with their families! It's picture-postcard perfect. Everyone wanted to be a part of decorating for your first Christmas back with the family!"

And just like that, Maisie had deftly lobbed the ball in his court. Now he had no choice but to join the others.

Nodding, he allowed her to grab his hand and lead him into the great room. Even with almost the entire family gathered, the huge room was cozy rather than crowded. A fire roared in the massive stone fireplace and box after box of glittering ornaments were spread all over the huge oak coffee table, along with numerous strands of white lights. The place looked like a scene from a holiday magazine. Homey, folksy and warm.

And he felt completely out of place.

As Damien entered, Maisie's teenaged son Jeremy threw open the back door, letting in a gust of cold air. "Here they are!" he shouted, grinning broadly.

Covered in a light dusting of snow, Damien's twin brother Duke appeared, half carrying, half dragging the bottom of a huge spruce tree. Wes Colton held up the top part of the tree, laughing and looking for his fiancée, Lily Masterson, who was helping Duke's fiancée, Susan Kelley, organize ornaments. Even Finn Colton had driven in from town. Their youngest brother had gotten engaged to Rachel Grant, who was helping him check the light strands.

It was, Damien thought sourly, a regular love fest in here. Damien couldn't help but notice how the three outside women took pains to try and include Maisie in their little group. To his surprise, Maisie seemed to be eating it up. A genuine smile of pure happiness lit up her face and put a sparkle in her aquamarine eyes.

Happy and festive, a perfect combination. Christmas carols played and there was homemade wassail simmering in a slow cooker on a table, along with various other goodies: Christmas cookies and fudge, dip and chips, and ribbon candy. Had they gone overboard for him? Damien wondered. Or was this the normal holiday celebration here at the Colton ranch these days?

Either way, they wanted to include him. He knew

he should feel touched, but instead he only felt empty. Everyone had paired off, it seemed. Everyone except Damien. Oh, and their stepmother, Sharon, who appeared to be single-mindedly focused on drinking an entire bottle of wine by herself. No one seemed to notice or mind Darius Colton's absence.

Wes, Duke and Finn lifted the huge tree into the stand while the women oohed and aahed. The children, belonging to various branches of the Coltons in town, chased each other and laughed. Damien took a step back, intent on beating a swift exit, but Maisie saw what he was up to.

"Come on." Grabbing his hand, she pulled him closer to the tree. "I'm sure the guys need your help, right boys?"

Amid a chorus of agreement, she left him, bouncing over to help the women with the ornaments. As he helped secure the tree in the stand, Damien felt his twin's gaze on him, though he refused to meet it.

This was no good. He planned to make a quick retreat as soon as humanly possible.

"What, not feeling too Christmassy?" His brother Wes, the town sheriff, punched him lightly in the shoulder. At Damien's questioning look, he shrugged. "It's written all over your face."

"Yeah, well it's been a long time." Damien's voice sounded raspy. Eyeing each of his brothers, he couldn't help but wonder if Darius had stolen their inheritance, too.

Underneath the sparkle and tinsel, there was something rotten and foul here on the Colton ranch.

"I've got to go," he told Duke, once the tree stood tall and straight and ready for the lights.

"Where to?" Glancing at his watch, his twin grimaced.

"I thought I'd ride out and check fences in the high pasture."

"Now? It's dark and snowing. That can wait for the morning."

Feeling increasingly uncomfortable, Damien tugged the collar of his shirt. "I've got to get out of here."

Instantly, Duke's teasing smile faded. "Are you all right?" he asked, low-voiced. "You're looking a little green."

"Green?" Damien scowled. He forced himself not to bolt. "I'll be fine as soon as I get some fresh air."

Duke nodded, but Damien knew his twin didn't understand. How could he, when he'd spent his entire life enveloped in the love of his family? It was Damien who was different, Damien who was the outsider.

A few steps and Damien stood in the foyer. Already, the sense of constriction had eased somewhat. But not enough. Since it was late and dark and snowing, instead of going for a ride, he'd head into town for a beer. His favorite watering hole, the Corner Bar, would be quiet and soothing.

The short drive took longer, due to the snow. But at least the streets were mostly deserted and his four-wheel-drive pickup handled the snow with ease. He parked, noting only two other vehicles in the lot.

Stepping into the Corner Bar, he glanced around the place appreciatively. Dark and quiet and mercifully short on holiday decorations, it was exactly what he needed after the festive frenzy at the family ranch.

Stepping up to the long, polished mahogany bar, he captured a barstool. "Kind of empty tonight."

"Sure is." Without being asked, Jake, the bartender, brought him a tall Coors Light.

"Business slow during the holidays?" Damien asked, taking a long drink, enjoying the light foamy head.

"Yeah, you're my only drinking customer," Jake said, wiping at the bar counter with a rag that once might have been white and now was a cross between gray and yellow. "Except for her, and all she's drinking is a Shirley Temple."

He pointed and for the first time Damien realized he wasn't entirely alone in the place as he'd first supposed. Eve Kelley, her skin glowing softly in the dim light, occupied the corner booth, which sat mostly in shadows. With her head bent over a notebook, her long blond hair hung in silky curtains on each side of her face.

"Eve Kelley," he mused, wondering why the girl who'd been the most popular in town was all alone.

"Yeah." Leaning forward, the other man groused. "She's been here an hour and she's not even drinking alcohol. That's her second Shirley Temple."

Intrigued, Damien studied her, wondering why she'd come to a bar yet didn't drink? A problem with alcohol? She'd certainly been a party girl back in the day. Back when he'd been a senior in high school, he and she had heated up the front seat of his Ford F150. She'd been pretty and popular and since she was a few years ahead of him in school, way out of his league.

Eve had been the only one in town who'd written him a letter while he'd been in prison. Though he'd never acknowledged it, he'd always wondered why.

"I'm going to join her," Damien told the bartender.

Though the other man didn't comment, he shook his head in disapproval. He probably thought, as did most of the people in Honey Creek, Montana, that Damien was tainted.

Crossing the room to where she sat, he willed her to look up and smile, or stare or something. Anything other than recoil in horror and disgust. Though he'd been back home almost three months, he could count on the fingers of one hand the number of people who didn't act as though he was a leper.

He made it all the way to her table without her noticing.

"Enjoying your Shirley Temple?"

When she did raise her head and meet his gaze, he saw her eyes were still the same long-lashed, sapphire blue he remembered.

"It's a seven and seven," she said, making him wonder why she bothered to lie. What did she care what he thought?

"Mind if I join you?"

A flash of surprise crossed her face, and then she lifted one shoulder in a shrug. "Suit yourself."

He slid into the booth across from her, taking another long drink of his beer. "Good. I missed that while I was in prison."

Stirring her drink absently, she nodded. "I imagine there are quite a few things you missed, aren't there?"

Since she asked the question with a very real curiosity, he felt himself beginning to relax for the first time in what felt like ages. When he'd been in prison, he would have slugged anyone who tried to tell him it'd be a hundred times more tense back home than in the joint, but in reality he thought more about running away than anything else. Except sex. He thought about that a lot. Especially now. Eve Kelley, with her long blond hair and T-shirt, instantly made him think of sex.

No doubt she wouldn't appreciate knowing that, so he kept his mouth shut, giving her a nod for an answer.

Leaning forward, she studied him. Her full lips parted, making him want to groan out loud. "What did you miss the most?"

A flash of anger passed and he answered truthfully.

"The feel of a woman, soft and warm, under me, wrapped around me."

Her face flamed, amusing him. But to give her credit, she didn't look away. "I guess I sort of asked for that, didn't I?"

"No, actually you didn't." Chagrined, he offered her a conciliatory smile. "I'm sorry. I think sometimes I've forgotten how to act in public."

"I guess that's understandable."

Finishing his beer, he signaled for another one. The bartender brought it instantly, setting it on the table without comment and removing the empty glass.

"My turn." He leaned forward. "Tell me, Eve Kelley. What are you doing all alone in a bar, nursing a Shirley Temple, with a snowstorm threatening?"

"I needed to get away." For a moment, stark desperation flashed in her expressive eyes, an emotion he could definitely relate to.

"Holidays aren't all they're cracked up to be, are they?"

She shook her head, sending her large hoop earrings swinging in that mass of long straight hair.

Glancing at her left hand and seeing no ring, he took another drink. "I'm guessing you're not married?"

"Nope."

"Divorced, then?"

"Never married. I guess I just didn't meet the right person." She sighed. "I've never really minded before, but the holidays can be tough on anyone, and it's worse when you're nearly forty and still alone. My mother is now on a matchmaker tangent. She's determined to marry me off or die trying."

Her voice contained such disgust, he had to laugh.

Watching him, her lovely blue eyes widened. "You should do that more often," she said softly. "It suits you."

"Makes me look less frightening," he replied, unable to keep the bitterness from his voice. "Isn't that what you mean?"

Now she was the one who laughed and when she did, her face went from pretty to drop-dead stunningly beautiful. He watched as the flickering light danced over her creamy skin, the hollows of her cheeks, the slender line of her throat, and ached. Damn, he'd been too long without a woman.

Talking to her had been a mistake.

Yet he couldn't make himself leave this train wreck.

"You aren't frightening. Not to me," she said softly. "I forgot how funny you are. At least you kept your sense of humor."

"Maybe," he allowed, studying her. Time had been kind to her. He remembered her as a tall, elegant athletic girl, one of the popular ones that every guy lusted after. She'd been a few years out of school, but that hadn't stopped them for getting together one hot August night at a party in someone's newly harvested field. Maybe because his life had all but stopped when he'd been sent to prison, but he remembered that like it was yesterday.

Hell, for him it *was* yesterday. Sometimes he felt like a twenty-year-old kid walking around in the body of a thirty-five-year-old man. Other times he felt like he was a hundred.

Tonight, it was refreshing to be with someone who didn't act as though he were fragile or dangerous, or both.

He lifted his glass, inviting her to make an impromptu toast. "To old friends."

With a smile, she touched her glass to his. "To old friends."

"You look good, Eve."

To his disbelief, she blushed again. "Thanks. So do you. It's surprising, but you're easy to talk to."

He laughed. "Do you always say exactly what you think?"

"No. Not always. I run a beauty shop here in town—Salon Allegra, have you seen it?"

"I don't get to town much."

"I see." She nodded. "After high school, I was going to go to college, but ended up attending beauty school instead. I worked at The Cut 'N' Curl for a long time. When Irene died, she left me the place. I fixed it up and renamed it."

"You never left Honey Creek?" he asked, letting his gaze sweep her face. "Didn't you ever want to live somewhere else, to get away?"

"Not really. I've traveled a bit, but it's so beautiful here. Where else can you have all this?" She made a sweeping gesture with her hand. "Mountains and valley and endless prairie. Big Sky Country."

Despite the contentment ringing in her voice, something seemed off. He couldn't put his finger on it, not exactly, but he'd bet dissatisfaction lurked underneath her complacent exterior. The Eve Kelley he'd known had been a bit of a wild child, not this staid, watered-down version sitting in front of him.

"But didn't you ever feel like you were missing out?"

She regarded him curiously. "On what? I don't like cities and crowds and pollution. I love the big open spaces. Honey Creek has all I need."

"Really?"

She thought for a moment. "Okay, sometimes I have to head into Bozeman or Billings to shop, but most everything I could want I can get here in town."

He dipped his chin, acknowledging her words but still watching her closely. "You don't get bored?"

"How could I? I have my family and friends, my business and my family's business. No other place could give me that. And the people are friendly."

"Ah, friendly. Maybe to you. Not to me."

"That both surprises me and doesn't. Even though everyone in town knows you didn't kill Mark Walsh, they're afraid of you."

She'd succeeded in shocking him. "Afraid of me? Why? I've done nothing to them."

"You've been in prison for fifteen years. That's bound to have changed you, made you...tough."

She licked her lips and he could tell she was speaking carefully. "Some of the people in town are really scared. They don't know what kind of person you are after all this time."

Incredulous, he stared. "Are you serious? I've lived here my entire life. They know me."

"They know who you used to be. Not the man you've become."

"What about you?" Nerves jangling inside him, he leaned forward. "Do I frighten you? Are you afraid of me?"

She swallowed. "Though part of you is dark and dangerous, I'm not frightened. Actually, you intrigue me."

As soon as she spoke, her face colored, making him grin. "I didn't mean that like it sounded. It wasn't a come-on, I swear."

"Too bad," he said lightly. Then, while she appeared to be still trying to absorb this, he raised his hand to signal the bartender.

"I'll have another. And bring the lady another one, too, whatever she's drinking."

Appearing relieved, Eve settled back in her seat.

"What was it like?" she asked. "What was it like, being in jail all those years for a crime you didn't commit?"

"What do you think it was like?" Though he kept his tone light, he could feel the darkness settling over his face. "Being there was no picnic."

"I'm sorry."

"Don't be. He waved away her apology. "I'd wonder, too, if our situations were reversed."

"And now? What are you going to do now?"

Their drinks arrived, saving him from answering her question right away. He waited until the bartender had moved away, drinking deeply before meeting her gaze.

"I'd like to buy my own spread. Maybe in Nevada or Idaho. I'm not sure. But I can't stay with my family forever."

"Why not? We're going to be family soon, you know, since your brother Duke is engaged to my sister Susan. She said they're moving to his place on the ranch."

"She's there at the main house right now, decorating the Colton family tree."

"And you're not."

Instead of answering, he shrugged.

"You know, I don't understand why you'd want to leave Honey Creek. Your life is here, your heritage. Why would you want to throw all that away?"

When she looked so passionate, her blue eyes glowing, he wanted to kiss her. Hell, he wanted to do much more than that, but he'd settle for a kiss for now.

"Kind of personal, isn't it?" he drawled, leaning back in the booth.

"Come on, it's not that personal. It's not like we're complete strangers. I've known you forever. I've always envied what you have, that connection to the land."

He studied her. "You're right about that. I do love the

land, my family's ranch. If I could stay there, out on the land, and never have to deal with my father or with the town, that'd be one thing."

"You really dislike Honey Creek, don't you?"

He noticed she let the reference to his father slide. Everyone must know about his father's deterioration. Everyone but him.

"Honey Creek has nothing to hold me. You know what? You're the only person in Honey Creek other than my family who ever bothered to try to make contact with me in prison, the only one who wrote me. I never thanked you for that. I'm doing it now. Thank you."

As though she wasn't sure how to respond, she simply nodded.

"About that letter…" Dragging his hand through his longish hair, he grimaced. "I appreciate you writing it and I'm sorry I didn't answer."

"That was a long time ago. I probably shouldn't have written that."

"No." He laid his hand across the top of hers, unable to keep from noting the difference, his big and calloused while hers was slender, delicate and warm. "You probably shouldn't. But I was glad you did. You let me know that at least one person in Honey Creek believed in my innocence."

"If you felt that way, why didn't you write back?"

"Because your belief, my knowledge, was all futile. No matter what I knew, no matter what you thought, I'd been convicted. I was going to do time. Hard time. For Christ's sake, I was twenty when I went in there. I'm thirty-five now. I went in a kid and now…I'm a man. That does things to you. Prison does things to you." He hardened his voice. "I don't expect you to understand."

Pity flooded her eyes. He hated that and would have

gotten up and left if he hadn't seen something more there
too, something besides pity.

"I'm so sorry," she said.

"Yeah. Me, too." Then, maybe because some demon
drove him, he did what he'd been wanting to do since he'd
seen her. He got up, crossed over to her side of the booth
and kissed her.

Chapter 2

When Damien came around to her side of the booth and leaned over her, Eve's heart skipped a beat. As he bent close, she froze, feeling the way she imagined a deer in the headlights of a hunter's truck might feel.

And when his lips slanted over hers…she melted.

For a second, she allowed herself to revel in the feel of him, the taste and wonderful masculine scent of him, before gently pushing him away.

"Don't do that," she said, her voice shaky.

Damien leaned back, but didn't move away. Dark eyes glittering, he gave her a slow smile. "Why not?"

"Because I can't get involved with you."

"But you want to." Again he moved closer, making her pulse kick up once more.

"Yes," she admitted, licking her lips. "But I can't get involved with you or anyone right now. In any way, shape or form."

Just like that, his expression shut down. Moving stiffly, he pushed himself to his feet. "I understand."

He thought she was refusing him because he'd been in prison.

"No, you don't. Believe me."

"Whatever." Draining the last of his beer, he set the mug back on the table with a thud. "I'll go take care of the bill. You have a nice night, Eve."

Watching him walk away, she knew she should just let him go. "Wait," she called, causing both the bartender and Damien to look at her.

She shot the bartender a glare that had him turning away, suddenly busy with rearranging something behind the bar. Since Damien made no move to come back to her, she rose and walked to him instead. "If you'd just let me explain—"

"You don't have to." He cut her off, flashing her a twisted smile. Cramming his cowboy hat back on his head, he grabbed his coat from the coatrack and headed out the door.

Inexplicably close to tears, Eve watched him go. Then, avoiding the bartender's gaze, she grabbed her coat from the booth and made her way outside into the swirling, blowing snow.

Outside, the snowstorm seemed to be gathering strength. She hurried to her vehicle, shivering against the blustering wind.

Her Ford Explorer was old, but she kept it well-maintained. There was no reason for it not to start, but when she turned the key in the ignition and got only a quiet click, she knew she was in trouble.

Just to be sure, she tried again.

Nothing.

Breath blowing plumes in the frozen air, she checked

her watch. Ten o'clock. Nothing to do but go back inside the Corner Bar and see if the bartender would give her a ride home.

It was either that or call someone to come get her, and then she'd have to explain why she'd been at the bar drinking by herself.

Cursing under her breath, she pushed open the car door. The icy wind hit her like a slap to the face, making her raise the hood on her jacket as a shield. Hunched against the cold, she made her way back in the direction she'd come.

"Car trouble?" Damien Colton appeared out of the darkness, snow dusting his hair and shoulders.

Miserable, she nodded. "It won't start."

"Mind if I take a look?"

She handed over the car keys, watching as he attempted to start her car with the same results. "It's either your battery or the alternator. Either way, it's too cold and stormy to do anything about it tonight. I'll give you a ride home and you can deal with your car later."

"Great." She followed him to his pickup. At least now, he'd have no choice but to listen to her explanation.

The first thing she realized when she saw his truck was that it looked awfully familiar. "Is this the same—?"

"Truck I had back before I got convicted? Yes." He unlocked the passenger-side door and opened it for her, waiting while she climbed up before closing it.

The cab of the older truck had a bench seat. Thoughts of what she and Damien had once done on that very same seat made her flush warmly.

Once he'd gotten in, she watched as he started the engine, waiting for him to elaborate.

When he didn't, she sighed. "Look, about what I said earlier—"

"No need to explain." He cut her off brusquely. "You of all people don't owe me anything."

"I owe you an explanation. I don't want you thinking the reason I—"

Muttering a curse, he slammed on the brakes, sending the pickup into a spin on the snowy roads. They did a nearly perfect donut, ending up facing the same way they'd been going. Damien inched them forward, until they were on what appeared to be the shoulder of the road.

Then, while she still reeled with shock, he reached for her, yanking her up against him and capturing her mouth. He kissed her long and hard and deep. When he raised his head, Eve couldn't find her breath.

"What was that?"

"Me proving to you that you want me."

"I never said I didn't." She bit the inside of her cheek to keep from smiling. "I said I couldn't be in any sort of relationship with anyone right now."

"Relationship? Hell, I don't want a relationship."

Confused, she looked at him, so brooding and dark and dangerous. "Then what do you want?"

"Sex," he said, his tone harsh. "I just wanted to have sex with you."

Stunned, she couldn't think, couldn't speak, couldn't move. "Sex?" she finally repeated. "Wow, you certainly don't believe in sugarcoating it."

"Why call a spade anything other than a spade? I want you, Eve. You want me, too, I can tell. Neither one of us is attached right now and we're both adults. Why not?"

For a second she closed her eyes, tempted beyond belief. Massimo in Italy had wanted the same thing, just sex, though he'd prettied it up with honeyed words and candy-coated lies. In the end, she thought, it might have been better, at least for her, if he'd told the truth. Then maybe she wouldn't have felt like such a fool when it ended the way it had.

"I appreciate your honesty," she said slowly. "And yes, I do find you attractive. Very much so."

He crossed his arms, watching her, waiting. She recognized the look she saw on his face. He was expecting to be hurt, wounded, as he'd been for the last fifteen years. He really didn't believe she'd sleep with him, and any explanation she'd give him would reinforce his apparently deep-seated belief that he deserved to be treated poorly.

Any explanation that is, but the truth.

"Damien, I'm pregnant."

This he hadn't expected. "You're…what?"

"This summer I went to Italy. I took the trip by myself, to celebrate the last year of my thirties. When I was there, I met a man. We had the kind of thing you just proposed, only I didn't know it at the time." To her chagrin, her throat closed up.

"You're pregnant," he repeated.

"I'm pregnant."

"Does the father know?"

Now she hung her head. "This is the hardest part of my story. He disappeared. I looked for ten days, but I couldn't find him."

"You didn't know his name."

"He called himself Massimo. One word. Silly, but I thought it romantic."

Damien let that one go, bless him. "Are you keeping the baby?"

"Oh, yes." Cradling her stomach protectively, she nodded. "I want this baby very much. And you're the only one who knows."

Again she'd surprised him, judging from the look on his face. "You haven't told your family?"

"No. I'm waiting as long as I can." Oddly enough, telling him made her feel as though a heavy weight had been lifted from her shoulders. "You know how this town can be. My mom will be thrilled—she's been wanting a grandbaby for forever. But I feel sort of foolish, goofing up so badly at thirty-nine years old."

The truck heater started blasting, making them both laugh.

"I'd better get you home," he said, putting the truck back into gear.

He drove slowly, the heavy vehicle making sure progress over the snowy roads. When they reached her house, he left the engine running as he walked her to the door.

"If you ever need someone to talk to," he began, making her smile.

"Thank you. Ditto for you." Then, unable to help herself, she reached up and kissed him on the cheek.

Unmoving, he watched until she opened the door and went inside, locking it behind her.

A moment later she heard his truck drive away outside. Eyes stinging with completely unreasonable tears, she listened as the sound faded, until all she could hear was the mournful howling of the wind as it heralded the approaching storm.

Arriving back at the ranch, Damien breathed a sigh of relief when he saw that most of the cars were gone, which meant most of the huge mess of family had gone home. Except for the resident ones.

Parking his truck, he puzzled over Eve Kelley. Of all the girls he'd grown up with, he would have expected her to be married with a bunch of kids by now. Large families were common around these parts—look at his own family. She'd been pretty, popular and fun. The guys had practically fought over the chance to date her back in the day, and now she was nearly forty, unmarried and pregnant.

Talk about the randomness of fate.

None of it, not circumstances or her pregnancy, did anything to dilute his desire. He still wanted her. He'd take her up on her offer to be friends, knowing if she'd give him a chance, he'd prove to her that they could be more. Friends with benefits. He grinned savagely, liking the sound of that.

The house felt settled as he walked in, shedding his coat and hanging it in the hall closet and placing his cowboy hat on the hat rack alongside all the others. Lights from the immense Christmas tree illuminated the great room. All of the earlier boxes and mess had been cleaned away and the decorated mantel combined with the tree to look festive and, oddly enough, holy. Damien couldn't help but remember the way he'd felt as a small boy, awestruck and overwhelmed at the beautiful tree. He'd used to lie on his back underneath the branches and peer up through them, marveling.

To his surprise, a spark of that little boy still remained.

He wandered over and stood in front of the tree, still thinking of Eve, then eyed the hallway that led to his father's office. Might as well do some poking around while the entire house slept. Darius never locked the door, believing his inviolable authority made him invulnerable.

Maybe so, but Damien had been screwed over enough.

Moving quietly, he slipped down the hallway and opened the door. Conveniently, Darius had left the desk lamp on.

Damien took a seat in the massive leather chair and started with the obvious—the desk drawers. A quick search turned up exactly nothing.

But, then, what had he expected? Darius was too shrewd

to leave incriminating documents anywhere they could be easily read.

Which meant there had to be a safe.

He turned to begin searching for one when a movement from a shadowy corner made him spin around.

Duke stood watching him, leaning against the wall with his arms crossed.

"What are you doing?" Duke asked, "You know the old man's going to be pissed when he finds out you went through his papers."

"Maybe," Damien allowed. "*If* he finds out. I'm not planning on telling him. I'm trying to figure out what happened to our inheritance."

"What do you mean?"

Since Duke didn't sound too perturbed, Damien figured his brother hadn't been given the same unlikely story as he'd heard today. "I asked Darius about it earlier today. You know how I've been wanting to buy my own ranch, maybe in Nevada or Idaho?"

"Yeah." Duke uncrossed his arms and came closer. "Don't tell me he refused to give you your money. He might be conservator, but you're well over the age of twenty-one. And you were in prison at the time you turned twenty-one."

"No." Damien watched his brother closely. "He didn't refuse to give it to me. He said it was all gone."

"What?" Duke's casual air vanished. Shock filled his brown eyes, so like Damien's. "How can three million be gone, just like that?"

"Exactly. Tell me, bro. Did you get your inheritance when you turned twenty-one like you were supposed to?"

"Hell, no. He offered to let me use it to buy a share in the ranch and I took it. Darius needed cash for some reason, and I wanted to make sure I'd always have my house and land. So I bought my hundred acres from him."

"Damn." Damien closed his eyes. When he reopened them, he saw his brother watching him, a worried expression on his handsome face.

"Are you okay?"

"No," Damien exploded. "I'm not okay. The entire time I was in prison, I was counting on this money being there for me when I got out. The money the state's going to pay me won't buy even twenty acres. How the hell am I going to make a fresh start without any cash?"

"Surely there's been a mistake."

"I don't think so." Grimly, Damien resumed his search for a safe. "How good are you still at guessing lock combinations?"

"What? You mean to break into Darius's safe?"

"Once I find it, yes."

Duke narrowed his eyes. "Well, then, let me help you out. I know where it is. I've been in here often enough when Darius had to open it." He crossed to the wall where a huge, ornately framed oil painting of the ranch hung. "It's behind this."

Removing the picture revealed a small wall safe, black, with a touch-pad combination. The entire thing was maybe two feet square.

Damien stood back. "Have at it, bro." As teens, Duke had exhibited an exceptional skill for picking locks and determining combinations. Within five minutes, he had the safe open.

"There you go," he said, stepping back.

Reaching inside, Damien extracted a leather-bound notebook and a sheaf of manila folders, held together by a rubber band. There was also a tiny metal box, like the kind used for petty cash. He removed everything and placed it on the desk.

"I'm out of here, man," Duke said.

"Will you just stand guard for me? I just need a few minutes." He started with the leather book. "Surely there's something in here that will tell what happened to my inheritance."

Inside the book were receipts for wire transfers. All of them were withdrawals from his account made over a period of three years. "Bingo," he said softly. "My money."

Though clearly reluctant, Duke moved over to take a look.

"How do you know it was yours?" Duke asked. "You know when Grandfather died he left all of our money in the same account. I authorized Darius to take mine, and maybe Wes, Finn, Maisie and the others did the same."

"But I didn't authorize anything. Yet Darius claims the account has been closed and there's nothing there."

"Did you see the bank statement?"

"He wouldn't let me." Damien flashed him a grim smile, reaching for the manila folders. "Oh, damn."

"That looks like a second set of accounting records for the Colton ranch." Duke scratched his head. "Why would he have that? Unless…"

Without answering, Damien continued digging. "Look here. A list of some sort of vendors and receipts for transactions."

"Transactions of what?"

"I don't know." But he had a good idea. The FBI had approached him shortly after he'd been released from prison, intimating they were investigating Darius. Damien, still smarting from his father's refusal even to visit him in prison, had agreed to act as their insider, an informant of sorts. This was exactly the sort of thing they'd expect him to report.

"I think our father has been running a little business on the side."

Duke cursed. "What are you going to do? You can't be thinking of turning him in?"

"I don't know."

"Damien, you know how the old man is. I doubt he'd survive a year being locked up. I'm not sure I could do that to him."

"But then again, he didn't steal your money, did he? You handed it over to him, lock, stock and barrel."

"Please, think about this before you do anything rash."

Flipping through the last of the folders, Damien reached for the metal box. Duke reached for his hand to stop him. "Hold up."

"What?"

"You've found enough. Put it back. I think we need to talk to Wes and Finn before we do anything."

Clenching his jaw, Damien stared at his twin. "I'm not asking you to do anything."

"This is a family matter." Moving with purpose, Duke took the metal box, folder and notebook and placed them back in the safe, exactly the way they'd been. "We—or you—aren't doing anything until we talk to the others."

"What about Maisie?" Damien asked. "She has a right to be involved, too."

Duke shot him a hard glance. "If you can trust her to keep her mouth shut, fine. But you know, she's been contacting that TV show, trying to get them out here to do an exposé on the town."

"She's been talking about that, but I don't think anyone there took her seriously."

"I know. Let's keep it that way, okay?"

Reluctantly, Damien agreed, watching as Duke resecured the safe and replaced the painting.

"Come on," his brother said, putting a hand on Damien's shoulder. "Let's go to the kitchen and see if we can rustle up a late-night snack. There are bound to be some of those hot wings left."

Feeling both disgruntled and slightly relieved, Damien agreed. A decision needed to be made about Darius, but he wouldn't have to make it alone.

The next morning the snowplows worked the roads bright and early. Eve woke to the peculiar blinding whiteness of sun on snow. As she padded to the kitchen to make a pot of decaf and get the hearth fire going before letting Max out, she couldn't stop thinking of Damien and his offer.

Just looking at the man made her mouth go dry. What he proposed was very, very tempting. The fact that she could even think like this should have made her angry with herself, but she was pragmatic at heart and believed in calling a spade a spade.

Damien Colton made her go weak in the knees. Always had, always would.

The knowledge unsettled her. So much so that after she'd finished her first cup of coffee, she started cleaning her kitchen. She knew she'd find comfort in the physical work and satisfaction in the finished results.

About ninety minutes into her cleaning binge, when she'd finished the kitchen and the two bathrooms and started on the den, Max's barking alerted her that a car had pulled up into the drive. Her mother. Perspiring and grungy, and knowing she could use a break, Eve went to the front door and opened it wide.

"You're out bright and early on a snowy morning," she said brightly.

Bonnie Gene's gaze swept over her daughter. "It's not morning. It's well after noon."

"Well, good afternoon then." Eve wiped her hands on her sweats. "You caught me in the middle of cleaning. What's going on?" Moving aside, she waited until her mother entered before closing the door.

"I have fantastic news!" Bonnie Gene gushed the moment she stepped inside. Sweeping into the foyer in her usual dramatic fashion, she eyed Eve's pitiful attempts at Christmas decorating before focusing back on her daughter.

"You are not going to believe this. Guess what I've arranged?"

"I'm almost afraid to ask."

"Can the sarcasm." Too excited to note—or care about—Eve's less-than-enthusiastic reaction, Bonnie Gene clapped her gloved hands together. "I've set you up on a blind date."

"Not another blind date," Eve protested.

"This is not an ordinary blind date—it's the coup de grâce of all blind dates! You are going out with Gary Jackson!"

"Who?"

"You know, Gary Jackson the attorney? He just moved here a few months ago and I know for a fact all the single girls want to go out with him. He's tall, handsome and—"

"Full of himself." Eve dragged her hand through her hair. "Mother, we agreed. No more blind dates."

"*You* agreed. I said nothing. And listen, this one is too good to be true. You can't pass this up."

"Does he even know?"

Bonnie blinked. "What?"

"Does this Gary Jackson even know he has a blind date

with me? Remember, the last guy you set me up with and forced me to go on a date with had no idea. I was never so embarrassed in my life."

"Oh, for Pete's sake." Bonnie Gene rolled her eyes. "It all worked out, if I remember correctly."

"No, it didn't. He was a stalker, mother. I had to get Wes Colton involved. Thank goodness that guy left town."

Removing her coat, Bonnie Gene wandered into the great room, standing in front of the fire. "Ahhh. That feels so good. Listen, both Gary's mother and I went through a lot of work to arrange this. I'd really appreciate you going on this date. As a favor to me."

The old guilt trick. Eve refused to fall for it. "No."

"Come on. What else do you have to do?"

Eve crossed her arms. "Do you really want a list?"

Dropping down onto the couch, her mother sighed, removing her gloves and scarf and loosening her coat. "You know I only want what's best for you."

"Yes, but you've got to stop this obsessive trolling to find me a husband. I'm nearly forty. I can find my own man."

"Oh, can you?" Bonnie Gene pounced. "Then tell me, what have you been doing to try and meet someone?"

"Here we go again. Mother, don't start."

"Fine. But you know I want grandchildren."

If ever Eve had been tempted to reveal her pregnancy, now would be the time. But her mother would broadcast the news all over town and right now, with the Mark Walsh fiasco in full swing, the last thing Honey Creek needed was more scandal. Nope, Eve just wanted to get through the holidays before dropping her bombshell.

"I know you want grandchildren, Mother. You've informed me of that nonstop for the last ten years."

"Well, then," Bonnie said brightly. "Since I've already arranged this date, will you please go?"

Bonnie Gene looked so contrite, Eve softened. As she always did. Sucker. "I'll go, but only if you give me your absolute word that this is the last blind date you arrange for me."

Grinning, Bonnie Gene nodded. "Do you want me to pinky swear?"

"Just give me your word, Mother."

"Fine." Huffing, Bonnie Gene grimaced. "You have my word. No more blind dates."

"Ever."

"Fine. No more blind dates ever." Her frown faded and she grinned. "Maybe this date with Gary Jackson will lead to something permanent and you won't *need* another blind date."

Oh geez. "Maybe. Who knows?" Sighing, Eve went into the kitchen. "Would you like a cup of tea?"

"I'd love one. Do you want my help picking out an outfit for your date?"

Midway to the kitchen, Eve paused. Turning, she eyed her mother, dreading the answer yet knowing she had to ask.

"When is this date with Gary Jackson, by the way?"

"Tonight."

Chapter 3

Eve nearly said a curse word in front of her mother. "Tonight? How could you do this to me?"

"Please," Bonnie scoffed. "You've got over six hours to get ready. It's not like you have to be there for lunch or anything."

"Where's there?"

"You're meeting him for drinks and dinner at the Corner Bar and Grill."

Of course. Her mother knew that was Eve's favorite place, as well as the second-most popular place in town, Kelley's Cookhouse being first.

Putting the kettle on the stove, Eve got out two mugs and two teabags of orange pekoe tea.

"Everyone will see me there," she groused, secretly glad her mother hadn't chosen to have her meet Gary at the family's barbecue restaurant. She'd done that before and Eve had spent the entire evening answering questions about what it was like to be part of the family that owned a famous franchised restaurant. Worse, her date had expected free food and had ordered one of everything on the menu. He'd been shocked, then angry, when Eve had informed him they still had to pay.

"Exactly! There's a live band tonight, the High Rollers, I think. So you know the place will be packed. Everyone will see you there with Gary," Bonnie enthused. "That man is quite a catch. The town will be talking about it for days!"

A catch? Mentally, she rolled her eyes. "Honestly, Mom. I'm not exactly fishing."

"No, you're not," her mother said with a wry twist of her mouth. "Which is why I have to help you. You've got me baiting the hook and casting for you. Now all you've got to do is reel him in."

Reel him in. Had they been mysteriously teleported back to the fifties when she hadn't been looking? Deciding to ignore the phrase, as she always did when Bonnie Gene started on this subject, Eve stared at the teakettle, willing it to whistle. A good cup of tea went far to sooth frazzled nerves.

Taking her silence for assent, Bonnie Gene came closer. "What are you going to wear? If you'd like, I could pick out your outfit."

"Oh, for—" Biting off the words, Eve forced a smile. "Mom, don't worry about that. I've got it covered."

Six hours later, standing in front of the mirror, Eve wondered why she'd agreed to this. She couldn't help but wonder if Gary Jackson wondered the same thing. If he was such a "catch," as her mother put it, she doubted he needed to be set up on a blind date.

But, heavens knows, Bonnie Gene Kelley could be pretty persistent when she wanted to be.

For her dinner date, Eve had chosen a thick sweaterdress with a cowl neckline in flattering shades of brown, cream and gold. Brown leggings and soft suede knee-length boots completed her outfit. She brushed her shoulder-length blond hair until it shone, swiped a tube of lip gloss over her lips, and told herself she was ready.

In fact, she'd rather be doing almost anything else. Even pooper-scooping Max's poo seemed preferable to yet another blind date set up by her own mother. How pathetic was that?

Still, she reminded herself, slipping on her parka and snagging her purse and car keys on her way out, none of this was Gary Jackson's fault. He could be a nice guy. She should give him a chance.

Thirty minutes later, covertly checking her watch, she knew she'd been wrong. From the instant she'd walked into the Corner Bar and taken a seat in the booth across from him, Gary Jackson had talked nonstop. About his law practice, what kind of car he drove, what stocks he'd invested in, where he lived and what kind of furniture graced his abode, blah, blah, blah. Every single time she thought he might be winding down, he'd start on another tangent. About himself, of course.

No wonder the guy couldn't find a date. She'd be willing to bet he'd jumped on the chance when her mother had offered her as the sacrificial lamb.

Poker-faced, she sipped her soft drink and tried to keep from yawning. Even on a weekend date, the man wore a button-up shirt and tie, along with a wool sport jacket and slacks.

"Anyway, when they asked me to help out with the Mark Walsh investigation…"

Finally, something interesting. "You're helping out with that? How? You're a lawyer, not a criminal investigator."

She'd barely got the words out before Gary was off and running. Not about the Mark Walsh case, which she might have been interested in hearing, instead, he rambled on about how anyone, even the lowliest criminal, needed an attorney and how lucky the people of backwater Honey Creek, Montana, were to have him. Because he was the best, the brightest, the most like a shark, etc.

While she sat, steaming and wishing she could drink alcohol. Since she couldn't, she practiced scathing remarks she'd like to say but couldn't.

Finally, she'd had enough. "Excuse me," she tried to interrupt. Either Gary had gone hard of hearing or was so involved in what he was saying that she had to repeat herself three times. In the end, she simply got to her feet, waved her hand at him, and headed toward the restroom. She could have sworn he continued talking to the air after she'd left.

This was a disaster. If it weren't that her mother would find out, she'd sneak out the back and leave him talking to himself.

The hallway to the restrooms was long and blessedly deserted. She took her time, aware that every second away from Gary was a second of peace and quiet. Finally she had no choice but to make her way back.

"Eve?" a deep familiar voice called her name.

Looking up, her heart skipped a beat. Her body, numbed by Gary's endless rambling, came gloriously, fully awake and alive. "Damien." She tried to sound casual. "What are you doing here?"

"Hoping to run into you," he answered, making her blush. "And here you are." He sounded so pleased, she had to smile. "Do you want to join me for a drink and a snack? Just to talk."

Talk about tempting. She had a brilliant idea. "I can't

join you, because I'm here with someone." Quickly she told him about her mother's scheme and Gary Jackson. "I want out of this, but I can't get him to shut up long enough to tell him so. Please, join us for dinner. Maybe then he'll get the hint."

Expression serious, he studied her face. "This is the second time I've helped you out, you know. After this, you'll owe me a date, just the two of us."

"Done." She'd have agreed to almost anything to end the torture of Gary, but a date with Damien seemed more like a reward than a payment of a debt. "So that means you'll help me out? I hate to ask, but…"

His smile took her breath away. "Sure, I will. But first, come here."

Pulse kicking back up, she didn't move. "No."

"Chicken."

"Maybe," she acknowledged. "But I need to know what you mean."

"A simple kiss. That's all I want."

"Here?"

He glanced around. "Sure, why not? We're in a dark hallway and unless someone comes down this way, no one will see."

Temptation. She realized suddenly that there was nothing she wanted more than to kiss him. But not the kind of kiss she could do here, standing in a hallway in the Corner Bar.

"My kiss," he reminded her. "Yes or no? Your call."

Moving closer, but standing far enough back that no part of their bodies touched, she leaned in, intent on making this a quick, touch-her-lips-to-his, peck-type kiss.

Instead, he yanked her up to him. "Real kiss," he growled. "I haven't been able to stop thinking about our last one. Now lay it on me."

At first she couldn't move. Paralyzed by indecision and the knowledge that the blind date from hell waited in the other room, she let panic immobilize her. For maybe all of three seconds.

Then she reached up and pulled him down to her. Slanting her mouth over his, she kissed him like they were alone in her bedroom, kissed him like she'd secretly been longing to do ever since she'd seen him, kissed him openmouthed and insistent and full of pent-up longing and desire.

When she finally raised her head, they were both breathing hard.

"There," she said, trying for a light teasing tone. "Now will you join me for dinner?"

Eyes dark and glittering, he nodded.

"Come on then." She took his arm. "Let me introduce you two. My date thinks he's an expert on the Mark Walsh investigation, though for the life of me I don't know what he has to do with it."

From the sudden tension in Damien's body, she judged she'd said the wrong thing. But there was no time to fix it since they'd almost reached the table.

Gary stood, appearing comically surprised that she'd already returned. Or, she surmised, watching his eyes widen as he saw Damien, shocked that she'd brought back an escort, especially one as big and muscular and male as Damien.

Speaking briskly, she made the introductions. "Gary Jackson, Damien Colton. Damien, Gary."

The two men shook hands. Then Damien pulled out a chair and, instead of taking a seat, turned it around and straddled it. "Let me buy you both a drink. What are you drinking, Gary?"

"Scotch on the rocks, neat," Gary responded. Since Eve

knew he'd been drinking a beer, she shot him a look, which he promptly ignored.

Trying not to watch Damien, trying not to think about that kiss and what else she wanted to do with him, she watched Gary instead. For once, eying Damien, her formerly talkative date appeared at a loss for words.

Signaling the waitress, Damien ordered. "Scotch for him, Coors Light for me, and a Shirley Temple for the lady."

"How'd you know that's what she was drinking?" Gary asked.

Damien shrugged. "Eve and I go way back. She was telling me you're involved in the Mark Walsh murder investigation? How so?"

"Part of my job dictates that I occasionally have to do pro bono work as a public defender. When—and if—the police find any suspects, I'm on call in case they can't afford an attorney." He spread his hands. "They won't even realize how lucky they are. I was the best criminal attorney in Fargo before I moved here and switched to private practice."

Eve glared at him. "So you're actually not working on the case then. You're just prepared to help if they need you?"

Before he could answer, Damien stood, waving. "Maisie. Over here."

Wearing a full-length fake fur and stiletto-heeled boots, Maisie Colton looked like a glamorous movie star. She breezed up to their table, giving Damien a quick hug before turning to face Eve and Gary.

"Hi, Eve," she said dismissively, turning to Gary, eyeing his clean-cut features and business attire. "Who are you? I don't believe we've met."

"Maisie Colton, meet Gary Jackson. Gary, this is Maisie, Damien's sister."

To Eve's amazement, Gary's face turned beet-red as he took Maisie's perfectly manicured hand. "My pleasure," he murmured, kissing her hand.

It took every bit of Eve's self-restraint to keep from rolling her eyes. She didn't dare glance at Damien to see his reaction.

For her part, Maisie appeared to be eating it up. Fluttering her long lashes, she took a seat, perching on the end of the bench. "I can't believe I haven't met you. Have you been in town long?"

Gary had to lean across the table to hear her breathy question, jabbing Eve with his elbow in the process.

"You know what?" Eve said, pushing to her feet. "I think I'm going to have to call it a night. It was nice to meet you, Gary."

"Likewise," he said, never tearing his gaze away from Maisie's perfect features. "Have a nice night."

"Excuse me." Damien nudged Maisie to get up so he could get out. "I need to be going, too."

Maisie slid out without protest, taking her seat back immediately after Damien stood. As Eve turned to go she saw Maisie reach across the table and capture Gary's hand.

"They deserve each other," Damien said, helping Eve on with her coat. "Let me walk you to your truck."

"This will be all over town by morning." Glancing around, Eve saw half of the place watching her and Damien and the other half staring at Gary and Maisie.

"Gossip. Don't worry about it."

"Easy for you to say. You forget, I run a beauty shop, aka gossip central. I will hear about this on Tuesday, both from my customers and from my mother." She brightened.

"Though at least I can blame Maisie for the failed date. That way I don't have to tell my mother that I thought Gary was a jerk."

One hand on the door handle, Damien stopped and studied Eve's face. "You seem to spend a lot of time pretending to be something you're not. That's not the Eve Kelley I remember."

Stunned, she could only retort with the first thing that came to her. "Maybe your memory's faulty."

Brushing past him, she slipped out the door.

She should have known he wouldn't give up that easily.

"Eve, wait."

"Oh, won't this give them something to talk about," she groused.

"Why are you so worried about what people think?"

"I'm not." With a sigh, she acknowledged her lie. "Okay, maybe I am. A little. But you have to understand what will happen when I open the salon tomorrow. Every one of my customers, whether or not they have an appointment, will be stopping by to ask about this."

"Are you sure you're not exaggerating?"

Tilting her head, she thought for a second. "I'm sure."

"What about him?" He jerked his head toward the bar. "Is he all right to leave with Maisie?"

"Oh, sure." Unable to suppress a grin, she shook her head. "Who knows? Maybe they're perfect for each other."

"Maybe. Eve, I—"

Suddenly skittish, Eve took a step back. "Damien, I've got to go."

One corner of his mouth lifted in an amused smile. "Have a nice night. I'll see you tomorrow then."

This stopped her short. "Tomorrow? For what?"

"Our date. Remember?"

Her stomach rolled. "You didn't say it would be so soon."

He took a step toward her, causing her to move back. "Eve, what are you so afraid of? Is it me?"

Oh, God, did he really think she was like some of the other people in town, frightened of him because he'd been in prison?

"It's not that. I told you, I don't want or need to get involved with anyone right now."

"We don't have to get involved." He held out his hand. "Just friends."

Blood humming, she stared at him. Then, slowly, she took his hand. "Friends," she said. Because the feel of his large, calloused hand enveloping hers made her want to touch more of him, she jerked her hand free. Moving so quickly she slid on the snow-covered ice, she headed for her car with the sound of his very male laughter following her.

Watching Eve drive away, Damien debated returning to the Corner Bar and finishing his beer. Finally, he decided against it, not wanting to interfere with Maisie and her apparent fascination with Eve's blind date. Still, he had to see if his sister wanted a ride home.

Entering the bar's warmth, he headed for the booth. Maisie and Gary were so engrossed in conversation that neither noticed his approach.

"Maisie, I'm about to head home."

"Oh." She pouted, slanting a look of invitation at Gary under her long eyelashes. "Then I guess I have to go."

"I can drive you home later," Gary gallantly offered.

In response, her brilliant smile was designed to blind. Tongue in cheek, Damien watched as the other man fell for it, hook, line and sinker. Poor guy could barely form a coherent thought, he was so taken with Maisie.

Kind of the way Damien felt about Eve.

Saying his goodbyes, Damien headed back into the cold and climbed into his pickup.

On the way home, acting completely on impulse, he turned down the road that led toward Eve's place. Yellow light beamed from the windows, warm and inviting. Cruising to a stop in front of her house, he eyed the beautiful log home. What would she do if he went up and rang the doorbell? Would she let him in or turn him away?

Debating, he finally put the truck in Drive and turned around, this time heading back to the Colton ranch.

Arriving at home, he parked and went around to the back door, knowing this way he had a better chance of avoiding Darius if he were skulking around and drinking. Coming in through the mudroom, off the back downstairs bathroom, he opened the door quietly, trying to make as little noise as possible, and just about ran into Jeremy, Maisie's fourteen-year-old son.

Even with the lights off, Damien could see the boy had been crying. Tears still glittered on his adolescent cheeks.

"Are you okay?" Damien asked, hating the inane question, but not sure if his nephew would welcome his intrusion.

"No." Jeremy sniffed, swiping at his face. "I'm not okay."

Which meant either Darius or Maisie had done something. And, since Maisie was still in town with Gary Jackson, his money was on Darius.

"What's the matter?"

"Darius," Jeremy snarled. "Darius is what's the matter."

The first time Damien had heard his nephew address

his grandfather by his given name, he'd been startled, but Maisie had told him Darius had forbidden the use of any name relating to grandfather. Figured. He'd always refused to allow his own children to call him Dad or even Father.

"What about Darius?" Damien asked cautiously. "What's he done now?"

"What hasn't he done? He makes my mother look like a saint. He's crazy."

Instantly wary, since he'd thought pretty much the same thing, Damien scratched his head. "Maybe so," he allowed. "But you still haven't told me what happened."

About to speak, Jeremy made a gagging sound and jerked away. He ran for the toilet and hunched over it while he threw up.

Alcohol? Food poisoning? Damien tried to remember all the crazy stunts he himself had tried at fourteen. He'd only been home a few months, but from what he'd seen of Jeremy, the kid appeared to be a real straight arrow.

Waiting patiently, Damien handed his nephew a paper towel to wipe his mouth.

"You've got to help me," the boy blurted. "Darius said he's selling my horse."

"What?" Damien drew back. "Why? What'd you do?"

Selling someone's horse was the worst possible punishment for a cowboy on a ranch. A horrible suspicion occurred to him. "Were you drinking or using drugs?"

"No." Now Jeremy appeared shocked. "Of course not. Darius caught me smoking cigarettes out by the barn."

Cigarettes? "When did you start smoking?"

"I didn't. I just wanted to try them to see what they were like."

"Ah, I see. I'm guessing he took them away?"

"No." The teenager gagged again, staggering back to the commode and retching. This started him crying again.

Through his sobs, he glared up at Damien. "Darius made me eat them."

"Eat them? I don't understand."

"He fed me the cigarettes. One by one. Made me chew and swallow each and every one of them, even the one I'd started to smoke." The kid started looking green again. He swallowed hard. "And now I'm sick."

Stunned, Damien couldn't understand his father's logic. "That's..."

"Crazy. I know, right?"

"Yeah." Damien, too, had tried cigarettes around that age. He hadn't liked it, and had never picked up a pack again, even in prison, where there were so little pleasures that men took whatever they could get.

He waited until Jeremy seemed all right.

"How long ago did this happen?"

"Half an hour. Why?"

"Just wondering where Darius is."

Anger flashed again in the teenager's eyes. "I don't know."

"Where's everyone else?"

Lifting one thin shoulder in a shrug, Jeremy gagged again. "Dunno."

Which meant no one else was around. Duke was probably out with Susan and Wes and Finn had long ago gone home. Damien and Maisie had both been in town.

Jeremy had been left on his own with Darius. Sure, Sharon had probably been here, but the woman stayed in her room ninety percent of the time.

Damn. Damien wanted to punch something. Or someone. He really didn't want another confrontation with Darius right now.

"If he sells Charger, I'm going to run away," Jeremy vowed. "I've raised that gelding from a colt."

"I know you have," Damien soothed. "I've heard he's a fine stock horse, too."

"He ought to be." Jeremy lifted his chin, furiously wiping at his tear-streaked cheeks. "I've spent the better part of three years working with him."

"That long?"

"Yep. Darius gave him to me for my eleventh birthday."

"That settles it. You can't take back a birthday present."

"I know. But you know what he said? If he gives, he can sure as hell take away."

"I'll talk to him," Damien heard himself promise. "I won't let him sell Charger."

Jeremy lifted his head. Hope flashed in his young face. "You mean it?" Then, before Damien could answer, the fourteen-year-old launched himself at his uncle, barreling into him and wrapping his arms around him tightly.

"I'll try," Damien choked out.

"Thank you, thank you," the boy muttered fervently. "I can't let anything happen to Charger. He's all I've got."

Something in the kid's broken tone reminded Damien of himself. Except Jeremy at least had a horse. Damien had nothing and no one. But then, he didn't need anyone. Jeremy plainly did.

"You have your mother," Damien pointed out. "She might have her problems, but she loves you."

"I guess."

Ruffling the kid's hair, Damien slung his arm across his shoulders. "No guessing about it. I know. Now come on. Let's see if I can rustle us up any of the mulled apple cider they were drinking the other day."

Jeremy nodded.

As they started walking toward the kitchen, they heard a scream. Loud, feminine and terrified.

"Wait here." Pushing the kid back, Damien rushed into the great room. There, cowering in a corner near the fireplace, crouched Sharon, Darius's wife. Darius stood over her holding a fire poker.

Chapter 4

"Darius." Damien spoke in a calm, measured voice. "What are you doing?"

When the older man swung his head around and attempted to focus his bloodshot eyes on his son, Damien realized his father was once again drunk.

Smashed, plastered, blotto.

Behind him, he heard a gasp. Jeremy had ignored his request to stay behind.

"Jeremy, go back in the kitchen."

"No." The fourteen-year-old's voice wavered, but he stood his ground.

Damien returned his attention to his father. "Put the poker down."

"This is a family matter," Darius snarled. "Nothing to do with you."

The inference being that he wasn't family. Used to his father's jabs, Damien ignored that, aware he had to steer

Darius away from Sharon. Redirecting his anger might be the only way to accomplish that. But first, he had to make sure Jeremy was out of the way.

"What are you doing, Darius?" Damien moved closer, praying his nephew had the good sense to stay back. "Sharon's your wife. Surely you don't mean to hurt her?"

Confusion briefly flashed across Darius's mottled face, before the alcohol-inspired rage replaced it. "She belongs to me, boy. I'll do whatever I damn well please."

Sharon made a soft moan of pain, drawing Darius's attention.

"Darius," Damien barked, taking another step forward. "Like hell you will. You'll have to go through me first."

"Fine," Darius snarled. "I will."

He swung the poker at Damien at the same moment as Damien kicked out his leg. The old man fell, the poker went flying into the bricks with a clatter, and Sharon Colton crumpled to the rug, unconscious.

Narrowly missing hitting his head on the hearth, Darius let out a bellow of fury and frustration and pain as he climbed toward his feet, starting for his wife.

After kicking the fireplace tool over to Jeremy, Damien grabbed his father, afraid Darius would start whaling on Sharon with his fists next.

Instead, as Damien wrapped him in a bear hug, the elder Colton folded up into himself, wrapping his arms around his own middle and rocking. Crying great sobs, he mumbled under his breath to himself, tears streaming down his face, all the while shooting an occasional death glare up at his son.

Not sure how to take this bizarre behavior, Damien glanced at Jeremy. The teen appeared flabbergasted and shell-shocked. Not good. He needed something to do.

"Jeremy, check on Sharon." Barking out the order, he saw his nephew jump. "Make sure she's breathing."

While Jeremy hurried over, Damien slowly let go of his father, who had hunched over and was now making a soft keening sound, like a wounded animal.

Obviously, he had more going on than a problem with alcohol.

"She's breathing," Jeremy said, checking his stepmother's pulse. "I think she just fainted."

"Okay, good." Trying to think what to do, Damien fished his cell phone out of his pocket and called his twin brother.

"Be right there," Duke said, after Damien explained the situation.

Darius's keening grew louder.

"What's wrong with him?" Wide-eyed, Jeremy stared at his grandfather. "Is he having a stroke?"

"I don't know. He's having something. Let's see if we can get Sharon to wake up. I want to make sure she didn't hit her head or injure herself in any way."

As soon as he got close to Sharon, Damien smelled the strong scent of alcohol. "She's been drinking," he said flatly.

"Maybe she and Darius were drinking together."

"Maybe." But in his experience, Darius's wife did as little as possible with her husband. In fact, she seemed to go out of her way to avoid him. His brothers had already begun taking bets as to how long she could hold out.

During his time home with Darius, Damien couldn't blame her. If he were in her shoes, he'd have hightailed it out of Honey Creek a long time ago.

Maybe she was like him. He took another look at her, still out of it and now snoring peacefully. Maybe she had nowhere else to go and no money of her own to make a new life. As with both his previous wives, Darius had most likely made her sign a prenup, ensuring she got nothing if she left.

"Hey, guys. What happened?" The tension seemed to dissipate slightly as Duke strode into the room. Ignoring their father, who'd gone silent and appeared to have passed out, he crossed to Damien and Jeremy.

Briefly, Damien relayed the night's events, letting Jeremy interject with his story. When they'd finished, Duke shook his head. "You know, Maisie's been trying to tell me things were getting bad here. I thought she was being her usual melodramatic self."

"If Maisie's been dealing with stuff like this, why the hell is she leaving Jeremy here alone?"

Duke looked directly at Jeremy. "Have you witnessed this sort of behavior much before now?"

"No, sir, not this bad. Lot's of yellin' and name-callin'. But nothing physical. Not like this at all. Darius hasn't ever acted so crazy."

"He's drunk," Damien said. "Not that being soused excused him acting like this, but it sure helps explain it."

"How do you know he's drunk?" Duke asked.

"Go take a whiff of him. He smells like he's taken a bath in Scotch."

"And Sharon's drunk, too," Jeremy added. "But she smells more like wine than hard stuff."

"I'll take your word for it. That's all the proof I need." Duke didn't even bother walking over to Darius. "Will you help me get Sharon to her room?"

"Sure," Damien nodded. "But what about him?"

"We'll come back and get him next."

Once they had both Darius and his wife safely in their separate beds, they all trooped in to the kitchen.

Rummaging in the refrigerator, Damien located the jug of apple cider and poured them each a glass.

"How long has this been going on?" Duke asked, dropping his large frame into a chair.

"You tell me." Crossing his arms, Damien faced his twin.

"Hey, I don't live here. You do. I knew his mental stability appeared to be shaky, but I had no idea he was this bad. I've never seen him like this. I don't want to ever see him like this again."

"He threatened to sell my horse," Jeremy put in. "And made me eat an entire pack of cigarettes."

"He did what?" Maisie, carrying her high heels and walking on stocking feet, entered the kitchen. "Where is that sorry sack of—"

"He's unconscious." Damien cut her off. "Passed out. He was stone-cold drunk when I got here."

"He attacked Sharon with the fire thingee," Jeremy put in. "We had to stop him from bashing her head in."

Maisie nodded, apparently unconcerned, then went to the cabinet, grabbed a glass and helped herself to some apple cider. "So where is he now?"

"Duke and I carried him to his room."

"I hope you left him on the floor. That would serve him right for what he did."

"Maise?" Damien leaned forward. "You're around here more than anyone. How long has he been this bad?"

Her angry smile faded. "A good while. But he seemed to get worse after you got out of prison."

"Has he attacked you?" Duke sounded horrified. And Damien noticed the way Jeremy suddenly seemed to find the kitchen floor absolutely fascinating.

"Nothing I couldn't handle," Maisie snapped. But her

heightened color told them all she was lying. Maisie always blushed when she wasn't telling the truth.

They all sat in silence for a moment, Damien trying to digest this sudden, radical shift in his world.

"You didn't know about this?" Duke directed his question at Damien.

"Hell, no. I spend as little time here at the house as possible. Most days I'm out riding herd on the cattle or checking the fences and pastures. What about you?"

"I don't live here. So no, I knew the old man seemed a little off, but not to this extent."

"He must have had an iron grip on his control all this time and now it's slipping. I've seen men like that in prison."

"We've got to do something," Duke mused. "But what?"

Maisie rolled her eyes. "As long as he doesn't hurt anybody…"

"He nearly hurt Sharon. And he made Jeremy eat an entire pack of cigarettes."

"True." She rounded on her son. "I want you to stay away from him, you hear me?"

Instantly defensive at her sharp tone, Jeremy's expression changed into that sullen, bored look all teenagers master. Damien remembered it well from his own childhood.

"I'd like to run away from here," Jeremy mumbled.

Perfect. "You know what?" Damien pushed to his feet. "Once I get the financial problem settled, I'm out of here. Maisie, Jeremy, you're both welcome to come with me."

"Awesome!"

"Financial problem?" Maisie frowned. "Just get your inheritance. That should be enough."

Damien exchanged a look with Duke. "Uh, yeah, about that. Maise, did you get your money?"

"No. Darius keeps it for me. He puts a monthly allowance

in my checking account so I can shop." She glanced from one to the other, narrowing her eyes. "Why?"

Damien told her about his conversation with Darius, finishing with, "I'm trying to find out exactly what happened to the money."

"Be careful," she said darkly. "I have a feeling there are things about Darius that we're all better off not knowing." She went to her son and put her arm around him, ignoring his sounds of protest.

"Come on, Jeremy. Time to go to bed. You've got school in the morning. As a matter of fact…" Her bright-aqua gaze pinned Damien and then Duke. "You two should turn in, too. Though the sun rises later this time of the year, you know how much work there will be in the morning."

She left, dragging Jeremy with her. After she'd gone, Damien glanced at Duke. "What do you know? Our big sister actually sounded practical."

"I know." Duke grabbed his Stetson and crammed it back on his head. "And she's right. I'm heading home. I'll see you tomorrow morning at the barn."

Locking the door behind him, Damien trudged up the stairs to his room, hoping the bone-deep exhaustion he felt would allow him finally to get a good night's sleep.

The next morning Damien woke pissed off and aroused. He needed a woman. Immediately, he thought of Eve. He'd been dreaming about her again. He couldn't help but hope that eventually, she might want him, too. Even if she had refused his offer to become his bedroom partner, he'd seen the desire in her beautiful blue eyes.

But for now, he'd leave her alone. As he'd done in the past, he'd find other outlets for his need. Meanwhile, he'd put in a call to his brother Wes, asking to meet him at the Corner Bar for lunch. He had several things he wanted to discuss with him, especially Darius's behavior.

Damien hurried through his morning preparations, showering and dressing in a hurry. On his way out, he stopped in the kitchen and picked up one of the sausage breakfast sandwiches the cook made for the ranch hands and a cup of hot coffee. Then he hurried outside, turning up the collar of his down jacket against the biting ice of the winter wind.

Walking to the barn, he finished the last bite of the sandwich, washing it down with the hot coffee. Fortified, he slipped on his gloves and went to saddle up his gelding. He'd ride out and join Duke and the other hands, aware they had to bring the cattle in from the pastures in the higher elevations before the forecasted blizzard.

They finished driving the cattle shortly before noon. Damien brushed down his horse and washed up in the barn washroom, before driving into town. He parallel-parked on Main Street and fed the meter, surprised that he'd managed to snag a primo parking spot, even if it was a block or two away from the Corner Bar. He didn't mind. Walking, especially in brisk, cold air like this, cleansed the spirit and cleared the mind.

Being in town wasn't so bad, he thought, feeling pretty upbeat for a change. Until he neared a group of Christmas shoppers and they crossed the street to avoid him.

Familiar anger filled him. Striding down Main Street, face lifted to the brisk December wind, he tried to pretend he didn't care, that he was just enjoying the invigorating winter day. It wasn't easy keeping his expression pleasant, trying not to notice how many people avoided his eyes, pretended not to see him or, worse, crossed to the other side of Main Street as the last group had, simply to avoid being in the same space as Damien Colton, ex-felon.

Going on four months out of prison and the citizens of Honey Creek, Montana, still treated him like a criminal.

Even though he'd known most of them all his life, to them he'd forever be branded Damien Colton, the murderer. It didn't matter to them that he'd been completely exonerated. Or that the body of the man he'd supposedly killed had turned up, really dead this time, fifteen years after his mockery of a trial. Now, even though the town was all abuzz while the authorities tried to find the real killer, all anyone around here saw when they looked at him was an ex-con.

He'd gone to prison a boy of twenty. Fifteen years later he'd emerged a man of thirty-five who might just as well have had a flashing scarlet letter—*K* for Killer—branded on his forehead.

Shrugging off the bitterness, he entered the Corner Bar, so different in the daytime, and looked around, helpless to keep from marking how many gazes slid past him the minute he looked their way. Every time he came to town, the reasons he needed to collect his inheritance and move far away became clearer and clearer.

His brother Wes waved him over from a booth in the back. Relieved to see at least one friendly face, Damien headed that way, head held high, shoulders back. In prison he'd learned many things, but the most important was the ability to present himself to others as full of self-confidence. It helped to behave as though his hometown's massive shunning of him didn't bother him at all.

His favorite bartender, a tattooed guy named Jack Huffman, who'd moved to Honey Creek from out of town and didn't care about any of the drama concerning Mark Walsh, the man Damien had supposedly murdered, saw him coming and met him at the table with a tall draft beer in a frosted mug.

"Ahhh." Sliding into the booth across from Wes, Damien took a long pull of the icy beer, reveling in the taste. Of all the things he'd missed while incarcerated, the taste of a good brew ranked right up there.

Both men ordered cheeseburgers, the Corner Bar's specialty, and another delicacy Damien had missed while locked up.

Would he ever stop thinking of things in that way? How everything related to the wasted years? As he did every day, he vowed to try. More than anything, he wanted to feel like a regular cattle rancher again. Unfortunately, he had begun to realize he'd have to leave Honey Creek to be able to do so.

"I haven't found out anything else about Mark Walsh's death," Wes said, assuming that's why Damien had asked to meet him. "The investigation is still ongoing. The FBI people have been a lot of help, but we still don't have anything new."

"I didn't think so." Absurdly uncomfortable, Damien dragged his hand through his longish brown hair, so different from Wes's closely shaven head, and sighed. Then he straightened his shoulders and transformed himself into the supremely self-confident, don't-mess-with-me Damien he embodied to confront difficult situations. "I need your help in another matter."

"Shoot. Does this have anything to do with you disappearing a couple of times a month?" Clearly intrigued, Wes leaned forward. "What's up?"

"I disappear every so often because I'm not a monk or a priest. Celibacy just isn't my thing," Damien drawled. "I went fifteen years without. After being locked up, I thought I was used to it, but I can't do it. So I drive up to Bozeman, sometimes Billings."

Wes sat back, shaking his head. "You haven't met anyone local yet?"

Trying not to think of Eve, Damien looked his brother

right in the eye. "You know as well as I do that every single woman in Honey Creek runs the other way when she sees me coming."

"Have you even tried?"

"Tried? Hell, I've spent so many nights sitting around this bar and a couple of others, that I've lost count. I can't even get a woman to dance with me, never mind take me home." Other than Eve Kelley, he thought silently. This was something he wanted to keep to himself for now.

"I think that might be your own fault." Now Wes pinned Damien with a stare. "I've heard you drink yourself blind, act surly and mean and scare away anyone—man or woman—from even talking to you."

Stung, Damien grimaced. "Where'd you hear that from? Your girlfriend?"

"Fiancée. And no, Lily hasn't been spying on you. A couple of my deputies have seen you."

Frustration nearly made Damien scowl. Instead, he used his poker face, knowing if he wanted Wes's help, he had to play nice. "Bottom line. When I need a woman, I head out of town. It's a long drive to Billings and I'm getting tired of it."

"Once or twice a month. Man." Wes whistled. "That's so—"

"I know. Cut the sympathy. You've got a woman."

Wes spread his hands. "What can I do?"

"Come on, you're in law enforcement. You've seen the seedier side of life. You know how back in high school there were girls who were…"

"Fast?"

"Exactly." He shifted his weight. "I've been away for fifteen years while you've been here. You know everyone. Surely you can point me in the right direction."

To Damien's chagrin and frustration, this time Wes laughed out loud.

"What's so funny?"

Wes stopped laughing long enough to answer. "You're really serious."

"Wouldn't you be, if our positions were reversed?"

"Maybe," Wes allowed.

"Maybe? Come on, tell the truth."

"Look." All trace of amusement vanished from Wes's face. "You just need to make friends with someone here in town. We've got plenty of single women. You could hook up with any one of them, if you'd just make the effort."

As if it was that simple. What Wes conveniently forgot to mention is that if any single woman in Honey Creek dated him, a Colton, she'd expect a lot more than a simple sexual relationship. Assuming she could look past the been-in-prison thing.

"I told you, I don't want anything complicated. I just want sex."

"Good luck with that."

"Then I guess I'll keep driving up to Billings."

"Or try harder to meet someone here in town. Maybe you should talk to Maisie."

"Surely you jest." Damien shot his brother an incredulous look. "I can't ask my sister to help me find a bed partner."

"True. Though you could ask her to help you get a few dates, you know. It's all in the way you put it. Since we were meeting for lunch today, I invited her to meet us here. She said something about you taking her Christmas shopping."

Damien groaned. "She's been hounding me about that."

"Then I guess now would be a good time to get started."

"What about you?" Damien leaned forward. "Maybe you should take her shopping. How much of your holiday shopping have you gotten done?"

As Wes was about to speak again, his fiancée, Lily Masterson, rushed up and interrupted, leaning in to give him a long, lingering and very public kiss.

Wes shot Damien a look that plainly said, *Speaking of sex...* Damn his hide. He might find this funny, but to Damien, it was no laughing matter. All he could do was clench his teeth and try to appear pleasant. "Hi Lily."

Her bright smile faltered a notch. "Hey, Damien."

Moving over so she could sit next to him, Wes draped his arm around Lily's slender shoulders before turning back to Damien. "Sorry. You were saying?"

Damien wanted to roll his eyes. Wes knew good and well he couldn't talk about this in front of Lily. Instead, he flashed her a quick smile. "Are you prepared for Christmas?"

As he'd suspected it would, the question sent her on a roll, listing what she'd bought and what she still needed to find and for whom.

Letting a clearly entranced Wes hang on to her every word, Damien tuned her out and slowly finished his beer. It was plain he wasn't going to get any help from his brother. He'd simply have to continue to find a woman on his own.

Again he thought of Eve Kelley and the kisses they'd shared. Just thinking of her heated his blood.

He wanted her. Though he claimed to be looking for a woman, any woman, right now only Eve Kelley would do.

Chapter 5

Watching through the window of Salon Allegra as the first snow flurries fluttered to the ground, Eve wiped a stray tear from her eye. Four months pregnant and already her hormones made her want to weep at the most inauspicious moments.

The approaching holidays made her feel even worse. She was alone and lonely, and because Honey Creek was such a small town, everyone knew. Most of the other women her age had families, some even had grandchildren. Most of them, especially the ones who hadn't been cheerleaders in high school, were either secretly glad about her situation or openly pitied her. On the edge of forty and still single! The shame!

Oddly enough, Eve herself hadn't really minded until the big four-oh had started to loom closer. She'd still had a sort of misguided faith that eventually the right man would come along. Which might explain why she'd been so eager to believe Massimo, with his honeyed promises and sensuous embrace.

Her mother, Bonnie Gene, kept bugging her to join the quilting group she'd started, refusing to let the minor fact that Eve had no interest in quilting deter her. Worse, despite her mom's promise, she knew she would continue to constantly network among her friends and in town, trying to set Eve up on one blind date after another.

So far, like the one last night with Gary, the dates had all been embarrassing disasters. Bonnie Gene refused to listen. She wanted grandbabies and would stop at nothing to get them.

If only she knew…

Eve rubbed her sore neck. Soon, she'd have her own little family of two. An unwed mother at thirty-nine. She couldn't help but wonder what her sister Susan would say. Recently engaged to Duke Colton, Susan had asked Eve to be one of her bridesmaids. Eve had agreed, but soon she'd have to ask Susan how she felt about having a pregnant bridesmaid in her wedding.

Despite her family and the fact that she'd grown up in Honey Creek, Eve had never felt so alone.

Turning away from the window, Eve turned up the thermostat and thought longingly of Italy's warm sunshine. She'd gone there alone on an impromptu vacation over the summer, and had met a sensuous Italian named Massimo. A chance encounter had turned into a whirlwind romance. Massimo had loved her for three wonderful, sun-drenched days before vanishing. She supposed she'd always understood a crazy fling like that would never last, that things had been too perfect to be real, but still…his disappearing act had hurt. She'd actually dared to believe that this time she'd found The One.

Instead, her infatuation had been just that. Starved for

attention, deprived of sex, she'd let physical attraction blind her to the fact that Massimo was a player. She'd come back to Honey Creek a little heart-sore, but wiser, completely unaware of the little life growing inside of her.

Now, nearly four months and three missed periods later, she knew she was pregnant with Massimo's child. Cupping her slightly rounded stomach, she paced the confines of her shop, marveling at the twist of fate that had brought her to this. She hadn't yet gotten used to the idea, despite having known for one month.

Part of her was mortified that, at nearly forty years old, she had gotten knocked up. She knew better and had, in fact, insisted on precautions.

Another part of her was secretly thrilled. Her own baby! Though the town—already a soap opera of gossip and intrigue with the whole Mark Walsh mess—would flay her alive with their wagging tongues, she was keeping this baby. She'd realized she might never find a man of her own. Who knew if she'd ever get a chance to have another baby? This son or daughter was hers. She'd be her child's sole parent, since all attempts to reach the man she'd known only by one name—Massimo—had been fruitless.

She wanted to celebrate, to revel in her pregnancy. Still, she kept it secret, not wanting to take away from Susan's wedding plans and the holiday. Plus, she wanted to enjoy the knowledge in private for as long as possible before becoming the object of pointing fingers and censuring eyes.

Her thoughts went to Damien. He'd certainly understand that. Though he'd been sent to prison through no fault of his own, the people of Honey Creek persisted in treating him like a pariah.

As they no doubt would treat her. Her body was changing. For now, she could hide that with loose clothing, but she wouldn't be able to hide it much longer.

She'd reveal her news in her own time. Until then, all of Eve's energy went toward appearing normal, at least until the holidays were over. Eventually, she'd have no choice but to go public, but for now, no one needed to know. Except... she flushed. Damien Colton. Why she'd revealed her secret to the one man who attracted her above all others, she didn't know.

The salon was quiet—too quiet. She'd finished all of her morning appointments and all the afternoon clients had cancelled due to the impending blizzard. Eve knew she should close down the salon and head home, but she couldn't seem to make herself move.

Just as she stirred enough to get up and go around shutting off lights and unplugging hair tools, her cell phone rang. It was her mother, inviting her to lunch at the Corner Bar. Since this would offer a respite from going home to her big, empty house and since the Corner Bar also served a mean burger, Eve agreed to meet Bonnie Gene in fifteen minutes.

Pulling on her down parka, she turned the sign on the door to Closed and went out into the swirling snow flurries. Though the weather wasn't bad now, with the blizzard in the forecast for that evening, everyone who'd remained in town was rushing around buying staples and trying to Christmas shop while they could.

The kind of snowfall being forecast could mean a complete shutdown of Honey Creek for a day or two, sometimes more if they lost power.

Eve wasn't worried. Even if she had forgotten to stock something at home, her pickup had four-wheel drive and she'd been driving in blizzards all her life.

Enjoying the pretty curtain of snow, she walked the

block and a half to the Corner Bar. A popular eating spot during the day and watering hole at night, the place was crowded, even for noon. Her family's barbecue restaurant was equally crowded, but no one in her family liked to go there except on special occasions. And when they did, they tended to close the back room. Otherwise, they were besieged by people wanting the secret recipe for their famous barbecue sauce.

Inside, she walked up to the hostess and requested a booth. Since they were all taken, she settled on a table near the back and out of the main footpath. She'd ordered a Shirley Temple, glad she got to give the order before her mom arrived. Watching the patterns the swirling fury of the snowfall made outside the windows, she fell into a daydream about decorating a nursery.

Fifteen minutes came and went. Her stomach rumbled a hungry protest, reminding her she was eating for two. Checking her watch for the third time, she sighed. Her mother was late again, which was a normal occurrence. Even the waitress had expected it and hadn't bothered her with requests to take her order.

Life in a small town. As she did every day, Eve reflected on how lucky she was to live here. Although she had enjoyed the cosmopolitan, old-world atmosphere in Europe, Montana would always be her home. She'd never been one of those who wanted to move somewhere else.

Twenty minutes crept past. Eve had her Shirley Temple refilled. Still no Bonnie Gene. She took to studying the menu, as though she didn't already have it memorized. Since she'd already decided on a hamburger and fries, she looked at the five different burger variations, trying to decide on which one.

The front door opened, sending a gust of icy air through the bar before it closed. The steady clatter of plates and glasses and people talking stilled for a second, then resumed again at an even louder roar. Eve glanced up and she felt a jolt go through her like a shockwave. For a second she forgot to breath and her heart skipped a beat.

Him. Looking as tall, dark and dangerous as a demon straight out of hell, Damien Colton strode into the room, drawing everyone's stare. He, of course, looked neither left nor right, pushing through the crowd like a broad-shouldered linebacker. For a moment, she thought she'd forgotten their date, but then realized it was far too early in the day for that.

As she had the night before, she contemplated how he'd changed. Prison had altered him a lot, she supposed. The earlier promise of his sulky beauty had matured, sharpened into a sort of rugged masculinity. He'd beefed up, no doubt from working out while behind bars, and if he'd ever had that prison pallor, the last three months he'd spent working on his family's cattle ranch had darkened his skin to bronze. Even the overcast skies of winter hadn't done much to dim his tan.

He was, she thought, absolutely, breathtakingly beautiful in a far different way than Massimo had been.

Dangerous for a woman like her. If she was smart, she'd stay far, far away from him. She didn't need that kind of trouble. Her hand drifted to her belly. Especially not now.

Still unable to look away, she sucked in her breath as he glanced over his shoulder, his dark gaze locking on hers.

Damn. Hurriedly, she looked down, cheeks flaming. Then, peeping up through her lashes, she watched as Damien took a seat across the room in a booth with his brother Wes. As he sat, the crowd of people obscured him from her view. Grateful he hadn't come over—heaven help her explain that one to her mother—part of her felt hurt that he'd ignored her.

Still, it took a while for her racing heart to settle back into a steady beat.

"Hey there, girl." Bonnie Gene breezed up, grabbing Eve in a fierce hug before she'd even had time to register her mother's arrival.

"Have you ordered yet?" Dropping into the seat across from Eve, Bonnie Gene snatched up the menu and flipped it open.

"Not yet." Eve couldn't keep her gaze from straying over toward the side of the bar where Damien sat.

Naturally, Bonnie Gene noticed. "What are you looking at?" Then, without waiting for an answer, she pushed to her feet to get a better look. "Damien Colton. I'll be."

Eve felt her face heat. Dang it.

"Hmmm." Her mother's shrewd blue eyes pinned Eve. "I feel really bad about what happened to that boy. Have you spoken to him yet?"

That boy was now thirty-five, and whether Eve had talked to him was none of her mother's business. Still, she couldn't outright lie. "A little, just in passing."

"I haven't. But I have talked to his sister. Just yesterday, in fact."

"You talked to Maisie Colton?" Surprised, Eve stared. Everyone in Honey Creek knew how much Maisie hated the Kelleys. Each and every single one of them. "When? How'd you manage to get her to talk to you? Was she… nice?"

Bonnie Gene signaled the waitress, who hurried over with a steaming cup of coffee, her usual drink, even in a bar. "Yesterday. And yes, she was nice. She's the one who approached me."

"Why?"

"She wants to join the quilting group."

Eve's mouth fell open. She couldn't have been more surprised if her mother had suddenly announced she wanted to take up hang-gliding. "Really?"

"Yes, really." Satisfied with her daughter's stunned reaction, the older woman sat back in her chair, smiled and sipped her coffee. "She's supposed to come visit our meeting next Thursday night. You ought to come, too. It'll be fun."

For once, Eve actually considered attending. But she knew if she started going now, her mother would expect her to go forever and always. Still, watching the train wreck of Maisie Colton trying to interact with a bunch of fervent quilters made it awfully tempting.

"Does she even know how to quilt?"

"I don't know." Supremely unconcerned, Bonnie shrugged. "If she doesn't, we'll teach her. It's about time that woman started trying to become a part of her community."

"Maisie Colton?" Eve couldn't wrap her mind around the image of long-legged, willowy, model-perfect Maisie Colton trying to make a quilt with her own exquisitely manicured fingers. "I hope this doesn't come back to bite you."

The waitress hurried over to take their orders. Eve ordered the California burger, with avocado and bean sprouts. After a second of consideration, her mother ordered the same.

After the waitress left, Bonnie Gene leaned across the table. "Are you going to go talk to him?"

"What? Who?"

"Damien Colton. You always did have a thing for him."

"Mother!" Horrified, Eve glanced around to see who might have heard. "I did not."

"Don't think I didn't know how you mooned over him when you were in high school."

Eve rolled her eyes. One fact of life—no matter how old she got, her mother could still make her feel like a little kid. "Drop it, Mom. Please."

Chuckling, Bonnie nodded. "Have it your way." About to say something else, she broke into a wide smile, jumped to her feet and began waving madly. "Well, look who's here. Maisie Colton. Yoo-hoo, Maisie! Over here!"

Instantly, the Corner Bar went silent. Voices hushed, forks stilled as all heads turned to stare at the door. Tall and statuesque, Maisie glided toward them. Her four-inch heels tap-tapping on the wooden floor was the only sound in the place.

For the second time that day, Eve wanted to let the ground swallow her up. Instead, since she had no choice, she lifted her chin, forced a pleasant smile and watched Maisie approach.

One thing about those Coltons, she thought. They were all lookers. With her exotically tilted aquamarine eyes, and perfect figure, Maisie would draw stares whether in New York, Paris or Bozeman, Montana. The hairdresser in Eve eyed the long, thick, brown hair cascading down Maisie's back, and longed to work with it. Since Maisie traveled to Billings once a month to have her hair done, she knew that would never happen. Eve's Salon Allegra was far too plebian for the likes of Maisie Colton.

"Bonnie Gene!" With a genuine grin on her bright-red lips, Maisie enveloped Bonnie Gene in a hug. "So good to see you."

"Come, join us." Scooting over, Bonnie patted the seat next to her. "I'm sure you know my daughter, Eve."

"I've seen you around, but I don't believe we've ever formally met." Maisie's smile turned cool as she held her perfectly manicured hand for Eve to shake. "You were a year behind me in high school."

"Pleased to meet you," Eve lied, suddenly overwhelmingly conscious of her short, unpainted fingernails.

They touched hands quickly, and Maisie sat down.

Luckily, Bonnie Gene kept the conversation rolling, and soon Maisie was chatting about everything from cattle wandering off in a blizzard to the latest winter fashions.

Meanwhile, Eve kept watching the kitchen while her stomach rumbled, waiting for her food.

Finally, the hamburgers arrived, dropped off by the hostess, as their waitress was busy waiting on other tables. Eve reached for her burger, ignoring Maisie's stare of disapproval as she raised it to her mouth and took a huge bite.

Heaven. It was all she could do to keep from rolling her eyes and moaning out loud.

Bonnie Gene, however, was a bit more gracious. "Maisie, would you like half of mine? We ordered long before you came in."

"No, thanks," Maisie drawled. "I don't eat beef."

That was too much, even for Eve. Swallowing her food, she couldn't resist pointing out. "Um, Maisie? You live on a cattle ranch."

Up went one perfectly shaped brow. "So?"

Staring at her, Eve tried to picture Darius Colton's reaction to a daughter who wouldn't eat beef. The autocratic cattleman had never been shy in proclaiming his contempt and disdain for what he called 'tree huggers' and 'vegans.' Was this her way of rebelling against an autocratic and dictatorial father? If so, Maisie was now a bit too old to be still playing that sort of game.

Either way, it wasn't Eve's business. "I just thought it was different, that's all. While I admire you for your principles, I could never do it. I love my meat too much."

"I can tell." Maisie let her gaze sweep disparagingly over Eve. Then, while Eve was still reeling from the incredibly rude comment—standard Maisie Colton—Maisie continued. "The way you're eating that burger it's almost like you're eating for two or something."

Eve froze. Panicked, she looked at her mother, to see Bonnie Gene also staring slack-jawed at the crazy Colton woman.

Blithely, as though completely unaware she'd said anything wrong, Maisie kept on. "Of course, you've got to actually have a man to get pregnant, and since everyone knows you're not dating anyone, unless you used a sperm bank or something—"

"Maisie!" Bonnie Gene barked, cutting her off. "I think that's enough. I'm shocked at your behavior."

Right. As if her mother had reason to be surprised. Maisie Colton would never change. Maisie was…Maisie. Beautiful, spoiled, unbalanced. She'd been that way as long as Eve could remember.

Yet, at Bonnie Gene's words, unbelievably, the glamorous Colton ducked her head, appearing contrite. "My apologies," she said, stiffly. "I meant no harm."

A shadow fell over their table. Damien Colton, grim-faced and impossibly handsome. "Ladies."

Eve's heart rate went into overdrive. His gaze touched on Eve, again briefly, sending a jolt directly to her insides. "Maisie, Wes and I are waiting for you over there. Lily's joined us as well." Holding out his hand for his sister, he waited patiently while Maisie made up her mind.

"I was meeting you for lunch, wasn't I?" she said in a sheepish tone, wrinkling her perfect nose prettily. "I'm so sorry I kept you waiting. I wanted to talk to Bonnie Gene for a second. She's going to teach me how to quilt."

To his credit, Damien didn't react to this news at all. He simply nodded, taking her hand and helping his sister to her feet.

"Sorry to interrupt your lunch, Ms. Kelley. Eve." This time, as his gaze met hers, Eve saw the hint of a promise in his. While she still tried to figure that out, he began to move off, Maisie on his arm.

"By the way," he said, glancing over his broad shoulder at her. "Do I need an appointment to get a haircut at that salon of yours, or can I just drop in?"

For one horrifying moment, Eve couldn't find her voice. Pulling it back somehow from somewhere, she managed a response. "How about Tuesday afternoon? Around four?"

He dipped his chin to acknowledge her words. "I'll be there." Then, with his sister's arm tucked in his, he left them.

Wow. Eve couldn't keep herself from watching him until the crowd blocked her view. "I've never cut a Colton man's hair," she breathed. "They usually go to the Old Time Barber Shop down the street. I can't believe this."

"Get your tongue back in your mouth, girl," Bonnie teased as she finally wrapped her hands around her burger.

"I know," Eve sighed. "Damien Colton's one kind of trouble I don't need." She'd need to keep reminding herself of that. Especially since every time she saw him, she turned to Jell-O inside.

"So," Maisie asked brightly, clutching Damien's arm as though she needed help to stay upright. Hell, trying to walk with those high-heeled boots, she probably did. "Are you ready to do some serious Christmas shopping?"

They'd reached the booth and the flurry of hellos and hugs saved Damien from answering. Maisie was the only one who acted as though he hadn't changed. She still treated him as if he was the same twenty-year-old boy who'd gone away to prison for fifteen years. As if she was trying to pretend that his long incarceration had never happened.

She and she alone appeared blind to how he'd changed. She didn't understand that he was different, that he'd become a bitter, angry man. Though he hated that, he accepted it, hoping with time some of the bitterness would fade. The only time he found any peace was on the back of a horse, riding the land, far away from people or buildings or anything even remotely resembling civilization.

But not only had Maisie been nagging him to go Christmas shopping with her, but he'd needed to meet up with Wes. As Honey Creek's sheriff, Wes was swamped at what normally was the slowest time of the year. With the Mark Walsh investigation going full-swing and the FBI in town, Wes hadn't been able to make time to get out to the ranch.

Fifteen years ago, a dead body had been mistakenly identified as Mark Walsh and Damien had been convicted of his murder. Then, some months ago, when the real Mark Walsh turned up actually dead and Damien had been exonerated, the search was on for his real killer.

Worse, the FBI had been in town. Damien had actually spoken to one of the agents again a while back, agreeing to help in the investigation any way he could. What he hadn't realized was that the Feds were in town for another reason, besides Mark Walsh's murder. They were looking into some of Darius Colton's business deals and had begun pressuring Damien to help them out. Not a day went by that he didn't regret his impulsive offer to help, especially since they were increasing the pressure.

Damien couldn't care less what his father might have done by making the wrong investment or whatever. The last thing Darius needed was to go to prison for some white-collar crime—Damien knew firsthand what prison could do to a man. And Darius was sixty—if he went behind bars now, he'd probably never get out. No, thank you. Damien wanted nothing to do with that mess. All he cared about was finding Mark Walsh's real killer. And, of course, finding out what had happened to his inheritance.

He had been hopeful Wes could fill him in on the investigation, hopeful they'd made real progress. He had a keen interest in finding out both who had actually finally killed Mark, and the identity of the body he had been accused of murdering fifteen years ago. Someone had killed that guy, whoever he was. Damien wondered what the tie-in was to the real Mark Walsh.

Had Mark set up the first killing, faking his own death? Surely he'd known Damien had taken the fall for his death and gone away to do hard jail time.

But evidently, Mark hadn't cared. People had believed him dead. Dead, he'd been free as a bird, while Damien's entire life had been ruined.

Nothing and no one could ever give Damien back what had been taken from him. Now, the burning drive to know the truth and a lack of ready funds were the only things that kept Damien in town.

Until his father had told him flatly that his inheritance was gone, he'd planned his entire future around that money. This, combined with the money his attorney said that the State of Montana would be paying him for his wrongful conviction, would be enough to start his own cattle ranch far away from Honey Creek. Someplace like Nevada or

Idaho. He'd already started pricing acreage, preparing himself for when he could shake the dust of this place from his heels.

Honey Creek, Montana, held nothing for him anymore. Nothing but painful memories. Except now that he had no inheritance, it looked like he was being held prisoner. Again.

Chapter 6

"Hellooo? Earth to Damien?" Maisie's voice, plus her fingers snapping in front of his face, brought him back to the Corner Bar.

"Sorry." He gave his older sister a rueful smile, noticing how Wes and Lily still couldn't tear their gazes away from each other. Love. Bitterness filled him. "What'd you need?"

"I asked if you were ready to go lighten your wallet after we eat?"

His wallet was already pretty damn light, but he didn't tell her that. The wage his father paid him for working on the ranch was the same as he paid all the other ranch hands. Not exactly a fortune. "Yes, I'm ready to go Christmas shopping," he lied.

She grinned, making his small falsehood worth the trouble. Just because he wasn't feeling Christmassy didn't mean he had to ruin the holiday for her.

They took their seats, Damien letting Maisie slide in first, so he could have the outside of the booth. Even before his prison experience, he hadn't liked feeling hemmed in. Now, if he wasn't careful, he'd feel trapped.

"Good. Shopping's my thing. Now, we've got to plan." Rummaging in her oversized purse, she produced a small pad of paper and a shiny silver Montblanc pen.

"Plan? Can't we just go?"

"Not when we've got as much to buy as you do," she chided. "Now let's see. I'm making a list of places we need to stop by." Scribbling furiously, oblivious to everyone else, she began plotting.

Damien exchanged a glance with Wes, who shrugged. Lily caught this and punched him lightly in the arm. Meanwhile, Maisie continued writing, unaware.

Finally, she raised her head and pushed the paper toward Damien. "Take a look. I think this will cover everything, unless there is someplace you want to add?"

Eying the paper, Damien groaned. "There must be ten different stores on this list," he groused, earning Wes's sympathetic grin. "Isn't there one place we can go and get everything? Like one-shop stopping?"

"The nearest Wally World is in Bozeman. That's twenty minutes away in good weather. With this snowstorm that's supposed to hit tonight, I think we'd better stay in town."

"That's pretty sensible," Lily agreed. She sounded surprised, which made Maisie grin. People outside the family saw only her eccentric, off-balance behavior. They'd been witness to enough emotional roller-coaster rides to label her crazy, which Damien could understand. Even in the short time he'd been home, he'd come to realize that his sister had some serious psychological issues.

Personally, he wondered if she might be bipolar. In that case, she'd be fine with the right medications. But the one time Damien had brought up the topic with their father, Darius had gone ballistic and the subject had been dropped.

So poor Maisie flew high and frequently dived low enough to scrape bottom. The entire town thought she was crazy. Damien believed she was actually sick. One thing he firmly intended to do before leaving Honey Creek was get Maisie the help she needed, even if he had to go against his father to do so. Thus far, though he'd been trying for the past few months, he hadn't had any luck. Maisie herself refused even to consider the possibility of seeking medical help.

Damn. Not for the first time, he reflected how complicated life was on the outside. Had he really believed when he'd been set free that he could go back to the simple days of riding the range and minding cattle?

"Damien?"

Again he raised his head to find everyone at the table eyeing him quizzically.

"You drifted off again," Maisie complained.

"Are you all right, bro?" Wes asked, concern furrowing his brow.

"Fine. Just tired. I was up all night with that sick cow."

Wes shook his head. "I'm so glad I don't have to do that stuff anymore."

"I missed it," Damien said simply.

"Yeah, out of all us kids, you and Duke were the only two who took to cattle-ranching. The rest of us didn't want anything to do with it."

"I agree." Maisie shook her head, sending her long hair flying and her huge, dangling earrings tinkling. "Nasty, smelly animals. I don't even like being in the same area as them."

This made the brothers both laugh.

"I can't even remember the last time you went to the barn," Wes said.

"I've been home almost four months and she hasn't been near the place in all that time," Damien seconded.

Lily reached across the table and lightly touched the back of Maisie's hand. "I don't blame you. Cattle are hell on manicures."

They all got a chuckle out of that, though the women didn't seem to understand why the men found this so amusing.

The waitress brought their food on a huge, circular tray. Damien realized with surprise that while he'd been woolgathering, Wes had evidently ordered them all burgers and fries, except for Maisie, of course, who had a huge bowl of broccoli-cheese soup and a small salad.

For the life of him, Damien couldn't understand how anyone could eat that way, but his sister made her own choices. If she wanted to be a vegetarian, who was he to judge?

He picked up his burger. The meat had been piled high with crispy bacon and mushrooms and cheese and smelled as close to heaven as a meal could. He dug in with gusto. Silence finally fell while the others did the same.

For some reason, while he ate his thoughts returned to Eve Kelley, sitting with her mother and Maisie earlier. God, she was beautiful. Each time he saw her he felt that familiar pull in his gut, signaling his desire. When she'd met his gaze, he'd recognized something in her face. As fanciful as it sounded, her eyes had looked…haunted. He knew haunted. Intimately.

"Maisie, I didn't know you and Eve Kelley were friends," he said into the silence.

Both Wes and Lily stopped chewing and stared.

Maisie scowled. "We're not. I told you, Bonnie Gene is going to teach me to quilt. I'm going to the first meeting this week, if we aren't snowed in."

Wes asked the obvious. "Why do you want to learn to quilt?"

At his question, Maisie's expression grew serious and determined. "For Jeremy. I want to make my son a quilt, so he'll have something to remember me by when I'm gone."

Concerned, Damien exchanged a glance with his brother. "Maisie, are you planning on going somewhere?"

She bit her lip, twisting the huge diamond ring that she always wore on her right hand. "No. You know what I mean. Someday we all die, right?"

Relieved, he squeezed her shoulder. "Someday. Just not any time soon, all right?"

"Of course." Then, in her usual way, she changed moods. From somber to giddy, lightning-swift. "I'm so excited about Christmas! I can't wait to get my gifts purchased and everything wrapped!"

He noticed Lily's wide-eyed stare. Though she and Wes were engaged, she obviously hadn't been around Maisie enough to get used to her.

Picking up his burger again, he nudged his sister. "And we'd better eat up so we can get started on all this shopping."

Munching happily, she nodded.

A short while later, food devoured, small talk dispensed with and heartily sick and tired of watching Wes and Lily hang all over each other, Damien and Maisie donned their heavy parkas and exited the Corner Bar.

It took every bit of self-restraint he possessed to keep from glancing over to see if Eve Kelley and her mother were still there. He could still remember her locked in his arms that night in the cab of his pickup. She'd been hot and willing and soft and beautiful.

Like a dash of cold water, he remembered that more than sixteen years had passed since that night. For him, it might seem like yesterday. But Eve would definitely have moved on.

Except she was still alone. And he wanted her.

Outside, the icy air and blowing snow hit him like a welcome slap in the face. Maisie kept hold of his arm.

"I love this time of the year," she enthused. "Look at all the beautiful decorations."

He squinted where she pointed, trying to make out what she meant. "All I can see is the snow. It's already a couple of inches deep."

"Spoilsport." Punching his arm, she began to sing "Jingle Bells," then stopped in mid verse to glare at him. "Feel free to join in at any time."

"I'm only here because of you," he groused.

"That and the fact that Christmas is only ten days away and you haven't bought a single gift. Sing along. Christmas songs might help you get in the spirit."

"I doubt that. You know I can't carry a tune."

A group of people, bundled in down coats and wearing knitted hats and scarves, hurriedly crossed the street to avoid them.

"Did you see that?" Damien glared after them. "The way people act makes me want to punch something."

"Just ignore them." Tottering along in her high-heeled, pointy-toed boots, Maisie used his arm like a lifeline. "People here always treat me like I have a disease. So, for sure, they'll treat you the same. Like prison's catching or somethin'." She giggled loudly at her own joke.

Even Damien had to smile. At least Maisie hadn't changed, other than growing older. She was the same eccentric wild child now as she had been when he went into prison, albeit now she was a grown woman with a teenage son.

"Besides," she continued. "Who cares what the townspeople think? You don't need to worry about them. You have us. You have family."

"True." That was the one rock-solid thing he'd hung on to while incarcerated. His family. Unlike most of the other inmates, he'd always have family. He'd known, despite their failure to win his freedom, that he could count on them. He knew they'd all tried to fight his conviction, knew they'd funneled money to various high-powered attorneys trying to force an appeal. They'd never doubted his innocence, or him. They'd had faith in him, which had given him faith in himself.

Everyone, that is, except his father. Though he'd harbored a bit of bitterness toward Darius Colton for not trying harder to get him free, Damien had emerged from prison ready to start over, forgive and forget and all that. But the passing years had not been kind to the patriarch of the Colton clan. Darius had grown colder, more autocratic, secretive and unreasonable. Of all the family, Damien felt, his father had become a stranger.

And after the incident last night, a mentally unsound stranger at that. Who might have stolen his own children's inheritance.

"Stop being a grinch and enjoy the holiday. Now, what's important today is getting your gifts," she reiterated, fluffing the snowflakes out of her long, dark hair and grinning up at him. "Especially the one you're buying me."

"Buying?" he teased. "I was going to make you something."

She pouted and he relented. Maisie knew he only had

the small paycheck his father allotted him for working on the ranch.

"Just don't be too extravagant, okay?"

"I won't." The mischief in her violet eyes told him she had something up her sleeve. "Though you could always charge it. That's what makes plastic so fun."

"You know I can't." He hadn't even bothered to apply for a credit card, not seeing a point since he'd planned to pay cash for everything once he got his inheritance.

Again he wondered why his father had dodged questions about that.

"I've lost you again," Maisie pouted. "Come on, Damien. It's not like I get you all to myself very often. Can you at least try to pay attention?"

Pushing all troubling thoughts out of his head, Damien forced himself to relax. "Sorry, sis. It won't happen again."

"Good."

Thirty minutes later, while the snow continued to fall in thick, wet flakes and pile up on the ground, Damien struggled to the car with his third load of parcels. Maisie's, all of them. She'd gone a little crazy once she got started, though since a good portion of her gifts were for Jeremy, he couldn't fault her.

He'd purchased exactly two things—a purple cashmere sweater that Maisie swore she couldn't live without, and the latest video-game console with two games for Jeremy. He made sure there were two controllers so they could play together.

"You still have Duke and Susan, Finn, Wes and Lily, not to mention Darius and Sharon. And Perry, Joan and Brand, of course."

"You're right," he said slowly. Though he was on the fence about Darius, he did need to get a gift for his father's wife. Though he barely knew the woman, third or so in a long line of wraithlike females who allowed themselves to be totally domineered by Darius, she'd always been civil to him. "What do you think I should get Sharon?"

"She likes scarves," Maisie pointed out. "What are you going to get Darius?"

"I'm not sure. I'm going to wait on getting him anything right now."

To his relief, she accepted that. "Okay. Then what about our brothers?"

"For the guys, I figured the feed store would have everything I need."

"The feed store?" Her expression mirrored her mock horror. "Surely you're kidding."

"I wasn't."

"You'd better be. Come on, you've got to get started. You've bought hardly anything," Maisie complained.

He stopped in his tracks, tightening his grip on her arm to keep her from falling. "You want to know something? I'm not sure about even celebrating Christmas," he teased. "Fifteen years in prison without the holiday made me kind of used to doing without it."

She slapped his arm with her purse, a huge, gaudy thing that seemed comprised of fake rattlesnake dyed a rainbow of colors, some natural, some not. "You are definitely celebrating Christmas, and you'll be happy about it. I insist. No arguing."

He hid a smile. "Yes, ma'am," he drawled.

"Here we are." She stopped in front of the Honey Creek Mercantile. "Our next stop. You should be able to get a little something for everyone here."

Since it was either that or listen to her complain, Damien nodded and pulled open the door, holding it for his sister and trying like hell not to notice how everyone in the store suddenly became busy doing something else. Something that made it impossible for him to catch their eyes.

Once again he stopped in his tracks, forgetting Maisie still clutched his arm and nearly causing her to fall.

"What's wrong now?" she asked.

Gesturing around the place, he shook his head. "I know you claim it doesn't bother you, but it does me."

"What does?" she asked, appearing honestly perplexed.

"This." Gesturing toward the packed store, he shook his head. "The way they act like I have a communicable disease."

"You'll be fine." Her firm, no-nonsense voice told him if she willed him to be fine, then he would. "Honestly, don't let them bother you."

"Easy for you to say. Coming to town makes me feel more like a criminal than prison did."

Maisie shot him a sideways glance. "It's not going to change any time soon, so get used to it."

He stopped, staring down at her. "That's where you're wrong, Maisie. I don't have to get used to it. And, like I've told you before, I'm leaving and you're welcome to come with me when I go."

Shaking her head, she only smiled and continued shopping.

After she'd finished her lunch with her mother, Eve switched her truck to four-wheel drive, glad she already had her snow chains on, and headed home, reveling in the bright white silence of the falling snow. Soon, if the storm gathered the strength the weathermen predicted, there'd be whiteout conditions, and no one would be going anywhere. But for now, it was a pretty typical Montana snowfall. Pretty, but nothing to get excited about.

At the house, she let Max, her boxer, out, smiling as the big, goofy fawn-colored dog bounded about, trying to catch the flakes in his mouth, whirling and bouncing and rolling in the snow. Watching him, with her gloved hands cradled protectively over her stomach, her worries fell away as if they'd never existed.

She smiled, her heart full. This dog was good for her soul.

The snowfall, now just a normal winter storm, was supposed to intensify as the night went on, eventually becoming a full-out blizzard, what the locals called a blue norther. A common enough occurrence in Montana in December. She had plenty of firewood, a pantry stocked full of food, and she wouldn't have to worry if she couldn't get into town to replenish her supplies.

Max bounded up, tail wagging, reminding her with a soft woof that it was his supper time.

"Come on, boy."

Inside, she poured the big dog a bowl of kibble. She kept an extra thirty-pound bag for occasions like this.

While her dog feasted, she found herself again thinking about Damien Colton. His aloof loneliness acted like an invisible lure, making her want to get closer.

Bad, bad Eve.

Still, she knew he had no friends. Everyone could use a friend and she was lonely. What would be the harm in that?

So she decided later to head into town and stop by the Corner Bar for a drink, despite the impending blizzard. Weather forecasts were often wrong and if they weren't, any Montana native worth their salt could drive in a snowstorm. If Damien was there, she'd join him.

She chose to ignore the fact that her heart rate accelerated at the thought.

* * *

"You're going back into town?" Maisie sounded incredulous. "We've only been back a few hours and you bitched the entire time we were there."

Before Damien could answer, Jeremy jumped up.

"Can I go with you, Uncle Damien?"

Gazing down into his nephew's bright eyes, Damien Colton glanced at his sister, Maisie. Her intense aqua gaze unfocused, she shrugged, in her own careless way giving permission.

Unfortunately, no way in hell he was bringing his fourteen-year-old nephew to a bar, even one like the Corner Bar and Grill.

"Not this time," Damien said. "Snow's on the way."

"So?" Maisie drawled. "Since when do we let a little snow stop us?"

"Maybe next time." Damien felt guilty disappointing his nephew, but he had no choice.

"Why not?" Jeremy challenged. "Mom gave me some money. I've got to get my Christmas shopping done, too."

"I'm not going shopping," Damien answered. "Sorry."

Maisie perked up at that. "Then where are you going?"

"Out for a drink." He squeezed his nephew's shoulder. Though he'd rather be dragged over broken glass than go shopping again, he had to do something to wipe the disappointment from the kid's face. "I'll take you tomorrow after school, okay?"

Jeremy nodded. "That'll work. I've got homework to do tonight anyway." Pushing back his chair, he got up and wandered off.

"He idolizes you, you know," Maisie pointed out, still absorbed in painting her fingernails a bright scarlet, apparently to match the cashmere sweater she wore.

"Ever since you got out of prison, all he ever talks about is you."

Damien frowned. "He has better examples in Duke, Wes and Finn."

Smiling, Maisie glanced toward the den at the twelve-foot-tall Christmas tree. Decked out all in silver and white with twinkling lights, the tree appeared to glow. "I don't know about that. I trust my son's judgment. Just don't disappoint him, okay?"

"I won't." Of all the family, Jeremy was the person Damien most enjoyed being with.

"Now tell me." Maisie cocked her head, eyeing him with interest. "Do you actually have a date or are you going trolling?"

"Trolling?"

"As in fishing. For a woman."

For half a second he thought of Wes saying he should ask Maisie to set him up. Just as quickly, he discounted that plan. Bad idea.

"Neither," he lied. "I'm simply going to town to have a drink. The Rollaboys are playing at the Corner Bar tonight."

"Oooh!" Maisie clapped her hands. "I can't believe I forgot that. I may go up there myself later."

Damn. Now he felt obligated to offer. "Do you want to go with me?"

She grinned. "No, but thanks for asking. I wouldn't want to cramp your style. Plus I want to make sure Darius isn't on the warpath. No way I'm leaving Jeremy here to fend for himself if our father is working into a good drunk."

"Smart move." He touched her arm. "Then I guess I'll be going."

"You'd stand a better chance of getting lucky if you drove up to Bozeman."

"I know." He raised a brow. "The question is, how did you know?"

Lifting one shoulder, she smiled. "You're not the only one with needs. None of the men in this town will date me."

"You seemed to be doing all right with that Gary Jackson."

"Oh, him." Her smile widened. "He's new in town and apparently doesn't believe all he hears. He and I have a date this Friday."

"Good for you."

"Yeah." Her smile tinged with sadness, she put the cap back on the bottle of nail polish. "I'll make it last as long as I can. Until I freak out over something and he takes off running."

"Maise." He touched the back of her hand. "Have you considered getting some help?"

Maisie's gaze slid away. "I don't need help," she muttered. "I'm a little moody, that's all. Leave me alone."

Before he could respond, she turned and stalked off.

Stalemate. Again.

He reminded himself he couldn't fix the world. Hell, he couldn't even repair his own problems—why did he think he could help anyone else?

Chapter 7

This Friday night was clear, crisp and cold. Eve drove into town feeling oddly reluctant, restless and not sure why. Since Damien Colton's handsome face kept popping into her mind, she figured the restlessness had a lot to do with her unfulfilled desire for him.

The parking lot was full. She lucked out into a spot near the entrance and parked, glad she'd taken extra care with her appearance.

At the door, she paused and surveyed the packed bar. Because she'd called ahead, the bartender had put a reserved sign on her regular booth and she headed for it, blowing him a kiss on her way.

Once he brought her Shirley Temple, Eve sat back and surveyed the scene. She waved at a family she knew as they snagged one of the last empty tables remaining. Unlike the other night, the bar was crowded. Even at 8:00 p.m., when the dinner rush would be beginning to die down, people milled in both the restaurant and around the bar area, elbow to elbow.

Tables were filling up fast. Tonight, the Rollaboys were playing. A local country-and-western band that had made good in Nashville, they'd returned home to visit family for the holidays and, following Honey Creek tradition, would play a free concert at the Corner Bar.

Since entertainment in their little town was pretty much limited to church nativity plays, ranchers and townspeople alike filled the room. The Rollaboys played an upbeat mix of country and rock that was enjoyed by all.

As the fifth person stopped by to chat with her, remarking excitedly on the band, Eve wondered if she should leave. She'd actually managed to forget the band was playing and would probably have stayed home if she'd remembered. She'd dated Ian Murphy, the Rollaboys' lead singer, on and off for two years a while back. The relationship had ended badly, with Eve refusing Ian's marriage proposal. She'd liked him well enough, and they were certainly compatible, but his lifestyle was the opposite of what she wanted for herself. She'd thought she'd been perfectly realistic, though Ian hadn't taken the breakup well.

She wondered if she should leave before Ian saw her. But the contrast between her big, empty house and the packed, boisterous bar was dramatic and she decided to stay. After all, it had been eighteen months since the breakup. Surely Ian had moved on by now. Deciding to stay, she settled back in her booth, hoping the shadows would keep her out of view of the stage.

Used to Eve's solitary ways, everyone waved and continued on to meet their group. A few people stopped by to chat briefly, but no one asked if they could join her.

Glad to be seated alone, Eve couldn't help but watch the door for Damien.

The waitress brought her another Shirley Temple. Eve found ordering them amusing since she associated them with Christmas. As a child, Bonnie Gene had served them to the Kelley kids in crystal wineglasses, always with a cherry as garnish. Eve planned to continue this tradition with her child when he or she was old enough.

The thought was enough to make her misty-eyed. Looking down at the table, she dabbed her eyes with her napkin, knowing she had to regain her composure quickly before someone noticed.

"Enjoying your Shirley Temple?"

The deep voice jolted Eve right out of her melancholy. She looked up and met Damien Colton's velvet-brown eyes. To her disbelief, she blushed and her heart skipped a beat.

"It's a seven and seven," she corrected out of habit, then realized as his smile widened that she'd said exactly the same thing the last time they'd met. Now he knew the truth. Had it been only yesterday?

"Mind if I join you?" he asked.

Her insides fluttered as she seriously considered his question. She glanced around, aware that the second he sat down the gossip would start. Finally, she shrugged. "Sure, why not?"

"Worried someone will see you talking to me?" He remained standing, balanced on the balls of his feet as though he meant to flee.

"Maybe." She owed him honesty, at least. "But not for the reason you think. Sit."

He studied her face for a moment, then slid into the booth across from her. "You really don't care?"

"They're going to gossip no matter what, so why not give them something to talk about?" Finding herself smiling, she leaned back in the booth. She realized she liked the way he made her feel. The sizzle of desire combined with a comforting sense of connection.

He smiled back, warming her down to the soles of her feet. "Aren't you worried about what they'll say?"

"Not really. Besides, even if you were Maisie, they'd talk. Because you're a Colton and I'm a Kelley, you know? Though I confess, I never actually bought into that whole feud thing like your sister did."

His smile dimmed. "Not only that. They're not going to like you sitting with me."

"Why not?"

"Because I'm an ex-con."

Incredulous, she could only stare. "Everyone knows you were exonerated. Mark Walsh wasn't even really dead."

"Someone was," he said grimly. "And though they used circumstantial evidence to convict me of a crime I didn't commit, no one seems to care about who the actual dead guy was or who killed him."

"Ah." She leaned forward, her earlier discomfort completely forgotten. "But you want to know."

"You'd better believe I do." Signaling the waitress, he held up his empty beer bottle. "I can't help but wonder if Mark Walsh himself set up the killing so he could disappear."

"That makes sense." Fascinated, she leaned forward. "But why? And now that Mark Walsh really is dead— fifteen years later—everyone is wondering who killed him this time."

"At least they can't pin it on me this time. I was already behind bars."

Impulsively, she reached across the table and laid her hand over his. "I'm so sorry. That must have been awful."

For a moment he simply stared at her, his expression

dark and unreadable. Abruptly, he stood, pulling his hand away as if her touch burned him. "It was. That's why as soon as I can, I'm leaving town. Excuse me," he growled. "I'll be right back."

Leaving town? She watched him cross the room, his masculine stride forceful and, if she admitted the truth to herself, sexy as hell. But then, even back in high school, she'd always had a thing for Damien Colton. Even her mom had been able to see that.

She smiled to herself at the memory. She'd been one of the popular kids, a cheerleader and a senior when she'd turned a corner with an armload of books and crashed into him. The attraction had been instant and hot and it hadn't seemed to matter a bit that Damien was a lowly freshman. She'd had a secret crush on him. Apparently, Damien hadn't felt the same. Of course, at the time, she'd been dating Mike Straum, the ex-quarterback of the football team. Kind of intimidating to anyone, even a Colton. Not to mention that Damien had started seeing Lucy Walsh.

Except one night at a field party, she'd had too much to drink and somehow, gloriously, she and Damien had ended up in the backseat of his truck.

When Damien had been arrested for Mark Walsh's murder, she'd been stunned and had protested loudly and often. Finally, Bonnie Gene took her aside and explained she wasn't helping Damien by complaining. If she truly believed him innocent, then she needed to try and figure out a way she could actually help him.

But someone else wanted Damien Colton convicted quickly. The trial had steamrolled on and he'd been railroaded right into prison. Then, the only thing Eve had been able to do was write him a letter, asking him if she could come visit.

Damien had never responded. Eve had decided to go visit him anyway, but Bonnie Gene persuaded her not to.

She'd always regretted that.

Still, moving away? She guessed the ever-present censure of their small town had proven too much for him.

Damien returned, sliding into the booth across from her and pinning her with his gaze. "Where were we?"

"We were talking about the murders."

"Yes. You asked why Mark Walsh would fake his own death. I think when they find that out, a lot of the other pieces will fall into place. But right now, no one seems to know. Not even my own brother, and he's the sheriff."

"Look on the bright side. At least you're lucky enough to have a brother who *is* the sheriff. That way, you'll find out as soon as they learn anything."

"Pollyanna," he mocked softly. "Are you always so upbeat?"

"So I've been told. I tend to wear rose-colored glasses. That's one of my biggest faults."

His gaze locked with hers. After a moment, he laughed. "You don't even sound too upset about that. So tell me, Ms. Glass-half-full-kind-of-person. What brings you out to the Corner Bar on yet another cold, snowy night?"

"I'm a barfly," she said flippantly, trying to get her stomach to quit doing somersaults inside her. "I hang out in bars because that's what I do."

"No, you're not. If you were a real barfly, you'd be constantly on the prowl for men."

"Maybe that's what I'm doing with you," she teased back.

Staring at her, his eyes darkened. Immediately after tossing off the words, she wished she could call them back. She used to be so good at flirting. Apparently, she'd completely lost her touch. And why did she want to flirt with Damien Colton anyway?

"Dangerous territory." His low, deep growl confirming her thought should have made her want to back off, but instead, it thrilled her in some deep, visceral way.

As she searched her mind for a response, a loud guitar riff sounded and the bartender stepped up to the microphone.

"Ladies and gentlemen, put your hands together and welcome home our friends the Rollaboys!"

The room erupted in cheers.

The music made talking at less than a shout impossible, so, as the dance floor filled, Eve sat back and enjoyed the music. She took care to stay in the shadows, ensuring that Ian couldn't see her and making sure not to make eye contact with him.

The first two songs were rollicking, boot-stomping numbers. After Ian addressed the crowd, the band segued into a slow, romantic ballad, making Eve sigh. "One Heart Too Heavy" had always been one of her favorites.

"Eve?"

Suddenly, she realized that Damien had gotten to his feet and now stood beside her.

Leaning in close, he spoke directly into her ear, his warm breath tickling her and making her shiver.

"Care to dance?" He held out his hand.

She eyed the mass of bodies swaying to the steel guitar. Suddenly, she didn't care if Ian saw her, if anyone saw her. She wanted Damien. Wanted to be held in Damien's muscular arms, to feel his broad chest against her cheek. The town would talk, Ian would most likely notice her, but she realized she actually didn't care.

For an answer, she slipped her hand into his and let him pull her out onto the dance floor.

* * *

Intensely aware of his unruly body, Damien briefly cursed himself for his foolishness. He should have known better. Then Eve looked up at him, her bright-blue eyes luminous with happiness, and he didn't care. She felt good in his arms—warm and curvy and...right. If holding her close meant he had to work to keep from becoming too aroused, then so be it.

The music went sweet, then sad, full of melancholy. For Damien, the music barely registered, other than a beat to which to move his feet. Eve Kelley, melting in his arms, was as close to heaven as he'd ever been.

The song finished and rather than launching into another, Ian, the lead singer, announced they were taking a ten-minute break.

Heart pounding, Damien led Eve off the dance floor and back to their booth. He couldn't believe how strongly she affected him. Obviously, he didn't have the same effect on her.

"That was nice," she smiled up at him. "I haven't had this much fun in a long time. "

"Take your hands off her," a male voice shouted.

They both turned. Ian Murphy. Fists clenched, complexion mottled, the other man looked ready to fight.

Still pressed close into Damien's side, Eve groaned. "Cut it out, Ian."

Instead, Ian moved closer, his mouth twisted with disapproval. "What are you doing with him? For Chrissake, Eve. He's an ex-con! I've only been back in town a few days, but even I've heard about him."

At the other man's words, Damien took a step forward. Eve's gentle squeeze on his arm stopped him.

"He was wrongfully convicted, Ian." To Damien's disbelief, she moved even closer to him, as if she wanted to meld into his side. "And who I date is absolutely none of your business."

Ian's fair complexion turned a violent shade of red, but instead of arguing or, worse, picking a fight he'd surely lose, he spun around and stormed off.

Damien would have welcomed the fight, though it wouldn't have helped his status around Honey Creek.

Next to him, he felt Eve relax. "I think I'd better leave."

"Old flame?" he asked, keeping his tone light.

"Really old. We dated before he went off to Nashville and made it big. That was eighteen months ago."

Back at their table, she gathered her purse and coat. "I'm sorry, Damien. I'd really better go."

Unable to help himself, he caught her arm. "Let me go with you."

As she peered up at him, her pupils dilated, and he caught his breath. Finally, she gave the slightest of nods. "Come on then."

He didn't wait to be asked twice.

On the way to the door, Eve had second thoughts. And again as she climbed in her truck. What on earth was she thinking? Half of the Corner Bar would have noted her and Damien leaving together. Worse, since he was following her home in his vehicle, if anyone drove past her house…

Stop it. Stop it right now. She was lonely, he was lonely. They wanted each other and were both adults. What would be the harm?

As long as Damien understood this could only be physical. No strings. Why borrow trouble when she already had enough of her own?

Snow flurries drifted in her headlights as she drove home. Aware her car heater wouldn't even kick on until she was nearly home, Eve shivered as she tried to stay warm.

Hitting the automatic garage-door opener, she pulled into her garage and parked, wondering yet again if she wasn't making a horrible mistake.

Yet, thinking of how she'd felt dancing close to Damien brought a rush of warmth, and she reminded herself she didn't care.

Damien Colton was addicting. Something about him… She'd given in to that craving sixteen years ago and now that he'd returned, she was beginning to think she hadn't ever gotten him out of her system.

Damien parked in the driveway behind her, his extended-cab pickup too large to fit in her garage. Heart in her throat, she watched him stride toward her. When he reached her, he didn't speak, but instead gathered her close and kissed her. Right there in her garage, both of them still bundled in parkas, his mouth covered hers with a hungry intensity that told her she wasn't alone in the fierceness of her need.

The feel of him, so big and male, made her shiver. As his lips blazed over hers, desire, raw and hot and heavy, banished all rational thought.

She wanted this man. Now.

Raising his mouth from hers, he gazed deeply into her eyes. "Are you sure?" he asked.

For one confused moment, she wondered if she'd spoken her thoughts out loud. Then she looked up at him and her heart lurched. Despite his apparent confidence, she sensed his vulnerability.

Instead of answering his question with words, she wound her arms inside his jacket and raised up to touch her mouth to his, giving him her answer with her body instead.

It was like kindling erupting into flame. Her body tingled, burned as she wrapped herself around him, yearning to be closer still.

Somehow, still kissing, they stumbled toward the door.

Though they were still wound around each other, she had the presence of mind to hit the close button for the garage door. As she did, she muttered a quick prayer that her mother wouldn't see Damien's truck parked in her driveway. Not that Bonnie Gene would mind, but a full-out interrogation would be sure to follow.

Then, as his mouth grazed her ear and burned a path down her cheek and neck, she forgot about everything else but the magnificent man in her arms.

They made it inside, though she didn't know how. She came up for air long enough to realize they were in her bedroom.

Shedding her coat, she let it fall at her feet, watching as he did the same.

"Come here."

Throat tight, she moved closer to him, aching for him to caress her.

Instead, he began to remove her sweater, helping her tug her arms free. He undressed her slowly, gazing at her with a burning intensity, as if memorizing her with his eyes.

Finally naked while he stood still fully clothed, she squirmed against him, seeking to taunt him into losing control. From the harsh intake of his breath, she'd succeeded, but still he didn't move.

"Easy now," he told her, his voice sounding like smoke and gravel, a contrast with the cool brush of his hands against her skin. "Patience."

She tried to hold back, trembling with both cold and need, but with her desire mounting, she simply could not. With a curse of frustration she tore at his clothes, impatient to see him, to rake her nails against his rock-hard abs and explore his muscular body with her fingers.

Lifting his hands, he let her undress him, the heat in his gaze promising all sort of pleasure when she'd finished. As she fumbled with his belt buckle, he helped her, and when she unbuttoned his jeans, and freed him, he made a sound of pleasure low in his throat.

Holding back her wildness, she caressed the hard length of him, marveling at the thickness and size of his erection, wickedly amused as he froze, as if afraid to move.

Then, grabbing her hands to stop her, he pulled her hard up against him, flesh to flesh, man to woman.

"I don't have a condom," he rasped. "I had a complete physical when I got out, and I'm still clean, but... Sorry, but I wasn't expecting..."

"It's okay." Her chest hurt from wanting him so badly. "I'm already pregnant. And they tested me for everything when I had the pregnancy confirmed, so we ought to be all right."

Fire in his gaze, he slanted his mouth over hers, both demanding and giving. Fire and ice, summer and winter, trembling with passion, they fell onto the bed. She sighed as she found herself underneath him, his aroused sex hard and heavy against her thigh.

Arching her back, she gasped as his mouth closed over her nipple, shuddering as he touched her, skimming the curve of her waist, stroking her moistness.

She cried out as he entered her, filling her.

"Perfect," he murmured, his lips curving as he began to slowly move.

As he did, the ache sparked by his kiss exploded into flame. Her body throbbed as he entered her completely and then withdrew, leaving her aching for him. Waves of passionate ecstasy filled her as they moved together, body-to-body, so close she couldn't tell where she ended and he began.

Her passion became mindless. She cried out, and he answered her with a deep thrust.

Just like that, she shattered into a thousand pieces.

As she clenched around him, he groaned, sending waves of ecstasy into her core with each long, deep stroke. A moment later, he found his own release, crying out and collapsing against her.

They held each other, their bodies damp from love-making, sated. She liked that she felt so comfortable with him, liked that she didn't feel the need to fill the space with vague conversation.

When he rose to clean up, she watched him walk to her bathroom and admired the view from behind. He turned and caught her watching and grinned before closing the door behind him.

This just might work out, she congratulated herself as she lay back in her bed, hands behind her head. All her life she'd gone into relationships with high expectations. Now, having learned her lesson, she had no expectations at all. Why ask for more when she'd never gotten more? Less heartache, more pleasure. Good all the way around.

Now, if only she could make herself believe it.

And if her heart gave a twinge whenever she thought of Damien moving away, she put it down to the newness of things, nothing more.

She'd been a fool back in Italy. She wouldn't make that mistake again.

Chapter 8

Working at the salon was becoming more and more difficult, the further along Eve got in her pregnancy. Her back was killing her. If she felt this bad at only four months, she wondered what she'd be like at eight.

She watched Mrs. Grant, her eight-thirty shampoo and set, walk to her car. Luckily her next customer wasn't due for another fifteen minutes, so Eve could take a quick apple-juice break and rest her feet.

The changes that had begun to take place in her body both amazed and thrilled her. Not only had she began to 'ripen' as she thought of it, with fuller breasts and a softly rounded stomach, but her ankles now swelled when she stood on her feet all day. And the exhaustion! It seemed she barely had time to finish her breakfast and begin her workday and she craved a nap.

Like now. Stifling a yawn, she grabbed her juice from the fridge and dropped into her desk chair, unwrapping her midmorning granola bar.

The sleigh bells on the front door jingled merrily. Lacy Nguyen, her part-time stylist, waved at her as she came in. "Good morning," she sang out. "Sure smells like snow out there."

Eve laughed. "When does it not? It's December in Montana. If it didn't smell like snow, I'd be more surprised."

"Still, I'd love some Christmas snow. Maybe we could build a magical snowman!" Lacy grinned as she hung up her parka. "I've got a full day booked today."

"Good." Barely stifling a yawn, Eve took another bite of her granola bar. "I do, too."

Lacy studied her. "You look… Hey, are you seeing someone?"

Eve almost choked on her granola. "What? No. Why do you ask?"

"Because you're glowing." Lacy shrugged. "You know, like you're in love or something?"

Relieved, Eve laughed. If Lacy only knew. "Nope. The latest on the dating front is that I went on another disastrous blind date my mom set up. This time it was with that new attorney, Gary Jackson."

"Ewww." Lacy made a face. "He hit on me once. Didn't seem to mind when I said I was engaged."

The doorbells jingled again. Both women looked up, and froze. Maisie Colton stood in the doorway, wearing a bright-orange full-length down coat and fuchsia-and-orange striped scarf and gloves. Even with her windblown hair, she looked as though she'd just finished posing for a glossy magazine advertisement on winter.

"Eve?" She stepped inside, her high heels clicking on the linoleum. "Do you have a minute to talk?" Her gaze cut to Lacy. "Privately?" she added.

Immediately, Lacy snatched up a load of freshly washed

towels. "I'll be in the back, folding these," she said, darting a meaningful look at Eve. "If you need me, just yell."

"What can I do for you, Maisie?" Eve asked carefully.

"I wanted to talk to you about Gary Jackson. I know you were out with him the other night—"

Now Eve understood. Maisie was interested and wanted to make sure she wasn't encroaching on Eve's territory. What was up with that? Since when had Maisie cared?

"Gary and I were on a blind date set up by our mothers. I have absolutely no interest in him and I have no doubt he feels exactly the same way."

"Really?" Maisie's heart-shaped face lit up, making Eve realize exactly how beautiful Damien's sister was. "I wanted to make sure. He asked me out for next weekend."

Curious, Eve decided to be blunt. "Why do you care what I think?"

The question didn't seem to faze Maisie.

"I know it might seem weird. In the past, if I wanted something, I took it." Her perfectly painted lips curved. "I guess I just realized I had to grow up sometime. I'm trying to repair the damage I've done to people in this town."

"That's why you joined my mother's quilting group?"

"Yes. And I haven't actually joined yet. I'm still trying to get up the nerve to go to a meeting."

Really? Maisie Colton, frightened of something? "What are you afraid of?"

Taking a deep breath, Maisie met Eve's gaze, unsmiling. "Those other women don't like me much."

Eve didn't know what to say. Maisie had spoken the truth and to try and dilute that with platitudes or reassurance would only undermine it. Still, she had to say *something*.

"Do you know how to quilt?"

"No." Maisie brightened. "But your mother promised

to teach me. I want to make a quilt for my son, sort of an heirloom thing."

Touched, despite herself, Eve nodded. "And you came here because you want me to help you figure out how to get along with all those women?"

"No." Maisie Colton shook her head, sending her wayward hair flying. "I came here because I want you to cut my hair."

Then, while Eve was still reeling from this shocking news, Maisie made a scissoring motion with her fingers, right below her chin. "I want it cut short. Very short."

Still staring, Eve swallowed. "Seriously?"

"Yes, seriously." Stalking over to Eve's chair, Maisie sat. "Let's get busy. You've got to get me finished before your next client comes in."

True. Shaking out the vinyl cape, Eve draped it around Maisie's shoulders. "Let's get you shampooed."

Maisie's hair was thick and lustrous, much like her brother's. Eve shampooed and rinsed and wrapped her in a towel, before leading her back to the chair and combing her out. "Now tell me what kind of a haircut you want."

Maisie grinned. "I'll do better. I'll show you." She grabbed her purse, rummaging inside and finally pulling out a folded square that had obviously been taken from a magazine. "Here you go. It's Rihanna. A pixie crop with a sweeping fringe."

"So it is." Eve glanced from the picture to Maisie. "You do realize this will involve me cutting off at least six inches?"

"Sure."

Relentlessly determined, Eve continued. "And you'll have to use styling products and a flat iron after you blow-dry?"

"I already do. Let's go for it."

"Fine." Eve grabbed her scissors and began. She couldn't help but wince as the long locks fell to the floor. "Does your brother know you're doing this?"

"Which brother?"

"Any of them," Eve said, refining her cut around the back. "Wes, Finn, Brand, Perry, Duke or Damien."

"No. But then I'm not in the habit of consulting my brothers before I get a new haircut." Taking a deep breath, Maisie closed her eyes. "He was with you last night, wasn't he?"

Eve was so busy snipping away that Maisie's words barely registered. "Who?"

"My brother. Damien."

Eve nearly cut off a huge swath of Maisie's silky hair. Accidentally, of course. "Ummm, maybe," she said hesitantly. "Why?"

Maisie opened her eyes. "I just want to know what your intentions are toward him."

Dumbfounded, Eve met the other woman's gaze in the mirror. "My intentions?"

"Yes. Damien's fragile. He doesn't really know how to react to the regular world. He's only been out a few months."

"Fragile. Huh." Resuming cutting, Eve couldn't seem to get past repeating parts of Maisie's words. "I think you should ask him."

"I tried." Pouting, Maisie sounded disgruntled. "He told me what he did in his spare time was none of my business."

Relieved, Eve began to shape the hair at the side of Maisie's face. "He's right, you know."

"Maybe. But someone has to look out for him. No one else will, so it might as well be me."

This struck Eve as both touching and funny, for some

reason. The image of Damien hiding behind his slender and glamorous sister made her want to laugh. Her mouth twitched, but she succeeded in holding it in.

Almost.

"Don't laugh," Maisie complained. "I'm serious."

"I understand." Brandishing her scissors high, Eve smiled. "Did it ever occur to you not to shock the woman who's cutting your hair?"

Maisie's perfectly made-up eyes widened. "You wouldn't," she breathed.

"No, of course not. I was just trying to get you to lighten up." She shook her head. "I'm a professional. Plus, I'd like you to come back. I know if I do a good job, you might."

Finally, Maisie's shoulders relaxed. "I *was* tense, wasn't I? I'm sorry. I try so hard, but I've never really gotten along with other women."

That was the understatement of the year.

The jingle bells signaled the arrival of Lacy's client. Emerging from the back room, Lacy did a double take to see Eve cutting Maisie Colton's hair. Eve shot her a warning look and the other stylist went to collect her customer, who also stared hard at Maisie. The news that Maisie Colton had gotten her hair cut at Eve's Salon Allegra would be all over town before the end of the day.

Finishing the cut, Eve sprayed Maisie's hair with a root booster and began blow-drying, showing the other woman how to style with a roller brush, then using a flat iron.

When she'd finished, she stepped back to survey the results before turning Maisie around to face the mirror.

"This might just be the perfect haircut for you," she said, letting Maisie see.

"Wow!" Maisie breathed, turning her head this way and that. "It looks really good." She shook her head, experimenting. "My head feels really light. I never realized how heavy all that hair was."

Removing the cape, Eve smiled. "I'm glad you like it."

After Maisie had paid and left, Eve checked her watch. Mrs. Peterson, her next customer, was late. As she was walking to check her appointment desk, the phone rang. It was Mrs. Peterson, canceling. Which meant Eve had an entire hour before Damien was due to arrive for his haircut. She went in the back to put her feet up and, she hoped, take a catnap.

She'd actually dozed off when the sound of the bells woke her. Peeking out front, she saw that Lacy's client had left. And the second she did, Lacy hurried back and plopped down into the chair next to Eve. "Tell me, tell me everything."

Covering her mouth while she yawned, Eve found herself feeling oddly defensive on Maisie's behalf. "Tell you what? There's nothing to tell. She wanted a haircut. I gave her one. That's what I'm in business for, right?"

Lacy looked unconvinced. "Well, yeah. But Maisie Colton never stoops to having her hair cut here. You know as well as I do that she always goes to Billings. We're not sophisticated enough for her."

"Maisie Colton is trying to change."

Lacy opened her mouth to argue when the bells jingled again.

Glancing at the clock, Eve stood. "My next client." She wondered if she should warn Lacy, then decided not to. It would be fun to see her face.

"Mine should be here any minute, too." Lacy would surely get her second shock of the day.

* * *

Usually having sex put Damien in a good mood, freed his pent-up tension and relaxed him. Not this time. The entire weekend, he'd been tense and restless, unable to stop thinking about Friday night and making love with Eve. Already he'd wanted her again; he'd reached for her first thing when he woke on Saturday morning. He'd never done that before and it worried him.

The rest of the weekend hadn't been any better. He'd wanted her at odd moments during the day. In fact, he'd had to force himself not to go to the Corner Bar on Saturday night, not wanting Eve to think he needed more than she was willing to give.

Evidently he hadn't gotten her out of his system yet.

Sunday and Monday had both been much of the same. He'd kept himself busy, rising at the crack of dawn and saddling up to ride out in the early-morning chill. He and his gelding had slogged through snow, keeping an eye out for any straggling cattle, and watching the sun come up over the mountains.

Days like these made him wonder how he could ever leave Montana or this ranch. The land was in his blood, as vital to him as fresh air. Sometimes he thought if he had the land, a horse and a few hundred head of cattle, he wouldn't need anything else.

Except sex, he amended. Again, he thought of Eve and shifted in the saddle. She could easily become an addiction. He craved her, craved the feel and scent of her, the satiny smoothness of her skin.

Again, he was struck by a sharp sense of need. Eve. No, he told himself. It didn't have to be her. Any woman would fit the bill. He wanted more sex. Lots of it, plain and simple. Not Eve.

But he knew he was only lying to himself.

Damn it to hell. She'd done something to him. Usually, the physical release after sex lasted him at least a week, sometimes longer if he kept busy.

But not this time. After making love with Eve, all he could think about was being with her again. He felt as if he'd been literally starving and she'd been a feast. A feast he couldn't get enough of.

He had to stay away, prove he could tough this out.

Still, he was glad he'd made the hair appointment with her for today. He needed a haircut and that would be a perfect time to prove he was immune to her lure.

After performing his morning chores, he'd plowed through lunch. All day he'd had an eagerness lurking low in his gut.

When it had come time to drive to town, he'd felt unaccountably nervous and edgy. He, who had faced down a three-hundred-and-sixty-pound enraged, territorial prison inmate, dreaded facing slender Eve Kelley. As if she could simply take one look at him and know he'd spent the last fifty-six hours thinking about her.

The walk from his truck to her salon door seemed far too long. Boots crunching in the frozen snow, he reached the door, wondering for the eightieth time why he hadn't just gone to the Old Time Barber Shop like he, and all the other Colton men, always did.

But he knew the answer to that. He wanted to see Eve.

Little bells jingled as he yanked open the door to Salon Allegra. Approaching the front counter, he saw the shop was empty and breathed a sigh of relief. The last thing he needed was to have a bunch of women with foil or curlers in their hair staring at him.

Then Eve emerged from the back, her smile so warm, so welcoming, he felt he could face down an entire army of gossiping women. He barely noticed a second woman following Eve, then stopping in her tracks and staring at him, openmouthed.

"You made it!" Eve sounded glad—and surprised.

Nodding, he smiled, managing to keep the smile plastered on his face while she introduced the other woman, Lacy Nguyen.

Eve whisked a cloak around him. "Follow me. We'll get you shampooed, then you can tell me how you'd like me to cut your hair." She took him to the back, waited until he had taken a seat, then ran the water.

Spraying his head with warm water, she began to massage his scalp with shampoo. Her deft fingers felt so good, he nearly moaned. Instead, he closed his eyes.

Apparently as nervous as he, Eve kept up a constant monologue as she worked. "Poor Lacy doesn't know what to think. First your sister, then you—"

He snapped open his eyes. "My sister? Maisie came here?"

"Yes. She had me cut her hair really short. The cut she wanted wouldn't work on just anyone, but on her it's fabulous. Wait until you see her."

"I'm more interested in what she had to say."

Eve colored, a dead giveaway. Rinsing his hair off, she wrapped his head in a white towel, then began to do a quick towel-dry. For a moment, he thought she wouldn't answer. Then, she lifted one shoulder in a quick shrug.

"She asked me what my intentions were toward you."

He laughed. "What did you say?"

Glancing around to make sure Lacy couldn't hear, Eve leaned in close and whispered in his ear, "I told her they were purely sinful."

Shocked by both her words and the quick flick of her tongue on his ear, he froze.

Her laugh was more musical than the bells on her door.

"Really?" he managed. "I can just imagine Maisie's reaction."

"Just kidding," Eve continued merrily, as if oblivious to her effect on him. "In a roundabout way, I told her it was none of her business."

"Did she take that well?"

"Well, she didn't throw a temper tantrum or anything, so I guess so." She ran her fingers through his hair, testing texture and length. "Now tell me how you want this cut."

Fifteen short minutes later, eyeing himself in the mirror, Damien admitted she'd done a good job. She'd trimmed his unruly hair into a much neater do, managing to make his longish style look both hip and clean. "I won't be spraying any of that stuff on it after I shower," he warned her. "I usually just towel-dry and go."

Her blue eyes widened. "You go out into the subzero temperature with wet hair?"

"It dries long before I head out." He got out his wallet. "How much do I owe you?"

She waved him away. "Nothing. It's on the house."

An awful suspicion worried him. "Did you cut my sister's hair on the house also?"

Eve grinned. "Nope. I charged her thirty-five bucks."

"For a haircut?"

Her grin widened. "No need to sound so shocked. She pays twice that at the place she normally goes." She licked her lips, a mischievous twinkle in her eyes. "I'm worth it."

"Yes," he agreed, even as his body stirred. "You are." He got out two twenties and placed them on the counter. "Here you go."

"Men's cuts are only twenty." She slid one of the bills back toward him.

He slid it back. "Then this is your tip."

Coloring, she nodded. "Okay, then. Thanks."

Conscious of the other woman watching, he leaned closer. "Are you busy later on? I was thinking we could hang out tonight, if you want."

Again she flashed him a smile as her lashes swept down to cover her eyes. But only for a second, then she lifted her chin and her clear blue gaze met his.

"I'd like that," she said softly. "Where and when?"

"I'll pick you up at your place. Say, seven? We'll go grab a bite to eat."

"Why don't you bring food over instead?" she murmured, apparently also conscious of Lacy's inquisitive stare. "I don't think I'm going to feel much like going out."

Zing. Just like that, she had the capacity to stop his heart. "Okay," he managed. "What time?"

"Six is good. The earlier the better." Then, while he was still reeling from the possibilities in her smile, she walked away, waving goodbye at him over her shoulder.

He left the salon in a daze.

"Do you have a date?" Lacy followed Eve into the back room.

"No, of course not." Eve knew her denial came too quickly. Another dead giveaway would be the rush of color staining her cheeks.

"I swear I heard Damien Colton ask you out," Lacy persisted. "And I'm pretty sure you answered yes."

"First off, we're not going out." Truth, since they were staying in. "And secondly, Damien and I are just friends."

"Since when?"

"Since high school," Eve shot back, shooting her employee a look that plainly told her to back off. "Nothing to gossip about. Just two old friends catching up."

"Okay, have it your way." Clearly skeptical, Lacy shook her head. "But let me point out that if the two of you are such good friends, Damien's been home for months and this is the first time he's been in the shop."

Since Eve didn't have an answer for that one, she let it go. Time to change the subject and try to put things back on a normal footing.

"Speaking of the Coltons, today's turning out to be a Colton Monday," Eve said, finger on her appointment book. "First Maisie, then Damien and next Sharon, though she's the only one who actually had an appointment in advance."

Sharon Colton, Darius Colton's wife, was due in for her usual highlights and cut. She had a standing appointment once a month and was meticulous about keeping her frosted blond hair looking exactly the same. Though some found her standoffish, Eve liked the older woman, who had a lot to cope with in marrying into the Colton family as she had, especially since she was Darius's third or fourth wife. She rarely left the ranch, and when she came to town, it was either to get her hair or nails done, or to eat at Eve's family's famous barbecue restaurant.

Even the Coltons were unable to resist the perfection of the Kelley's slow-cooked brisket or smoked ribs. The restaurant was especially busy this time of the year with its smoked holiday turkeys.

"Better you than me," Lacy said, yawning and apparently giving up. "This has been a long day. I'm ready to call it a day."

"Me, too. I just have this one more customer, then I can lock the place up and head home."

The bells over the front door tinkled, telling them Sharon had arrived. Hurrying out into the salon area, Eve stopped short at her first glimpse of her client. Usually,

Sharon Colton looked like a less dramatic version of Maisie—perfectly put together, remote and fashionable. Not today.

Though she wore one of the many full-length fur coats her rich cattleman husband had given her, her heart-shaped face looked drawn and pale. The huge circles under her blue eyes made her look tired, and every tiny line stood out in stark relief. Many of the townspeople believed she went to Bozeman on a regular basis and got Botox treatments, but looking at her this morning, Eve doubted it.

"Are you all right?" she asked softly.

Sharon looked up, swaying slightly. "I think so. Or I will be, once I finish getting pampered." Her tight smile didn't reach her eyes. As usual she spoke with a hint of a Southern accent, the kind that blurred her words and softened consonants.

If she didn't want to elaborate, Eve wouldn't make her. "Well, come on then." Eve patted her chair. "Have a seat and let me mix up your color. I won't be a minute."

Sharon complied, sitting quiet and stiff while Eve draped a cloak around her. Eve left her there, going into the back room to prepare the color, returning with the mixture and her box of precut foils. They'd do the highlights first, as usual, then shampoo, color and style.

Sometimes Sharon chattered away, sometimes not. Today appeared to be one of the latter times, since Sharon closed her eyes while Eve began painting on the highlights, then wrapping them in foil. Because of her pregnancy, Eve wore two layers of rubber gloves and a mask to protect her, not wanting to take a chance. To her shock and amazement, Sharon fell asleep, dozing while Eve completed the highlights.

When she'd finished, she gently touched Sharon's slender

shoulder, waking her. "All right, it's time to go under the dryer."

"Give me a minute." The older woman blinked, speaking as though she were drugged.

"Are you sure you're okay?"

"Yes. No. Something's wrong at home," Sharon confessed abruptly, the anguish in her eyes wrenching Eve's heart. "Darius has been worse since Damien came home. I don't know what to do."

She actually sounded afraid. Even terrified. Then, before Eve could comment, she continued.

"I think my own husband is trying to kill me."

Chapter 9

"Trying to kill you?" Eve repeated, shooting Sharon a shocked look. "Why do you say that?"

As if she regretted saying anything, Sharon's expression shut down. Carefully blank, she shook her head. "Forget I said anything, all right?"

As if. Still, what else could Eve do?

Carefully considering her words, Eve slowly nodded. "If you need help, or just someone to talk to, call me. I'll write my cell phone number on the back of my card, all right?"

Instead of answering, Sharon looked away, her remote expression indicating the conversation was over. Eve led her to the dryer and left her, setting the timer for fifteen minutes.

In the back of the salon, Lacy had just finished removing the last load of towels from the dryer and folding them.

She looked up as Eve approached, then hurried over to take Eve's arm.

"Are you all right? You look awfully pale."

"I'm…" Eve had to think for a moment. "I'm fine. Just tired. I've got Sharon Colton under the dryer. After I finish with her, I'm going home."

Lacy studied her. "I was going to leave, but I'm thinking I'd better hang around in case you faint or something. Maybe you should sit down." She pulled out a chair.

Without even arguing, Eve sat. "Ah," she breathed. "That's better."

"Maybe you've been working too hard." Still concerned, Lacy fluttered around her like a mother hen. "You should consider taking a day off."

Eve waved her off. "I haven't been working too hard and I'll have plenty of time off for the Christmas holiday. Today's just been a rough one."

"I guess, with all the Coltons coming in and all." Finally, Lacy moved away. "Then if you really are all right…"

"You can go home. I've still got to rinse Sharon Colton, then cut and style her hair. I should be thirty more minutes tops."

Lacy eyed her slyly. "And then you can get ready for your big date with Damien Colton."

"It's not a date," Eve began automatically, stopping as Lacy burst into laughter.

"Call it whatever you want. Just have a nice night." Still giggling, Lacy waved as she headed toward the door. "See you tomorrow."

As she finished up with Sharon, Eve remained quiet, hoping to give the older woman a chance to talk if she wanted to. But Sharon said nothing else, her closed-off expression indicating she wasn't open to questions.

When Eve finished styling her hair, Sharon laid a crisp, one-hundred-dollar bill on the counter as she always did.

"Merry Christmas," she said, her attempt to appear carefree falling short. Swirling her fur coat around her shoulders, she sailed off.

Locking the door behind her, Eve wondered about Sharon's earlier remark. Surely she hadn't been serious, though her fear had seemed real enough.

Still, her own husband? Darius had been married three or four times, but all the marriages except the first one, the one who'd been the mother of most of the Colton children, had ended in divorce. Had Darius threatened Sharon? Was he abusive?

The answer to that, Eve didn't know. No one except his own family and maybe his business associates truly knew Darius Colton. Reclusive and secretive, the man seldom left the ranch. She'd heard gossip, but she didn't know what to believe about him, negative or otherwise. Maybe she should ask Damien.

Or, she told herself, shaking her head, maybe she should keep her nose out of other people's business.

Still, the fear in Sharon's eyes haunted her as she drove home.

Though he had a few more end-of-the-day chores to finish before he could clean up and head over to Eve's place, Damien couldn't concentrate on any of them. He felt like a teenager about to go on a date with the most popular girl in school.

Despite an outdoor temperature in the low twenties, he took a cold shower, trying to control his unruly body.

Then he had to decide on food. Honey Creek wasn't big enough to have a huge selection of fast-food places. Besides Kelley's Cookhouse and the Corner Bar and Grill, there was a pizza parlor, a hamburger joint and the newest place, a Mexican cantina. Guadalupe Torres and his wife, Angelina, had moved to Montana from Laredo, Texas, and wanted to introduce Mexican food to Honey Creek. Damien hadn't tried it yet and he was willing to bet neither had Eve.

Perfect. He phoned in an order for beef and chicken fajitas. He'd pick them up on the way to Eve's.

The drive from the ranch back into town went quickly, though it seemed agonizingly slow to him. But the food was ready and before he knew it, he was on his way.

The spicy aroma filled his car, making him realize he was hungry. This, oddly enough, relaxed him. Grinning as he pulled into Eve's driveway and parked, he grabbed the box of food and went to her front door.

He'd barely pressed the doorbell when she opened the door, wearing a red silky bathrobe. As she stepped back to let him enter, she closed the door behind her and took the food out of his hands, carrying it to the kitchen.

Not sure what to do, Damien waited in the living room, taking in her Christmas decorations. A fire roared in the stone fireplace and a slender Christmas tree stood in one corner, decorated in red, gold and green. He liked the simple, uncluttered look of the room, so different from his own family's all-out Christmas attack.

Behind him, Eve made a sound. When he turned, she strolled over to him, expression determined, and then, gaze locked with his, she stepped out of the robe.

Slipping her sleeves from her robe felt like one of the most daring things Eve had ever done. Heart pounding in her throat, she trembled as she lifted her chin and met Damien's glorious brown eyes. Then, taking a deep breath, she stepped out of her clothing, feeling way out of her comfort zone baring herself to him. She felt naked in more than her body—she felt naked in spirit, too.

She needn't have worried. Damien inhaled, a harsh sound, then his gaze darkened and he pulled her into his arms.

This time when they made love, she couldn't believe the way they immediately found an exquisite rhythm, a mutual harmony that made each kiss, every caress magic.

Now that the first rush of heady desire had become a steady, pulsing thrum, they were able to take their time exploring each other's bodies. She let herself luxuriate in the feel of him, gliding her hand over his muscular abdomen, caressing his broad shoulders and perfect abs. She delighted in teasing him, bending over him to take his nipples in her mouth, trailing kisses down the hard length of him until he shuddered and told her no more.

"My turn," he rasped, and nearly turned the tables. His lips traced a sensual path down her throat, to her breasts, and she let out a soft moan as he took her in his mouth.

Now she couldn't go slowly any longer. With fierce cries she urged him on. He shook his head and continued his teasing torture, until she'd finally had enough.

Pushing him over on his back, she straddled him. Poising herself over the hard length of his body, she lowered herself onto him, taking him deep within her and riding him until he bucked like a rodeo bronco.

Seconds later she found her release and as she did, he cried out and did the same.

Later, she microwaved the now-cold food and they feasted on fajitas. Covered by only a blanket, they sat on the rug near her fireplace and cuddled.

"How's Sharon doing?" she asked without thinking.

"I don't know. We hardly ever see her. She and Darius

have an entire wing to themselves and she keeps mostly to herself. Why?"

She knew he felt her tense. "No reason," she lied. "I cut her hair this afternoon and she wasn't feeling too well."

"Hmmm." He nuzzled her neck. "I'm sorry to hear that."

Though she knew she should let it go, she couldn't. "Sharon was worried about Darius. She thought he might... be angry at her."

Now he drew back. "There's more that you're not telling me, isn't there?"

Miserable, she nodded, then blurted out the whole story.

Damien listened, his expression thoughtful. "Please don't tell anyone else what you've told me."

"I won't," she hastened to reassure him. "But poor Sharon seemed so terrified, so I thought I'd better let you know so you could keep an eye on things."

"I will, believe me." Once again Damien pulled her close, holding her. The way he held her made her feel as though she was the most precious thing in the world. For half a second, before she took herself to task.

She was done wearing rose-colored glasses and she no longer believed in fairy tales or happy endings. It was time to call a spade and spade and be grateful for what she did have.

"About our arrangement..." Nervously, she pushed out of his arms and cleared her throat. "I think we should have some ground rules."

One corner of his mouth quirked in the beginning of a smile. "Okay. Shoot."

"First off, this is for fun. The minute it stops being fun for either of us, we can call it off, no hard feelings."

He nodded.

"Two, no emotional entanglements. Three, once I start showing, you can't make fat jokes. That is, assuming you still want to continue seeing me once I'm showing."

Now he did laugh. "Come here."

More afraid than she'd realized, she allowed him to pull her close once more. As he nuzzled her neck again, she found thinking difficult.

"You worry too much. One day at a time, Eve Kelley. One day at a time."

Then he covered her mouth with his and she gave up trying to think.

Back at the ranch after spending a few wonderful hours with Eve, Damien enjoyed a perfect night's sleep for the first time in ages. He awoke on Tuesday morning sated and refreshed and craving coffee.

Later, as he sipped his coffee and had to stop himself from whistling out loud, he realized that the world couldn't have gone completely crazy. If he tried really hard, he could just about convince himself that the two episodes with Darius were the result of his father being out of sorts due to having had a bad day and/or drinking too much.

Darius had long been the patriarch of the Colton clan, and was a well-respected rancher. He'd try talking to his father again. Surely, this time Darius would be more reasonable.

Even if he wasn't, Damien had no choice but to confront him. He had to find out where his money had gone. Darius owed him that much. If he couldn't replace the inheritance, he needed at least to provide a reasonable explanation for its disappearance.

He knew he could catch Darius in his office at this time of morning, attending to ranch business. Prudently, he gave the older man time to ingest a few cups of coffee, not sure if morning crankiness might be another of his sire's recent bad traits.

At least this time he'd be sober.

Tapping on the heavy oak door, Damien waited until Darius looked up from his paperwork. "Do you have a minute?"

Darius frowned, but he motioned to the chair in front of his desk. "What do you want?"

The rude question made Damien feel like a panhandler, let in from the cold and begging for a handout, but he forced himself to let the feeling slide away.

"I wanted to talk to you about my inheritance."

Immediately, Darius's expression twisted with anger. "That again. I've already told you, the money is gone. Live with it and quit bothering me."

"Last time we spoke, you'd had a few drinks." Damien kept his tone level, even soothing. "I understand the money is gone. What I'd like to know is where it went."

With a snarl, Darius removed his glasses and threw them onto the desk. "That is none of your business."

Damien felt as if the bell had just rung for round two. Why did all dealings with his father have to disintegrate into arguments and fights?

Taking a deep breath, Damien tried to tamp back his instinctive reaction to his father's behavior—his own anger. Maybe if he refused to let the old man goad him, they could eventually have a civil conversation.

Maybe.

"This *is* my business," he insisted. "It was my money and I'd like to know what you've done with it."

To his surprise, Darius actually nodded.

"Fair enough." Darius's expression smoothed over and his tone became pleasant. "As conservator, I invested it for you, hoping to make more money. As you know, the stock market tanked. I lost it. Every single penny."

Finally. A reasonable explanation.

"I'd like to see the transaction records."

Darius's expression hardened and his mouth thinned in displeasure, though his tone remained civil. "When I have time, I'll locate those and get them to you."

And now Damien had a choice. He could agree, aware Darius was putting him off and had no real intention of finding anything, or he could insist on seeing the records now. While the latter would be the most productive, it also was the most likely to provoke Darius into a rage.

Still, Damien hadn't come this far to back down now. Maybe if he kept everything calm and rational, Darius would follow his lead.

"Actually, I'd like to see them now."

"Actually," Darius mocked him. "That's not possible. I don't know where they are."

Now came the tricky part. "This is your office. I'm sure you must have a file for your stock transactions. If you'll let me review the file, I can make copies of anything pertaining to my money."

A flicker of horror flashed across the older man's face. "No. I'm too busy to deal with this right now. Plus, no one makes copies of my personal financial records. No one. Understand? Now go away."

Damien didn't move. "I'm not going anywhere. I'm well within my rights to ask to see records of my own money."

"You have no rights," Darius spat, his gaze full of contempt. "Now get out."

"Don't start this—"

"You started it by coming in here and demanding, in my own office, in my own house. How dare you demand anything from me. You ought to be grateful I give you a roof over your head, boy."

Face a glowering mask of rage, Darius stood and pointed toward the door. "Go away before I say something I might regret."

"What, you haven't already?" Damien didn't bother to hide his disappointment. "All this shadow-dancing makes me think you really do have something to hide."

"You don't even know the half of it," Darius sneered. "I could snap my fingers and have you killed, just like that."

This stopped Damien cold. "What are you saying?"

"I'm just saying, don't go poking your nose in places it doesn't belong, understand me?"

"You're my father." Damien felt as if a heavy weight pressed against his chest. "How can you talk like that to me?"

In reply, Darius gave a nasty chuckle. "I can't allow personal relationships to get in the way of business. This is business. I told you to leave before you heard something you didn't want to hear. The truth isn't always pretty, now, is it?"

"I wonder if you even know what the truth really is." Finally, realizing that if he wanted answers, he'd have to get them on his own, Damien pushed to his feet. "I just hope that when I find out what really happened, I don't discover you have been lying to me."

"Or what?" Darius crossed his arms, his face hard. "You gonna treat me like some of your prison buddies no doubt treated you?"

Instead of dignifying this awful statement with a response, Damien slammed out of the room, Darius's mocking laughter following him, making him want to hit something.

In the kitchen, he grabbed the wall phone and dialed the sheriff's office. Wes answered on the second ring.

"I'm calling a family meeting," Damien announced.

Wes cursed. "Not now. I don't have time for this."

"Make time. Things are worse here than you realize."

"You don't understand. I'm working a murder investigation."

Damien didn't pull any punches. "You'll be working another one if we don't deal with Darius now."

Shocked silence. Then, as Damien had known he would, Wes agreed to be there.

Finn was easier. "Sure," he agreed. "As long as it's at night or on a weekend, I'll drive out to the ranch."

"Tonight, seven o'clock."

"That soon? Things must really be bad. Okay, count me in. I'll be there."

Two down, five to go. Next, Damien phoned Duke.

"Tonight, Susan wants me to help her pick out food for the wedding." Duke sounded as though he'd rather wallow in pig excrement. "If I tell her I have an emergency family meeting, I think I can get out of it."

"I'll need you to back me up on what's been going on around here."

"Can do." Sounding relieved, Duke hung up to go find his fiancée and tell her the news.

Last, Damien went looking for Maisie. He'd been surprised when Eve had told him she'd cut his sister's hair. Last he'd heard, Maisie had been paying over a hundred bucks for a haircut at some fancy salon up in Billings.

When she opened the door after his knock, and he saw her, he was shocked speechless.

"You like it?" She preened, spinning around so he could get the full effect. "Eve did a wonderful job."

"Wow! When she said she'd cut your hair, I had no idea,"

he began. The look of glee in his sister's eyes made him realize his mistake.

"You saw her?"

He crossed his arms. "Yes. Yesterday. She cut my hair, too. Why?"

"She didn't say anything about seeing you. I even asked her about her intentions."

"You did what?"

"Asked her about your intentions. When did you get your hair cut?"

"After you." Swearing under his breath, he shook his head. "I already told you, none of your business." He shook off his irritation. This was Maisie, after all. She'd always danced to the beat of her own drum. "We're having a family meeting at seven tonight. Perry, Joan and Brand aren't around, and you and Jeremy need to be in attendance, all right?"

She nodded, then looked dubious. "Is Darius going to be there?"

"No. Darius is the reason we're having a meeting. We're going to discuss him."

"Behind his back?" Maisie scrunched up her nose. "He won't like that."

"He's not going to find out. Just be there, Maisie. Okay?"

Finally, she agreed. "Make sure you have something to eat. I'm usually hungry around seven," she said. Then, claiming she needed a nap, she closed the door in his face.

That evening, waiting in the kitchen as everyone straggled in, Damien tried to plan what he wanted to say. The others had to understand that Darius was ill and apparently had been for quite some time.

Maisie arrived last, after the others were seated. Since

he'd called the meeting, Damien remained standing. Pacing helped him articulate better.

Damien cleared his throat. When everyone had fallen silent, he began. He told them about the disappearance of his inheritance, then recounted the scene with Darius in his office that morning.

"He threatened to kill you?" Duke's tone reflected his shock.

Even Maisie appeared stunned. Only Jeremy gave no reaction, but continued stuffing his face with gingerbread cookies.

"Yes. He intimated that he could have someone do the deed. Like he'd done it before."

"Now wait a minute," Wes pushed to his feet. "This is crazy. Darius may be a lot of things, but he's still our father. I know he's been growing increasingly unstable, but murder—whether for hire or otherwise—is a serious crime. Darius knows that. He won't risk the ranch and our futures, not to mention his own, for something like that."

"I don't think Darius gives a rat's ass about any of us," Damien said. "And as for risking the ranch, I believe he already has."

Finn shook his head. "You have no proof. You're saying that based on what happened with your inheritance."

"That, and the fact that he won't let me examine the books. Have any of you seen the books for this ranch?"

"No. Sharon does them for him. She used to be an accountant. Have you asked her?"

"No." Damien dragged his hand through his hair. "But I will, now that I know." He took a deep breath, meeting each of their eyes, one by one.

"Back to Darius. We need to get him in for medical tests. I think there might be something wrong. Either that or he's a sociopath." He attempted a chuckle, failing miserably.

"Finn, since you're the doctor in the family, you should handle that."

Finn gave an inelegant and decided un-doctorlike snort. "Just how do you propose I do that? Even if there is something wrong with him, which is a distinct possibility, he's a sixty-year-old adult man. I can't force him to submit to medical tests."

"You know Darius," Wes added. "He'll tell you to go to hell. I don't see how we can convince him to get help."

Duke spoke up. "Maybe Maisie can. She seems to have more sway with him than anyone else."

Before he'd even finished talking, Maisie shook her head. "He just views women differently, that's all. We're—me, Joan and Sharon, that is—his possessions. Objects in a way, not real people. If you think for a minute that he would allow me to try to tell him what to do…" She shuddered. "Not going to happen. I don't want to be the next one he comes at with a fireplace poker. No, thank you."

Jeremy lifted his head and swallowed the last bite of his cookie. "I think we should just leave Darius alone. He doesn't like any of us anyways. Maybe we could all move to a new ranch with Uncle Damien."

As one, they all turned to look at Damien.

"Move to a new ranch?" Finn frowned. "What's this all about, Damien? Why are you filling the kid's head with such nonsense?"

Even Maisie looked askance at him. "Honestly, you can't go around telling my son we're moving without even talking to me. You know I love Honey Creek. I'm not planning on going anywhere."

Before Damien could answer, Jeremy slammed the heel of his hand on the table. "That's typical, Mom. You do everything you can to ruin my life." He ran out of the room.

No one spoke as they watched him go. "Teenagers," Maisie said, to no one in particular. "What can you do?"

Finn steered the conversation back to Darius. "I'll talk to him, tell him it's time for him to have a physical. I'll run every test I can on him to make sure there's nothing wrong."

"Oh, there's definitely something wrong," Damien and Duke said at the same time. Sheepishly grinning at each other, they shrugged. As twins they finished each other's sentences all the time. Or had, until Damien had gone away to prison.

"What I'm trying to say," Finn continued, "is whatever is wrong with Darius may be mental rather than physical. If so, then nothing will show up on my test results."

"Even Alzheimer's?" Maisie asked.

"There is no test that can definitively diagnose Alzheimer's disease." Finn paused for a moment, thinking. "Though if I order a CT scan of his brain, it might be able to detect Alzheimer's plaques and tangles. It's all a crap shoot when it comes to that kind of stuff."

Still, it was the best they could do and they all knew it.

"There's more," Wes added slowly, sounding reluctant. "The Feds aren't in town just for the Mark Walsh murder. They're investigating Darius. It sounds pretty serious."

Chapter 10

"Investigating Darius? Why?" Duke asked. He, Finn and Maisie reacted with varying degrees of surprise and/or shock. Damien said nothing. How could he? The Feds had approached him days after he'd been released from prison. At the time, he'd thought they were crazy, so he'd readily agreed to help them. Now, he regretted that. The longer he was home and the more he tried to talk to Darius, the more he suspected the old man truly had something to hide.

"For what?" Finn sounded incredulous. "He's just a rich rancher. What could he possibly have done?"

"Besides stealing my inheritance?" Damien interjected dryly.

"You don't sound surprised," Wes said.

"I'm not, actually. The last I heard, they were looking at him for several things. Racketeering and money laundering being just two of them."

Wes narrowed his eyes. "You knew about this? How long have you known?"

With them all staring at him, Damien kept his face expressionless. "The Feds approached me right after I got out of prison. They wanted me to be their inside guy."

Wes swore. "They said they had someone on the inside. I didn't believe them." He cursed. "Especially you, of all people. The last person I would have suspected. Tell me, have you been reporting back to them?"

Crossing his arms, Damien studied each of his siblings. Their expression bore various degrees of surprise, shock or, in Maisie's case, disinterest. Still, the fact that Wes had to ask hurt. "I can't believe you asked that."

"Answer the question," Wes barked.

Pushing away a flash of anger, Damien shook his head.

"No, I haven't told the Feds a damn thing," he sighed.

"Why not?" Maisie interjected. "You know he's hiding something."

"Because I have nothing on him." Damien told the truth.

"Would you have told the Feds if you did?" Duke sounded merely curious, rather than condemning.

"I don't know. Personally, I think they should be kept out of this. Whatever he's done, I refuse to believe it's illegal. Darius might be acting crazy, but he's our father. We're all family here and all we have is each other. No matter what."

"I agree," Duke said. "Whatever he might be guilty of, it can't be that bad. This is family business and, bottom line, family is family."

Family is family. The Colton family's creed. Even if Darius himself appeared to have forgotten it, there was no reason any of them should betray him to the Feds.

Unless he actually hurt someone. That aspect needed to be addressed.

"That goes without saying," Wes seconded. "Unless of course, Darius does something completely crazy, like he's been threatening to do."

"Like kill me?" Damien asked. "Something has to be wrong with him. Something medical. I hope we get a handle on it before it gets to that point."

"We will." Duke sounded certain. "You've had a rough enough time of it already. It's a shame you're having to deal with this, too."

Damien silently agreed with that statement.

"I'll see if I can get him to agree to letting me do a complete physical. But for now, I've got to go." Finn glanced at his watch. "Rachel is waiting for me." The eagerness in his voice struck a chord of envy in Damien, making him wonder how it would feel to have a woman you loved waiting for you.

"Yeah, me, too." Wes walked to the door with his brother, turning when he reached the doorway. "We're all good, right? Medical tests from Finn and stonewall the Feds."

"Exactly," Damien answered. Still, Maisie said nothing, apparently engrossed in her nail polish.

The others all left, too, talking quietly among themselves.

Maisie said goodbye absently, picking at the polish on her index fingernail.

"Maise?" Damien moved closer. "What's wrong? You've been uncharacteristically quiet."

When she lifted her head to meet his gaze, her expression was troubled. "I think something really is wrong with Darius. You saw how he threatened to kill Sharon the other night."

"Like he did me."

"Yes." Maisie dragged her hand through her perfect hair, rumpling it. When she raised her gaze to meet his, fear shone in her eyes. "Damien, I think he really meant it. Sharon did, too. She looked absolutely terrified."

"I'll talk to her."

"No, don't." Maisie touched his arm. "I've already tried and she shut me out. I think she wants this to all just go away."

He sighed. "Don't we all."

"I know I do."

"Take it easy. Try to enjoy yourself. It's nearly Christmas. Do you have a date tonight?"

"Yes." For an instant her smile lit up her eyes, but then her face fell. "Only I'm not sure I want to see him anymore."

On alert, Damien watched her closely. "Has Gary Jackson done something to hurt you?"

"No, it's not that. It's just that he seems to have it in for you. He's really intense about it, Damien. He says he's assisting the Feds on an investigation concerning you. I'm worried they'll try to pin some crime Darius might have committed on you."

"Wouldn't that be par for the course?" He gave her a grim smile. "That's all I need. I've already been wrongly convicted of one crime."

Then, seeing how anxiety tightened her face, he tried to lighten the mood. "Come on, you know and I know that's not gonna happen. After all, what's the likelihood of lightning striking twice?"

"I don't know, but this still has me worried."

"Me, too." He thought for a moment. "I am kind of curious. Do you have any idea what Gary Jackson has against me, or why?"

She shrugged, avoiding his gaze. "I don't know."

Rising, she carefully placed her water glass in the

sink. Still not looking at him, she made a beeline for the hallway.

"Where are you going?" he asked, once again confused by her mercurial mood swings.

"To bed."

"I thought you had a date."

"I'm going to cancel it." Head held high, she sailed from the room, shooting him a look that dared him to follow.

He didn't. Though every bit of her demeanor suggested she was hiding something, Damien let her go. He was tired of drama, tired of secrets and hidden meanings. He longed to saddle up his gelding and take off for the open range, where only cattle and eagles would be his companions.

If it had been summertime, that's exactly what he would have done. Since it was winter and already dark, not to mention twelve degrees outside with the temperature falling fast, he did what he really wanted to do.

He got in his truck and headed over to Eve's. She was fast becoming an obsession with him. He dreamed about her at night, thought about her a hundred random times during the day. He ached to hold her, touch her, feel her lush body pressed up against him.

Though he desired her, Eve was special. He wanted more. More than just for sex, he wanted to be with her—after all, she was the closest thing he had to a friend.

The knock on her front door roused Eve from a deep sleep. She'd fallen asleep on the sofa again, with a Christmas special playing on the TV and her Christmas-tree lights twinkling in the background. Yawning, she rubbed her eyes and pushed to her feet, feeling ungainly and ungraceful, even though she'd only gained six pounds. Tightening the belt on her robe, she padded to the door and peeked through the peephole.

Damien. Snow dusting his cowboy hat, he looked good enough to eat. Beautiful and sexy, a wounded, lost man. Exactly the kind that always got her in trouble.

For no reason at all, her eyes filled with tears. Sniffing, she opened the door and let him in.

"What's wrong?" Sounding concerned, he pulled her close. He smelled of snow and leather, an outdoorsy, manly scent that embodied his essence.

"Nothing." She took a deep, shaky breath and wiped at her eyes. "Pregnancy hormones, I guess." Grabbing the old quilt she used to keep warm on the couch, she swung it over her shoulders and sat down.

"Were you asleep?" His deep voice rumbled with humor.

She glanced at the mantel clock before answering. "Maybe."

His grin warmed her more than any quilt. "Do you want me to leave?"

She punched him lightly in the arm. "I think you know the answer to that."

Taking off his cowboy hat, he hung it on her coatrack. As he removed his parka, he shot her a mischievous look. "Got any room under that blanket?"

Instead of answering with words, she lifted a corner of the quilt. Grinning, he came over and sat next to her, jeans-clad thigh next to her pajamas.

"You feel cold," she told him, snuggling against him. Then, as he lifted his hand to her cheek, she gasped. "Dang. Didn't you wear gloves?"

"No. I was in too big a rush to get here."

She searched his face. "Why? Did something happen?"

"I missed you, Eve." He kissed her. Taking his time,

letting the drowsy heat of her warm his cold lips. "I've really missed you today."

He sounded truly perplexed, which made her smile. Pleasure filled her for a moment, until she got a grip on herself and shook her head. No warm and fuzzy feelings here. Men said stuff like that all the time as a prelude to wanting sex. They didn't mean it. He didn't mean it either. She had to remember to take everything he said with a grain of salt. Otherwise, she'd end up hurt, with Damien running as far away as he could, leaving her alone with a broken heart.

Unfortunately, even thinking about doing without him made her feel weepy. "Damn hormones," she sniffed, while tears slowly tracked down her cheeks.

"Are you sure you're all right?" Big fingers gentle, he wiped the tears away.

"It's being pregnant," she explained, taking his hand and letting him feel the soft swell of her belly. "I'm a little past four months along now and the hormonal changes are making me act...different."

He nodded, his dark gaze finding hers. "Do you ever miss him?"

"Who?"

"The father of your baby. Massimo."

He remembered the name? She shook her head. "I barely knew him. I went to Italy because I was upset that I'm going to be forty soon. He was hot, we hit it off and the next thing I knew, we were in bed. He said all the right things, I wanted badly to believe him, and..." Lightly, she touched her belly. "Here I am. Hopefully wiser."

"When are you going to tell your family?"

"After New Year's. Since my sister and your brother are getting married on January second, I wanted to wait until that was over. Susan doesn't deserve me stealing her thunder."

"Ah, yes, the wedding." He pulled her closer. "I'm assuming you're a bridesmaid. I'm a groomsman. Wanna go together?"

For a second she couldn't breathe. "You mean...be each other's dates? In public?"

Now he watched her closely, his expression guarded. "Yes. Unless, of course, you're ashamed to be seen in public with me."

"Of course not. But I want you to consider this, Damien. Once I tell everyone that I'm pregnant, I'm not going to name the father."

"So?"

"Well, now you and I have an agreement not to get serious. But what if we ever started dating heavily, people might assume this is your baby." Grasping at straws, not even sure what was driving her.

A muscle worked in his jaw. Uncoiling himself from the couch, he stood. "I see. And for your child's sake, you don't think that's a good idea."

"It's just that..." Spreading her hands, she tried to find the right words to explain.

"Don't bother. You don't want people to assume your baby was sired by an ex-con. I get it. Don't bother getting up. I can find my own way out."

And he was gone.

Stunned, feeling as though she'd been hit by a ton of bricks, Eve huddled under her blanket, staring at the spot where he'd just been. What had all that been about? She'd only been trying to be practical, in keeping with their no-strings agreement. Damien was just out of sorts. Apparently she wasn't the only moody one in Honey Creek tonight.

* * *

Back home, insides churning, Damien parked next to an unfamiliar black sedan. Someone had company. Probably Maisie. After all, hadn't she mentioned she'd had a date with Gary Jackson tonight? Since she'd said she was going to cancel it, Gary had probably come to her.

His stomach rumbled, reminding him he hadn't eaten. He went to the kitchen and pulled out sandwich fixings. In the middle of making a sandwich, he heard the tap-tap-tap of Maisie's high heels headed his way.

"Hey, Maise." He greeted her as she strode across the ceramic tile. "Whose car is that in the driveway? Gary's?"

"No. Listen, there are a couple of men here to see you." Maisie looked worried. Moving closer, she said in a loud, stage whisper, "They say they're with the FBI."

Damien froze. The black car. "They're really pushing it, coming out here. Tell them to go away."

She shook her head, shooting him a weird look over her shoulder as she headed toward her room. "Tell them yourself. I put them in the study off the great room. That one guy scared me. He's built like an NFL linebacker."

Special Agent Donatello. It had to be. Maisie could charm most people and considered herself fearless. If someone frightened her... Donatello was a stereotypical law-enforcement official in love with his power. From his flat-top haircut and round spectacles, down to the long black trench coat he affected, he tried to appear a badass. In the entire time he'd been out of prison, Damien had never seen the man smile or crack a joke, and his humorless, no-nonsense attitude probably didn't win him any friends.

Damien had met Donatello when he'd first gone to talk to the Feds, willing to assist in the Mark Walsh investigation. Hell, he'd felt compelled to offer to assist in the investigation, and had been furious when they'd turned him away.

At the last second, they'd reconsidered and called him back. They did need his help on another investigation, they said. They were investigating his father. When Damien had demanded to know for what, they'd listed racketeering and money-laundering among a long list of other crimes.

Shocked, Damien had told them he'd help out. He'd gone home, regretting his words, and had managed thus far to avoid them.

Apparently, they'd gotten tired of waiting and had sent out the big guns.

Feeling as if he were heading to an execution—his own—Damien headed down the hallway toward the study. Two men, both wearing long black overcoats, waited with barely concealed impatience.

"What can I do for you gentlemen?" Damien asked.

Donatello swung his cold gaze around. "Why don't you tell us? You seem to have fallen off the grid."

The other agent, an older, gray-haired man, stepped forward. "What my colleague is trying to say is that we're close to finishing our investigation. We were expecting certain information from you. So far, you have not come forward with this information. Therefore, we are coming to you."

Seriously?

Aware he had to tread carefully, Damien manufactured a casual smile. "Could you be a little more specific? What information are you talking about?"

"Cut the crap, Colton," Donatello snarled. "You know what we mean." He took a step forward. "You agreed to help. We've done our part and stayed off your back. Now, unless you start producing, that will change."

"A threat is only effective when the person you're threatening understands what you're talking about," Damien felt obligated to point out. "Begin with explaining what you mean by 'stay off my back.'"

The two men exchanged a look. Then Donatello laughed. "We can put you under twenty-four-hour-a-day surveillance. Always watching, always waiting for you to make the slightest mistake. Do you want that?"

"Why me?" Damien spread his hands. "I'm not part of my father's financial dealings. I know nothing about them. His wife does the books, I think." Though he secretly doubted Sharon knew anything about his father's finances, he had no choice. "You might talk to her."

"Don't stonewall me." Donatello gave him a menacing look, which didn't bother Damien. After fifteen years in prison, he'd learned that looks alone couldn't hurt him. It's what came after the look that he had to worry about, and Donatello wouldn't touch him. Not here, not in front of witnesses.

"Look, I've been home since September." Damien smiled slowly. "I haven't seen anything out of the ordinary, so I have nothing to report to you." He put on a pained expression. "I don't understand why you can't comprehend that."

Though Donatello flushed beet-red, he knew there wasn't anything else he could do. "Come on," he told his partner. On the way out the door, he aimed one last parting shot at Damien. "We'll be back."

Damien couldn't resist one of his own. "Next time, you'd better have a search warrant."

Donatello slammed the door behind him.

As Damien walked to his room, Darius stepped in front of him, blocking his way.

"We need to talk," his father said, his commanding tone leaving no room for refusal. "In my office. Now."

Steeling himself for another round of threats, Damien followed Darius into the lushly appointed room, mildly surprised when the older man locked the door.

"Wouldn't want to be overheard," he said. Crossing to the window, he pulled the shades closed, then drew the curtains. "You should know I have this room periodically swept for electronic bugs or any kind of video-recording devices."

"A bit paranoid, aren't you?" Damien couldn't resist asking.

As expected, Darius frowned. "When you're a man in my position, you have to be."

"Really? And what position is that?"

"Enough already," Darius snarled. "I want to know what the FBI was doing here."

"Surely you're aware they're investigating you?"

Moving more swiftly than Damien had ever seen him move, Darius crossed the room until he stood toe-to-toe with his son.

"What did you tell them?"

Though he knew he was pushing it, Damien couldn't resist another jab. "What are you so worried about?"

Instead of answering, Darius cocked his graying head. "Let me say this. If you value that pretty little Kelley girl you've been nailing, you'll keep your mouth shut."

"That's it." Damien had had enough. "What the hell is wrong with you? Leave her out of this. Threatening me is one thing, but she's not involved in this at all."

Darius gave him a sly smile so cold it didn't even touch the flatness of his eyes. "You try to do anything to hurt me or betray this family, and the girl will die. Worse, I'll see to it that she suffers."

Stunned, Damien eyed the man who had sired him. No hint of humanity remained in his father's calculated gaze.

Damien realized Finn could run all the tests at his disposal and they wouldn't reveal any medical reason for their father's behavior. Darius was a sociopath and had no doubt always been one. He'd just never expressed it so violently before. He probably meant what he said and would have no compunction about torturing and killing an innocent woman.

Shaking his head, Damien turned and went to the door. Unlocking it, he turned and gave Darius a look he'd perfected in prison. "I take care of my own, understand?" Then without waiting for an answer, he left, closing the door behind him.

When he reached the safety of his own room, Damien unclenched his fists and realized he was shaking. He needed to talk to Wes and convince his brother that it was time for the sheriff's office to step in. His entire family appeared to be disintegrating around him. Damien, having lost fifteen long years that he could never get back, had come home halfway expecting things to be exactly the way they'd been when he'd gone to prison. Now, almost four months out and counting, he realized he'd been a fool.

His brothers had all found women they wanted to spend the rest of their lives with. People change, grow older and move on. Because of his time behind bars, he was the only one who hadn't.

In his room, he started to undress, then stopped. The walls of his room, an average-sized bedroom in the huge ranch house, felt as though they were closing in on him. Too close, too confining. He felt trapped, the way he had often felt while in prison.

Eve… No. He had to figure this out on his own.

If this were during the summer months, and claustrophobia was making his chest tighten, he'd simply saddle up one of the horses and go for a long ride. Now, he couldn't, because the forecast was for an arctic blast, with temperatures dipping well below freezing. The utter darkness compounded with the cold made riding after sundown impossible. Instead, he could walk to the barn and spend time with the horses, perhaps even ride in the covered arena. Or… Deciding, he snatched his car keys from the dresser. He'd go for a drive in his pickup and cruise the streets of his hometown with the stereo blaring. That had always made him feel better when he'd been a teenager. It shouldn't be any different at thirty-five.

But, although he found the hum of the truck's engine soothing, the feeling of nowhere to go unsettled him. After thirty minutes of aimless driving, passing by Eve's house twice, he found himself back at the Corner Bar. Since there were still a couple of hours until last call, the place was still open, even though the parking lot only had five or six cars.

A beer would taste mighty fine right about now.

Parking, he debated whether or not to go inside. Just as he was reaching for the handle to open the truck door, the bar's side door opened and his brother Wes came outside, accompanied by Agent Donatello and his henchman.

Chapter 11

What the hell. Keys clenched tightly in his fist, Damien froze. A knot settled in his stomach as he watched his brother the sheriff laughing with the man who, less than an hour before, had threatened him.

After a few more seconds of talking in the cold night air, Donatello and his partner got into their black sedan and drove away. Hands in pockets, breath making plumes of mist in the freezing air, Wes stood and watched them go, then made his way toward his own truck.

"Wes." Opening his door, Damien called him over. "What was that all about?"

Expression closed, Wes came over and climbed up into the truck next to Damien. "I was about to ask you the same thing. I still can't believe you were their inside informant."

Relief flooding him, Damien snorted. "They wish. They must have come to you right after they left the house."

"What happened?"

As succinctly as possible, Damien relayed the evening's events, including Darius's crazy threats and menacing behavior. "I'm beginning to think our father is a true sociopath."

"Whew." Sitting back in the seat, Wes rubbed the back of his neck. "If he is, that would mean he's dangerous, and I don't like to think that about my own father."

"Me neither. But something's going on with him. While he's been odd ever since I got home, things are getting worse fast. He's hiding something."

"I wonder what Darius knows that's got him so worried."

"You and me both."

A chime sounded and Wes checked his phone. "Lily," he said with a sheepish smile. "She's reminding me we have to be out at the ranch at the crack of dawn to help with the preparations for the big feast this weekend."

At Damien's inquisitive look, Wes laughed. "It's so good to have you home. Sometimes I forget you were gone so long. Tomorrow the preparations start for the annual Christmas lunch."

"Already?" At Wes's nod, Damien groaned. "Why so early?"

"Because it's huge now. You remember how every year on the Sunday before Christmas, no matter their faith or lack of—"

"The congregations of a bunch of churches get together for a holiday meal. I know, I remember."

"It's bigger now. Actually, the entire town of Honey Creek holds one huge celebratory service."

The tradition had started in the early eighties, when Mrs. Murphy and the ladies of the Lutheran Church had held a joint Christmas supper with the ladies of the Catholic and Baptist churches. Each had invited their respective congregations.

The next year, the small Pentecostal Church joined, as well as Honey Creek's lone nondenominational church. The annual event became so popular that by the end of the eighties, men and women of all faiths, including those who didn't even celebrate the holiday, attended.

"That's hard to believe. The last time I went, it was at the high-school cafeteria," Damien mused.

Wes laughed. "Not anymore. The dinner's grown so huge that for the last several years, the town uses the Colton ranch's indoor riding arena. That's what they're doing tomorrow, setting up rows of buffet tables and folding chairs and getting everything ready. We even had heating installed."

"But tomorrow's only Wednesday. That's a long way from Sunday."

"You've been gone fifteen years," Wes pointed out gently. "Like I said, the thing's blossomed and grown."

"Now I'm really looking forward to Sunday." Damien squeezed his brother's shoulder. "Thanks, man."

"Any time." Serious now, Wes checked his watch. "It's late. If I'm going to head out to the ranch at dawn tomorrow, I'd better go home and get some rest."

"Me, too." Suddenly weary, Damien told Wes goodbye and started the truck.

Driving home, he again turned down Eve's street and coasted to a stop in front of her house. Already he regretted storming out on her earlier. He needed to apologize, but her house was dark. Plus, he'd already shown up unannounced once tonight and didn't want to do so again.

Instead, he put the truck in Drive and headed home. He'd apologize to her tomorrow. He hoped she'd understand.

He rose the next morning a full hour before sunrise.

After showering and dressing, he padded down to the kitchen to make coffee and found Jeremy waiting, also fully dressed and munching on a stack of waffles.

"What are you doing up so early?" Damien asked, pouring a steaming cup of coffee.

"I can't wait." The teenager practically jumped up and down with excitement. "This year Uncle Duke said I could help park the cars. I might get to drive one and everything! It's going to be so wicked!"

Grinning back, Damien ruffled the boy's hair. "Let me drink a cup of coffee and grab a muffin. Then maybe we should head out to the barn and see if Sharon needs any help."

Barely concealing his impatience, Jeremy nodded. He fiddled in his chair while Damien ate, slurping at his glass of milk while Damien sucked down a second cup of coffee.

Finally, Damien stood. "Are you ready?"

The boy needed no second prompting. He ran for the coatrack, snatched off his parka and Damien's, then ran back to hand Damien his coat.

Chuckling, Damien bundled up against the winter morning.

Outside, even with the pole lights lit, the sky was still inky-black. Even at this early hour, a crew had already started getting the first field off the road ready to be turned into a massive parking lot. Metal gates, usually locked, stood wide open.

Wind buffeted them as they strode toward the barn. Though the air was cold and crisp, it was dry. The clear sky revealed several constellations sparkling like diamonds in the still-dark sky. With such a big event scheduled, Damien supposed it was a good thing they weren't expecting snow.

As they neared the barn, they saw what looked like close

to thirty people, mostly women, bustling around unloading boxes from two white panel vans. The barn opened to reveal people already hanging decorations inside.

No one noticed them, so engrossed were they in their own tasks.

Damien exchanged a look with Jeremy. "I don't think they need us," Damien said, surprised to see so many people already at work at such an early hour.

At that, Jeremy looked so disappointed that Damien relented. "Of course I'm sure there's always a spot for an extra hand."

But now Jeremy wasn't listening. He'd fixated all of his attention on a petite blonde girl in a hot-pink ski jacket and hat.

"Who's that?" Damien asked, hiding his amusement.

Jeremy tore his gaze away from the teenager to grin sheepishly at Damien. "Nobody. Just a girl from my school."

Cuffing the boy lightly on the shoulder, Damien let it go. "If you want to go help her, go ahead."

"Okay." Needing no second urging, Jeremy sauntered over to the shyly smiling girl.

Whistling under his breath, Damien went inside the barn. Christmas carols were playing from a portable stereo set up on a table. He wandered over to where three men were setting up a series of long buffet tables. They'd already done two rows of ten and were starting on a third.

"Need any help?"

The instant the men looked up, the easy camaraderie vanished from their faces. "No, thanks."

Studiously avoiding meeting his gaze, the trio went back to work.

Pretending it didn't bother him, Damien moved away. Even here, on his own ranch? Though it stung, this would be his first Christmas in fifteen years as a free man, and he refused to let anyone—especially small-minded fools—ruin it for him.

A second group of men were assembling small artificial Christmas trees. There had to be at least thirty boxes stacked near them. Approaching, Damien didn't ask this time. He just reached for a box and opened it, getting right to work, ignoring the way their carefree banter stopped, then started up again, haltingly, when he made no effort to join in.

"Hey, handsome!" A feminine voice called, barely discernable over the rowdy version of "Jingle Bell Rock" playing.

When he didn't turn, someone tugged on his sleeve.

Turning, his eyes locked with Eve's bright-blue ones, and his mouth went dry.

She didn't appear to notice. "When you get finished over here, will you come help me?"

Dumbstruck, he nodded. Had she already forgiven him for storming out the day before? "I'll help," he managed.

"Fantastic!" She smiled, sending his heart rate into double time. "I'm over there, unpacking napkins and paper plates, but I'm going to need someone to help me put the tablecloths on the tables once they're all set up."

"Give me a minute and I'll be there," he said, aware of the other men's interested stares. "I'm just about done with this tree."

With a nod and a wave, she moved off.

Finishing the tree in record time, he forced himself to stroll over slowly. When he reached Eve, she was rolling plastic cutlery sets inside holiday napkins.

"There you are." Reaching out, she touched his arm.

Hands in pockets, he nodded. "Listen, I need to apologize for what I said last night."

"No need." Her smile never wavered as she gestured around the room. "I saw how they treated you. I didn't understand before. Now I do. No worries."

He wanted to hug her. Not wanting to start gossip, he restrained himself.

In the course of the afternoon, as Eve dragged him from group to group, chore to chore, he realized she was single-handedly making sure everyone accepted his help and, more importantly, him.

She didn't know it, but she'd given him a present greater than gold.

Hours later, when all the tables were in place, and fifty artificial trees had been covered with white lights, everyone gradually left to go home. Damien stood next to Eve, watching his father's wife check on all the finishing details.

"Are you coming over later?" Eve asked him quietly. "I put fixings for beef stew in the slow cooker and made a loaf of bread in my bread machine."

Heart so full that it hurt, he nodded. "I'm starving." And he was, for more than food. "What time?"

"Give me an hour to shower."

He tried to hide his eagerness. "Do you want me to bring anything?"

For an answer, she winked. "Just your big ol', bad self."

Showering and changing in record time, Damien found himself in the truck on the way to Eve's house in forty-five minutes. He stopped at a small grocery store and purchased a bottle of alcohol-free wine. As he drove toward town he caught himself whistling, and he shook his head, grinning.

He parked in her driveway and his grin widened as Eve opened the front door before he'd made it halfway up the sidewalk. She'd changed from her jeans into a soft sweaterdress the same blue as her eyes. Her long blond hair was still damp from the shower. And her welcoming smile starting a slow burn of desire deep inside him.

"Hey," she said softly, stepping back to let him inside. He gave in to the impulse and kissed her.

When they broke apart, both were breathing heavily.

"Wow." Blinking up at him, she shook her head. "You're amazing."

"I was going to bring you a bottle of wine," he said. "But I remembered you couldn't drink it, so I brought this instead." He lifted the alcohol-free wine bottle, wishing he'd bought it earlier so he could have had Maisie put it into one of her fancy bags or something.

"Wonderful." Beaming at him, Eve carried the bottle into the kitchen. "This will be perfect with the beef stew."

"It smells great." Damien inhaled appreciatively. "Fresh baked bread and homemade stew. You can't ask for more than that."

At his compliments, Eve positively glowed. He followed her into the kitchen, where she had a perfectly set table with a large candle burning as a centerpiece.

"Do you need any help?" he asked.

"Nope. I've got it under control. Why don't you go sit in the den and I'll holler at you when it's ready to eat."

Though he didn't want to leave her side, he nodded and wandered into the other room. A fire blazed in the fireplace and he took a seat on an overstuffed chair, watching the flames and thinking.

This could be his life. Sharing this home with the woman.

If he hadn't been sent to prison, he'd probably be a dad by now, with a couple of kids and a life full of love.

An ordinary life. Something he hadn't even realized he craved until recently.

"It's ready," Eve called, breaking him out of his reverie.

As he took a seat at the table, it occurred to him that he'd been given a second chance. Being with Eve made the impossible possible.

The fragrant stew tasted delicious and the crusty French bread she'd made in her bread machine was the perfect complement. Damien had seconds, which clearly pleased her.

When they'd finished, he insisted on cleaning up and ordered her to take a seat by the fire. As soon as the last dish was stacked in the dishwasher, he joined her.

As he put his arm around her and side by side they leaned back, full and content, he felt a glimmer of hope brighter and stronger than anything he'd felt since being imprisoned.

Lost in his thoughts and enjoying the feeling of closeness, he looked down at Eve and realized she'd fallen asleep. Moving carefully, he covered her with a light blanket and let himself out of her house through the back door, since he could lock it behind him.

On the drive home he cursed his foolish optimism. It was all very well and good to hope for the future if you were an ordinary man. But with all his baggage, Damien knew that this would probably be only a dream for him. That didn't stop his chest from aching as he parked and went inside to go to bed alone, already missing Eve.

Finally the day of the big feast dawned. Montana weather, never the most reliable, gave them an early Christmas gift of clear skies and unseasonably warm temperatures, with a forecast of highs in the fifties.

All Honey Creek's shops and businesses closed early, and a great feeling of festivity filled the air. Outside, the men tended to the huge smokers, ensuring that the meat was cooked, while inside the arena the women set out tray after tray of cooked dressing, sweet-potato casserole, green beans and rolls.

As the celebration approached, most of the ranch hands were given a break from their daily chores. Working abbreviated three-hour shifts, they rode out in groups of three or four to check on the herd and the fence, and spent the rest of their time engaged in friendly poker games under Darius's radar.

Since the ranch hands had begun to treat him like one of their own, Damien tried to participate in the games. He wanted to relish the experience, so fresh and new after years of confinement, but although he'd honed his poker skills during the years in prison, he couldn't concentrate. He could think of nothing but Eve, her beautiful bright-blue eyes gazing so expectantly at him, her full lips curving in a smile. When they were last together, they couldn't stop touching each other.

He couldn't help but wonder if they'd sit together, which would mean she'd have to sit at the head table with the rest of his family. Her sister Susan would be there with Duke, as would his Wes's and Duke's fiancées. Of course, if Eve sat by his side, that would be akin to making a public statement, something they hadn't really discussed.

The other alternative, which he liked better, would be to sit with her among her family. Same statement, but less visible.

Or, he reflected glumly, they could sit separately, which would be the most sensible option if they didn't want gossip.

He didn't really care if people talked about him, but Eve was a different matter. He'd do what he had to do to protect her even if he didn't like it.

Eve arrived at the Colton Ranch an hour early, hoping to catch Damien alone, but as she waited in a long line of cars on the road leading to the ranch, she realized several others had chosen to come early as well.

Teenagers were hard at work directing cars to one of the two pastures designated for parking. After Eve pulled into her slot, she checked her reflection in the rearview mirror. Her new green sweater looked good with her blond hair and she'd tucked her jeans into a pair of furry boots.

One hand on the car door, she swallowed. Oddly enough, she felt nervous. Though she and Damien had been getting together nearly every single night, she wasn't sure how to act here at his home with the entire town watching.

Would they sit together? The entire Colton clan usually held court at a long, raised table in the front of the crowd. Her sister Susan would be up there this year, next to her fiancé, Duke Colton, as would Lily Masterson with Wes, and Rachel Grant with Finn, and the other Colton children, Joan, Brand and Perry. If Damien asked Eve to sit there, it would mark her as of special significance, something she wasn't sure she was ready or willing to accept.

No complications, she reminded herself. Damien understood that as well. All would be good. Still, that didn't stop her from wiping sweaty palms down the front of her jeans as she walked up to the barn.

Inside, townspeople milled around, gathering in small groups to talk. Some were claiming their seats, saving places for their friends and family. The only Colton she saw was Sharon, busy directing a small army in the placement of the large trays of food with their accompanying warmer candles.

Moving off into a corner, Eve pulled out her phone and sent him a text. *I'm here. Where are you?*

Look behind you, came back.

Slowly she turned. He stood in the entrance, alone, watching her. Her heart leapt into her throat and she had to forcibly restrain herself to keep from running into his arms.

Keeping her expression as casual as possible, she strolled over to him. "Hey, you."

"Hey, yourself." His velvet-brown gaze searched her face. "Want to sit together?"

Eve froze. "Up at your family's table?" she squeaked. "I don't..."

"We don't have to." He touched her arm, his fingers gentle. "If you don't want to sit up there, we can sit somewhere else."

For the first time she considered what this meant to him, that he was willing to give this up. For the first time in fifteen years, he had the right to sit with his siblings and his father at the family table. Eat with them, be with them, celebrate the holiday with those closest to him. And he wanted to give this up to be with her?

Part horrified, part humbled, she looked away. Her clan, with all her brothers and sisters and their spouses, as well as extended family, usually took up two entire tables. This time, her sister Susan would be eating up front with Wes. This was to be expected, since the two were engaged to be married.

But if Eve were to sit with Damien, people would assume...

When she dragged her gaze back to him, she saw an impassive cowboy, trying hard to pretend not to care. She knew this man and, as much as she might try to deny it, she cared about him. As a friend and…more. The realization both terrified and exhilarated her.

"I'll sit up front with you," she said, impulsively deciding. "It's time I stopped worrying so much about what people think."

Pure joy flashed across his face, so quickly she might have imagined it. He gave a slow nod, then took her hand, threading his large, calloused fingers through hers. Giving her a mischievous grin, he led her toward the front of the huge indoor arena.

"Let's really give them something to talk about," he said. Then he kissed her.

Time both stood still and rushed forward. For the space of several heartbeats she couldn't move, couldn't react, then the heat of his mouth moving across hers seared her, bringing her to life.

"Ahem." Someone cleared a throat behind them, yanking Eve right back to her surroundings. Face flaming, she pushed away and looked up, straight into her mother's curious face.

"Bonnie Gene." Damien stepped forward. "Sorry about that. Eve looks so pretty, I just had to kiss her."

If the ground could have opened up and swallowed her, Eve would have taken a nose dive for it. "Hi, Mom."

Ignoring Eve, her mother looked Damien up and down. "Staking a claim?" she asked, eyes twinkling.

He gave her a wicked grin. "Maybe I am."

She nodded. "Good." Without another word, she turned and walked away.

Shocked, Eve stared after her. "What the heck was that about?"

His grin widened, inviting her to join in. "I think your mother just gave me her stamp of approval."

Shaking her head, Eve began to move forward, not touching him this time. "Let's go find our seats."

"Regretting your decision?" he asked, his voice suddenly serious. "Because if you are…"

"You'll let me go back and sit with my mother? How fun would that be now?"

"No. I was going to say that I'm not letting you out of it." He took her arm, ignoring her resistance. "Sweetheart, if you're going to do something, you might as well do it up right."

With that, he led her up to the front. As she took her seat next to him at the long table, she felt a bit like royalty of olden times. Banishing the feeling, she smiled at Finn and Rachel, just arriving.

Damien got up to talk to Finn, and Eve took the time alone to calm herself. She'd never been a coward and hated that she felt so nervous now. It wasn't as though she and Damien actually were an item.

The room began to fill up as more and more townspeople arrived. Sharon Colton, still busy making sure the serving lines were set up correctly, would be one of the very last to take her seat. Her husband, Darius, would, as usual, make a grand entrance and once he made it to the front, he'd tap on his wineglass to get everyone's attention. Only when the room became completely and utterly silent, would he announce it was time to eat.

After that, pandemonium would reign.

"What are you doing here?" Her sister, Susan, appeared behind Eve, eyes wide. "I saw you sitting up here all by yourself and thought I'd better rescue you. Mom and the rest of the clan are at our usual table," she hinted.

Fidgeting, Eve felt like a little kid. "I'm here with Damien." There. She'd said it.

Smile faltering, Susan did a double take. "With Damien? Colton? Are you sure?"

Just then Damien came up behind them. Putting his hand possessively on Eve's shoulder, he smiled. "Hi, Susan. Where's Duke?"

"He, uh, went to see if Jeremy needed any help parking the cars." She darted a look from Damien to Eve and back again. "Eve says you're here together?" Voice rising on the last word, she made this sound like they'd just announced they were submitting to bizarre experimental drug testing in the Yucatan.

Glancing from one sister to the other, Damien frowned. Only the quirk at one corner of his mouth told Eve he was trying not to crack up. "Yes, we're together. Why? Do you have a problem with that?"

Susan immediately began backtracking. "Er, no. It's just that I didn't know Eve was seeing anyone. And I don't think Duke even knows you're dating Eve." She began looking around wildly, trying to find her fiancé. "We need to bring him over here and fill him in, don't you think?"

Trying to keep from laughing was a battle and Eve finally lost it. "Susan," she managed between chortles, "relax. Damien and I are just good friends."

Before anyone could say another word, the rest of the Coltons hurried to their places. A commotion at the entrance to the arena let everyone know that Darius was preparing to make his grand entrance.

And, exactly as he'd done every other year, he did. Moving up the center aisle, shaking hands on one side and then the other, and basking in the adulation as if he were a rock star. Completely used to this, Eve sat back and watched, amused. Beside her, she felt Damien's sudden tension and remembered he'd been in prison for the last fifteen years. The entire production, with its familiar ceremony and almost ritualistic feel, would seem strange to him.

She wondered what he'd done while in prison. Thinking this made her realize how little he talked about his experiences there. Maybe because the memories were too painful.

Then Darius climbed the steps to the platform and the Colton family table. As he made his way to his seat in the center, his gaze locked on Eve, and the hard look in his eyes wasn't the least bit friendly. In fact, he looked downright dangerous.

Chapter 12

Luckily, Sharon Colton bustled up to the table next, drawing Darius's gaze away from Eve. Troubled, Eve looked down at her plate, wondering if she'd imagined the disturbing malice in the look the Colton patriarch had given her. Surely she must have. After all, what reason would the head of the Colton family have to dislike her? If it was because she was a Kelley, she'd think her sister Susan would draw more of his ire—especially since Susan was actually marrying his son Duke. Eve was merely Damien's guest.

Darius intoned the traditional blessing, finishing as he always did, with a request to form lines at the buffet. When he turned to take his seat, his gaze drifted impersonally over his collective family, before narrowing on Eve.

Again, she felt the force of his glare. Telling herself it was due to an overactive imagination didn't help—not when the man kept shooting her venom-filled looks. Resolving to ask Damien later, Eve decided to let it go for now.

Next to her, Damien talked with his twin brother, Duke, her own sister's fiancé. Eve forced herself to relax, leaning back in her chair and watching as the crowd surged to form lines near the self-serve buffet tables. A veritable army of servers stood by, carving meat and constantly refilling trays of food, making sure everything was hot.

The Coltons, as hosts of the banquet, had the right to go to the head of either line whenever they wanted. Maisie and Jeremy went first, followed by Finn and Rachel and Wes and Lily. Duke and Susan, contentedly holding hands, waited a few minutes longer until the first group came back with their plates.

"Are you coming?" Duke asked Damien, giving Eve a friendly smile.

"In a minute," Damien answered, his voice tense. With a nod, Duke moved off, one arm around Susan.

"What's wrong?" Eve murmured, wondering if Damien, too, had noticed his father's odd behavior.

"Nothing." He smiled, but it didn't reach his eyes. "Are you ready?" Though he asked the question in a light voice, Damien touched her arm, as if giving her a warning.

Dubious, she glanced around him to where Darius and Sharon still stood, like benevolent rulers surveying their kingdom. As ashamed as she would be to admit it out loud, she was afraid if she moved that she'd once again draw Darius's cold stare.

"I'm not sure," she admitted with a slight grimace. "Shouldn't your father and stepmother go first?"

Glancing at him, she saw him eyeing his father, who now had started once again to glower in their direction.

"What's the matter with him?" she asked. "Is he mad about me being here?"

"Who knows?" His attempt to sound unconcerned fell flat, especially since he tightened his arm around her. "He's been acting kind of weird lately. It's probably best if we ignore it. Do you want to eat?"

She nodded, getting slowly to her feet at the same time as Damien. Trying to avoid glancing out into the crowd, she still felt as if she had a hundred pairs of eyes on her, many of them mirroring the disapproval she'd seen in Darius's. No doubt the gossip had already started.

She told herself she didn't care, reminding herself she'd better get used to being an object of scandal. The speculation and rumors would start to swirl in earnest once people realized she was pregnant. And when she refused to reveal the father or the circumstances concerning her pregnancy, the rumors would become outrageous. At some point she expected to be asked if her baby had been fathered by aliens. No lie.

As Damien turned to help lead the way down, a shadow fell over the table. After pushing her chair back in, Eve looked up. Darius had stepped in front of them, back to the crowd, completely blocking their way down.

"Son, aren't you going to introduce your little friend?" Darius asked, tone dripping venom.

Wary, Eve instinctively moved closer to Damien as he performed a quick introduction.

"Pleased to meet you," Darius said, sounding anything but. Giving her hand a quick squeeze, the older man quickly released it, returning his attention to his son.

"Well, well, well. I wasn't aware you were this serious," Darius smirked. "Good for me, bad for you."

Though his words made no sense, Damien's sudden tense grip on her arm told Eve that he at least understood what his father meant by the odd statement.

"Don't even go there," Damien warned. "This isn't about her."

"You keep your nose out of my business, and I'll keep

mine out of yours." Suddenly affable, Darius held out his hand. "Deal?"

Stone-faced, Damien made no move to accept his father's offer.

As the silence stretched out, Darius's smile faded. Finally, he lowered his arm, his expression going hard again. "I should have known. So that's the way it's going to be?"

"Excuse us," Damien said firmly, steering Eve around his father. "We're going to go eat."

Darius stepped aside without a word.

On the way down, they passed the others returning. Even though Damien stood protectively close, Eve swore she could still feel Darius's rancor-filled gaze burning into her back.

"What was that all about?" she asked softly as they made their way toward the buffet table.

"I'll tell you later." Squeezing her arm in a too-hard gesture that he'd no doubt meant to be reassuring, he gave her a smile tinged with anger.

Filling her plate with the piping-hot food, Eve tried and failed to recapture her earlier contentment. The look in Damien's father's eyes had been tinged with madness, a very real, almost feral look that seemed as dangerous as an actual physical threat.

No one else appeared to have noticed a thing. Following Damien's lead, she smiled and chatted with several people in the serving line, ignoring the question in many of their gazes. None of them were quite bold enough to ask her outright why she was sitting with the Coltons, but she knew that would wear off by Tuesday. In fact, she anticipated twice the amount of traffic in her hair salon, with women stopping by just to "visit."

Plates filled, she and Damien made their way back to

their seats. Throughout the entire meal, despite the friendly overtures made by Damien's brothers, she couldn't help but feel conscious of Darius's hostile glare, especially since he sent it her way every time she looked toward him.

When they'd finished eating, pastors of the various churches announced the date, time and meeting location for each of their annual Christmas carol sings. The Coltons' church traditionally had theirs Christmas Eve, with caroling that afternoon, before the holiday service.

Sitting at the front table was a completely different experience for Eve. Her family's table, situated in the thick of things, usually ended up empty as various family members socialized with their friends and neighbors. Once everyone had eaten, they roamed, standing in small clusters and talking, before moving on to the next group.

The Coltons were different. As if they were forbidden to leave, not a single one of them left their seats. Instead, everyone came to them, swarming the table like bees to a hive. Bemused, Eve caught her sister's eye. Susan shrugged and went back to looking for her friends so she could wave them over.

Meanwhile, the food was cleared and trays of desserts brought in. Pumpkin, pecan and apple pies, and there had to be at least ten cakes, most baked by the attendees. When all had been set out, along with coffee, many people went for the sweets while others continued to visit.

All in all, Eve thought, a pleasant way to spend an afternoon. In the past, this particular event had been the galvanizing event to give her a dose of the holiday spirit.

This year should have been no different, but as she glanced uneasily at Darius, holding court over his cronies, she realized it had been. If it weren't for Damien, she would have scurried back to her own family like a chastened mouse. Instead, she sat calmly, viewing a group of six dowagers from her mother's quilting club who were bearing down on her. The glint in their eyes promised she was in for the kind of grilling only a true gossip hound can produce.

As if he saw them coming, Damien put his arm around her and joined her in facing them. This didn't slow them one bit in their determined progress and Eve steeled herself for the questions.

To her surprise, just as they approached the table, Sharon Colton stepped in front of them, asking them something about the Christmas-caroling committee.

"Divertive missile launched," Damien muttered dryly. "You are so lucky."

Watching as Sharon led them away, Eve couldn't help but laugh. "Yes, I am."

As the afternoon wore on, more and more people took their leave. Bonnie Gene came up and gave both Eve and Susan a hug before leaving.

"You look good together," she whispered in Eve's ear, indicating Damien with a thumbs-up sign.

To her dismay, Eve felt her face flush. "Thanks," she managed.

A few minutes after her family left, finally Eve felt as if it was time to go.

"Are you ready?" Damien asked, making her wonder if he'd read her mind.

She nodded, keeping her head high as she rose, feeling Darius's malevolent glare on her back all the way to the door.

Damien followed her home in his truck.

Max greeted him in the enthusiastic way boxers have, overjoyed to see his new friend. Eve measured out her dog's kibble, then, while he ate, she poured two glasses of nonalcoholic wine and carried them into her living room, where Damien had lit a fire.

"This is nice." Accepting the glass, Damien sat on the couch, stretching his legs. "You were a trouper today."

"Thanks. I actually enjoyed it," she said honestly. "Except for the weirdness with your father. What was all that about?"

What he told her next stunned her.

"Your own father stole your inheritance?"

"Not just mine, but possibly my brothers' and sisters', too." He looked grim, taking a long drink of wine. "And when I asked him about it, he threatened me."

"What do you mean? Threatened you how?"

"Like he wanted to kill me." The bleakness in his deep voice tugged at her memory.

"You know, Sharon said something similar when she was in for her hair appointment the other day. She said she was worried her own husband was trying to kill her."

"Since he attacked her with a fireplace poker, I'm not surprised. Something's got to be done about Darius, but I don't know what. We've had a family meeting about it, but nothing got resolved."

Though hesitant to do so, she knew she should tell him everything she knew. "You know, I've heard the FBI is investigating him. No one in town is sure what for, but that's the ongoing rumor." She lifted one shoulder in a shrug, just to show he shouldn't take her seriously.

To her surprise, he did. "They *are* investigating him. Racketeering and money-laundering are just two of the items they've mentioned. They actually approached me about being an informant."

Her mouth fell open. "On your own father?"

"Yes," he said bitterly. "On my own father. What's worse, at one point I actually considered it.

Hurriedly, she took a sip of her drink, trying to compose her expression. "You did?"

"At one point. But not now. Darius's problems are family business. If he's broken the law, they'll need to prove it without my help."

Aching, she touched his arm. "You sound as though you think he has."

"Broken the law?" He gave a harsh laugh. "A man who would steal from his own son? I have no doubt Darius has done things he should go to prison for. But I've been in prison, and no matter how evil he seems to be, I wouldn't wish that on any man, especially not my own father."

"It must have been awful for you," she said softly. Sitting shoulder to shoulder, hip to hip.

Staring off into the distance, he didn't respond. The pain etched in his rugged face tore at her heart.

She loved this man. The realization hit her like a lightning bolt, so awful and glorious and strong she had to push herself up off the couch. When had this happened and how? Galvanized into motion, she strode into the kitchen, needing the comforting ritual of making coffee, something, anything, to keep her hands busy and purge her mind.

"I should go," he said from behind her.

For one terrible instant she froze, on the verge of unreasonable and unwarranted tears. Then, getting a grip on herself, she nodded, making herself turn and face him with a completely insincere smile.

"I am kind of tired," she lied. Throat aching, she managed to keep the smile in place as he uncoiled himself from the sofa and headed toward her.

"One kiss." Low-voiced, more of a command than a request.

She could do this. She could, without giving herself away. Walking into his arms was easy, as was lifting her face to his. But when his mouth covered hers, soft and warm, familiar and beloved, her self-restraint vanished.

Now fully aware of her feelings, heat and passion flooded her. Her burning desire ignited his own, and they wound up back on the couch, naked limbs intertwined, making love with such a deep yet tender urgency that she wanted to weep.

When it was over he held her, silent. Lying in his arms felt good and right, making her hate herself for betraying her own rules. No strings. They'd both agreed. Worse, she knew if she told him her feelings had changed, he'd run fast and far. So she kept her mouth shut, cherishing the feel of him, and steeled herself for the moment when he had to leave.

As if he sensed her turbulent emotions, he kissed her softly before easing out of her arms. "Don't worry so much."

Startled, she stared at him. "What do you mean?"

"I can see it in your face. You're worried about something. If it's my father, don't be. He has as little as possible to do with my life, and vice versa."

Relieved, and feeling somewhat better, she nodded. "Okay." She swallowed, then gathering up her nerve, she said, "Stay."

"Not tonight," he said, kissing her hard on the lips. "But I'll take a rain check, okay?"

She nodded, wishing she didn't feel so foolish.

Dressing hurriedly, he left, giving her one final kiss before breezing out the door.

Smiling to herself, she watched until his taillights disappeared. Then, locking the front door, she turned and made her way back to her bedroom, intent on trading her clothes for a comfortable pair of well-worn sweats. At the last minute, she remembered she needed to let Max in, so she detoured to the back door.

Shaking off snow, the big dog bounded in. Laughing at her pet's antics, Eve finally gave him a bully stick to settle him down. The fire had burned down to embers and she banked these, yawning.

Damien had barely left and already she missed him. She could get used to having him around. Pulling herself up, she gave herself a sharp talking-to. She didn't love him—she couldn't love him. Having relationship hopes always led to disappointment and pain. She'd sworn she wouldn't do this again, not with him. Especially not with him.

Distracted, she prowled around her house, putting everything back in its place, rinsing out the wineglasses before placing them in the dishwasher.

Satisfied that her tidy little world was back in order—this was one of the few things she *could* control—she whistled for the dog and padded off to bed.

Max circled three times before settling into his dog bed. She pulled back the covers and got her own bed ready, before brushing her teeth and washing her face.

Abstractedly—for curiosity's sake only—she allowed herself to wonder what it would be like to climb into her bed at the end of a day with a warm and drowsy Damien waiting for her. Cutting off the thought because the rush of pleasure it brought alarmed and worried her, she climbed beneath the covers and turned off the light.

Sometime later, Max's low growling from his bed woke her. Instantly alert, she lay still in her bed and listened.

Max sprang to his feet, entire body tense. He took a step forward, lips lifted in a snarl.

"Wait," she ordered softly. Sliding her feet into her slippers, she grabbed her robe from the end of the bed and moved slowly toward the doorway. Honey Creek had been virtually crime-free her entire life. No robberies, break-ins or assaults. Certainly, other than the Mark Walsh case, no murders. Of course, there had been cases of various kinds of wildlife crashing into people's homes—deer, moose, bird, even the occasional mountain lion or bear.

She suspected this might be just such an instance.

Though she'd trained Max well and didn't think he'd disobey her commands, she closed the bedroom door, shutting him in. If the intruder was larger than her dog, she didn't want to take a chance that Max would be injured or killed.

Moving carefully, as any wild animal was sure to already be in panic mode, when she came to the curve in the staircase, she peered around the side to below. Eyes already adjusted to the darkness, she froze at the sight below.

A tall shadow, human rather than animal, stood silhouetted below. Male, stocky, wearing a black hoody. And holding something that looked like a crowbar or a baseball bat.

As she registered these details, the man lifted his weapon and swung, shattering her flat-screen TV. Heart pounding, she tried to catch her breath, cursing the fact that she hadn't grabbed a cordless phone or her cell. Moving back into the shadows, she watched as he took out her lamps next, then the Christmas tree, walloping the branches until he'd shattered just about every single ornament. Branches cracked and snapped and her beautiful tree looked whipped and beaten.

At some point it dawned on her that he wasn't taking any pains to be quiet or hide the fact that he was systematically destroying her home. Which meant he didn't care if she caught him, in fact he'd probably welcome the chance to hurt or even kill her.

Why? Cradling her stomach protectively, Eve backtracked her steps, moving swiftly. Once in the relative safety of her bedroom, she locked her door and released Max from his stay, uncomfortably aware that her seventy-five-pound dog might be her—and her unborn child's—only protection.

Snarling louder, as if he sensed her distress, Max faced the doorway. With the hair on his back raised, he looked ready to attack. Keeping her eye on the door, Eve snatched up the phone and heard the dial tone with relief; part of her had assumed the intruder would have taken out the phone line. She punched the number for the sheriff's office.

A second later, Wes Colton's dispatcher came on the line. Speaking in a hushed voice, Eve urgently relayed the situation and begged them to hurry.

Once she'd hung up, still clutching the phone, she searched her bedroom for something to use as a weapon, pitifully aware of her shortcomings in the self-defense department. The best she could come up with was a large, heavy flashlight.

Through the closed bedroom door, she could still hear crashes, telling her the man was still savagely wrecking her belongings. Though the thought stung, better that he struck inanimate objects rather than her or Max. Still, why? What had she done to make someone that angry? This didn't make sense.

Suddenly conscious of the phone still gripped in her hand, Eve dialed Damien's cell. He answered on the second ring.

"Miss me already?" he teased.

Tersely, she told him what was going on. "I called 911 so Wes or one of his guys should be here soon."

"I'm on my way. I'll be there in ten," he told her. "Stay

put. Don't leave your bedroom, okay?" He hung up without waiting for an answer.

Knowing rescue was on the way didn't settle her nerves. She could still see the man in his black hoody swinging his crowbar, as if the image had been permanently burned on her eyeballs.

Why, why, why? She rubbed her eyes.

A few seconds went by without any crashing sounds. Then a few more. Outside, a motor roared to life. Motorcycle? Hurrying to the window, Eve saw the taillights of some kind of big bike flash red before disappearing into the distance.

After that, everything seemed to happen at once. The sound of sirens growing closer, flashing lights—red and blue—as two Honey Creek squad cars pulled into her drive.

Voices yelling, a crash, a shout, Max barking wildly, all the while she stood in her darkened bedroom, unable to move except to tremble.

Downstairs, the police called her name, alternating between *Eve* and *Miss Kelley*. Still she could do nothing but clutch her flashlight so hard her hands hurt and stare at the door.

Max went into protective dog overdrive, launching himself at the door, snarling and growling. Still she stood frozen, a statue of shock. Only when she heard Damien's voice calling her name could she take a deep breath and move forward, moving Max back and putting him on the down command, then stay. Though the tension in the boxer's body showed he really didn't want to obey, he'd been well-trained and so he did.

Opening her door slowly, she peered out. Downstairs she could hear men's voices, recognizing Wes and one of his deputies, Charlie Calhoun. And Damien, calling her as he ran for the stairs, taking them two at a time. As he rounded the curve, barreling up to the landing, she launched herself into his arms.

"Are you all right?" He smoothed back her hair, kissing her cheek and her neck and finally her mouth. "Jesus, Eve. Downstairs looks like a tornado went through it. Did he touch you?"

"No, no." She hastened to reassure him, unable to stop her trembling even now. "I'm so glad you came."

"There's something you need to see."

Tempted to refuse, to hide her face and try to withdraw like a turtle seeking a shell, she nodded. Sooner or later she'd have to deal with what had happened, and she sure as heck would rather face this with Damien by her side.

With Damien holding her arm, she slowly descended the stairs. Stopping at the bottom to look up at him.

"This way," he told her, steering her toward the living room.

Tell him to leave town, or else.

Staring at the six-inch black letters written in marker on her living-room wall, Eve flinched. Only Damien's solid body behind her kept her steady on her feet.

"Any idea what that means?" Wes Colton asked, his voice gentle.

Speechless, Eve shook her head.

"What about you, Damien?" Wes pushed.

"No idea," Damien answered, deadpan. Glancing up at him, Eve knew instantly he was lying. He knew exactly what this meant.

Following this thought, an image of Darius Colton and his malicious glare popped into her head. Had Damien's father had something to do with the break-in? The idea seemed so ludicrous she nearly dismissed it, but a niggling seed of doubt told her she'd better discuss it with Damien later, when his brother the sheriff wasn't around.

"Take a look around, Eve," Wes said gently. "See if anything is missing."

Nothing was. Her belongings had been shredded and destroyed.

"Seems like it was personal," Wes commented, watching her closely.

"Maybe, but I can't imagine who would do such a thing. I have no enemies."

"That you know of."

Looking around at the mess that had been her living room, Eve had to agree. "That I know of."

Once the report had been written up and the scene processed, Wes and his deputy helped Damien tape up the back window while Eve vacuumed up pieces of glass. After one more circuit around the house looking for clues, Wes and his deputy climbed into their cars and left.

As soon as the police were gone, Damien pulled out his cell phone.

"What are you doing?" Eve asked, blinking.

"Calling that sorry SOB." Expression furious, he punched in a number. Listening, he shook his head and disconnected the call. "It went straight to voice mail. I'll talk to him personally when I get home."

She sighed, feeling stunned and strangely detached. Must be shock setting in. "You don't know for sure it was him."

A muscle worked in his jaw. "Oh, yeah? Who else would have done this? He wants me out of here. But he should know that I can't leave without my money."

"But to give you a warning through me? How is that effective?"

Pulling her into his arms, he kissed the top of her head. "Because it's a barely veiled double threat, sweetheart. He's letting me know he's not above hurting the people I care about to get me to leave."

"I don't understand."

"My inheritance is missing and Darius is worried that the Feds are investigating him. He's even threatened to have me killed."

Shocked, she gasped. "Your own father?"

"I think he's losing his grip on reality," he said. "Though I hate making excuses for him, that's the only explanation that makes sense."

"I can't stay here now," she told him. "Will you wait while I grab a few things? I'm going to spend the night with my mother."

"That's an excellent idea." He hugged her again. "Though I don't think you're in any real danger now that the message has been given. I want you to be safe. Do you want me to drive you?"

"No." She shook her head and pushed out of his arms. "I need to have my own vehicle. I'll be fine."

Still, he followed her all the way over to Bonnie Gene's, driving off only once she'd stepped inside. Eve couldn't help but wonder what would happen once he got to the ranch. She had no doubt he meant to confront his father. Closing her eyes, she prayed he'd be safe.

Chapter 13

On the drive back to the ranch, Damien struggled to get a grip on his rage. He believed he'd successfully hidden his fury from Eve. Somehow he'd kept his voice calm even when he'd wanted to explode.

Someone hurting Eve was a thousand times worse than anything Damien had ever imagined. He knew without a shred of doubt that Darius had been behind the break-in and the message. Threatening Eve. Pregnant, vulnerable, beautiful Eve.

How. Dare. He.

Pulling up fast, tires crunching on gravel, he parked under the barn light, strode to the house and threw open the front door.

"I know what you're thinking." Materializing from the shadows, Wes stepped into his path. "But Darius isn't here. I've already checked."

This stopped Damien in his tracks. "Where the hell is he?"

"Billings. He left right after the luncheon to go Christmas shopping."

Damien swore. "How freakin' convenient for him."

"Yeah." Hunched against the cold, Wes accompanied his brother into the house.

"His cell phone goes directly to voice mail."

"I know. I tried to call him, too. Sharon said he's probably visiting his mistress."

Damien shook his head as the two men headed inside. "Now, why doesn't that surprise me?"

"What, that he has a mistress or that Sharon knows about her?"

"Both. Damn. Nothing about him should shock me. Anyone who'd threaten a pregnant woman—" Too late he realized his mistake.

"Eve's pregnant?" Wes cocked his head. "Yours?"

"I shouldn't have said that. As a matter of fact, forget I did."

"You didn't answer the question."

Swearing, Damien turned away. When he faced his brother again, he took a deep breath before speaking. "That wasn't my secret to tell. So no, I won't be answering the question. Can we get back to Darius and what the son of a bitch did?"

"You don't know that it was him."

"Like hell I don't. You know as well as I do that he hired someone to do his dirty work for him. He conveniently left town to give himself an alibi."

"Again, you have no proof." Wes crossed his arms. "None of us needs to be jumping to hasty conclusions that have no basis in fact."

"Oh, come on." Damien rounded on his brother. "You know as well as I do that the old man's behind this."

"No, I don't. Yes, I agree it seems probable—"

"Probable? Who else would have done such a thing?"

Ignoring him, Wes continued. "We can take hunches, guesses and probabilities under consideration. But that's all we can do. Until we have proof—cold hard facts—we can't go off half cocked." Wes gave him a hard look. "Understand?"

Without agreeing, Damien relayed what had happened earlier at the Christmas luncheon.

"He *threatened* you?" Wes sounded as if he didn't believe it.

"And Eve. What about your need for proof now?"

"It makes a difference. I will have to talk to him about this."

"When?"

Wes shrugged. "When he gets back."

"But—"

Rounding on him, Wes looked as if he wanted to take a swing at Damien's jaw. As furious as he felt now, Damien thought he'd probably welcome it.

"I'm not going up to Billings to hunt him down." Wes swore. "Do you have any idea how it's going to feel, questioning my own father?"

"Do you have any idea how it feels being threatened by my own father?" Damien shot back.

They each took a deep breath, striving for calm. When Wes spoke again, he sounded curt and professional.

"Actually, no, I don't. Darius has never threatened me or, to my knowledge, anyone else in our family before this. But I do know we can only operate on facts, not on guesswork."

Damien managed a small smile. "That's the law-enforcement officer in you."

"Yes, but that's also the realist in me. Come on, Damien. This is your *father.* You got sent to prison based on circumstantial evidence. You of all people should know how it feels to be wrongfully convicted."

This brought Damien up short. He started to argue, changed his mind then shook his head. "What can I say? Darius has all but admitted he's behind this."

"Has he? Has our father admitted to breaking and entering and terrorizing your girlfriend?"

"No, but—"

Relentlessly, Wes cut him off. "Has Darius admitted to stealing your inheritance or laundering money?"

"Not in so many words."

"Then you have nothing. Without proof, it's all just as circumstantial as the evidence they used to convict you of a crime you didn't commit."

With that parting shot, Wes grabbed his coat, lifted his hand in farewell and left, leaving Damien sitting alone in front of the Christmas tree.

The next morning Maisie confronted Damien in the kitchen, catching him as he was pouring his first cup of coffee. Today she was wearing a soft brown sweaterdress and over-the-knee, high-heeled boots. Without her makeup, she looked like a cross between a Victoria's Secret model and the big sister he remembered from their childhood.

"What's going on with you and Eve Kelley?" she demanded.

He rolled his eyes. "Nosy, aren't you? How's Gary Jackson?"

"Touché."

He grinned, watching as she poured herself a cup of coffee, liberally spooning sugar and cream into it before stirring and taking a sip.

"However," she said, slowly raising her gaze to meet his, "I didn't invite Gary to sit at our table at the Christmas luncheon. You know what that means. The entire town will be talking."

Confused, he frowned. "She sat with me because we're together. We like each other. Nothing more than that."

"Have you bought her a ring?"

"What?" Damien let his mouth fall open. "Of course not."

"Well, you've just proved to the entire town that you're serious about her. No Colton invites a woman to sit at the family table for the Christmas luncheon unless they're engaged or married. You know that."

Did he? "Maybe that rule came into place while I was locked up," he finally said. "Why didn't she tell me?"

Maisie looked at him for a long second. "I don't know. Maybe she's hoping for a ring."

The thought sucked the breath from his chest and made him dizzy. He took a drink from his coffee mug to steady himself. Remembering Eve's attempt to tell him why she didn't want to sit with him, and his own reaction, he knew that wasn't the case.

Before he could summon up something to say, Maisie dropped another bombshell. "Damien, I need your help with something. You know I had an affair with Mark Walsh fifteen years ago? Should I tell Jeremy that he's Mark's son?"

Damien could only stare. Sometimes he felt as though he'd been dropped into a carnival fun house filled with twists and turns. "You and Mark Walsh?"

"Yes. It went on for over a year, right before he was supposedly murdered. I thought he loved me. He said I was irresistible but he was scared of my craziness, as he called it. Turns out he also had another lover in Costa Rica."

A horrible thought occurred to Damien. "Did you know

he wasn't really dead?" The depths of such a betrayal would destroy him.

"Of course not." Maisie looked at him as if he'd suddenly grown horns and a tail. "Do you honestly think I could have known that and let you rot in prison for fifteen years?"

Relief flooding him, Damien managed a shaky smile. "No. Sorry. I had to ask." Then another thought occurred to him. "That son of a bitch knew you were expecting his child and he still faked his own death?"

"No. I didn't find out I was pregnant until after his supposed murder.

"What about Darius? I'm guessing he was not too supportive."

"He was furious. It would have been ten times worse if he'd known who the father was. He wanted me to give up the baby. That's the only time in my life I've ever really stood up to him."

"You never told him Mark Walsh was Jeremy's father?"

"Nope. And Jeremy doesn't know either."

"Surely he's asked by now."

"Oh, yes." She gave him a wistful smile. "Many times. I keep telling him I don't want to talk about it."

"But now you want to tell him? Why?"

When she met his gaze, hers was direct and clear and honest. "Because I think he has the right to know. He's fourteen, old enough to handle it."

"But there's more, isn't there?"

"Maybe." She gave him a wistful smile. "I've been told that secrets are like poison to people like me."

"True enough." Damien didn't know if he should congratulate her on her insight or ask for specifics on who was advising her.

"That's why I've been trying to get that TV show, *Dr.*

Sophie, to get a camera crew out to Honey Creek. They need to reveal all the secrets."

"Are you still obsessed with that?" he asked.

"No. I've finally realized that they're only going to continue to ignore me. Apparently TV-watching America isn't interested in the goings-on of a small town in Montana."

"You're probably right," he agreed. "I've got to tell you, sis, I'm really glad you gave that one up."

"Whatever." She shrugged. "So I'm asking your opinion," Maisie continued. "What would be the best way to tell Jeremy the truth about his father?"

"Wait until he asks. Don't rush it, make him sit down and tell him slowly, but talk to him like he's a man."

"He is. My little man." She laughed. "Will you tell him for me?"

Only Maisie could ask such a thing and be serious.

"No." Reaching out, Damien touched her shoulder. "That's between the two of you. I can't be involved."

"I thought you'd say that." She sipped her coffee. "But it was worth a shot."

Time to change the subject.

"Wes said Darius is gone. When did he leave?" he asked as casually as he could manage.

"Right after the Christmas luncheon. He said he was going to do all of his Christmas shopping in Billings. Why?"

"Somebody broke into Eve's place last night while she was asleep in bed. They trashed it pretty good and left a message on her wall."

Maisie's jaw dropped. "Are you serious?"

"Deadly serious."

She closed her mouth. "What kind of message?"

He told her.

"And you think Darius is behind it."

Instead of answering right away, he refilled his coffee mug. "Yeah, I do. Don't you?"

She shrugged. "I don't know. It all seems kind of pointless. I mean, you and Eve aren't serious or anything, so why threaten her?" Narrowing her eyes, she studied him. "Unless Darius knows something I don't."

"Darius knows nothing about me or my life." He thought of something else Eve had said. "Wes said he talked to Sharon last night, and she said something about Darius being with his mistress. Do you know anything about that?"

Making an inelegant snorting noise, Maisie made a face at him. "Looking for something to use against him? Don't waste your time. Everyone knows about Darius's little 'indiscretions,' as he calls them. He *always* has a mistress, though none of them lasts long. He'll have a new one by February."

"Have you seen Sharon lately?"

"No, why?"

He relayed what Eve had told him Sharon had mentioned while having her hair done.

"Damien," Maisie said with exaggerated patience. "You saw him attack her with a fireplace poker. Of course she'd say he's trying to kill her."

"But that was an isolated incident, wasn't it? He was drunk. So was she."

"Like that excuses it?" Maisie huffed. "And for your information, that was not an isolated incident."

Damien stared. "You've seen others?"

"Not that violent, but yes. I've witnessed a thousand small cruelties. So has Jeremy. And remember the cigarette thing, how Darius made my son eat an entire pack of cigarettes."

"So Darius is off his rocker," Damien said glumly. "Finn's supposed to get him to allow tests. Until then, that doesn't mean we have to excuse his behavior."

"No, of course not." A tinge of bitterness colored Maisie's tone. "No one excuses mine."

Gently, he put his arm around her slender shoulders. "Maise, I know you don't think you need it, but have you thought about getting help?"

This time, instead of automatically shaking her head or getting angry, Maisie nodded. "I talked to Finn. He doesn't think I'm bipolar."

Careful to hide his surprise, Damien waited for her to say more.

"Of course, he isn't ruling that out. Apparently, diagnosing that sort of thing is pretty complicated. But he did say he leans more toward Borderline Personality Disorder."

"He didn't mention anything about this."

"Finn? Of course not. There's this little issue called doctor-patient confidentiality."

"Did he recommend any course of treatment?"

"Yep. He referred me to a psychologist up in Bozeman. I go once a week. I've gone twice so far."

He hugged her. "Did he give you any medicine?"

"Yep." Looking up at her brother, she smiled. "It took it a while to work, but I feel better now than I have my entire life." She made a motion with her hand, mimicking a mountain and a valley. "The ups and downs aren't as dramatic."

"Good for you, Maise. I'm really happy for you."

Moving toward the coffeepot, she glanced at Damien over her shoulder. "Now, you've just got to get your life in order, bro. Once you do, all the Coltons will be happy."

"Except for Darius," he reminded her.

"Except for Darius," she echoed. Looking sad. "I just wish things could be different for him."

"Me, too," Damien said, surprising himself. "Me, too."

Eve spent Monday morning unable to stop smiling. Despite having to clean up the mess the intruder had made, despite waiting for the glass company to show up and fix her window, she kept thinking about what Damien had let slip the night before.

He cared about her.

What that might mean, she wasn't sure. However, she was pretty certain they'd moved beyond the friends-with-benefits stage. She definitely had.

Her salon was closed that day, so after a cup of coffee and an English muffin, she tackled cleaning up the mess. She hoped to have her living room back in some semblance of order by lunchtime. Bonnie Gene had offered to help, but Eve really hadn't wanted her mother fussing with her things. Also, Eve felt that doing this herself might help her heal.

First, she worked on her poor, broken Christmas tree. Once she removed the damaged branches, the formerly stately fir took on a dejected and battered look.

Removing all decorations and garland from it, she vacuumed up pieces of tree and shards of broken ornaments, sorting what was left whole into neat piles on her coffee table.

When she'd finished, she turned the tree again, wondering if she could somehow make it look halfway presentable.

Finally she settled on facing the most broken part back against the wall and fluffing up what would now be the front. Plugging in the lights, she realized she only had to make a minor adjustment to those. Her ornaments were mostly destroyed, but she had a box of pine cones in her garage that she could use. With Christmas only a few days away, she didn't want to go buy new ornaments now, so she'd improvise.

While the pine cones were drying, she turned her attention to the rest of the room. She'd have to toss a few things that had gotten broken, and she'd have to buy a new lamp, but after cleaning her wall and erasing the warning, she felt she'd done all she could.

Her stomach growled. Glancing at her watch, she saw it was nearly noon.

Her cell phone chirped. Caller ID showed an unknown caller. Eve answered anyway. "Hello?"

"Ten thousand dollars," a distorted male voice said. "Deposited into your bank account or left on your doorstep, no questions asked, whichever you prefer. You'll receive this if you are successful in making him leave town."

Darius Colton. Though she didn't recognize the voice, who else could it be?

"What?" Though she felt she should have had some witty comeback, Eve was too stunned to do more than stammer. "Who is this?"

"Don't concern yourself with that," the voice snarled. "Do you want the money or not?"

She took a deep breath, trying to keep herself from shaking. "Don't call me again."

"Twenty-five thousand. That's my final offer."

"Are you crazy?" By now she was gripping the phone so tightly it hurt.

"Not crazy, just determined. I want Damien Colton gone by Christmas, and you'll have an early cash present."

She pressed the disconnect button without replying.

A moment later, she dialed Damien's number, heart still pounding.

"I'll be right there," he said, when she'd finished relaying the story. "Don't move."

He must have driven at twice the speed limit, because barely ten minutes had passed before he rang her doorbell. When she opened the door, he took one look at her face and pulled her into his arms.

"Get your coat. Let's go somewhere and have a cup of coffee."

Relieved, she nodded and went to get her jacket. "How'd you know that getting out of the house is exactly what I need?"

Instead of answering, he kissed her cheek.

Because it was after lunch and the donut shop had already closed, they chose the Corner Bar and Grill over the Honey-B Café. After all, it was "their" place.

"We have fresh-baked peach pie," the waitress told them as she led them to a booth. "Just out of the oven."

"Sounds lovely." Eve smiled at the girl. "I'll take a piece, along with a cup of decaf coffee."

"Just coffee for me," Damien said. "Regular."

After the server left, Eve leaned back in her chair. "Thanks for being so kind," she said.

"That's what friends do," he teased, though she couldn't read the emotion that darkened his eyes. "And anyway, what happened to you is my fault. I shouldn't have made you sit with me at the Christmas luncheon."

Friends. Oddly enough, his words made her want to cry. Damn hormones. Clearing her throat, she managed a smile and a nod as the waitress returned with her pie and their drinks.

"Mmm, pie." Though her appetite had deserted her, Eve picked up her fork and dug in. When she glanced up, Damien was watching her intently. Meeting his gaze actually made her chest hurt with physical pain.

Fool. Returning her attention to the pie, she made herself go through the motions. Fork to mouth, chew and swallow. Repeat. Though she was sure the peaches were delicious, she couldn't taste anything.

Once again, she'd fallen in love with a man who thought of her as a friend. And she had no one to blame but herself. After all, she'd set up the rules. Too bad she hadn't been able to live by them.

The waitress bustled up to the table, standing almost as if she was trying to block them from seeing the door.

"Don't look now," she muttered, leaning in close. "But Lucy Walsh just walked in."

Lucy Walsh was Mark Walsh's daughter. She'd once been Damien's girlfriend, before he'd gone to jail for supposedly killing her father. Mark had discovered their relationship and had, according to local gossip, gone ballistic, threatening Damien. Based on this story alone, a jury had convicted Damien of murder and sent him to prison.

These days, Lucy had a lot to deal with. Not only had she learned her father had been alive all these years without contacting her or anyone in the family, but she'd had to cope with his recent murder all over again.

Rumor had it that Lucy had believed Damien guilty and had never gone to see him in prison. Until Eve had been seen in public with him, most of Honey Creek also believed Damien had harbored both an unrequited love for Lucy and an acrid, bitter resentment.

Now it seemed everyone in the Corner Bar wanted to see how Damien would deal with this.

Wary, Eve glanced at Damien. She wasn't sure how she'd react if he showed signs of pining after Lucy. The waitress, too, watched him intently, no doubt hoping for a reaction.

Appearing both unaware and completely unconcerned, Damien simply lifted his cup and asked for a refill.

Crestfallen, the server walked off to get the coffeepot.

Then, to Eve's shock, Lucy herself came over to the table.

"Afternoon, Eve. Damien." A pretty girl, Lucy had a youthful attitude and style of dress that made Eve feel ancient and dowdy.

"Hey, Lucy." Damien smiled. "How have you been?"

Though Lucy glanced curiously over at Eve, she gave the appearance of being completely at ease. "I'm good. I noticed you both at the Christmas luncheon. Even though I couldn't make it up there to say hi, I was glad to see you two together."

It was on the tip of Eve's tongue to tell her they weren't together, but she merely nodded.

"Any news on the investigation?" Damien asked.

"Not so far." Everyone in town knew Lucy was very tuned in to the murder investigation. Some speculated it was to make up for being so ready to believe Damien guilty.

"Well, I won't take up any more of your time. Merry Christmas to both of you!" With a jaunty wave, Lucy moved off. As she went, everyone in the place alternated between watching her and eyeing Damien and Eve.

"Lucy and I made our peace a while ago," Damien said, again making Eve feel as if he'd read her mind. "We were both young and foolish. She lost her father and didn't know who to blame. End of story."

"I still can't believe the police haven't been able to find out who killed him. Of course, there were a lot of people who would want Mark Walsh dead."

"This time, I suspect they're being more careful." His

smile tinged with bitterness, Damien eyed her pie. "Aren't you going to finish?"

"No." Suddenly feeling queasy, she slid the plate toward him. "Help yourself."

Flashing her a grin, he picked up his fork and dug right in.

Funny how something so simple as sharing a piece of pie could seem so intimate, so homey. Dang, she was in deep.

Chapter 14

As she'd predicted, the women started dropping by Salon Allegra around ten o'clock Tuesday morning, about an hour after she opened and thirty minutes after her first shampoo and set. Arriving in small groups of two or three, they made no pretense of needing to get a haircut or being interested in purchasing styling products. Instead, they all wanted to know about Eve and Damien.

The first bunch, three elderly ladies from Bonnie Gene's quilting group, asked Eve point-blank, completely disregarding the fact that she was in the middle of a hair-cut.

Fortunately, Eve had prepared a standard, noncommittal response. "We're just good friends," she said, smiling a carefree smile.

By Tuesday afternoon, not only were her ankles swollen and her back aching, but she thought if one more person asked her about her relationship with Damien, she would scream.

At least she had her work to distract her. Traditionally, the week leading up to Christmas was busy for her little salon. This year was no exception, but as the days flew by, the steady stream of gossip-hungry visitors far eclipsed her appointments.

By Christmas Eve, they'd finally begun to taper off.

For years she'd made it a practice to work only half a day on Christmas Eve, and she had just finished her last appointment. Finally, she could close the shop up and go home, where she had a date with some mulled apple cider.

The phone rang, which, since she had no one else listed for the rest of the day, most likely meant someone wanted to schedule a rush appointment. This happened every holiday. Someone realized they needed highlights or a cut before church services or the big day and panicked.

"Salon Allegra," Eve answered. Nothing but silence from the other end. Wrong number? "Hello?"

As she was about to hang the phone up, a small sound, almost a cry, close to a gasp, made her freeze.

"Hello?" she said again. This time, instead of silence, someone sobbed. Then the voice—feminine and low— whispered an unintelligible phrase.

Every nerve standing on alert, Eve strained to hear. Silence.

"I'm sorry? I didn't understand you." She kept her voice gentle and soothing. "I couldn't hear you. Please, what did you say?"

"Help me. Please, help me." And the phone went dead.

Slowly replacing the receiver, Eve tried to calm her pounding heart. Sharon Colton. It had to be her. She'd said her husband was trying to kill her.

Grabbing her cell phone, she dialed Damien. The call went immediately to voice mail, which probably meant he was out in the mountains checking on cattle. He'd said the ranch typically gave the hands half a day off on Christmas Eve, so they rushed to complete all their chores in the morning.

Pacing the confines of her small reception area, Eve eyed the phone as if she thought the handset might suddenly grow wings. For the first time ever she wished she had caller ID on her business phone.

What to do? Her choices were clear: she could do nothing or she could take a drive out to the Colton ranch and make sure Sharon was all right.

The thought of confronting an enraged Darius Colton was daunting. Then she realized she could call Wes Colton. And say what? That she'd had a mysterious phone call and she wasn't sure, but she thought it might be his stepmother and oh, by the way, his father might be trying to kill her.

He'd think Eve had lost her mind. No, thank you. Pacing, Eve tried to figure out a course of action—after all, she had her unborn baby to protect. Grabbing her parka, purse and car keys, she had just turned the sign on her door from Open to Closed when the phone rang again.

"Eve?" The voice sounded weak and wavery, but closer to normal. "This is Sharon Colton. I've had a bit of an accident with my hair."

"A bit of an accident?" Eve repeated. "What do you mean?"

Silence, then Sharon Colton answered, her voice low and full of pain. "Darius took scissors to it." Her breath caught in a sob. "I look a fright and I have to put in an appearance at the big caroling thing tonight. Can you come by and fix me up?"

Cautiously, Eve agreed. "Did you call a second earlier?"

After a moment's hesitation, Sharon admitted she had. "I'm sorry if I frightened you."

"You said 'Help me.'" Choosing her words carefully, Eve tried to figure out what to say. "Are you in need of some help?"

Another short hesitation, then Sharon said, "No."

"Is he there?"

"Darius?" Sharon gave a short laugh which ended in a hiccup. "No. He went down to his office."

"Are you hurt?" Eve persisted.

"You know what?" Sharon sighed. "I'm sorry I involved you in this. Forget I called."

She hadn't answered Eve's question.

"Wait, don't hang up. I'll come and fix your hair." Taking a deep breath, Eve tried to think. "That is, if it's safe for me to be there."

"Safe?" Weary impatience tinged Sharon's voice. "Of course it's safe. Why would he want to hurt you?"

Good question. Unfortunately, Eve kept seeing the rancor in Darius's stare. Still, the older woman needed help. "I can be out there in twenty minutes, all right?"

"Thank you. And I'm sorry to bother you on Christmas Eve. I'll double your usual tip for this."

"That's okay," Eve said. Hanging up the phone, she grabbed her parka, locked the door and headed out to her SUV.

An hour of her time doing a Christmas Eve favor to a woman she liked. What could be the harm in that?

Course decided, she headed out.

The drive out to the ranch took fifteen minutes. As she turned down the long driveway leading toward the main house, snowflakes appeared in her headlights. No flurries, these, but a steady, blanketing snowfall that carried the promise of becoming a storm.

Had the weathermen predicted this? She couldn't remember. In a matter of moments, the wind picked up and the snow started falling in earnest. Though snow was as common as cattle to Montana, snow on Christmas Eve was relatively rare. Magical.

Parking near the barn, she noticed the place seemed almost deserted, the ranch hands having been given the afternoon off so they could begin their holiday early.

Climbing from her SUV, she stood for a moment in the swirling snow, enjoying the crisp purity of the air, the cleansing beauty of the white curtain of snow. Then, she went to the house and rang the front doorbell.

No one came. She pressed the bell again and waited, but no one answered the door. Nerves prickling, she tried the handle, knowing it would be unlocked. Should she go inside or call Sharon on her phone to come let her in?

Remembering the humiliation in the older woman's voice, she decided to search her out on her own. Stepping into the huge marbled foyer, she closed the door behind her.

Wow. Awestruck for the space of a heartbeat, she gaped at the huge ranch house. Though her family was wealthy in their own right, the Coltons' ranch house was as different from the Kelley mansion as night and day. Though they were similar in size, there the resemblance ended.

Done in warm tones of oak and cedar, the Coltons' home exuded warmth and country living. The casual Western style reminded her of their state. Eve always thought Montana's true spirit was the unusually strong bond between the people, the animals and the land.

A huge evergreen tree dominated the great room, decorated in a rustic style that perfectly complemented the room's decor.

Inside, she circled the huge den, making her way into the kitchen, which was also empty. From there she went down a short, carpeted hallway, thinking it might lead to a guest bedroom or office of some kind.

As she rounded the corner, she heard Darius Colton's distinctive voice and froze, praying he wasn't about to hurt Sharon again.

"You know, I thought trashing the Kelley girl's place would make my son realize he needs to quit poking his nose where it doesn't belong, but no." Darius made a sound of disgust.

Eve crept closer. The older man stood in front of a wall of floor-to-ceiling windows, phone in hand.

"I agree. Though I hate to do it, I see no alternative. I'll have to kill him like I did Mark Walsh and that first guy, whoever he was." He chuckled. "Yes, I did just say I'd have to take out my own son. Hell, I made sure he got sent to prison, didn't I?"

He laughed, a malicious chuckle. "One good thing about him is that we can make it look like a suicide. Since he just got out of prison, I can claim he was having trouble making it on the outside."

Involuntarily, Eve gasped, the sound escaping her throat in a high-pitched squeak.

Darius turned. He pinned her with his gaze.

Oh, God. Eve took one step back, then another. She didn't hear what he said next, but he hung up the phone and moved swiftly toward her.

"Well, well." On his way toward her, Darius snatched up a heavy ceramic-and-brass lamp from his desk, ripping the plug from the wall.

Eve turned to run, aware she was far too late.

Darius grabbed her arm, yanking her feet out from under her. As she spun to face him, the last thing she saw was his arm raised, lamp in hand, before he hit her.

Though the Christmas carol sing wasn't slated to begin until dusk, Damien was rushing through his chores. Though the ranch hands had all been given leave to knock off work at noon, it was generally understood that all assigned chores must be completed, and Damien and one other man had driven bales of hay up into the pastures for the cattle and the horses. Each had taken a flatbed pickup with two huge round bales and spread the hay out for the animals' daily feed.

Though snow had started falling heavily, Damien completed his task, then returned to the ranch to park the truck next to several others in back of the barn.

At least three inches of snow had fallen during the time he'd been out in the pasture, blanketing the equipment and the vehicles. Though the parking lot in front of the barn had grown rapidly more deserted as ranch hands took off for town, a few remaining vehicles were covered in white snow, making them indistinguishable from their surroundings.

Back at the ranch house, Damien whistled as he washed up in the mudroom, before heading toward the kitchen to grab a quick snack.

Behind him, the back door blew open, slamming against the outside wall. He must have not closed it right. Frowning, he turned back around and came face-to-face with Darius, disheveled and covered in snow.

"What happened to you?" he asked, curious. In the entire three-plus months he'd been home, he'd never seen his father looking like this, not even at his drunken worst.

Instead of answering, Darius grunted something unintelligible and hurried away to his office, trailing snow and leaving tracks of mud.

The back of Damien's neck prickled. Something was wrong. Going against his better judgment, he followed his father.

Rounding the corner, he spied Darius, still wearing his coat, hurriedly picking up broken pieces of glass and china.

"What happened?" he asked, moving forward to help.

"Leave it alone," Darius snarled. "I'll get it. I broke my desk lamp."

"Out in the hallway?" Struck by an even stronger sense of trepidation, Damien moved closer. "What really happened here?"

"None of your damn business," Darius snarled. "If you know what's good for you, you'll get out of here."

Just then, Sharon Colton rounded the corner. Seeing her husband and her stepson, she froze, one hand to her mouth. Her left eye was swollen, raw and purple, and her mouth looked as though it had had a run-in with a fist.

"Did you hit her?" Damien asked, voice low and furious. "For the love of God, tell me you didn't hit your wife."

As he advanced on his father, Sharon gave a low cry.

Damien froze. Darius had produced a Smith and Wesson revolver and now had it pointed straight at him.

Eve came to slowly, wondering why she was so cold. Dang heater must be on the blink, which meant she needed to put in an emergency call to Rusty's Air Conditioning and Heating Service. She was trying to rise when the blinding pain in her head made everything spin.

What the...? Suddenly she remembered. Testing her arms, she found they were tied behind her back and she couldn't move them. The same applied to her legs. Darius

Colton had hit her with the lamp, knocking her out. Which meant she was...where?

Eyes adjusting to the darkness, she slowly looked around. She lay on a bale of hay, surrounded on three sides by other large rectangular bales. Since the huge round bales were used for the pastured livestock and these large squares were used to feed the barn-penned animals, she had to be close to the main barn. A hay barn, most likely.

Listening, she heard only silence, the heavy snowfall outside blanketing all sound. No livestock here, confirming her earlier guess.

She could only wonder what Darius Colton meant to do with her, especially since she'd overheard him not only confessing to a murder, but planning to have his own son killed.

Protectively cradling her stomach and the unborn life growing inside her, she began looking for a way out. Christmas Eve was a time for living, not dying. No way she would go out without a fight.

"What are you doing?" Damien asked, stopping in his tracks and eyeing the gun. Behind him, Sharon Colton began to cry, soft gasps of sound that barely drew the old man's attention.

"What I should have done months ago," Darius snarled. "You should have stayed in prison. Poking your nose around where you don't belong, just like your stupid girlfriend."

Damien's blood turned to ice. "Eve? What has she got to do with this?"

"I asked her to come out here and fix my hair," Sharon's broken voice answered. "I was just looking for her now."

Glaring at the man who'd sired him, Damien took a step forward. "What have you done with her?"

"Stay back."

"What have you done with her?"

Darius laughed. The guttural, malevolent sound sent a chill up Damien's spine.

He took a step closer. "Darius, what have you done to Eve?"

"Don't worry, I didn't kill her. Yet. Though with the storm raging outside, she may freeze to death before I have to. Rest assured, I will take care of her. Just like I'm going to have to take care of you."

Darius lifted the weapon, squinting at Damien as though he was about to fire.

"She's pregnant," Damien blurted, thinking fast. Back in the old days, before he'd gone to prison, his father had really cared about family and the Colton dynasty. "Eve is pregnant. You can't kill a pregnant woman."

This startled the older man. "Pregnant?"

"With my son," Damien lied, wishing with all of his heart that it was so. "Your grandson. Eve is carrying the next Colton."

For the first time a glimmer of humanity showed in Darius's flat, cold eyes. Slowly he lowered the gun.

Now! Damien moved, knocking the gun from his father's hands and slamming the older man into the floor.

"Where is she?"

Instead of answering, Darius struggled to free himself.

"Sharon, go call the police," Damien ordered, tightening his grip.

Wide-eyed, the woman stood frozen, staring at her stepson who had her husband wrapped in a choke hold.

"You will not," Darius rasped. "Sharon, get my gun and take this son of a bitch out."

Slowly, as though his voice compelled her, Sharon Colton moved toward the weapon.

"Bring me the gun and go and call Wes." Damien urged. "Do it now, Sharon, before anyone else gets hurt. We've got to try and find Eve. We've got to save her."

Shaking her head as if coming out of a trance, Sharon nodded. Turning, she went for the revolver first, handing it to Damien, who accepted it with one hand before pushing up and off his father.

Sharon then moved toward the office. She reached for the phone and started dialing, keeping a wary eye on her husband, who remained on the floor. Her single act of rebellion appeared to knock the remaining wind from Darius's sails.

A moment later, she returned to the hall. "Wes is on his way. And Jake Pierson is with him."

"Good." Damien liked Jake, who had been one of the first FBI agents to arrive in town. Since then, he'd left the Bureau and now he had a private security business and worked with Wes in the Sheriff's Department, intently focused on solving the Mark Walsh murder. If anyone deserved to find answers, Jake did.

"Where're Maisie and Jeremy?"

"At church. She volunteered to head up the organization for the Christmas carol sing this year."

"Good. I don't really want them to see this."

Keeping the gun trained on Darius, Damien backed away. "We've got to find Eve," he told his father's wife. "If he left her somewhere outside, she won't last long in this weather."

"She's probably already dead." Darius sounded gleeful. "You may have won this round, but in the end, I've won the battle."

"What battle, Darius?" Sharon rounded on her husband. "You've alienated and injured your entire family, all in the pursuit of your business. I've lied long enough for you. I know where you keep the second set of books. Heck, I helped you set them up. I'm ashamed of that now. I'm going to turn in my CPA license, as soon as I turn those books over to the FBI."

"You wouldn't dare," Damien snarled. "Or I'll kill you, too."

Shaking her head, Sharon ignored him. "I'll go see if I can rustle up a search party. Don't worry, Damien, we'll find your girl."

With all his heart, Damien had to believe that. A moment later, Sharon returned.

"I got hold of Duke," she announced. "He's gathered up the ranch hands who were still here and they've split up into search groups."

"Good." He felt a sliver of the tension ease. He wouldn't feel anywhere near normal again until he held Eve in his arms. "I'll join them as soon as reinforcements show up."

In what seemed like an hour but was really only ten minutes, Wes and Jake arrived. Turning over the gun and Darius to his brother, Damien watched while Jake handcuffed the patriarch of the Colton Clan.

"How far the mighty have fallen," Jake muttered. "I've contacted several of my old coworkers in the Bureau. Most of them have gone home for Christmas, but they'll be back on the twenty-sixth to wrap part of this investigation up. Sharon's willingness to share the books and testify will help tremendously."

Damien nodded, barely hearing the other man. He ran for his parka, cramming his hat onto his head and shoving his fingers into gloves. "I'll be out searching. If you can get together more men to help search, I'd be grateful."

"They're already on their way." Wes clapped his brother on the shoulder. "Jake can keep an eye on Darius. Let's go."

"Wait," Darius cried as they turned to go. "I'll tell you where she is in exchange for my freedom."

"No." The two brothers spoke in unison. "No deals."

"Wes, Damien, you're my sons," Darius pleaded. "Let me go. I promise I'll disappear quietly. I'll sign over all this to you and you'll never hear from me again."

"Tempting as the offer is, we'll pass." Damien spoke through clenched teeth, knowing without asking that Wes felt the same way. Darius had bullied the family long enough.

Together, he and Wes headed out. At the doorway, Wes stopped.

"Are you sure you want to add murder to your list of crimes?" Wes asked quietly, turning to look at his father. "You have a choice here. You can tell us where Eve is and save her life, or you can let us search. If she dies, I'll make sure you're brought up on murder charges, do you understand?"

Instead of answering, Darius turned his face away.

"Come on, man." Damien took off, no longer caring if Wes was behind him. He barreled outside, into the midst of a blizzard.

"Damn." Wes came up beside him. "This got worse fast. On the way here, we had some visibility. Now it's whiteout conditions."

"I don't care." Damien started blindly in the direction of the cattle pens. "We've got to find Eve."

"I'll take the cattle pens," Wes told him. "You go check the machinery barn and the hay sheds."

Without another word, Damien turned and went the other way.

The angels of Christmas Eve must have been with him that night. Barely five minutes into his search, he pushed open the door of the hay barn and found Eve, trussed up and freezing, but alive and drifting in and out of consciousness.

Gathering her close, he freed her arms and legs, massaging them to bring circulation back, hoping she wouldn't have frostbite. She cried out in pain as feeling returned, violently shivering.

"Damien," she croaked, nearly unintelligible because of the shudders racking her body. "Darius killed Mark Walsh and the first guy, a homeless man that everyone thought was Mark Walsh. He let you go to prison knowing you were innocent. And now he was going to have you killed, I heard him."

"Shhh." Hushing her by placing one gloved finger against her mouth, he tried to determine the extent of her injuries. "We'll deal with that later, once we get you inside."

Then, lifting her, he carried her out into the snowstorm. When they reached the house, he carried her into the den, where he gently lowered her to the rug in front of the roaring fire.

Seeing her, Sharon wept with relief, heading into the kitchen and putting on a pot of hot water for tea. When she returned, Damien put her in charge of calling in all the searchers and letting them know Eve was safe.

With the Christmas tree shining brightly in the background, Damien crouched by the fire, helping Eve sip her tea and rubbing her legs, feet and hands, watching as her color slowly returned and her trembling subsided.

"You're safe now, sweetheart," he whispered, kissing her cheek. "I'll tell Wes what you heard."

Her beautiful blue gaze searched his face. "Are you all right? It must be a shock, knowing your own father wanted to kill you?"

"No worse than knowing he let me go to prison for a

crime he committed. But you're safe and that's all that matters."

Drowsily, she snuggled against him. Contentment filled his heart. He felt complete and at peace for the first time since he'd stood in that courtroom, fifteen years ago, and watched a prison sentence being handed down, sending him away for a crime he hadn't committed.

"I told them you were pregnant," he whispered into her hair.

"That's okay." Smiling, she kissed him. "It's about time I stopped worrying about tarnishing the family name."

"I, er, told them the baby was mine."

She froze, then turned in his arms to gaze up at him. "Why'd you go and do something like that?" she whispered softly. "It'll only make it worse when they find out the truth."

"Maybe they don't have to find out the truth." He kissed her lightly on the lips, then the nose, then the curve of her neck.

"What are you saying?"

Tightening his arms around her, he closed his eyes, inhaled her scent and took the leap. "Because I'd like that baby to be mine. He can be the first of our children, Eve. That is, if you'd like more."

"Damien?"

To his dismay her gorgeous eyes filled with tears, spilling over and trailing silver down her cheeks. Despair filled him as he realized he'd made her cry, which could mean only one thing.

She didn't want him.

"I'm sorry, I—" he began stiffly. "I didn't mean—"

"Don't you dare apologize, cowboy." Putting her arms around him, she kissed him full on the mouth. "That's the nicest thing anyone has ever said to me. But I need to know, are you suggesting we live together, or are you wanting to make an honest woman out of me?"

Hope slammed into him, hard, nearly making him gasp.

"You mean you'd marry me?"

Cocking her head, she gave a soft chuckle. "If you ask me right, I just might."

Slowly, he grinned. "How do you think your sister would feel about a double wedding? Her and Duke and me and you."

Eve's answering smile warmed his heart. "I guess we'll just have to ask her, now won't we?"

Epilogue

Valentine's Day dawned clear and cold, without a single cloud to mar the bright blue perfection of the sky.

The entire town of Honey Creek gathered at the town square, cameras in hand, ready to record the historical day.

Coltons and Kelleys, wed in a double ceremony. A joyous occasion which they hoped would go a long way toward erasing the shadow that had hung over their town for so long.

Though clearly ill, Darius Colton had gone to jail and was awaiting trial for the murder of Mark Walsh, as well as for the murder of the unknown drifter fifteen years ago. The twists and turns of this soap opera-like story had finally drawn the attention of the popular television show, *Dr. Sophie,* and they'd actually sent a camera crew to do an exposé on the scandal, much to Maisie Colton's delight. She'd even managed a cameo appearance. "The Scandal at Honey Creek," as their episode had been named, would air in the spring.

Eve Kelley's pregnancy had been announced, and though she'd refused to let Damien take responsibility for the baby, he made it clear to her that he'd be raising the child as his own.

Susan and Duke were jubilant when Damien and Eve had decided to marry, and this joint wedding would be the culmination of months of planning on Susan's part, one wedding easily stretched to become two, though she'd had to change the date slightly.

Sharon Colton remained at the ranch, finally emerging from her shell now that she was no longer under Darius's grip. She'd started a support group for battered women and traveled often to Bozeman, where she'd headquartered her office.

Church bells chimed the hour and a hush fell over the crowd. Finally, the sound of hooves on pavement filled the air. Two white, horse-drawn carriages turned the corner, decorated with white and peach roses, clattering down Main Street. The two brides, Susan and Eve, both decked out in ornate white gowns, rode in the first. The grooms, Duke and Damien, wearing matching gray tuxedos, followed in the other. They would arrive at the church, where the rest of the family and wedding party waited, seconds apart, and the ceremony would commence.

Because both Susan and Eve had wanted small weddings, the ceremony itself was by invitation only and had been limited to family and close friends. Later, everyone in town was welcome to attend the huge reception at the Colton ranch. The Rollaboys had been booked to play, Kelley's Cookhouse would be catering the reception, and the open bar provided by the Coltons ensured the celebrations would last long into the night.

Inside the church, two nervous brides prepared to walk up the aisle at the same time, sharing their father's arms. They knew two loving cowboys waited for them, both wearing identical looks of love on their handsome faces.

And Duke and Susan Colton, Damien and Eve Colton, were pronounced husband and wife. Both couples kissed sweetly.

When the ceremony was over, everyone lined the streets to watch them go past before racing to follow them. For the first time in recent history, the ranch house would be opened to the public, and the two newlywed couples would receive guests for two hours, before joining the party.

Despite the double wedding, the two couples were taking separate honeymoons. Duke and Susan were traveling to Jamaica and Damien and Eve had chosen Ixtapa, Mexico.

And when they returned, Damien would be moving to Eve's house. He'd agreed to continue to work on the ranch, side by side with the rest of his family.

He planned to persuade Eve to let him adopt her unborn child, giving him or her the Colton name. Once she'd agreed, which he had no doubt she would, he looked forward to good-naturedly needling all his brothers that he would have the first Colton baby. He had no doubt one of his brothers and their new bride wouldn't be far behind.

All in all, Damien planned to live a life full of happiness and love with his beautiful wife, Eve, and their baby. A normal life in the Big Sky Country, exactly as he wanted. Happily ever after. Of course.

* * * * *